FRICTIO

Stories by Women

Rhea Tregebov

Maya Khankhoje

FRICTIONS
Stories by Women

Edited by

RHEA TREGEBOV

SECOND STORY Press

CANADIAN CATALOGUING IN PUBLICATION DATA

Main entry under title:

Frictions: stories by women

ISBN 0-929005-07-4

1. Short stories, Canadian (English) – Women authors.*
2. Canadian fiction (English) – Women authors.*
3. Canadian fiction (English) – 20th century.*
I. Tregebov, Rhea, 1953–

PS8321.F75 1989   C813'.01'089   C89-095387-2
PR9197.3.W65F75 1989

Printed and bound in Canada

Published by
SECOND STORY PRESS
585 1/2 Bloor Street West
Toronto, Canada M6G 1K5

CONTENTS

Introduction
Rhea Tregebov
13

My Father Rescued a Cat
Debby Dobson
21

A Long Story
Beth Brant
26

Sleeping Beauty
Clare Braux
34

Butterfly on a Pin
Claire Harris
42

Glenda
Joan MacLeod
54

Worm
Lee Maracle and Siddie Bobb
57

Coupling
Marlene Cookshaw
60

In Such a State
Jan Bauer
63

The Mammal Stories
Claudia Casper
81

That Shaggy Look
Suniti Namjoshi
94

Hide and Seek
Carole Corbeil
96

Music from Below
Susan Glickman
102

The Meaning of the Marriage
Cynthia Flood
105

Mirror, Mirror
Rachna Gilmore
115

Sooner or Later All Bodies Tend
To Move Toward the Centre of the Earth
Libby Oughton
127

Mikalyn
Frances Rooney
132

Against the Tooth of Time
Ruth Millar
137

The Earthquake
Lake Sagaris
146

Canada Day
Maya Khankhoje
154

Summer Wages
Caroline Woodward
161

Me and Mine
Sara McDonald
171

Spring Forward, Fall Back
Sarah Sheard
176

Pretty Goldfish
Libby Scheier
181

Pictures
Gertrude Story
188

The Tallest Man in the World
Susan Swan
200

To a Fairer Place
Helen J. Rosta
210

Guatemala
Susan Perly
226

The Orphan Boy
Marina Endicott
233

Contributors
261

PUBLICATIONS

Beth Brant's "A Long Story" was previously published in her collection of stories, *Mohawk Trail* (Firebrand: 1985) and in the anthology *A Gathering of Spirit* (Firebrand: 1989; The Women's Press: 1989).

"Sleeping Beauty" by Clare Braux appeared in *Waves*, January 1987.

Marina Endicott's story, "The Orphan Boy," was previously published in the anthology *Sky High* (Coteau Books: 1988).

"Glenda" is derived from Joan MacLeod's play *Amigo's Blue Guitar*, which is to be produced at Toronto's Tarragon Theatre in January, 1990.

The first section of "Me and Mine," by Sara McDonald, was published in a slightly different version in the anthology *Open Windows* (Quarry Press: 1988).

"Pretty Goldfish," by Libby Scheier, was previously published in *Canadian Women's Studies*, Volume 8, Number 3.

Sarah Sheard's "Spring Forward, Fall Back" appeared in the February 1988 issue of *This Magazine*.

ACKNOWLEDGEMENTS

The editor would like to thank all the members of Second Story Press for their encouragement and advice, and for the opportunity to once again work with them. I would especially like to express my appreciation to Liz Martin for her enduring enthusiasm and her commitment to literary publishing. Thanks also to Margie Wolfe and Lois Pike for their hand-holding and knowledgeable advice through the various stages of development of this manuscript.

Second Story Press would like to express its gratitude to the Director/Producer for the Association for Native Development in the Performing and Visual Arts, Viola Thomas, for her assistance in providing the editor with referrals for Native writers.

Thanks also to Thomas King of the Department of Native American Studies at the University of Lethbridge for his help in outreach to Native writers and for setting an inspiring example.

PREFACE

Frictions is Second Story Press' first collection of short stories by women. With its publication, we affirm our commitment to feminist fiction, providing a forum for women's words and stories. We share an interest with Rhea Tregebov, the editor of this anthology, in writing that challenges how we construct our own sense of the world. In *Frictions*, the reader will find works of fiction representing a diversity of age, sexual preference, class, race, ethnic background – voices to stimulate and provoke us. We wanted stories that would challenge the idea of a fixed female identity, that would show that in our differences we can find strength and celebration.

Three of the stories presented in *Frictions* – "In Such A State," "Against The Tooth of Time" and "Guatemala" – have been the subject of controversy in another anthology published in 1988. While The Women's Press had already signed contracts with these authors, agreeing to publish their work in *Imagining Women*, the stories were subsequently rejected. They were charged with being 'structurally racist' because the authors had either attempted to delve into experience not their own or used a genre of creative writing allegedly belonging to another culture. To protest this banning, two other contributors to that collection withdrew their work; the stories "Mikalyn" and "The Earthquake" are also included in *Frictions*. The controversy helped to precipitate the lockout of eight long-time members of The Women's Press, leading to the genesis of our new feminist publishing house – Second Story Press.

It is with great pride that we present this entire collection. We hope that the arrival of *Frictions* will be followed by other such collections, as women carry forward the work of re-visioning our world.

Elizabeth Martin, Lois Pike, Margie Wolfe, Carolyn Wood,
Judi Coburn, Connie Guberman, Graziela Pimentel,
Christa Van Daele

Second Story Press
September 1989

INTRODUCTION:

Changing the Possible

Rhea Tregebov

[It would have been ...] virtually impossible to take a feminine character as a central figure, to make Plotina, for example, rather than Hadrian, the axis of my narrative. Women's lives are much too limited, or else too secret. If a woman does recount her own life she is promptly reproached for being no longer truly feminine. It is already hard enough to give some element of truth to the utterances of a man.

Marguerite Yourcenar
"Author's Reflections on the Composition
of Memoirs of Hadrian," 1951

Memoirs of Hadrian is an extraordinary piece of literature; Yourcenar an extraordinary writer. Her powerful first novel, a fictional autobiography of the Roman emperor Hadrian, established the young Frenchwoman as a major writer. Yourcenar's talent, the irresistible force meeting the immovable object of her culture's sexual bias, eventually led her to rise above the entrenched prejudices of her culture. She was accepted by the literary establishment – so much so that, in 1981, she became the first woman to be elected to that paradigm of elitism, the Academie Française.

13

We have always had 'talent'; we have always been able to write.
Whether or not we granted ourselves permission, or were socially
granted permission to write, whether we felt free in the choice of
subject as well as form is, however, a separate question.

I would not wish a word of *Memoirs of Hadrian* changed. But I
would wish the young woman who began the task of writing so
many and so few years ago wider options. Thirty-eight years ago,
the female subject was "too limited" or, alternatively, "too secret."
Either not worth speaking of or unspeakable. The internal and
external censorship against writing the female experience was, at
the time, to this author and to far too many others, overwhelming.

I was born in 1953. Yourcenar's position is where I and the writers of my generation come from. Simone de Beauvoir's *The Second
Sex*, the starting point and the keystone of much feminist theory,
was first published in 1949. (In 1953 the first American edition
appeared.) Since then, what was "virtually impossible" for Yourcenar, in France, in 1951, has become, for us, in Canada, in 1989,
commonplace. Perhaps we can see the triumph of feminism in the
fact that the 'possible' has changed.

Here I must stop and qualify. We are not in any paradisiacal age
of post-feminism. Despite the battles we have won, the war has just
begun. And in the case of many of those battles we might have once
thought, naively, we had won – abortion, equal pay, decent daycare – we are finding we must begin the struggle over again. The
patriarchal structures may have wriggled uncomfortably from
our pressures a number of times, but they have not yet substan-
tially changed.

What have changed are our minds, and the weapons of our
struggle. We have, for one thing, a vocabulary: *patriarchy, chauvin-
ism, sexism*. What can be named can be altered. Change cannot
come about without belief in the possibility of change. To this end,
some of our best allies have been our writers. The ability to imagine
a different world – namely *our* world, the living experience of
women's lives – is a potent tool for change. This gut evidence, this
visceral experience, *women's lives*, is, as this book and the many
others like it give witness to, no longer unspeakable, no longer
unworthy of being spoken.

Our ability to see ourselves as different, to express the individu-
ality of our lives, began with seeing ourselves as different from the

male standard. Since then, it has expanded into an ability to see the differences among and between us – in terms of our sexuality, class, race, ethnicity, age. This ability has become our greatest strength. The validation of difference is clearly evident in the depth, breadth and range of the stories in this anthology.

◊

Frictions is not representative of a single theoretical school of feminist writing, or even any single vision of women's experience. It is more an expression of the editor's great good luck in receiving (in a extraordinarily short space of time) many extraordinarily good submissions than it is of any critical position or manifesto. I believe this book is an indication of the health and the vital good spirits of writing by women in Canada today.

I am exhilarated by the scope as well as the quality of the work represented in this collection. We have a variety of authors from across the country; authors for whom this is a first publication and authors of international repute. I am also delighted at the diversity of voice, of background, origin, age, and point of view. I do, however, regret that constraints of time and resources made it impossible to include work in translation from writers in French.

◊

Perhaps the most heartening evidence in these stories of the empowerment of women writers is the availability of humour as a tactic and mode for tackling a variety of less than simple issues. Susan Swan's yarn about an intrepid female reporter who encounters and vanquishes "The Tallest Man in the World" explores our fears of sexuality and our continuing difficulties with body-image. And it does so with a sense of the inherent comedy in *la condition feminine* that might well have been inaccessible to us thirty or even ten years ago. Libby Scheier's funny, gentle tale, "Pretty Goldfish," deals with the trials and tribulations of a child's first encounter with death. Its humour asserts both the straightforwardness of the most profound issues as seen by a child and the no-nonsense self-awareness of the narrator-mother. This refreshing directness and lack of sentimentality about child-rearing is also evident in Sara McDonald's work. "Me and Mine" goes straight to the heart of the bliss, isolation, frustation and heroism of the stay-at-home mother and comes up grinning. We have even come to be able to poke fun at our own foibles, as Suniti Namjoshi adeptly shows in "That Shaggy Look," her parable about feminist fads and trends.

We have come to expect an inevitable wry humour in every piece of work from the veteran writer, Gertrude Story. "Pictures," the story of the sexual awakening and adventures of an escapee farm wife, is no exception. While the economics of marriage are a constant subtext in this fine piece, the more intricate economics of erotic desire are the focus of Story's frank, unerringly perceptive eye. In Caroline Woodward's "Summer Wages" the grim reality of wage slavery is tempered but not undercut by the savvy of the working-class narrator. Because not enough has changed in a generation, the narrator's hard-earned wisdom, wit and cynicism about the working world may or may not save her daughter from undergoing the same oppressive apprenticeship. Joan MacLeod's "Glenda" is impossible to read without laughing aloud. It is also a penetrating critique, through the fresh and hilarious voice of a teenager, of the terrible human cost of the terrorism wielded against the people of El Salvador. "Glenda" ends by offering the young narrator's moving, possible vision of a better world.

◊

The political is inescapable, and many of the writers in this collection concern themselves explicitly with bringing to life stories the headlines desiccate. In "Guatemala" Susan Perly comes to the issue of authorized atrocity against a people by their government from a very different literary method than does Joan MacLeod. Her motivation, however, is much the same. Both writers share the desire to provoke in their readers a passionate, compassionate response to the destruction of 'Others' with whom, through the power of their writing, they allow us to identify. Beth Brant brings the issue of legalized oppression close to home. "A Long Story" is the powerfully juxtaposed narrative of two women who lose their children to the authority of the state: the first to the barbaric paternalism which resulted in the American government's removal of Native children from reserves in the 1890s; the second to contemporary homophobia.

Maya Khankhoje's "Canada Day" adroitly brings together politics at home and abroad. The young protagonist is forced by economics to emigrate from Mexico to Canada. Her hard-won change in status from domestic visa worker to Canadian citizen serves only to illuminate the enduring hypocrisy of her establishment employers. The tragedy that such complacency, such easy assumptions can lead to is uncovered in Rachna Gilmore's strong and unsettling "Mirror, Mirror." A young emigrant housewife daydreams of the good life back home in India. Her reverie is disturbed by memories of the servant girl her friendship and naiveté destroyed.

Such issues of power and powerlessness dominate Helen Rosta's intricate narrative, "To A Fairer Place." A young girl grows up on the Prairies during the dying days of the Depression. She sees her beloved older brother anonymously, inexplicably annihilated by the war that follows. She also is witness to the slow destruction through poverty of a neighbouring family. This powerful story, which convincingly conjoins personal and public morality, can be read as a meditation on courage and the failure of courage. In "Music from Below," Susan Glickman takes a similar enlightening leap from the intimate to the historical. A young woman's protected reality is invaded by another's tragic past. The author deftly leaves us speculating on the enduring issue of power, as well as the intriguing question of how the interpretation of reality affects and creates reality.

◊

Claire Harris' intriguing, multi-layered story of the counterpointed lives of two emigrant cousins focuses on the interplay of realities. "Butterfly on a Pin" presents a startling and stimulating challenge to our ideas of authorial responsibility, as well as our conventional notions of narrative, of simple-minded cause and effect. Carole Corbeil's "Hide and Seek" even more explicitly invites the reader to question the creation of a reality, particularly the fictional reality. A magician's assistant, finding herself infinitely replaceable, decides simply to redefine magic. The author invites the reader into the story, offering alternate resolutions to the plot. The credibility of the fictional narrative is deliberately undermined.

Lee Maracle's "Worm," a tender, gentle vignette of her young son's struggle to comprehend mortality and loss, was co-authored with the child. By doing so, Maracle disrupts our assumptions about authorship and offers a more cohesive view both of the integration of the natural with the human world and of the evolution of story.

◊

The tensions inherent in heterosexual relationships continue to perplex. In "Spring Forward, Fall Back" Sarah Sheard writes with eloquence and passion of the first days of motherhood. She also provides a clear-sighted appraisal of the balance of power between a couple whose love is unlivable once the tenuous peace that produced the child ends. Marlene Cookshaw's brief, lyrical "Coupling" capsulates the gulf in eroticism between the sexes, proposing habit as the death of desire. Clare Braux's "Sleeping Beauty," however, suggests a more hopeful scenario. Braux writes, refreshingly, from the point of view of the man. The tentative gestures toward communication and warmth of her rigid, almost speechless protagonist do find reception. With the war planes buzzing overhead, with the promise of death all around, Braux proposes the possibility of connection, of love.

Jan Bauer's compelling, taut political parable, "In Such a State," allows for no such proposition. Two women are destroyed by the vast, greedy conspiracy of the male power-seekers who surround them. In this setting, the companionship of women is the only enduring value. Female solidarity is also the basis for Frances Rooney's poetic fable, "Mikalyn." In it, the author envisions a society of women whose model of emotional and physical desire allows it to integrate all aspects of female love. In Rooney's mythic society, love does not end with physical death, but continues at the level of spirit.

Libby Oughton's "Sooner or Later All Bodies Tend To Move Towards the Centre of the Earth" proposes a similar spiritual quest. The narrator, a recovering alcoholic, finds emotional centring in the craft of pottery. Ruth Millar's sensitive portrayal of a woman's lack of resolution, of her wavering between choice and passivity, also ends in spiritual renewal. In "Against the Tooth of Time" the protagonist risks the comfort of her mundane existence to take on the challenge of development, both political and personal.

◊

The conflict integral to the structure of the family is taken on with a mixture of hopefulness and realism by a number of authors. In Lake Sagaris' "The Earthquake," a family survives the aftermath of the Chilean coup d'état through the strength of its women. When natural disaster follows political disaster, the metaphor of survival amid the wreckage takes on new life. Sagaris offers an intimate vision of the ordinary heroism that fuels rebellion – against all odds.

Marina Endicott provides a deeply perceptive view of the intricate mechanisms by which a family's love can either support or destroy its members. "The Orphan Boy" is a stunningly-written story of family loyalty and betrayal and of the complexity of sisterhood. Claudia Casper's "Mammal Stores" takes us through a complex web of significant anecdotes of the coming of age for the various members of her matriarchal clan. Mammals all (with the exception of Auntie Dot), the women sense, despite their differences, the commonalities of their physical being, of the curious physical particulars – live birth, suckling, sexual maturation – that characterize us as and among animals and mold our perceptions. Cynthia Flood's "The Meaning of the Marriage" also carries us through the maze of family lore to the possibility of character, of meaningful relationship, that such tales proffer.

◊

I will leave the last word to the first story in our collection. The narrator of Debby Dobson's "My Father Rescued A Cat" may seem, at the end of her story, overwhelmed by the constraints that govern her. She's dropped out of school to work as a cleaner at the mental instituation to which her father has been committed. She speaks, however, as a survivor. She speaks also as a woman of authority, a woman whose time to speak, if it has not yet come, is just around the corner;

And they talk, these women I work with. Mostly I just listen to them and their strong sure voices but sometimes I feel like saying something myself, telling a story too. They talk about people who are different: real people and TV people ... and my father. They don't know who I am. I haven't said anything but I want to. I know good stories about him too.

MY FATHER
RESCUED A CAT

Debby Dobson

O NCE MY father rescued a cat from a tree. No one saw him but
the cat scratched him and he'll show you the scars to prove it.
It ran away as soon as he put it down but he read the next day in the
paper that this woman's cat that had been lost for two years
showed up. It had to be the same cat and he had to tell everyone
about it.

I think I was with him the day he rescued the cat but I was very
little. He must've set me down somewhere while he climbed the
tree. Or maybe it was one of those old-fashioned telephone poles
with metal bars sticking out to climb up with. I hope so. About the
pole instead of the tree. I don't like to think I lay there worrying
that he would fall if a branch broke, lying on my back in the damp
grass (someone had just moved a sprinkler), watching his feet disappear up the pole. Yes, I'm sure it was a pole. That memory is
quite strong. We have the biggest arguments about what I remember and what he remembers. I'm good at details and he's good at
plot. Like the cat story; he doesn't remember the wet grass, but
then again, he didn't have to lie in it. That always helps a memory,
if there was some discomfort or other.

For the longest time he didn't send me to school. "They won't
know what to do with you," was what he told me. Since I didn't
know who They were or what School was, I didn't argue with him.
I was only a child and listening to a child wasn't going to change

anything for him. He never said that to me, I just felt it. And I got resentful till I had views too and I knew I didn't have to change them for anybody because he never did. No matter what.

When he didn't send me to school, he realized he had to do something with me. The first thing I remember is him teaching me the alphabet and not starting with the letter A. He started with T because he told me it was a very popular letter. I believed him: his name started with T, so did mine, and our cat was called Tickle. He let me name the cat but then he never used the name. That was how he showed he didn't like something. He didn't use it or wouldn't have anything to do with it. That's how I know he loved me, because I didn't have to go to school; he kept me around him even when he wasn't teaching me things.

Most of the time he wasn't teaching me things. I didn't know that though. I thought school would be sitting around watching the teacher do something they wanted to do and the kids had to be quiet and watch. Or a kid could wander away quietly and do something else.

It was better when I was alone. I could go to my room and do things like listen to the radio or play with Tickle. Once I wrote down all the things a cat could do, like poke things under the edge of the rug with one paw or stand like a ballet dancer with toes pointed out. And then the next day I had to do all the things I'd copied down in the order I'd seen Tickle do them. He was a good student too, Tickle was. He lay on the bed and watched me poke things under the rug. Or he slept quietly.

Maybe the neighbours talked. One year after Christmas, he took me to school and left me there. I found my own way home and he never asked me about my first day. Ever. Or any other day after that. It was like I went into space as soon as I left the house. School didn't exist. He wouldn't sign anything that came from the school. He wouldn't come to anything that happened at the school. I bet I was the only kid in grade four who could write their own notes for illness or appointments. I guess they figured I was more responsible than he was. Most of the time I was pretty responsible but in high school it got too tempting.

My mind wasn't into school by then. I only went to school because he had taken me the first day and left me there. That was his way of saying this was a place I had to be. I thought that's what he was saying. Why else would he have done it? When I started asking questions, that's when I stopped going to school all the time. I went most of the time but by then I had developed an imaginary disease that required lots of tests at the hospital. For days I would stay home in my room listening to the radio, sending in letters to Morningside or calling in to the talk shows.

One day he came home in the middle of the day. There was a man with him and they talked for the longest time in the kitchen at the table where my lunch dishes still sat. The man was angry about something. Something at work. It was like my father wasn't there; he only said a couple things in a voice so low I could barely hear it. When the man left I went downstairs.

"It's all over now," my father said and got up and went outside. I followed him.

"It wouldn't be so bad but it took such a long time." He started to rake leaves from the birch at the back.

"Why do you think it took them so long to find out?" He asked me a question. He stopped raking and looked at me. He'd never asked me a question before and now he wanted an answer. Was waiting for it.

"Find out what?" I asked but he didn't want another question. He wanted an answer. I think he was missing my mother. I think he wanted her there. I think for a moment he thought she was there.

Then I had to go back to school because he was home every day. I went every day for a while until the Guidance Counsellor asked how I was feeling. He meant the tests. I told him they were waiting for some results from Montreal. Then I tried staying home a couple days and my father never said anything. Maybe he thought I'd graduated or something. It wasn't as nice as having the house to myself but it was better than going to school.

But I got older; I used up the house. My room wasn't magic anymore; Tickle was dead. I could listen to music on my Walkman anywhere, and did. It felt crowded with him there, him and his crazy schemes that had taken over the day when he could've been out working. Bodybuilding in the basement, a stationary bike in front of the TV. A model village in the back yard; that was his way of socializing, of getting people to visit. He built these miniature houses complete with streets and sidewalks and a park. I guess it was kind of neat but I was too old then to appreciate it. He even tried keeping it open in the winter, built little snowmen outside the houses, put Christmas lights out. The dogs kept peeing on one of the corner houses until it was a solid yellow icicle. But it was too much work for the few people who could be encouraged up the driveway in the dwindling afternoon light. People trusted him, though. They believed he had something to show them, that it wasn't a trick to kidnap them or molest them. In all his rambling and wandering no one called the cops. He always kept just this side of what was right.

Maybe that was why nobody asked me what I was doing; they knew whose daughter I was.

Then I discovered the mall. Not a grand elaborate mall, just a common shopping mall – a Met at one end and a SuperValue at the other. There was a twin cinema with walls so thin you could hear the chase scene in Theatre One when you were sitting in Theatre Two. I got tired of just standing around buying watered-down cokes so I lied about my age and got a job at a women's clothing store. Cheap stuff. Garish. It looked great till you put it on. That was my job; to tell the young girls who came in how nice they looked, how trendy, how thin even when the pants bulged and the hems dragged at the back of fat thighs.

One day he came to the mall. I wouldn't have seen him because I was stocktaking at the back. But I heard him: End of the World Part Two. All the other clerks were laughing at the old man in dirty jeans and a deerstalker who was shouting at nobody about nothing. This time he'd gone too far. For sure he'd be arrested and then where would I be.

He wasn't surprised to see me and didn't mind helping me tag clothes. He always settled better if his hands were busy.

"So what's happening?" I asked him.

He snapped a couple more plastic security tabs on sleeves.

"You try the muffins I made this morning?" I asked.

And then he started to cry. My boss thought it was kind of strange, this man crying, even if he was helping for free. I couldn't explain so I quit.

We just stayed at home. I watched Sally Jessy Raphael in the morning and All My Children in the afternoon. He slept till supper and then watched TV all night, it didn't matter what was on, he didn't choose anything, he just watched.

But we weren't getting by.

I have another job now, at the hospital, cleaning stuff like beds and toilets. They give me their flowers sometimes, the patients I mean, when they're leaving. But usually they give them to the nurses. We have to wear these bright yellow uniforms and we sit there in the cafeteria and drink coffee we buy and eat sandwiches from home.

And they talk, these women I work with. Mostly I just listen to them and their strong sure voices but sometimes I feel like saying something myself, telling a story too. They talk about people who are different; real people and TV people ... and my father. They don't know who I am. I haven't said anything but I want to. I know good stories about him too.

But just when I think I might say something, just when I think I might tell my own story, someone will start one about my father, and they'll be off and running with it before I've had my chance. Before I can tell them what I think. I suppose it doesn't matter. It never has before. Mattered, I mean, about what I think. It doesn't matter because if it did I would've done something about it, I guess. That's what I think.

A LONG STORY

Beth Brant

"About 40 Indian children took the train at this depot for the Philadelphia Indian School last Friday. They were accompanied by the government agent, and seemed a bright looking lot."

The Northern Observer (Massena, New York, July 20, 1892)

"I am only beginning to understand what it means for a mother to lose a child."

Anna Demeter, *Legal Kidnapping*
(Beacon Press, Boston, 1977)

1890

IT HAS BEEN two days since they came and took the children away. My body is greatly chilled. All our blankets have been used to bring me warmth. The women keep the fire blazing. The men sit. They talk among themselves. We are frightened by this sudden child-stealing. We signed papers, the agent said. This gave them rights to take our babies. It is good for them, the agent said. It will make them civilized, the agent said. I do not know *civilized*.

I hold myself tight in fear of flying apart in the air. The others try to feed me. Can they feed a dead woman? I have stopped talking. When my mouth opens, only air escapes. I have used up my sound screaming their names – She Sees Deer! He Catches The Leaves! My eyes stare at the room, the walls of scrubbed wood, the floor of dirt. I know there are people here, but I cannot see them. I see a darkness, like the lake at New Moon. Black, unmoving. In the centre, a picture of my son and daughter being lifted onto the train. My daughter wearing the dark blue, heavy dress. All of the girls dressed alike. Never have I seen such eyes! They burn into my head even now. My son. His hair cut. Dressed as the white men, his arms and legs covered by cloth that made him sweat. His face, streaked with tears. So many children crying, screaming. The sun on our bodies, our heads. The train screeching like a crow, sounding like laughter. Smoke and dirt pumping out of the insides of the train. So many people. So many children. The women, standing as if in prayer, our hands lifted, reaching. The dust sifting down on our palms. Our palms making motions at the sky. Our fingers closing like the claws of the bear.

I see this now. The hair of my son held in my hands. I rub the strands, the heavy braids coming alive as the fire flares and casts a bright light on the black hair. They slip from my fingers and lie coiled on the ground. I see this. My husband picks up the braids, wraps them in cloth; he takes the pieces of our son away. He walks outside, the eyes of the people on him. I see this. He will find a bottle and drink with the men. Some of the women will join him. They will end the night by singing or crying. It is all the same. I see this. No sounds of children playing games and laughing. Even the dogs have ceased their noise. They lay outside each doorway, waiting. I hear this. The voices of children. They cry. They pray. They call me. *Nisten ha.* I hear this. *Nisten ha.**

1978

I am wakened by the dream. In the dream my daughter is dead. Her father is returning her body to me in pieces. He keeps her heart. I thought I sceamed ... *Patricia*! I sit up in bed, swallowing air

* Mother

as if for nourishment. The dream remains in the air. I rise to go to her room. Ellen tries to lead me back to bed, but I have to see once again. I open her door. She is gone. The room empty, lonely. They said it was in her best interests. How can that be? She is only six, a baby who needs her mothers. She loves us. This has not happened. I will not believe this. Oh god, I think I have died.

Night after night, Ellen holds me as I shake. Our sobs stifling the air in our room. We lie in our bed and try to give comfort. My mind can't think beyond last week when she left. I would have killed him if I'd had the chance! He took her hand and pulled her to the car. The look in his eyes of triumph. It was a contest to him, Patricia the prize. He will teach her to hate us. He will! I see her dear face. That face looking out the back window of his car. Her mouth forming the words *Mommy, Mama*. Her dark braids tied with red yarn. Her front teeth missing. Her overalls with the yellow flower on the pocket, embroidered by Ellen's hands. So lovingly she sewed the yellow wool. Patricia waiting quietly until she was finished. Ellen promising to teach her designs – chain stitch, french knot, split stitch. How Patricia told everyone that Ellen made the flower just for her. So proud of her overalls.

I open the closet door. Almost everything is gone. A few things hang there limp, abandoned. I pull a blue dress from the hanger and take it back to my room. Ellen tries to take it from me, but I hold on, the soft blue cotton smelling of my daughter. How is it possible to feel such pain and live? "Ellen?!" She croons my name. "Mary, Mary, I love you." She sings me to sleep.

1890

The agent was here to deliver a letter. I screamed at him and sent curses his way. I threw dirt in his face as he mounted his horse. He thinks I'm a crazy woman and warns me, "You better settle down Annie." What can they do to me? I am a crazy woman. This letter hurts my hands. It is written in their hateful language. It is evil, but there is a message for me.

I start the walk up the road to my brother. He works for the whites and understands their meanings. I think about my brother as I pull the shawl closer to my body. It is cold now. Soon there will be snow. The corn has been dried and hangs from our cabin, waiting to be used. The corn never changes. My brother is changed. He says that *I* have changed and bring shame to our clan. He says I should accept the fate. But I do not believe in the fate of child-stealing. There is evil here. There is much wrong in our village. My brother says I am a crazy woman because I howl at the sky every evening. He is a fool. I am calling the children. He says the people are becoming afraid of me because I talk to the air and laugh like the raven overhead. But I am talking to the children. They need to hear the sound of me. I laugh to cheer them. They cry for us.

This letter burns my hands. I hurry to my brother. He has taken the sign of the wolf from over the doorway. He pretends to be like those who hate us. He gets more and more like the child-stealers. His eyes move away from mine. He takes the letter from me and begins the reading of it. I am confused. This letter is from two strangers with the names Martha and Daniel. They say they are learning civilized ways. Daniel works in the fields, growing food for the school. Martha cooks and is being taught to sew aprons. She will be going to live with the schoolmaster's wife. She will be a live-in girl. What is a *live-in girl*? I shake my head. The words sound the same to me. I am afraid of Martha and Daniel, these strangers who know my name. My hands and arms are becoming numb.

I tear the letter from my brother's fingers. He stares at me, his eyes traitors in his face. He calls after me, "Annie! Annie!" That is not my name! I run to the road. That is not my name! There is no Martha! There is no Daniel! This is witch work. The paper burns and burns. At my cabin, I quickly dig a hole in the field. The earth is hard and cold, but I dig with my nails. I dig, my hands feeling weaker. I tear the paper and bury the scraps. As the earth drifts and settles, the names Martha and Daniel are covered. I look to the sky and find nothing but endless blue. My eyes are blinded by the colour. I begin the howling.

1978

When I get home from work, there is a letter from Patricia. I make coffee and wait for Ellen, pacing the rooms of our apartment. My back is sore from the line, bending over and down, screwing the handles on the doors of the flashy cars moving by. My work protects me from questions, the guys making jokes at my expense. But some of them touch my shoulder lightly and briefly as a sign of understanding. The few women, eyes averted or smiling in sympathy. No one talks. There is no time to talk. No room to talk, the noise taking up all space and breath.

I carry the letter with me as I move from room to room. Finally I sit at the kitchen table, turning the paper around in my hands. Patricia's printing is large and uneven. The stamp has been glued on halfheartedly and is coming loose. Each time a letter arrives, I dread it, even as I long to hear from my child. I hear Ellen's key in the door. She walks into the kitchen, bringing the smell of the hospital with her. She comes toward me, her face set in new lines, her uniform crumpled and stained, her brown hair pulled back in an imitation of a french twist. She knows there is a letter. I kiss her and bring mugs of coffee to the table. We look at each other. She reaches for my hand, bringing it to her lips. Her hazel eyes are steady in her round face.

I open the letter. *Dear Mommy. I am fine. Daddy got me a new bike. My big teeth are coming in. We are going to see Grandma for my birthday. Daddy got me new shoes. Love, Patricia.* She doesn't ask about Ellen. I imagine her father standing over her, coaxing her, coaching her. The letter becomes ugly. I tear it in bits and scatter them out the window. The wind scoops the pieces into a tight fist before strewing them in the street. A car drives over the paper, shredding it to garbage and mud.

Ellen makes a garbled sound. "I'll leave. If it will make it better, I'll leave." I quickly hold her as the dusk moves into the room and covers us. "Don't leave. Don't leave." I feel her sturdy back shiver against my hands. She kisses my throat, and her arms tighten as we move closer. "Ah Mary, I love you so much." As the tears threaten our eyes, the taste of salt is on our lips and tongues. We stare into ourselves, touching the place of pain, reaching past the fear, the guilt, the anger, the loneliness.

We go to our room. It is beautiful again. I am seeing it new. The sun is barely there. The colours of cream, brown, green mixing with the wood floor. The rug with its design of wild birds. The black ash basket glowing on the dresser, holding a bouquet of dried flowers bought at a vendor's stand. I remember the old woman, laughing and speaking rapidly in Polish as she wrapped the blossoms in newspaper. Ellen undresses me as I cry. My desire for her breaking through the heartbreak we share. She pulls the covers back, smoothing the white sheets, her hands repeating the gestures done at work. She guides me onto the cool material. I watch her remove the uniform of work. An aide to nurses. A healer of spirit.

She comes to me full in flesh. My hands are taken with the curves and soft roundness of her. She covers me with the beating of her heart. The rhythm steadies me. Heat is centring me. I am grounded by the peace between us. I smile at her face above me, round like a moon, her long hair loose and touching my breasts. I take her breast in my hand, bring it to my mouth, suck her as a woman – in desire, in faith. Our bodies join. Our hair braids together on the pillow. Brown, black, silver, catching the last light of the sun. We kiss, touch, move to our place of power. Her mouth, moving over my body, stopping at curves and swells of skin, kissing, removing pain. Closer, close, together, woven, my legs are heat, the centre of my soul is speaking to her, I am sliding into her, her mouth is medicine, her heart is the earth, we are dancing with flying arms, I shout, I sing, I weep salty liquid , sweet and warm it coats her throat. This is my life. I love you Ellen, I love you Mary, I love, we love.

1891

The moon is full. The air is cold. This cold strikes at my flesh as I remove my clothes and set them on fire in the withered corn field. I cut my hair, the knife sawing through the heavy mass. I bring the sharp blade to my arms, legs, and breasts. The blood trickles like small red rivers down my body. I feel nothing. I throw the tangled webs of my hair into the flames. The smell, like a burning animal, fills my nostrils. As the fire stretches to touch the stars, the people come out to watch me – the crazy woman. The ice in the air touches me.

They caught me as I tried to board the train and search for my babies. The white men tell my husband to watch me. I am dangerous. I laugh and laugh. My husband is good only for tipping bottles and swallowing anger. He looks at me, opening his mouth and making no sound. His eyes are dead. He wanders from the cabin and looks out on the corn. He whispers our names. He calls after the children. He is a dead man.

Where have they taken the children? I ask the question of each one who travels the road past our door. The women come and we talk. We ask and ask. They say there is nothing we can do. The white man is like a ghost. He slips in and out where we cannot see. Even in our dreams he comes to take away our questions. He works magic that resists our medicine. This magic has made us weak. What is the secret about them? Why do they want our children? They sent the Blackrobes many years ago to teach us new magic. It was evil! They lied and tricked us. They spoke of gods who would forgive us if we believed as they do. They brought the rum with the cross. This god is ugly! He killed our masks. He killed our men. He sends the women screaming at the moon in terror. They want our power. They take our children to remove the inside of them. Our power. They steal our food, our sacred rattle, the stories, our names. What is left?

I am a crazy woman. I look to the fire that consumes my hair and see their faces. My daughter. My son. They still cry for me, though the sound grows fainter. The wind picks up their keening and brings it to me. The sound has bored into my brain. I begin howling. At night I dare not sleep. I fear the dreams. It is too terrible, the things that happen there. In my dream there is wind and blood moving as a stream. Red, dark blood in my dream. Rushing for our village. The blood moves faster. There are screams of wounded people. Animals are dead, thrown in the blood stream. There is nothing left. Only the air echoing nothing. Only the earth soaking up blood, spreading it in the four directions, becoming a thing there is no name for. I stand in the field watching the fire, The People watching me. We are waiting, but the answer is not clear yet. A crazy woman. That is what they call me.

1979

After taking a morning off work to see my lawyer, I come home, not caring if I call in. Not caring, for once, at the loss in pay. Not caring. My lawyer says there is nothing more we can do. I must wait. As if there has been something other than waiting. He has custody and calls the shots. We must wait and see how long it takes for him to get tired of being a mommy and a daddy. So, I wait.

I open the door to Patricia's room. Ellen and I keep it dusted and cleaned in case my baby will be allowed to visit us. The yellow and blue walls feel like a mockery. I walk to the windows, begin to systematically tear down the curtains. I slowly start to rip the cloth apart. I enjoy hearing the sounds of destruction. Faster, I tear the material into strips. What won't come apart with my hands, I pull at with my teeth. Looking for more to destroy, I gather the sheets and bedspread in my arms and wildly shred them to pieces. Grunting and sweating, I am pushed by rage and the searing wound in my soul. Like a wolf caught in a trap, gnawing at her own leg to set herself free, I begin to beat my breasts to deaden the pain inside. A noise gathers in my throat and finds the way out. I begin a scream that turns to howling, then becomes hoarse choking. I want to take my fists, my strong fists, my brown fists, and smash the world until it bleeds. Bleeds! And all the judges in their flapping robes, and the fathers who look for revenge, are ground, ground into dust and disappear with the wind.

The word *lesbian*. Lesbian. The word that makes them panic, makes them afraid, makes them destroy children. The word that dares them. Lesbian. *I am one.* Even for Patricia, even for her, *I will not cease to be*! As I kneel amidst the colourful scraps, Raggedy Anns smiling up at me, my chest gives a sigh. My heart slows to its normal speech. I feel the blood pumping outward to my veins, carrying nourishment and life. I strip the room naked. I close the door.

Thanks so much to Chrystos for the title. Thanks to Gloria Anzaldúa for encouraging the writing of this story.

SLEEPING BEAUTY

Clare Braux

JOSEPH is holding a stubby index finger against his small, pursed mouth, making kissing movements. There are tiny lines running from his nose to his lips. Gives him a buttoned-up look. But when he was a boy .... He pumps his eyebrows. On the sand of the almost empty beach, in a white shirt and grey slacks, he sits stiff-legged and barefoot, one ankle crossed over the other. He watches the woman looking for treasures in the ebbing slosh. How can she put her hands in that muck? A shiver runs along his spine. He shifts his weight, jabs a clenched fist into his left side, trying to dispel the knot in his stomach. Relax for godsake, he tells himself. You're 59 and away from home in the country of anything-goes. She waves to him. At this distance her face is blurred. He waves back feebly. He bends forward, farts and rolls up his pant legs. He pokes at a tiny snail straining up its dune of sand grains. It retracts its eyestalks and is still.

He met her three days ago; adjacent apartments, the Bonjour Motel, Hollywood Beach, Florida. He'd noticed her on the plane from Montreal. Who could miss her? Continually changing seats, she talked to anyone who would listen. Gossip about her neighbours in Joliette. Her father had been half-Irish she told the bald man in the seat ahead of Joseph's.

She's bending toward the dark, choppy water again. Her heavy body in the swimsuit looks like a red beach ball from where he's sitting. Everything around her is grey, an angry grey, the water, the sky, even the beach is colourless in this light. Who could miss her, he thinks, smiling to himself. She's very pretty and young-looking

34

as fat women often are right up into their seventies. She says she's 54. She looks 34, with her smooth skin and stylishly cut auburn hair. But even at his age he's fussy.

In summer, when he was a boy, his father would wake him at four every Friday morning and the two of them would load the produce and leave the farm in Bécancour for the city. They would drive in silence for miles in the old truck to catch the five o'clock ferry for Trois-Rivières. His father's stern profile. On the ferry they would stand against the guardrail and watch the wake. His father said, one time, "You're a fine-looking boy." Joseph remembers blushing.

Here she comes. Take a deep breath. She's running in her droll way, her legs angling out from the knees, her thighs pressed close, her arms flapping. She looks like a wind-up toy. She twirls, facing the four compass points.

"So! You won't even wet your feet, Joseph?" Margaret-Rose whoops, standing over him. She says her mother named her Margaret-Rose after the princess. Her bulk, her breath, her warmth, fill the vast dull sky above him. He hears the faint drone of what he thinks is a fighter plane above her head. He shivers again. He can't think what to say to her.

"I'm not dressed," he says, flustered, and removes dead crab claws from under his right calf. She ignores his comment and plumps herself down beside him, spraying his legs with sand and seawater. He brushes it all away, patting and scrubbing, while she hollers,

"I love the sea! It cures all my big troubles!" She's hugging her fat arms, looking toward the horizon, clutching something shiny in her hand. A little halo of darkening sand outlines her smooth thighs. Why doesn't she sit on a towel? She cries out,

"Oh, Joseph, don't you just love this beach? We'll come every February, you and me."

Her voice carries. He looks around. Only a few scattered couples are lying on the warm, sunless beach. It *is* a nice, wide beach. Miles and miles of coarse golden sand that massages your feet. He smiles thinly, hoping the she-devil in her'll be appeased.

"You know," she continues, "I deserve this. I've always worked so hard. I brought up my sisters and brothers when my mother had to go to work. Now I'm going to live!"

There goes a father with his little blond daughter. A cigar in his mouth. He's proud. He bends down to say something to her in English. His wife walks by herself, her feet splashing the water of the strand. Us men, Joseph thinks, we like our women sweet and innocent.

"When I get back," Margaret-Rose is saying, addressing the ocean, "the first thing I'm going to do is move into this building I told you I bought. Then I've got to invest twenty-five thousand dollars on renovations. I'm going to have my apartment at the back and my real estate office in the front. I'm going to be rich and in five years I'm going to sell the whole shebang and retire."

They sit together in silence. Scudding whitecaps ripple and flatten as the wind dies. Gulls shriek and wheel.

She pokes him in the ribs. "Well! Joseph. What do you think?" She gives a little jump and grabs her beachbag. She's still holding the object she brought from the shore. She rummages and comes up with a stick of gum. Thrusts it at his face. He moves his head back and looks at it. "Want some?" she says. "I've only got the one. We can split it." She leans heavily against him and whispers, "I'll unwrap it and put it between my teeth and you can bite off your half." She laughs uproariously, her dancing dark eyes peering into his glasses. Can she see his two poor eyes behind them? He shades his face with one hand and squints at her.

"Scratch my back," she says, turning her body away from him, her bare back a huge expanse, looking over her shoulder and grinning, the gum visible between her cute teeth. He strokes with the sides of his fingers not to get too much of her grease and dead skin cells under his fingernails. She soon gets tired of the unsatisfactory service and, good-humoured as always, she slaps his thigh smartly and lies down, her head on his lap. He gasps. Maybe she'll feel his pot swelling and subsiding with his breathing. He can feel the side of her head, her ear, against his abdomen. He tries to breathe as shallowly as possible, inching away from her.

Arriving in Trois-Rivières, his father would park the truck on rue Radisson at the best stall still available. Joseph would help his father lay out the strawberries, the cucumbers, the cauliflower, the green onions, everything to look nice so people would buy from them. His dour father had nervous hands, patting the vegetables, moving crates, smoking cigarettes. Sometimes Joseph thought his father had chosen him, the youngest, over his brothers because of his good looks. He had this straight nose and full lips and nice, round chin. Girls and women stopped at their stall, even when he was 9 or 10 years old, and flirted with him.

She's sitting up again. "Joseph," Margaret-Rose says loudly, "Why don't you put your arms around me? There's nobody for miles to see!" She giggles. Is she joking? Is she making fun of him? What does she want from him? She's made a pot of Bourguignon stew, and invited him for supper. Is a man who's masturbated all his life still a virgin?

When Joseph was 13, his life with his father, the hotel and the restaurant dinners every Friday night, ended. His father sold the farm and went into construction. Eventually he became a contractor, moving the family to Châteaugay, near Montreal, where he'd prospered.

That last Saturday in Trois-Rivières; Joseph can still see the girl's angry face, her rabbit teeth. She looked older sitting there. She was the girl who'd hung around the stall teaching him English. He was proud of his growing ability to speak it, especially since his father would smile in that tight way of his and nod at the English girl. Joseph felt that his father admired the English. That day, Joseph went into the indoor market and walked into the Ladies Room by mistake and saw her, her stall door open. She screamed. There was flushing and two of her friends came crashing out of other stalls. He ran. The three came after him, down the wide corridor, pounding and yelling, "You dirty little Frenchie! You dumb peasoup hick!" They laughed like banshees, shrieking, "You stupid Frenchie! Stupid! Dirty Frenchie!"

Joseph did not answer his father's question: Did you go in there on purpose? That was what made his father so mad. He grabbed Joseph and beat him with the flat of his hand, the back of his hand, he punched him on the side of the head. Joseph's cries and tears only seemed to inflame his father more, and the people standing around gawking. Joseph fell against the truck's lowered back panel. His body turned once and he lost consciousness as the grass came up toward him.

A finger is running around his ear. He flinches.

"You know Joseph, I like you. Why don't we pretend we're married?" Margaret-Rose sits up and grins at him.

He smiles sadly, mysteriously, he hopes. He doesn't want her angry, abandoning him for someone else. She leans on him again.

"I'm leaving my husband in the spring. That's definite. As soon as I get settled in my new apartment. I told him, I've had enough. But he doesn't care. He comes home tired, wants his supper, sits in front of the TV with a beer and snoozes. Then he goes to bed. I can do without that, don't you think? I need a real man. I'm through, Joseph, do you hear? His name is Freddie. He's ten years younger than me. I should never have married that baby. He's only 44. He's got no experience of anything. Not like you, Joseph. You're a mature man. I can see that. Tut, tut. How come you never got married? My first husband, I caught him in bed with the babysitter, a woman older than both of us put together. I threw them out, I can tell you!"

Joseph nods. "That was the right thing to do," he says. A monstrous coast guard helicopter roars by at low altitude. They follow it with their eyes. Are there drug smugglers in those yachts? Joseph wonders. Maybe spies in submarines offshore? Nuclear warheads? Maybe we're sitting on a time bomb.

"I'm sick of these babies. I'd like an older man." Margaret-Rose muses. "He's lazy. Four years ago, when I was 50, I finished high school and took real estate courses at the same time. I was a waitress then. Before that I worked as a dressmaker for rich people and I did char work too. I've been saving my money all my life for this. I sell houses easy. I'm a good salesman. Saleswoman, I guess you'd say." She laughs again, a loud peal, throwing back her head. Where her throat meets her shoulders are two soft rolls of flesh. She finds a lipstick in her bag and, holding a small mirror with the hand clutching the object she found on the shore, paints her lips bright orange. She dabs at the corners of her mouth with her little finger. She smiles at Joseph.

"I like to make people feel good. I like to make them laugh. What's life all about, Joseph?" She sighs and looks up at the rushing clouds. She shakes her head. "We're no longer innocent, you and me and *le genre humain.* Now we know that those clouds are only a cover-up. We know there's only black space up there, full of crazy suns. So big, so big. We're so small, teeny-weeny, you and me, Joseph." She brings her thumb and index finger together, an eighth of an inch apart and squints at it. "We know there are no angels to blow trumpets and tell us what to do. We have only each other. But you know, Joseph, I can't keep it down. All this joie de vivre in me. I'm not very ladylike." Her hand, coming up to touch her hair, is trembling. "Most people want to be thought respectable. Me, I can't control the fun in me, this urge to touch people. I should keep my hands to myself, eh, Joseph? I can see you don't like it."

Joseph turns his head toward her. He doesn't see her. He shivers again. A howling starts up on the beach, a baying back and forth on the wind that blows down from the north. He runs pell-mell, his heart racing, away from loud, incomprehensible, loud, ugly words. Pushing his way, punching a giant father away, punching. He's punching.

"Joseph! What are you doing?"

"Nothing." He looks away. Why does he titter? He knows men don't titter. He can still hear the cruel laughter. He must have been a slow-witted child. He closes his eyes tight. He listens inside himself as he often does. He hears words like stones that don't connect, that he cannot speak. Sometimes when he listens, his words are hard and angry and they frighten him. Joseph took over the firm when his father died. He discovered a creative business sense in himself and tripled the company's assets. Sold it four years ago and now he's a rich man. Poor man, he tells himself. Never married, no children; what is he anyway? Self-absorbed, self-tormented. Poor, poor, poor you, you poor fool, he thinks. He turns toward the woman.

She's digging in the sand. Burying her legs. One hand clenched over the small object she's holding. She sits up. "Bury me, Joseph." She digs with both hands behind her. "Help me," she says. He digs with the sides of his palms. She lies down.

The English family passes by, going the other way. The father waves to them. Margaret-Rose, raising her head, waves back. The little girl looks several times from them to her parents. Joseph slowly lifts handfuls of sand from around the woman and drops them on her. She pats it down.

"Come on, Joseph. Pat me down. Make the shape of me in the sand. It's so warm down here. I think I'll stay here forever. Make a pillow for my head." She stretches. The sand cracks a little. Joseph smooths some of the crannies along her arms.

"Now Joseph, you're alone on the beach."

There is no one in sight. The little English family has disappeared. He's conscious of the huge mound beside him. She's closed her eyes. And her mouth. He relaxes. It's nice when she's quiet. He breathes the damp air of the warm, cloudy day. Hears the breakers for the first time. The eternal shushing. The huge helicopter roars by again. It disappears down the coast toward Miami.

"Go away, Joseph."

He stiffens. Looks around. Her mouth speaks again, "Go away, Joseph." Her orange lips close. They open again. "It's all hopeless isn't it?" she says quietly.

He sees the soft rise and fall of her breathing. It moves him in the strangest way. How can he tell her he likes her? Her arms come up above her head, scattering sand. The object in her hand glints in the pearly light from high above the ocean. A round, flat stone, a little bigger than a silver dollar. It fits neatly in her small, plump palm.

"Let me see," he says. She doesn't move.

"Let me see your little stone."

She sits up, sand streaming off her, her eyes searching his.

"You mean this?" She shows it to him. "I thought it had a pretty pattern on it. I found it in a narrow rivulet in the packed sand down there." She smiles. She moves its silvery face back and forth, its flowerlike pattern coming and going depending on the way the light falls on it. She angles it for him to scrutinize, but doesn't relinquish her hold. Then she looks at it a long time.

"It's a fossil, Joseph. Look! It's scary-looking. If it was bigger I mean. It's a millipede. See? There in the middle of the stone."

"It's two bugs."

"You're right, Joseph. And they were mating when they died. Look!" Margaret-Rose laughs and points with a long vermilion fingernail. He shakes his head.

"It's possible, Joseph. Wouldn't it be nice to think that our ancestors were making love, maybe squeaking from the stab of pleasure, when doom came for them, millions of years ago? Joseph, stop shaking your head! And you're blushing! Oh, Joseph!"

Margaret-Rose frowns, she holds the mirrored stone like one holds a dart. She stares at Joseph, her orange mouth pursed.

"Lie down," she says and reaches up and places the flat of the stone against his forehead, pushing him down until he lies on the sand. She scrambles up to a kneeling position beside him. "Now close your eyes. Close your eyes. Relax, Joseph," she says, softly. She begins to stroke his face ever so gently, like a tiny millipede crawling on it and he tingles all over. Down his neck, her two soft hands barely graze his skin and unfasten the buttons of his shirt. His whole body shudders. He can feel the round stone, hot from her hand, in the middle of his forehead. Margaret-Rose whispers in his ear, "Let me in, Joseph. You have to be in there yourself, to let anybody else in." She smiles at his closed eyelids. "It's like a quickening, Joseph. At our age, we can ignore the rest of the world." She puts her hand on his chest.

Her words soothe him. His First Communion portrait in a navy-blue knee-pants suit with the big white bow at the neck and the white and gold armband and shiny patent leather shoes appears in his mind's eye. His mother examined the photograph and said, "He looks like a little prince." Joseph smiles at the memory. He sinks into a peaceful torpor, the warm sand gives way under him and he floats, his head heavy and enveloped in darkness.

Margaret-Rose sits on her haunches, her hands on her lap. She looks at his face, newly handsome in its slackness; he looks twenty years younger. The beach is deserted except for the wheeling gulls, a flock of them squabbling over some sea offal three yards away. Joseph begins to snore softly. High up, flying through wisps of ragged underclouds, Margaret-Rose sees a squadron formation roaring toward the east. She moves closer to Joseph. She bends over him, supported by her two arms on either side of him. She lowers her face over his and slowly kisses him on the mouth. She watches him awaken.

BUTTERFLY
ON A PIN

Claire Harris

I N such dream quickened dark
      everything looms   streetlights
corner bank   drugstore   even small houses in small
gardens gather their skirts   lean
in their intent night-windows a scythe-moon
glitters   and this is where a poem begins   innocent
insistent   *she finds herself at the corner*   dream
sense of stifled horror   how doom swirls   to know
once and for all what it is that eludes
and teases   in such a space the night is wet   dank
streetlights are blue / orange / red in pavement   a wind
a plastic bag that lifts and skids and blows
gleams   *ghostly as flimsy as i in the schoolyard*
twirling   twirling to music that not even the dream
reveals   what is a dream *without revelation*
i watch as from a great distance above how *she*
comes face to face with her self   *that other that*
in the dream *is glimmering*   trailing   not always
there   not all there   sudden as dreams are sudden
the city glows in her forehead
her eyes are islands   *dark Caribbean seas*
a yellow light on her face   *deft peculiar grace*
my mouth opens straining to fit in to   reach what

is there   on that street corner in Calgary below
the bluffs and dry poplars   *to fit into*
infiltrated by the bitter orange glow of midnight streets
to reach what there is teasing beyond the edges and
heaven's bruised light spilt i am crying   *i am Enid*
Thomas   my voice rising i think it is my voice   *i am*
Enid Thomas   voice as if my hands were tied behind
my back as if someone were denying me
a name *i am Enid Thomas*

◊

She wakes. She is not. Not Enid Thomas. Let's make that clear. She
is Patricia Williams. Patricia Whittaker-Williams. Narrator of her
own story. And Patricia has never met, never even heard of Enid
Thomas. As if she didn't have problems enough. What with a principal trying to get rid of her. And a publisher (m)ucking up her
book. If she smoked this would be a good time for a cigarette. Bars
of moonlight across the bed. The cross from her father's coffin
handed to her mother before the mattress and the shovelfuls of
earth and stone. Now, since her mother's death, passed on to her.
Mysterious in grey blue light. She is hot, throat sore, dry. The secret
dream-life as strenuous as other rebellions.

◊

The bed is a ghostly galleon floating the moonlit sea
Enid Thomas comes sailing   sailing
sailing
Enid Thomas comes sailing up to the old Bounty

◊

When she wakes for the second time, grey light fills the room like
an unwanted visitor. Her head is stuffed, bulging with the night's
images. Walking about the room she touches everything, claims
the bright spines of detective fiction, the Inca head, the Warri
beads. She runs her hands over the television screen, the Brecht,
the Spaniards. Reads the titles of all the Africans. Then stands

shivering before the open window trying to pierce the storm-driven torment of snow to the bluffs and sentinel towers. As if to reassure herself. As if some vital truth of herself, some proof susceptible to the hand, the eye, lingered on the surface of things. So could bear witness.

◊

When she first come to tell me this story, she say, "Great Aunt, what happen here? What it is that really happen?" Is a question Patricia always asking, as if she suspicious, she want the whole world to have meaning. She is a child that never believe in accident, in chance. She tell me she read somewhere "God don't play dice." Well, if it ain't dice He playing, is card He pulling. But she can't believe that yet. It going to come. She got some more living to do.

Well to go back to the beginning. The whole trouble start with this dream she have. Simple as that. Patricia have a dream. Everybody have nightmares, but hers have to be dramatic! They have to have atmosphere! Is a worse thing: they have to have meaning! So she set like a comet on somebody path. She got to interfere with Enid Thomas. While she standing there at that window, pretending that everything she see is hers ... she seeing changing it, you understand ... laser eyes ... that poor woman, Jocelyn, who don't even know her, who is getting out of bed, pushing those heavy blankets back, pulling her pink brushed nylon nightgown up over her head, and struggling a little, seeing as she forget the buttons at the neck, and liking how it soft, and how she smell she own sweetish warm scent, and wondering if is so Lloyd does smell it when he sleep over, and how she got to get that Ashley out of bed, and the porridge on the stove; that woman who don't believe in this cornflakes thing, and the child only picking up, picking up from that damn TV, *but porridge does stick to the ribs, and she going to put an egg in it, no child of hers going to school hungry, and blast! the child have a dentist appointment this morning, she hope Marylyn, since she owe her one, going to cover when she take Ashley ... that place so far, is the LRT she going to have to take and then a bus, it go take two hours, if she go early and use the lunch hour perhaps sourface Garth ain't going to mind, but is a kind dentist, she talk real soft and she Black, and not stuck up because she professional, but is so damn far; that woman who don't have no time for water trouble now, so is what wrong with the tap ... is only hot water coming, she ain't got time for this fiddling fiddling this morning, she really got to get in early ... ah is now the water coming good; that woman who stand under the shower who throw she head back who let water fall on she face like rain on the banks of the Lopinot river, the water pockmarked the cocoa trees darkening and glistening in the rain and the sound of it like a kind of thunder ... you see what I mean this Jocelyn who thinking like a normal person about what is real: what happen already, what she know going to happen again because it happen already, whose life ain't no fantasy, that woman going to have to deal all unexpected with Patricia who think she and God in this together. Together they creating everything she see, everything she touch. I tell you life ain't no equal contest. Just think how no Carib, no Iroquois, could ever imagine that somebody could leave their own place, come thousands of miles to this place and think to take he land from him, think he have a right to take he land, not only he land, he world, he very self. And calling he 'Indian.' In the same way this poor woman who once call she self Enid Thomas can't even imagine what go happen to she, can't even prepare she self for this thing what coming.*

◊

This morning she puts on the loose floating African gown she affects, then drifts into the kitchen. From the door of the broom closet she takes the huge barbecue apron and fastens it on. This is an egg morning. There is the unexpected school holiday, the snow on the balcony banked up against her glass wall, the soft muffling sound of sky slanting into heavy white drifts, wind-howl rising every now and again to penetrate the triple windows. As if it were a whisper, a secret breathed in her ear, she begins to hear words, phrases, the poem she dreamt last night. She connects the blanks, begins to design the whole, to lay the poem out in her head.

While the water for her poached egg boils, she cuts the crusts off whole wheat slices. That done, she drops creamy Danish butter into the small china jar, breaks an egg into the butter, hesitates over thyme, a drop of tobasco, a sprinkle of cheese; or salt, white pepper, a dusting of paprika. She decides on a plain egg, but at the last moment fishes the jar out of the boiling water, unscrews the stainless cover and adds a twist of black pepper to the orange-yellow yolk. One part of her quietly enjoys the breakfast ritual, the silence, the other part of her works furiously at the poem she intends to write.

◊

I can see Patricia now sitting there prim as prim, looking like she mother and planning something. The next thing you know she pick up the phone. She tell me it have twenty-three E. Thomas in the phone book, one E.J. Thomas, one Edwin Thomas, one Ethelridge Thomas, one Edgar, one Eulah. She figure it have to be one of the E. Thomases, but Ethelridge sound like a West Indian name so she try there first. Well, is an English man answer, she ask for Enid anyhow, but she knew was a waste of time. In she mind, Enid single. I have to tell you she ain't think twice about any of this. She have a writing plan, nothing else matter. I know how this shaping up it sound bad for my girl. You have to remember what they teach she there. Is a big country is Canada, is advanced, people there think theory matter more than human being. She learn a writer have a right to write anything, do anything for the writing. Never matter who life it bruise, who life rough up. Is freedom of speech all the way. If words does kill, she ain't grow enough to know that. Bull in a china shop. I tell you now, is so people delicate. Is easy to mangle them, and words does mangle better than iron. It ain't have no cripple like a soul-cripple, and no one so dangerous. But she ain't think so far yet. Patricia like a child. She want every life she see, every life she dream. She ain't want to live it, no, just to lay it out on paper, like a butterfly on a pin.

◊

"Hello."
   "May I speak to Enid Thomas, please?"
   "It don't have no Enid Thomas here."
   "Is this Eulah Thomas?"
   "Yes. Whom am I speaking to, please?"
   "I represent the Heritage school. It runs on Saturdays at the Multicultural Centre from 9:30 to 3:30 p.m. Its purpose is to put

African and Caribbean children in touch with their heritage and themselves."

"Well, we don't have any kids in this house. But it sound like a good idea."

"Please tell your friends: we rely on word of mouth."

She writes down the dialogue for nuance and flavour. Then continues the long trek through the E. Thomases.

"Hello."

"May I speak to Enid Thomas, please?"

"I'm sorry, you must have the wrong number."

"Oh, I'm sorry."

"Goodbye."

The brisk Northern formula speeds things up, but there are no more West Indians, no possible Enid Thomas.

The slender dark-skinned woman with the high cheekbones and great dark eyes is not present in any voice she has heard. Yet she knows she is there somewhere. And a great story with her. It has taken one and a half hours to phone. If she is to get anything done today she must hurry. She calls the various West Indian associations, she calls a few 'spokepersons,' she calls the food bank, the battered women's shelters (who incidentally would give out no information). She calls the Remand Centre, the hospitals, Unemployment Insurance. In all these places she is trying to get in touch with her cousin who came to Calgary and vanished. Sometimes she is surprised and cheered by the helpfulness. But she cannot find Enid Thomas. She has a cup of tea and decides to phone Immigration. Somebody must have a record of a West Indian woman, a recent immigrant to this country. Outside the snow has stopped. Blue, blue sky, white and cold. "Bone-chilling" the radio says. She is so keyed up, so excited by the search, that her hands are trembling as she dials the Department. Somehow the very elusiveness of her dream-woman makes the search more important, the possible story looms fantastic in her mind. It never for one moment occurs to her that Enid Thomas may not exist. That she may be simply the figment of her dream, a name she once heard and last night put to a use of her own. Normally brimming with the psychological imperative, she does not recognize it now.

The Immigration Department is cautious; she is put on hold, then a man comes to the phone. Brennan wants to know where last she saw Miss Thomas. When she tells him Trinidad, he begins to suggest places she might check. They are chatting, getting on quite famously, reviewing various possibilities when she suggests the Multicultural Centre. He tells her they've moved to larger quarters, gives her the new address. She thanks him and is about to ring off when he says "You will of course let us know if you find her." When she hesitates, he tells her withholding information is a criminal offence. She has not of course given them her real name. Ethelready Thomas, she had said. Now outraged by the menacing tone, she simply puts down the receiver. "Her own status may be in jeopardy." She notes the weasel words as she writes it down. It is clear she will be able to find a use for it.

◊

If it had stop there, if only. Ain't those the saddest words. And every story have them, even if they ain't said aloud. But no, she had to put on she coat. In spite of all that snow and cold and wind, all what it had for weather, she cover she face with ski mask. Patricia don't ski, but she have ski mask to mind poor Jocelyn business. She put on big high boots and go down to the Multicultural Centre. She say she think perhaps somebody there could tell her something. All this because of a dream. Life is something, yes! Somebody dream and you life mash-up! Patricia tell me it was only eight blocks from her, and she couldn't call a taxi, so she walk. This is the same girl, everybody have to leave whatever they doing to come with the car and carry she wherever she want to go. That was when she in Trinidad, and she wasn't walking no place. Now she leave she warm house to walk eight blocks in ice. The same distance as from here to the river. I remember how I used to see Jocelyn coming there to the ledge, every Thursday with that boy from town ... Burri. Everybody know he was no good. Woman get under he skin and he jumpy. First one flower, then another, then another. When he get in that accident, the only person surprise was he. Jocelyn mother send she to she aunt in Calgary. Was for a visit: to have the child in secrecy. When she never come back, the poor mother tell everybody she going university. I don't know who believe that! By the time Jocelyn leave here, the child rounding she arms and thing, she hair thick and shining. A pretty-pretty girl .... They say if you don't trouble trouble, trouble wouldn't trouble you ... is a long penance that girl pay and paying still and for what ... she young, she innocent, she trust where she love.

◊

Sheets of steel blow off the Bow river. Patricia is thrust forward by each gust, and in the end the wind carries her along the icy pavement at a half trot. Today ice frosts the mouth holes of ski masks, forms icicles on beards and moustaches. Normally noisy with the bustle of Adult Vocational Students on the way to class, the streets are lonely. Only the cars sweep by in the blue cold, and the heavy trucks grind past. Many of those who are out, red-faced and smiling, carry a jaunty air. Below the din of the asthmatic traffic, they exchange quick amused glances with her. There is an air of secret triumph, of camaraderie, as if this were an adventure. She smiles absentmindedly at everyone who glances at her, and while part of her mind notes every stance and gesture, she is busy plotting the discovery of Enid Thomas. She expects the Centre will have employment records, volunteer lists, mailing lists. If she can only get a lead, she is certain she will find Thomas. In any case, someone there may have heard of her. It's such a relief to escape the cold that she finds her way through the maze of corridors and security doors where her back door entry has led her, with ease. Finally, she comes to a hall enlivened with the bright, clear art of children. She passes through a half-opened door to a small reception room furnished with green plastic chairs, mustard walls, with posters of functions both past and future. On the receptionist's desk there is a brave croton. The person at the desk is about 50, well groomed. With great poise and assurance, Patricia introduces herself as a writer who has lived in the city for many years.

◊

"I have been asked by my aunt, quite old actually, to get in touch with a cousin, Enid Thomas." The lie trips off her tongue, dances in the air. "We know she's in the city, but no one has heard from her for years. Such a pity when families drift apart, don't you think."

The receptionist agrees, "Family is really important to ethnic people. We have gathering with children every Sunday. First the Mass, then the big dinner."

"Do you really? Where are you from? Are you Latvian?"

The woman is surprised.

"How you know?"

"A friend whose father is Latvian. They farm outside of Beiseker. When I lived in the islands, we did the gatherings. I miss it now. I wonder if I could see your mailing lists? Perhaps my cousin is on them?"

"Today, everything is on computer."

"Is the manager of the Centre in?"

"Oh yes! She got in early."

◊

Half an hour later Patricia sits at a long table in the bare conference room beyond. Through the open door she can hear and see what is obviously the multicultural daycare centre. No doubt because of the storm, there is an unusually wide age range of child painters happily attacking large sheets of brown paper tacked up on the walls of the corridor. She has already gone carefully through the mailing lists. No Enid, no E. Thomas. She has begun to work her way through a varied list of volunteers, paid workers, and possible volunteers.

"We update this list every three years. So anyone who has done anything here, even attending a meeting, is on this. We haven't done the deletions yet."

Patricia is half-way through the list, and still certain that she will find Thomas, when she becomes aware that a woman is standing in the doorway of the daycare centre arguing with a furious small girl. The girl is about 8, and is making her feelings clear about staying in a daycare for toddlers. Something about the child's eyes, the diamond slant of her face, trigger a memory. Eight years old and still Pat to all and sundry, she is standing on the verandah of the house at Lopinot, staring horrified at a girl she doesn't know. A girl her own age, who, eyes glazed with admiration, is holding out a gift, two firm, plump mangoes, a spray of hibiscus. A girl, whose face marked with the same awe, the same suppressed excitement she has seen on the faces of the white girls chosen to present flowers to the Governor's wife, she never forget. She is told the girl's name is Jocelyn, Jocelyn Romero. And Jocelyn's shy smile comes and goes, but she stands there her hands rooted to her sides, making no effort to take the fruit from her. Finally, mother pushes her forward, she takes the fruit, says a low "thank you." Jocelyn runs back to her mother smiling hugely. Mrs. Romero smiles at her parents on the verandah, and with her daughter continues on their way to the village. But she stands staring after them, tears pouring down her cheeks. She has begun to sob uncontrollably.

◊

That was the first time she meet Jocelyn, far as I know, was the only time they ever talk, if you can call it talk. Jocelyn give her the fruit, and she stand there bawling like somebody do her an injury. Embarrass everybody that child. Is not one cry she cry you know. After the mother take her inside, and she can't stop the child crying, I go in after them. I tell the mother leave her with me. I get a glass of cold water, a wash rag, and a towel. I pick her up off the pillows, and make her stand up. I wash she face and make her drink the glass well slow. And I ain't talk at all. Then I hold she hands by she side, and I make her breathe with me. Slow-slow breathing. Then we wash the face again. I say to her "Tell me the truth, what take you so?" She look like a misery, but she ain't say nothing. I hold both she soft little hands in my cocoa hands, an I say "So tell me, just tell me how it come." She say Jocelyn just like she. "What you mean? You is a girl, Jocelyn is a girl. All-you-two the same age. How you mean that?" She say it ain't have no difference. She could be Jocelyn, Jocelyn could be she. She look in Jocelyn eye and feel she self Jocelyn. What if she wake up one morning and find she self Jocelyn? She ain't want to be poor. What it have to say to child like that? Everybody know it have rich and poor in the world. She 8 years old and she see is accident. Come to think of it, must be that what make her decide God don't play dice! Is a idea she don't want to risk. Anyway, I hold she hard-hard in my arms, rocking she. She say she ain't no "royal personage." Is so she used to talk. Plenty-plenty words. Read too much. I know right then that child go see trouble. The world is a hard place for them what see further than the eye. And for who have to live with them.

And is that same seeing that lead her to Jocelyn. For is Jocelyn self was there standing in the doorway with Ashley. Jocelyn who once, just once, call she self Enid Thomas.

Is when Burri leave she pregnant by the river and go he way. The mother know one time was disgrace. A child with no name for she one daughter. And she proud. She sit down and write she sister in Canada.

Just as they getting everything together, the registry office burn down in Arouca. Well! The government announce how anybody could replace their papers with two sign pictures, and two important signatures, in any registry office in the area. They see they chance, Jocelyn and she mother. They seize it.

Is so it start, this Enid Thomas thing, so easy-easy. First, they take pictures with she hair crimp and comb up in a big Afro. Then they fool the headmaster to sign is Enid Thomas. You can't expect the man to remember everybody what pass through a district school. Children coming from everywhere. Next, they went quite Port-of-Spain to a real fashionable hairdresser to get it straighten and so. With that they take pictures and get the priest to sign is Jocelyn Romero. Is so she get the two identification, and the two passport to go to Canada. Once she pass in the country, was a easy thing to burn up Enid Thomas. She just go back to being she. The mother say she go to school nights. She bear a real pretty-pretty girlchild, that one, and intelligent for so. With nobody to help she. Is so when you too proud. They ain't even apply for immigration. Just sneak in the people country. Live like a thief. Always frighten-frighten. Prouder than pocket! It don't pay. Then one day Jocelyn look up and see my great-niece.

◊

The two of them just start moving towards each other. They hold out their hands and they move across the room. Like is a magnet. Like they can't stop. They on track and they can't stop. People say thing like that is God's will. If I was God, lightning and thunder! That is slander, yes! Think about it. Something lead to blood and guts in the street, and you saying is God's will! What kind of God is that? Such a God! Too much like people for people to be safe. If He was wanting her to dead, you ain't think He could let her dead in bed. Private like! With some dignity! God! My foot! You ain't think is time priest come up with a reason what better than that?

◊

They are laughing, their hands still clasped together, all of home in their palms, when she feels Jocelyn stiffen, sees her face go rigid. Ashley too is still, her eyes wide. She looks over her shoulders, sees two men hurrying down the long hallway towards them. Perhaps it's their slight swagger. She knows immediately. Immigration!

Immigration! Immig .... Jocelyn grabs Ashley, races down that long hall.

"STOP! STOP! IMMIGRATION! ENID THOMAS! ENID THOMAS! STOP! IMMIGRATION!"

Shouldering Patricia aside, sweeping her against the wall, they run past. Startled, horrified beyond belief, she stands for a moment, and sees Jocelyn, her dark green coat flying out behind her, half dragging Ashley as she tugs at the heavy doors. The child struggles with her red back-pack as she runs.

At the door, Ashley looks back, her small face intent, terrified. Patricia begins to run now, through halls that seem to narrow inexplicably, are dark, towards the brilliant patch of light at the door. She pushes the door open and finds that she is on Sixth Avenue, where cars and trucks come pounding through to the overpass, sweep over the Langevin to Memorial. As she reaches the curb, Patricia sees Jocelyn's scarf on the street, and looks wildly around. Then in the gap left between two trucks, she sees Jocelyn herself on the median. Such a look on her face! Together, their mouths widen into a scream. When the trucks move on she sees the Immigration officers on the opposite sidewalk, their lips shaped in an O, their eyes wide and staring. At first she does not see Ashley. And always afterwards Patricia is to believe she called "Jocelyn come back! This way! Come back!" but she can never be sure what if anything she says before the tableau is complete.

On the far side of the far lane, a brown car has caught the child. She cannot see her head, her face; only the one arm lifted, a red rag of coat, a foot like a doll's in a white stocking. There is blood and mud. The snow clots and burns. Cars, trucks, buses are grinding to abrupt halt. The shrieks of tires, bang, jangle, crash of metal is repeated again and again as cars crash into the backs of cars. It seems to her that Jocelyn falls in slow motion to her knees in the snow; that the wind picks up, sends loose-leaf sheets whirling into the air; that the sky begins to fall in thick white drifts; that the distance between her curb and Jocelyn is all the years between that girl on the verandah, and that woman who dreamt.

GLENDA

Joan MacLeod

M Y NAME'S Glenda. I live on Campbell Island which is like an hour from Vancouver on the ferry. Perhaps you read about Campbell in a recent issue of Rolling Stone because David Bowie practically bought a place here but then he didn't. This is a fairly big deal unless you're me and think David Bowie's a complete and utter asshole. You might also have heard of Campbell as being a draft dodger community – my dad being the very first one.

Until eleven days ago I attended Capilano College on the mainland but I am now very, very happy to tell you I quit. It was a personal dream of mine to study geography, which I have a gift for, but this did not work out.

It is now my personal dream to get my Industrial First Aid Certificate. Here's the deal on industrial first aid – putting on minor bandaids is okay but anything big, I mean if someone really got hurt, it's completely illegal to even touch them. So basically you don't do anything, ever. This is my idea of the perfect job and I hope to be employed at it full time in the near future.

I am also somewhat of an expert on the Heimlich manoeuvre, the hug-of-life. Say you choked on a big bone or something – I could hug it right out of you. On Thursday Elias is practically dying over a muffin gone down the wrong way and I made it sail right out of him. Like a little wet bird thumping against the window.

Today was the first snow, which means something but I can't remember what. I am quite a spiritual person. On the Granville

54

Mall once I met some scientologists and they hooked me up to a machine that measures your emotional and spiritual honesty. I passed.

So for Elias this is the first snow in his whole life because he's from El Salvador which is basically snowless. We go down on the dock to watch it blow. Elias is a refugee and he just got here so my main job these days is showing him the ropes. He speaks only Spanish and is also abso-fucking-lutely gorgeous. Guys, eh?

I think guys that can cry are fantastic. My last boyfriend had a great deal of trouble with emotional honesty. We went out for seven weeks and when it all ended he couldn't cry. I do not have a problem in this regard. I cried for fourteen hours nonstop until my mum put a paper bag over my head. It was a gesture of love. One of the few she has managed since I was born. I'm telling you about crying because sometimes Elias does. We can hear him at night, crying soft and sort of pretty.

On Wednesday Elias was helping me out with my first aid – Saw Mill Accident Number Six. This is when your hand is chopped right off and I was following the book, swabbing the stump, which I know sounds gross, but if this happened to you you would be glad of my cool head. This is also the first time I had seen the scars and some other white marks on his back but they are very light, like drops of rain.

This also ties into my gift with geography. This is how it works. You see, these islands, I think normal people just think they're just floating out on the ocean. But I know how to imagine what's lying underneath; all the parts that you can't see are real clear to me.

So. I have Elias all bound up in white gauze and he turns weepy. I know I just said guys crying is no problem but I can't look at him. I start thinking about the islands, all this rock going down and meeting up with the ocean, the American border snaking around. When the draft dodgers were pardoned I was pretty little still and fairly dumb and I thought this big red rope – like in a bank lineup – had been let down forever.

Kay-ree-ah k 2, kay-ree-ah k 2 then something about *el pecho en la boca*. Elias is saying this over and over and so we try and look up the right words in the dictionary. *I would like to, I would like to ...* that's the beginning but we sort of give up after that and watch St.

Elsewhere. When he goes to bed I'm looking up *pecho* and *boca* and it finally all goes together. He's been saying to me *I would like to place your breast in my mouth*. Guys, eh?

But I don't think he meant it that way really. You see it's the same as with my gift with geography, I could see what was under there, lying inside those scars on his chest and believe you me it isn't horny, it's just a very sad place and I'm thinking of all these damn borders and how they really screw people up. My dad; Elias. I also have this basic rule: anyone who's been tortured and that, they're allowed to say whatever the fuck it is they want to say.

My grandma's American so of course she's completely bug-fuck over Kitty Welles. She's always singing her stuff, making like a little concert. Grandma'd say, "Pretend my hair's dark. Pretend I'm beautiful" then she'd sing into her fork, sing us a whole string of Kitty Welles songs.

Today Elias and me we stayed down on the dock until way after the snow stopped even. Elias is looking quite foreign in his new ski jacket but also happy and we just have this amazing spiritual connection even though we never know what one another is talking about but I am fairly used to this with guys. The moon comes up over the water like a big aspirin and Elias probably thinks I'm completely nuts and I can't sing for shit but it's the only thing I know that's half-way Spanish. I say, "Pretend my hair's dark, pretend I'm beautiful" and then I sing for him:

Tonight they're singing in the village,
Tomorrow you'll be gone so far,
Hold me close and say you love me,
While Amigo plays his blue guitar.

Aye-yiii, ay-yiii the moon is so lonely,
Tomorrow you'll be gone so far,
Mañana morning my darling,
I'll be blue as Amigo's guitar.

WORM

Lee Maracle and Siddie Bobb

All of my stories were written to entertain and teach my children. "Worm" is special to me because it is a synthesis of a story given to me by someone else and worked up in my own imagination. It is the story of the momentous struggle my 3-year-old son had coming to grips with life and death and with the loneliness that separation from his sisters gave rise to. It took him two weeks to tell me the story. Because he knew I was a writer he kept saying, "Write this down, this is my story." The language is partly mine, partly his; likewise we share the story in its telling.

A FAT, GLOSSY, peach-coloured worm with a blue vein encircling his middle rises from the ground, pushing aside small bits of earth that cling momentarily to its sticky body, unmindful of the eyes studying him. Insistently, doggedly, he wriggles his front; middle and rear follow suit. Another inch of turf is covered.

"Worming ... worming ... worming along." Siddie's words come punched between cheeks squeezed by delicately clenched fists pressed hard against his face. Lips flupping out mumbled sounds at worm, who's just inching along.

"Doin' his bizness," flups through his contorted little face.

"Worming his way out of dirt bizness. Trouble must be dirty," he surmises, "dirty bizness, cuz mom always sez, 'you mustn't try and worm you way out of trouble.' Wormin' is when you move up and down and sideways but your body someways goes straight." It was for the crouched little boy a revelation, though he did not see

57

or feel its significance. Worm showed him by doing his business.

"He is so shiny and pretty pink, nice and wigglesome. I wonder how cum big people don't likum?" Fat, pink worm stops and the tip of him worms forward to wiggle in the thin shaft of sunlight that has squeezed itself through the myriad of salmonberry leaves to the black earth below. Sunshine, so little of it gets squeezed to this corner of the yard.

The yard. The little fellow's mind, like a moving camera, travels back to the time when the yard was a tangled mass of roots and spikes he kept tripping over. Then uncle Roge, 'n' uncle Dave, 'n' Wally, 'n' Brenda 'n' Lisa 'n' Tania, 'n' Cum-pa came. Everyone was rushing around, digging and pulling roots and carrying them to where the fire was going to be, only Dennis didn't know it wasn't a fire yet, cuz he kept saying, "Take roots down to the fire." Siddie chuckles to himself at the image of his step-dad.

"That Dennis, he just kept hollering, 'take it down to the fire' and everyone took the roots to the fire." Siddie knew it wasn't a fire. It was a stick mountain, but he didn't want to hurt Dennis' feelings, so he pretended it was a fire just like everyone else. He looked up. Stick mountain is still there, a lonely sentinel watching out for the return of all the people. A great wrenching clutches his small chest, twists itself into unspeakable pain.

"Tania ... Cum-pa," he whispers mournfully to fat worm and silent tears wash both little fists that press themselves tight at the touch of his tears. The realization that divorce has separated him from his beloved sisters falls on him with terrible force.

"The back of my hands is wet and shiny like you, fat worm ... are you lonely too, fat worm?"

An alert, red-breasted robin from her perch in the apple tree overhead has decided the crouched figure below poses no threat to her mid-noon meal. In one graceful motion she sweeps down and snatches the worm out from under the boy's gaze.

A tiny piece of earth drops on his face, mixing with the tears that course across his cheeks to splat on his grimy hands. A scream swells from inside, gains volume, but is stopped in his throat by the picture of gold and green overhead at the centre of which a cheeping pair of gaunt babies cry out their incessant need for food. "Worm death is pain, baby birds are joy and somewhere in between wiggles loneliness." A little cloud scuttles across the sky, blocking out the brightness of nature's colours and the tears clean his cheek of earth's trace.

A large pair of hands scoop him up in their arms. He buries his face on the chest of the big guy. The soft murmurs of the man erase the remnants of the lonely scream the boy could not cry out.

COUPLING

Marlene Cookshaw

THE MAN WORKS overnight but comes home for supper, full of what he's heard on the car radio. He removes his shoes while the woman begins to ladle a fish broth in which carrot slices float like yellow coins. He follows her to the table, pepper grinder in hand, and waits till she's seated to begin.

"Apparently," he tells her, "you can present someone with a fixed visual pattern of alternating black and green stripes running, for instance, vertically, have the person stare at the pattern – you know, *immerse* himself in it – and when you then present him with the same pattern of stripes, this time black and white, he doesn't see white at all, but magenta."

"Magenta?" The woman looks up from spooning her soup.

"The afterimage of green," he explains, "its opposite. But there's more."

"Keep talking," she says from the kitchen where she's gone to fetch the butter and turn out several lights. "I can hear you from here."

"The person retains the memory of this image for some time – hours, occasionally weeks; whenever he's presented with the black and white pattern, he sees magenta."

"Imagine."

"Providing, of course, that the pattern is again presented in the original manner, in this case, vertically. If the person is shown the pattern askew, or horizontally, his eye reads the colours correctly."

The man's tie is knotted slightly to the left of his Adam's apple; his cowlick is more pronounced than usual. Perhaps the Friday

60

night traffic tailgates his thoughts. Perhaps she has put too much cumin in the soup.

"Scientists suspect," he says excitedly, "that the part of the brain which is the optical receptor simply gets bored. That when the eye is forced to regard the repetitive green and black image for longer than interest demands, the brain memorizes the image and, in effect, disconnects. And that, when you present the subject again with what he reads at first glance as the same object, the brain immediately cuts in to supply the memorized image."

The man's jaws close repeatedly on flatbread, without grinding, delighted at this intricate game of mind and eye. No horizontal movement, just the *snap, snap* of his teeth clamping on rye and sesame shaped with water, baked in a slow oven.

◊

The next morning they meet in bed. He opens the curtain, sheds his clothes just as the light is forming. As usual his body vibrates with the energy of night work; as usual hers yawns toward waking. Long hills and rain in her dreams, some bright cloth draped over branches to be washed. She tries to narrow the focus of her thoughts.

The curtain and bed grow white as steam. He is intent. Maybe if we skip the preliminaries, she thinks, pulling him onto her. It'll be like jumping on a moving train; we'll arrive somewhere.

But he's too attentive, pushes back her hair, strokes her neck. His eye reads the aura between her limbs as magenta, and *this does not bother him*. He wants to look at her face, wants to kiss her: her mouth revolts. Against the man she'd hold for hours if he did not insist they lie like two dark stripes against the sheet.

Green, cries her brain, green, and outside their window the rain hurls itself vertically at the grass, loving the earth absolutely, though it will lie neither with it nor to it.

◊

"What are you thinking?" he asks, his hand quiet in hers. She says, "*Dodeska-den*," her mind billowing with Kurosawa's delirious filtered colours. Was it train smoke that spewed a fevered rainbow over the crowded slums? She recalls train; he recalls trolley and poisoned fish and the black and white litany of the child walking the city in search of food for his dying father.

What he recites appears gradually before her as a delicate etching on worn glass. She *remembers* only the colours.

IN SUCH A STATE

Jan Bauer

I

NOT TOO MANY years ago, there lived a man of great wealth and influence – Benito Domingo Hidalgo. Owner of the country's largest hacienda and a third of the mahogany forests, he steadfastly refused to allow himself to be elected president. It was in his interests, and in the interests of his family and country, for he was a patriot, that he and a few others like him remain in their private offices, bringing to power by what seemed to be a democratic process lesser men, though ones of reasonable intelligence. Ones who wouldn't lose the country to another either by war, or by a naive belief in peace without resistance.

Unfortunately, his son, Tomás Salvatore, didn't agree with his father, and had become an idealist instead of a pragmatic man, a man of good sense. The list of things Tomás had set out for himself and others to accomplish was really quite impressive. The only thing that was stopping them was Benito Domingo – and all the other men like him.

It was said that Tomás fired the first shots in what became, to a greater or lesser degree, a continuing state of bloodshed. The shots were fired one evening as Benito Domingo had just finished dressing for a formal reception in honour of several similarly wealthy men who were visiting the country and considering investing in the cotton industry, or perhaps a chemical plant. Benito Domingo was killed, murdered by his son in the marble foyer of his beautiful home, as he put the final touches on his wife Isabella's appearance, snapping closed the clasp to a silver necklace.

Within three months of his death, of the moment when Tomás had done what he did and then fled to the hills and mountains to become leader of *los compañeros*, the memory of Benito Domingo Hidalgo was bronzed and his image preserved in granite. Within three months, what few recalled and what fewer have recalled since, was the death of Isabella. She died in more or less the same way as she had lived – unnoticed. It seemed the perfect sum of her life to die like this and that her death should be an accident. A bullet had strayed into her head. If there was anything at all remarkable about the event, it was only that her skull hadn't shattered and her brain hadn't bled.

After one winter and four months had passed, Tomás Salvatore Hidalgo was seated in an office of the Casa Rosata, in the president's chair, head of a new government. Before the mud on his boots could dry and even before removing his two bandoliers, Tomás decreed that the mall surrounding the building would from then on be known as Plaza de la Victoria del Pueblo. Having decreed that, it was logical to say that in a plaza commemorating the victory of the people there was no room for the statue of a traitor, an imperialist. Also, since there was already such a state of euphoria at having won the country, a celebration was clearly in order. So there would be that night an enormous display of fireworks, commencing with the bombing of the statue of his father, followed by more traditional pyrotechnics – Catherine wheels and Roman candles. All the children in the capital, Vida Nueva, were to be given sparklers.

Not long after, and though at first he demurred, then, feeling it was best to accede to the wishes of the people, Tomás Salvatore Hidalgo allowed a statue of himself, smaller and more modest, to be raised in the very place where before had stood his father's.

For a time, all seemed well. The land that had traditionally belonged to the great haciendas was divided into small parcels and the titles given to the people. As he had promised, Tomás did fully intend to carry out the nationalization of the privately owned banks but, as with some of the other things he had promised, there were quite a few obstacles to be overcome. In his speeches on the radio or from the balcony outside his office, he exhorted the people not to succumb to despair and asked them to be patient. It was a slow business, he said, but they were making progress.

Friends of Benito Domingo, those who had survived and had not fled, smiled to themselves. Tomás was learning what they had always known, what he had been too innocent to guess. Running a country required a great deal of talent and an infallible instinct for knowing who was enemy and who was friend. For Tomás Salvatore Hidalgo, none of them would lift a hand. Each of them, alone and together, would sit by, waiting their chance.

In a short while it became painfully obvious even to the most fervent of the optimists – things were going to hell in a handbasket. True to the promise that under the leadership of a popular government, all across the country all would share equally, everything had become chaos and everyone had an equal share in it.

So it was very easy for General Matute to lead his army into Vida Nueva and take the Casa Rosata. Only a dozen shots were fired. Three from the roof of the building, to signal to the troops that the coup had been successful. One shot was heard when a sidearm was dropped and discharged accidentally. The other eight shots came about a little bit later and in a slightly different manner.

Those who had helped Tomás were hauled to prison and killed quietly, without ceremony. He was not. He was hanged by his ankles from a newly-built scaffold in Plaza de la Victoria del Pueblo. Upside down, with the legs of his trousers bunched at his knees and his hands dangling close to the ground, Tomás Salvatore Hidalgo was forced to watch as his own statue was bombed off its moorings. After that the other shots were fired, one at a time into his living body, with care not to puncture his heart. He didn't die until many hours later, long after Vida Nueva was very, very quiet, deeply asleep on a warm summer's night.

And that left only Inez Hidalgo.

Inez lived in an unholy church. It had once, many many years ago, been a missionary chapel, abandoned when the reach of the church moved deeper into the villages and the lives of the Indians and mestizos. It was situated on an old post road travelled by only a few people. Having allowed the chapel to fall into desuetude, Archbishop Oribe had finally been convinced to make the journey from Vida Nueva and to perform a kind of exorcism in reverse, desanctifying it, welcoming demons and devils should they decide to move in.

At the time Inez went there, no one thought of her as a bane, though she was, to many, a great inconvenience.

While her father had been alive, Inez had remained aloof from his business, which hadn't greatly disturbed him since he hadn't considered business suitable for women. What had bothered him was Inez's disinterest in marriage, her preference for spending time alone, reading many of the many books in his library. Worse was her insistence, at the age of 23, that he allow her to attend university. She wanted to study the humanities and take one or two courses in science, to leaven the abstract with proven realities. Neither of them could decide who was the better liar. Her father to her, because he said he had finally accepted that she would never marry and give him grandsons. Or she to him, because she promised to devote all of her energy to the pursuit of a suitable husband, if granted just two more years to think before putting her mind into storage, busying herself with the tasks of having his grandchildren and, in her spare time, embroidering new vestments for Archbishop Oribe.

At the time of the shooting, she did grieve not only for Isabella, but also, in some ways, for her father. Yet, at the same time, living alone in the large house, she did feel a greater sense of freedom. So it was that she went into a kind of reclusion. In the months prior to Tomás Salvatore's triumphant arrival in the capital, she refused to attend rallies or to make speeches on behalf of the president and his government, tottering badly in the absence of Benito Domingo Hidalgo. Each time she was asked, she gave the same answer. Before her father's death, if she were to believe them, she had only been meant to marry and produce children. The death of one man, no matter how important, no matter a parent, hadn't changed her abilities and talents. If before her father had been killed she had had no thoughts worthy of anyone's attention, then still she had no such thoughts and preferred to remain silent.

When Tomás Salvatore rode into the capital, Inez remained deaf to similar pleas from him for a show of family solidarity. She would, she told him, as any good woman and as all men wanted, remain home with her needlework and invitations to noncontroversial, soporific brunches. He could run his fingers through the lives that he governed without her, and play King of the Mountain until someone pushed him off the other side and into a chasm.

Since there had been no funeral for Tomás, Inez was spared the problem of whether she should or should not, for the obsequies, make an appearance.

It was shortly after Tomás' death that Inez moved from the large house in Vida Nueva to the abandoned chapel.

Her move there was accomplished through negotiations between herself and those who were in control of the situation. General Matute agreed to it because he said it was for her own protection, removing her from the centre of potential conflict. Archbishop Oribe agreed and said it was apt: he had never considered her a very devout or holy woman. Others, when they heard of the move, said it was exile, some said it was prison. Inez herself simply said it was a bargain.

She would, she had promised, refrain from attending rallies or making any speeches either against the church or in favour of revolution. In exchange, she only asked for three kegs of nails, one hammer, two barrels of lime wash instead of madeira, one paintbrush, a ladder, a shovel and a hoe. She would, she added, be glad enough to live alone, yet in a place on a road where, with a little effort, everyone could come watch her just to be sure she wasn't subverting any of the causes they supported. A kind of remote yet accessible fishbowl. She had no need for welfare and would ask nothing from anyone. Not Matute nor Oribe. Nor Sanchez, the new leader of *los compañeros*, snug in his hiding place somewhere in the hills and mountains.

And so, with her hammer and nails, by trial and error, with the ladder and lime wash, the hoe and shovel, Inez reclaimed the place from its ruins. When she ran out of materials or needed different ones she drove a small truck into Vida Nueva, the trip to the capital being her one negotiated freedom. Inez didn't find this limited travel a constraint, but rather saw it as the definition of a small and manageable world in which she was the sole survivor.

She was content. With her books, the work, and the silence around her. With simple meals – fresh fruit, especially mangoes.

The unannounced interruptions didn't really bother her and were, in fact, occasions for private humour. She served tea and was careful not to betray her amusement.

There was General Matute's aide-de-camp, who came to ask if she had everything she needed, was there anything they could do for her. In the course of his visits it was usually contrived as an innocent and impromptu question: Had she, by the way, happened to hear anything of *los compañeros*? Meaning: Inez Hidalgo, are you plotting with those who still invoke the name of your brother?

There was the young priest, secretary to the archbishop, who came offering to hear her confesssion and bringing communion. She, with thanks, declined to partake of either ritual. In the course of his visit the rumours were usually mentioned. The mestizos were turning more and more to ideas preached by a renegade priest or so. There were two Gods: *el Dios de los ricos*, who lived in the archbishop's cathedral, and *el Dios de los pobres*, who had nowhere to live at all. Had any of the few peasants who happened to pass on that road murmured such a thing to her? And more, what were her thoughts on that subject? Inez Hidalgo, do you believe there are two Gods and if so, which one will you follow?

There was Sanchez's marathon runner close on the heels of the first two. He brought her greetings from the one who was carrying on the good work of her brother. And, by the way, any news of Matute or Oribe? Inez Hidalgo, how close are you to Vida Nueva and those two old jokers? How far are you from those of us hiding in the hills and mountains? How much do you hate the memory of your brother?

Many questions, none of them spoken.

To each of her visitors she always said she had heard nothing and in fact, this was so. But none of them could believe she was so innocent and unconcerned, and so none of them believed her. After a while these visits became so well improvised that, to Inez, they became utterly predictable.

◊

Some months after Inez moved to the chapel, and while she was still absorbed in repairs and making things comfortable, the aide-de-camp mentioned, during one of his visits, that General Matute was suffering a profound and personal sorrow. His daughter had died while giving birth. That was bad enough, but what was worse was that the child, a son, had also died. Horrible sorrow. The loss of a future fine soldier. There was, the man said, such a shortage of doctors. So many were dying in the field hospitals, accidently bombarded by the government's own forces or intentionally strafed with machine gun fire by *los compañeros*. Or, doctors were simply dropping from exhaustion while tending to the severely wounded who were daily evacuated to Vida Nueva. And, of course, some doctors were simply too busy with full caseloads in the prisons – keeping detainees alive and sufficiently well to undergo another round of interrogation.

Inez murmured a few sympathetic phrases and asked that her condolences be conveyed to the family and most especially General Matute. She suggested that in future a midwife might be a useful utensil, like the box of candles one kept in the event of a power failure. The man laughed and Inez smiled. Her smile was insincere, his laugh genuine. After so many visits he had begun to find her a pleasant companion. It was only with some effort that he was able to remember she was a threat to them and most specifically to *his* general.

It wasn't that Inez had planned to become a midwife, though she did know something about it, from reading, from having taken several basic science and medical courses. But, as was true for many people at that time, it wasn't what Inez intended that really mattered.

One evening the aide-de-camp arrived not just to visit but to take her to Vida Nueva, where the wife of one of the officers was in the first stages of labour. As usual, no one could find the doctor. Inez protested, saying she had no experience, but he was adamant and fully confident. Besides, if either the child or woman, or both of them died, Inez would have done no worse than the missing doctor. So that was how Inez came to deliver her first child, from the womb of a woman who was a perfect stranger. And that was how it went on, from one child to another. She was calm, efficient, seemed to be knowledgeable and best of all, reliable: they always knew where to find her.

But, when the woman named Maria came one morning, it wasn't for help in childbirth. Maria had been at work the day Inez had been called to help deliver Doña Adélia's third child. Maria had walked all the way from Vida Nueva to speak to Inez, to ask for help, because she already had eight children and couldn't possibly provide for another. Maria crossed herself many times and understood perfectly well that what she was asking was profane and would join her forever with the devil. But eternal life with the devil couldn't possibly be any worse than temporal life with a husband who couldn't keep a job because he was much too busy drinking beer with his friends at the local *taverna*.

There was a silence that lasted only a few moments. In that silence all of Inez's thoughts were practical. She glanced at the bag where she kept the instruments she had had to buy when it had become clear to her that she was going to be a midwife. In that bag, too, there was a small bottle in which she kept an emulsion made from amaryllis. More than one woman, after a difficult birth, had been grateful for it, but she wasn't sure it would be enough to deaden the pain for Maria.

To those doubts the woman replied that pain was relative.

In this way Inez's name was quietly passed from one woman to another, from Maria in the kitchen to women in the barrio and by a circuitous route into the rooms of fine and elegant houses.

II

After so much uncertainty and so many changes, passages through variations on the words freedom and regime, some in the capital believed that things had finally settled and the country was at last on its way to prosperity.

Ursula believed nothing. All she knew was that the place in which she lived couldn't even be called a barrio.

It was more like an improvisation. There had been only a few people at first, with a bit of tin here, some cardboard there, a roof made of tar paper. Those people had believed that shabby though they were, their lives would get better. But nothing seemed to go right, nothing seemed to work out as they had thought it would. Finally, one or two tore down the few crudely painted signs that one or two others had put up in a moment of optimism over the future. Esperanza. Hope. And one or two others had crudely painted new signs, warning all those who entered that they were coming into Miseria and from there, there was no exit in sight. Yet more and more did come, crowding into shacks little bigger than shipping cartons, a city of large boxes attaching itself to the edge of Vida Nueva practically overnight.

Ursula moaned. She was in labour and she knew the child would be stillborn, like all the others, save for her daughter

Estrella, who was hunkered down on the mud floor beside her. The fathers of all her children, those who had died and the one who had not, had each told the same story, had each asked the same question. Could he have the use of a woman's body, hers, in exchange for a few centavos or, from some, a small bundle of firewood, just one last time before he went off to become a hero, fighting on one side or the other. Or, faced with the mindlessness of the war, perhaps fighting both sides from the middle as a profitable adventure, or dying in a moment of lethal confusion, a government bullet in the back, and a rebel bullet in the chest.

It had been the only way to survive. To lie with each of them. But even then somehow, each day, instead of having more and getting ahead, she had ended up with less, until nothing was left. From a poor neighbourhood, to one poorer, to the worst, and finally to the very edge of the city beyond which, she was sure, there was no life, only desert.

It was the thought of the desert that finally consumed her. The pain in her loins receded, leaving only the pain in her mind. She wrapped the half-formed child in an old piece of cloth and with the wood that was left built up the fire. As she had done before, she burned it, listening to it sputter, the only thing that sounded moist. She then glanced at Estrella but try as she might she couldn't imagine what the child's future would be like. Her only advice to her daughter was, "If you need help, find the woman named Inez. They say she lives in the unholy church. Go at night."

Then Ursula lay down again, her head very close to the fire, very close to the flames. There was no need for her to do anything. Her mind was so hot, her body and her hair very brittle and dry.

That was how Estrella remembered her mother. The flames in Ursula's hair, the ragged clothes burning, in the end believing in nothing, least of all in the God who had given her such a life.

For a while, Estrella didn't move, only rocked on her haunches, singing a song she had written herself. "La Mujer, Maria." The Maria of her song could read the future in the flight of birds. She tended a bestiary of fantastic creatures, healing their wounds, making potions, and selling likenesses of them as icons to travellers who became lost and stopped to ask directions. The melody of the song was simple, the words colourful, the overall effect enchanting, as was the girl herself.

The night Ursula died, Estrella wasn't especially worried. She would, in the days to come, sit in one of the parks and make up one or maybe even two new songs. She would sing on street corners as she had often done and inevitably a couple of passersby would give her a few centavos. When she became tired, there was a church that straddled the line where Miseria started and the actual city stopped. At that church the door was always open. She could take shelter there, sleep on one of the benches in the light of votive candles. In the morning she could avail herself of one of the communion wafers for breakfast. If thirsty, there was always the holy water in the font.

◊

The pastor of that church, Father León, was young and ambitious. Behind his mask of inexhaustible affability, he was writing his own bible. It began with the parable of the young priest who, by his own labours and astute observations, became master of the game: who would be pretender, who king.

Father León had seen Estrella once, not far from his church. He could only vaguely remember the tune and the words of her song because at the time he had been far more occupied with two other things: the colour of her hair and eyes, and the fact that men were watching her.

When he saw her in his church after the Mass that morning he could only be amazed at how quickly a man's fortunes could turn. Noticing that she lingered after the others left, he asked her if she was alone and she, ingenuous, said yes. She described Ursula's death in a calm voice, as though it hadn't happened merely the day before but many years ago. He invited her to join him in the rectory, where they had some tea and toasted bread.

Her father, Estrella said, had been just one of the many bandits her mother had taken to her bed. A man she had never known and, according to Ursula, a man of rifles, words, swaggering dreams and a moment's success – briefly adored, suddenly dead.

The priest smiled to himself at that and thought: Tomás Salvatore Hidalgo. The child was a perfect likeness of the man who had been the priest's closest boyhood friend. In a country of Latin darknesses, there had been Benito Domingo, his eyes lazuline, though black-haired and darkly complected. And Tomás, the hair not black but a rich and dark mahogany, his eyes as blue as his father's. And there was Estrella, seated across from him. Her hair a very deep, very rich wine red. Her eyes a dark blue, almost lavender near their centres.

He allowed her to bathe and then told her to sleep, helping her into his own bed, on which he had put fresh sheets. He left her there and went into his study to calculate his chances not only of dethroning Archbishop Oribe but perhaps to become a cardinal. Cardinal León. That in itself would be quite an achievement. Once there, if it seemed right and conditions propitious, he could always cast a glance even further, all the way to the Vatican, St. Peter's.

He had never understood why men wanted to be presidents or generals. It was so much harder to win over the people and, once having won them, to keep things in order. Acquiring power in the name of God really only required nimble fingers, a certain dexterity when handling symbols.

It was in this way that Estrella became one of those symbols adeptly handled.

Because what Father León understood about Benito Domingo and Tomás Salvatore was that even in death, or maybe more so in death, both men still had their followers. He knew a number of those who had supported one or the other of the Hidalgos, those who believed the future was found in the past.

For them, bedding Estrella was pleasant; she was nubile and winsome. But bedding Estrella was also an act of imagination – each saw himself remaking the nation yet again. She was, some told themselves, the granddaughter of Benito Domingo, patron saint of wealth, the accumulation of wealth and honourable profession. She was, others said, the daughter of Tomás Salvatore, who, though an egalitarian, had recognized that even in equity some were privileged. If only, each sighed as Estrella dutifully stroked them, they could be sure of Archbishop Oribe's position. In every battle with General Matute the church held the balance and everyone knew it. It was on that point Father León reassured them. All paid him for an hour's services from the child. It was, he said to each of them, an investment. When General Matute was toppled, Archbishop Oribe would be silent. A careful campaign. The money to those who had nothing but *el Dios de los pobres* and the walk along the most holy Via Crusis. Some money perhaps to a few who knew a bit about prelates, how to discredit. All the gold on the high arches over the altar in the great cathedral wouldn't be enough to save him. Archbishop Oribe. An obstacle removed, leaving a clear path to the Casa Rosata for the man who decided he most wanted to be the next president.

To Estrella all the men were the same and it was all the same cut with the same knife. When there were no men for whom she had to sing "La Mujer, Maria," she was left alone seated cross-legged on her own little cot and at all times her belly was well fed. All in all, Estrella decided that her life there was about as perfect as any life such as hers could get.

With so little asked of her and with so many hours on her hands, she would write not one new song but a whole collection. She would eventually copy them from her notebook onto pieces of special lined paper like the ones she saw in the choir, on the music stands. When they were all done she would sneak out one morning as Father León was saying Mass. She would take them to Café de Oro and sing them for Señor Morazán. She had heard people say he was a good man, with a good eye for talent, so maybe he would give her a chance. If he did, she would stand confidently and prettily on the stage and sing very well. And it would be so nice when people clapped in appreciation and pressed money into her hands.

But Estrella was distracted from her plans. Two months went by and she didn't bleed. She didn't bleed. She knew what that meant.

Father León forced himself to be calm when she told him but for a moment he was disgusted.

It had been such a perfect plan.

The last and most perfect revolution. Such a revolution wasn't made in war rooms, or scratched in the dirt on a trail somewhere in the mountains or discussed in whispered conversations in private clubs. It wasn't won in battles in the streets of Vida Nueva nor in the hills and in those mountains. It was made and won in the mind of the man who most completely believed he could do it. Who said to himself: *I am the one, I am chosen.* Estrella was a young girl, a nice interlude, a pleasure. But more than that, for those men, Estrella *was* a state of mind, an illusion. Each time a man took her, he took his country with her and some day one of those men would owe everything, his present and his future, to a priest very few others even knew existed.

No. Estrella couldn't be pregnant. There was no time for that. Everything was ripening. In the hills and mountains the fighting had become much worse, the losses becoming enormous, both sides losing by attrition. In the villages, in Miseria, in the barrio, and even in the better neighbourhoods of Vida Nueva, people were complaining more frequently, more loudly, lamenting such a liberal and pointless use of resources. Even the most common provisions were become scarce.

It was, to Father León, merely a question of timing. It wouldn't be long. In a little while the country would be there for the taking. And behind the man who took it there wouldn't be a banker, or a dreamer, or an old archbishop cozy in his cathedral and dotage. Behind that man would be Father León who, in order to get where he would be, would have had to do nothing.

"There's a woman named Inez," the priest said.

As she left Father León's house Estrella recalled Ursula's words, "Go at night." But it was only a little past noon and the sun was quite hot and, happily, he had given her a few coins; they were jingling in her pocket. So she sat in the shade of a tree and ate a cup of orange sherbet, the first thing she had ever bought for herself. She chewed on the end of her pencil and wrote in her notebook, intent on writing verses for a new song she had started. From time to time she thought that if the Inez she was to see was a nice woman, she might share with her her plans to approach Señor Morazán. More than a few centavos, she might become rich. She might become a star. One of the men had said that was her name in English.

III

Inez was stunned.

She was stunned first by the appearance of Estrella. It was like looking at a small and effeminate image of her brother, or looking at herself as a child. She was stunned when the young girl said she had walked all the way from Vida Nueva alone, first in the dusk and then in the dark. She was more stunned to hear Estrella recite in an even voice the events that had taken place at the home of the priest. Father León, Estrella said, had told her that there would be a miracle and when she woke up the next morning the baby would be gone and everything would be fine again. Would Inez like to hear the song "La Mujer, Maria"? The men had liked it quite well. Inez said that it wouldn't be a miracle, that what had to be done would be painful.

Once it had been briefly explained, Estrella nodded knowingly. "Will you do it with a stick?" she asked. Ursula had once dug at her own body with a stick and had, for weeks afterwards, been very sick.

Inez tried to conceal her horror and said she would never think of using a stick. She asked Estrella if she really wanted her to "take care of it." And wondered why she felt she had to use euphemisms since it seemed that Estrella knew all the sorrier details of life, had an intimate understanding of them.

In answer to the question Estrella simply said, "Never have babies unless you're rich."

It was unnerving to hear Estrella grunt a bit while contentedly floating in the cloud of mescal Inez had given her to drink. And it was unearthly that the girl could just lie there humming a kind of singsong as Inez probed and scraped, the only time in the many times she had done it that her hands trembled. Inez couldn't decide whether her hands were shaking because Estrella was so young, or because Estrella was her niece and because the clearest words in her singing were "Benito Domingo" and "Tomás Salvatore." Drunkenly, Estrella said they were going to be two minotaurs in a new song, though she didn't use that word, minotaur. She only said they were fantastic – half-man, half-bull – very strong, and that they vied with each other for control of all the people who lived in a volcano.

All Inez could think, as she washed away the blood and tucked Estrella into bed, was: you aren't very far from the truth.

◊

The following day, when Estrella seemed impossibly cheerful and energetic, though happy enough to stay in bed, she said that rather than returning to Father León she would much rather stay there with Inez. She said Inez was beautiful and nothing smelled of incense and she really would like to have a friend.

Inez smiled, somehow grateful. With the young girl, she didn't have to be wary, weigh every word, pretend. They were two against the world and the use the world wanted to make of them. There was no chance Father León would come in search of his nymph. There was no one to whom he could complain that the child had been taken from him.

And so they lived together, watering the flowers and making a flotilla of small boats from bark and leaves and sending them out on the river's current. When Inez was called to Vida Nueva to attend to a woman in childbirth, Estrella went with her and sat quietly by, less interested in what was going on than in writing more verses in a new notebook, one Inez had given her as a welcoming present. And when a woman came to Inez, Estrella stood sturdily next to the table and held the woman's hand, just as she had done for Ursula before her mother had turned brittle and shunned all contact.

IV

Although conditions were deteriorating and some concern was expressed, General Matute, Archbishop Oribe and Sanchez, each in his own thoughts, was sure that he and he alone was secure in his job and in control of the situation.

Father León, on the other hand, had no such secure thought nor any feeling at all of being in control of what had become a very uncomfortable situation. He was, that morning, facing a delegation of two, democratically elected, he supposed, from all the men who had paid him, one man from each of the two camps. But at that moment he found little difference between them. Their anger was impressive and he was, he sorrowfully and silently confessed, feeling a little daunted. Word had passed along Miseria and into the kitchens and from there into the drawing rooms. A child named Estrella was living with Inez and between them there was a remarkable resemblance. Somehow, one by one, one man had admitted his chagrin to another and before long they had all banded together – against him.

The two men facing Father León wanted to know how and why it had happened. To make matters worse, one intoned the name of Benito Domingo and the other Tomás Salvatore, and as they raved at him, the priest had the distinct impression that his house of cards was about to collapse. In this he was right, because each man had been led to believe that he and he alone was privileged to have access to Estrella and the assurances of the priest that he would champion each man's cause. In order to get them even to consider stopping the shouting he had to confide to them the whole distasteful story of Estrella having become pregnant, of his having to send her to Inez for the abortion. He was disgusted to hear his own voice whining as he explained that he had thought Estrella would trust only him, that she would hate Inez for the pain, and would naturally return gratefully to him. He finished pleading his case weakly, with the declaration that he could hardly have gone chasing after his nymph.

It was pointed out to him that more important than the loss of Estrella was the fact that he had taken each man's money – considerable sums of money – and then had lied to each of those men.

Father León blanched white then, white as the alb he wore when saying the Holy Office.

Near the end of the discussion it was phrased as a choice, though Father León was hard-pressed to find any alternative in it. He had, they said, shown a formidable lapse of good judgement. He really could no longer be trusted by any of them. It seemed to the men seated across from him that the world would be a much better place were he not in it. He could jump from the Puente de la Paz that spanned the great river – in which case at least he wouldn't land on cement but hit water, through which it was earnestly hoped he would continue to fall until he met Satan. Or, he could be stubborn and refuse – in which case the men, in a rare show of oneness, would denounce him and accuse him of trying to overthrow the government, the cause of *los compañeros*, and Archbishop Oribe and General Matute, all at one stroke. Should that happen there was no way to tell who would get to him first and what kind of death he would have, though most assuredly it wouldn't be pleasant.

The view from the Puente de la Paz was rather splendid. He had sometimes stood there facing east, thinking he could see all the way to Rome and the dome of St. Peter's.

◊

It was at the moment when Father León's body was found near the quay at the back of the Casa Rosata that the country entered a period where anyone could have toppled it with just one finger. There were so few provisions in the stores. So many dead, dying and wounded. So many marauding groups of civilians and disgruntled soldiers breaking into houses looking for something to eat, steal, or kill in their frustration.

It was the fault of the government, some said. No, it was the fault of *los compañeros,* said others. No, it was the fault of *el Dios de los ricos,* said the disadvantaged. No, it was the fault of *el Dios de los pobres,* said those who had managed to cling to their last remaining privileges.

The three heads bent together, deep in conversation, were a strange sight – General Matute, Archbishop Oribe and Sanchez. Something had to be done. The people were becoming unruly and unwilling to play along. Fortunately, the discovery of the body of Father León and several subsequent and skillful interrogations of those still living revealed the truth behind the priest's death. And in the reasons for that death those three, whose names were ubiquitous and increasingly synonymous, found the ultimate gambit.

Inez and Estrella had murdered the nation. They had killed that child, the embodiment of every side's aspirations. They were assassins of dreams and together they were the incubus that was draining the country of all its resources.

Yes?

Agreed.

The three men shook hands and parted. There was no time to sit around gabbling like old women. It was an awesome task: to create just the right kind of mass hysteria, and to direct it at two rather small, innocuous targets. Still, it could, no doubt, be orchestrated.

Their problems had begun when the river had started to run backwards, just after it had received the body of Father León who had tried but failed to save the life of the unborn Hidalgo child.

Their problems worsened because the harbour became clogged with boats run aground, their cargo holds empty, and no way to sail to other ports in other countries to fill them and bring back what the people needed.

It was because the hills and mountains were red with the blood of aborted foetuses, thrown there by Inez Hidalgo.

It was, in the final analysis, because of Estrella and that woman Inez.

Things were going so badly that in fact it was relatively easy to incite superstition and give free rein to a primitive resort to a belief in magic, a belief that was soon spreading with the swiftness of contagion.

V

Of all the small boats made of bark and leaves that Inez and Estrella had launched there really was only one that had, improbably, survived the river's currents and had come to an uneventful stop on the bank not far from the Casa Rosata. The river was not running backwards because they had, in their callous murder of the nation, given a figurative push in the back to Father León. The land was becoming excessively dry not because the water was draining back into the mountains, back into its sources, but because the summer was unusually arid, the sun unusually hot. If, in any of the previous years, a proper irrigation system had been provided, not so many crops would have been lost and not so many shelves in the stores would have remained unstocked.

But no one listened to the few who spoke with reason.

◊

So finally, Inez and Estrella watered the flowers as they did each day in the late afternoon once there was shade in the garden. They then stood in front of the unholy church and watched as people gathered on the road, coming from Vida Nueva, coming from the hills and mountains, led by their leaders, each with his emblems. Archbishop Oribe with his mitre and crozier. General Matute with his medals and chevrons. Sanchez with his beard, bandoliers and rifles. Determined as ever to return to their game, once this unpleasant business was over.

Inez and Estrella were lynched and killed in the light of torches. One remarked to the other, just before they died together, how little things had changed. The only one not to be seen among all those who had come for the festivities was Torquemada, but then he had been dead for a long time. Still, it was an auto-da-fé and, like Ursula, at the last, Inez and Estrella did feel flames in their minds.

THE MAMMAL STORIES

Claudia Casper

THE EARLIEST STORY Sally knew came from before she remembered things.

It was a lush garden, misty and cool. Bright shaggy flowers bowed towards her. She sat right on the mucky earth near the back. The slug was stuck to a plant that looked like broccoli, and it was very big and brown and juicy. She wrapped her fat baby hand round it, put it in her mouth and crunched down. Blood and ooze mixed with her drool and dripped onto her smocked dress. Her mother Louise ran toward her.

Years later, on rainy autumn nights when a damp, earthy, fermented smell rose from the sidewalk and she couldn't distinguish between soggy brown leaves and the dark bodies of slugs, Sally walked in the middle of the road. She was afraid of stepping on them; she didn't want to feel the brief round resistance they offered against the ball of her foot, and then their thin moist skin, giving, a slimy squish on her shoe's sole – similar, she imagined, to what would happen to her own body if someone big were to step on her.

◊

Peggy, Louise's mother, was the first woman in Toronto to sue for divorce. The grounds were sexual incompatibility. Louise stopped understanding what the teacher was saying. All she could think about was how her friends shunned her and said things behind her back to the boys. When she said hello, they turned away and started conversations with each other. A month after the divorce her mother married a man named Sid Dandy.

Louise decided to break her arm in order to get out of school. She passed the milkman on her way. His sleeves were rolled up and he was sunning himself on the stoop of his milk truck. He twirled a maple seedling between his thumb and forefinger. All around them the twin blades of seedlings were breaking out of the earth, a fleet of helicopters unearthing themselves, growing into the warm air.

Sid Dandy's arm moves round her back and under her arm and then reaches a little further to where her breasts will be in a year or two. "My dear little Louise, you're such a wild little girl." When he kisses her, he makes her mouth all wet.

The milkman dropped the seedling onto the grass and climbed wearily back into his truck. Louise noticed the seedling was a similar shape to the paper-thin veined keys that spun down in autumn. There was a crumbling brick wall in the empty lot down the street. Near the bottom was a crevice with dust and stones sifting out and for a long time she stared at the dark shadow inside the hole.

She buttoned down her shirt sleeve so her skin wouldn't get too scratched-looking and smashed her arm against the wall. It hurt, but it didn't break. She bashed it again and again as hard as she could, but she was holding back a little. She walked home with bruises coming up yellow and purple on her arm.

◊

Peggy's maiden name was Shaw. When she was still a child her father Edward Shaw died trying to rescue someone in a hotel fire. The three sisters, Peggy, Sylvia and Dot, and Naomi, their mother, entered genteel poverty, living on the insurance settlement. This pittance had to be supplemented by the oldest sister Dot's income from teaching piano.

Before her father died, something happened in their family. Peggy, her big sister Dot, her little sister Sylvia and her baby brother Tom went to Cherry Beach. The day was humid and overcast. Cherry Beach had no sand; it was a pebble beach with a long

THE FAMILY TREE

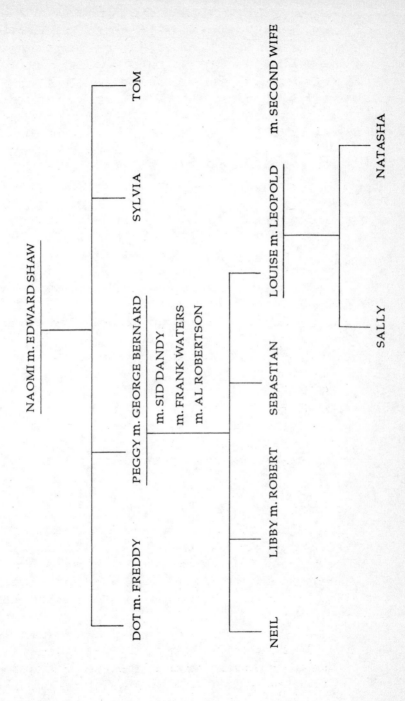

NAOMI m. EDWARD SHAW

DOT m. FREDDY

PEGGY m. GEORGE BERNARD
m. SID DANDY
m. FRANK WATERS
m. AL ROBERTSON

SYLVIA

TOM

NEIL

LIBBY m. ROBERT

SEBASTIAN

LOUISE m. LEOPOLD   m. SECOND WIFE

SALLY

NATASHA

wooden pier. Peggy played with her bucket and shovel, making loud rattling noises with the stones. Then she got bored and looked around for something different to do.

A crowd of men had gathered at the end of the pier. Her father was there in his suit and tie. He dove into the water. She would have started playing again except she knew grown-ups didn't go swimming with their clothes on. The way her father was diving in, again and again, going under the surface for a long long time made her feel bad. They found the body when it was almost night. It was her baby brother.

Afterwards, Peggy got an odd feeling when she thought of him, how he had been in the world, a small quiet boy, and then one cloudy day he didn't exist any more. Everything was a dream and the whole world seemed to be made out of a single substance – bread dough or cork or cardboard, painted the right colours, green for grass, blue for sky, flesh colour for people, greeny grey for lakes.

◊

Her step-cousin slapped her across the face for changing the channel. It was the last straw for Sally. She slammed every door as she stormed through the huge house down to the kitchen where the maids looked up from their potatoes.

Sally ran out to the garden where the huge wicker chair hid her in its shadow. The air was cool and smelled of cedar. The swimming pool had a lapping sloshing voice in the breeze and the white moon was reflected in its waters. Animals shuffled in their cages. In the dark the pool belonged to no one – not her step-cousin or his mother.

The search party spilled from the house. They turned on the outdoor lights and yelled her name in every direction. Her father Leopold cursed her stubbornness. He shouted, "stop being silly girl, come on now," then they turned out the lights and went back inside. A peacock walked into the moonlight on the other side of the pool, his tail dragging in the dust. He'd left the pen where the other birds slept and roamed the garden alone, pecking at beetles.

The peacocks were moulting. Every morning Sally went to the garden before anyone else to look for tail feathers. In two weeks she had enough for a bouquet of feathers; a miraculous spray of dark eyes amid shimmering gold, copper, electric blue, emerald and turquoise – treasures to store for the future when she would be home with her mother Louise, her holidays over.

She was a guest in the dark garden, a pair of eyes and ears, tiny hairs sensing a warm night breeze; her companions: the peacock in the moonlight and his fellows dozing in the pen, the dogs shuffling in their cage, the moon and the pool pulling each other close. Here no one told her the swimming pool did not belong to her, or the peacocks and the tail feathers.

She crept out from behind the chair and went back into the house.

◊

Peggy put on her blonde bathing cap. Blonde, because it was a novelty bathing cap with platinum blonde hair attached to the outside. She waded step by step out to her rock, Peggy's Rock because it lies at just the right depth for her to stand on. She shivered a little. Her bathing suit had a short skirt attached at the hips and in the green water it billowed and ruffled like seaweed. Her thighs and arms were marbled by ripples across the lake's surface, fleshy, soft, phosphorescent.

She looked up at her daughter Louise on the dock and gazed through her as though she were air. The girl's hair sparkled in the sun and Peggy thought of a dragonfly, the light catching its beautiful body, opalescent wings – a strange other-worldly form; she looked at the child with that kind of distant wonder.

She turned toward the middle of the lake, pushed away from her rock and glided as though the water were velvet. The fake hair on her bathing cap trailed behind her like cornsilk, unsubmersible. The sky had clouded over. The lake was still.

Peggy had never been one for exercise, yet she kept swimming plush, swish, plush, swish, plush, swish, out into the middle of the lake.

Louise was already in her bathing suit because at the cottage that's all anybody ever wore. They'd wake to the sound of green leaves brushing against each other, to the crackle of the hot Ontario sun heating and drying the forest and perhaps, across the lake, the sound of an electric chainsaw. They emerged from their warm sleeping bags, skins hot and clean from swimming the night before, and picked their bathing suits off the floor. Where the elastic was tight, the top of the thighs, the shoulders, the suit settled into familiar indentations. They slipped on rubber flip-flops and wandered into the kitchen for breakfast.

Louise was already in her bathing suit. She jumped off the dock and swam hard. When she reached half-way she yelled, " Come back Mommy!" She yelled so loud that everyone on the lake must have heard and run down to their boats to save them. But no one came. She couldn't tell if her mother heard or not.

Peggy stopped swimming though. She duck-dived and stayed under until the lake's surface was smooth. Yet her blonde bathing cap eventually bobbed up. She dove again but her warm plump body was too buoyant and her arms weren't strong enough to keep her down. Hers was the soft body of a woman who over-indulged in trifle and sherry and bridge with girlfriends, who had a maid to scrub her floors, wash her clothes, knead her bread and bring up her children.

Louise swam back to shore, wrapped a big towel round her and waited. When Peggy came out of the water her daughter noticed she had been crying.

◊

Memory floated up – a great white balloon pushing itself slowly out, a strange reversal of the way a snake eats things – whole. It came from Louise's mouth, unburst, clean, an empty white womb. Now that she remembered, she was lighter, more compact, her body less a tomb.

◊

When Natasha turned 15 she and a friend cut her hair into a mohawk and dyed it orange. She pierced her nose, got a butterfly with a death's head tattooed on her hip; she wore chains, dog collars, spikes and steel-toed combat boots. Drugs made her confused and absent-minded; she spoke in the same breath of suicide and kicking people's heads in.

Sally and Natasha left early one morning and drove all day, stopping once for buckwheat pancakes and coffee. Through a two-hour stretch of fast food joints and new motels they grew morose, and then felt empty in the big dull national park. As the sun set they drove down a long flat road past a tiny windblown town called Ocean Beaches. They drove right out onto the beach, parked beside a sand dune and got out of the orange Volkswagon beetle.

The sun sank, bloated, into the heaving ocean. Natasha ran into the dark water. She leaned into each wave oblivious of the cold water seething round numbed calves. The sky was infused with pink and purple. Huge waves swelled above their heads and they could not see the horizon.

When Natasha returned to the car the mohawk no longer looked strange. It looked like hair, cut like other people's, according to their idea of beauty. Her eyes sparkled with tears and her voice when she spoke was full and deep.

Sally remembered when Natasha was 6 and she 16. They left the house after dinner and rode their bicycles top speed, the cheeks of Natasha's face shining and red as her 6-year-old legs whirred round to keep up. They were like wind together. They rushed into the musky changerooms, got into their bathing suits and raced up sun-warmed steps, through the shower, one splash, two, into the cold water. Eglinton Swimming Pool was a turquoise jewel in the hot dusty city.

This was the first time since then they had shared a similar feeling – except they weren't quite sharing any more – Natasha claimed her part all her own while Sally watched. What hadn't changed was the intensity. Seeing Natasha's eyes sparkle and her cheeks shine through the makeup, chains and spikes made Sally want to cry.

On the way home the moon shone into the back of the car. Natasha put her socks and wet combat boots by the heating vents and as they dried they began to stink like a beach in the hot sun when the tide's out.

◊

Sally discovered her breasts at Peggy's house just after Peggy's third husband, Frank Waters, died. The family was worried the old woman would get too depressed so Sally, as oldest granddaughter, stayed in the spare bedroom for a while. She got to watch TV and eat pizza and jello with Rich's topping. At night she phoned her mother Louise and said goodnight, kissed her grandmother and inserted her body between the cold sheets. She wrapped her arms round her knees until the sheets returned her warmth.

One night she felt small mounds of flesh where nothing had been before. Did they really exist or was it just the way she'd been lying, scrunching up flesh that had always been there?

A couple of years later, when she had definite breasts, Sally discovered a special connection between herself and her grandmother: on the outward slope of each breast toward the underarm was a pink mole-sized bump with a tiny indentation in the centre. "They're secondary nipples dear," Louise said. "Your grandmother has them too." The tiny nipples seemed to link Sally and her grandmother to other mammals. They were personal proof of evolution.

◊

When Louise was in nursing school she visited her father, George Bernard, Sunday afternoons. Around one she put away her anatomy books and changed into one of her good wool skirts, tight across the hips, a tiny pleat behind the knee, and a matching lambswool sweater. She put on silk stockings and pointy-toed pumps, wound her brown hair round a hot curling iron, applied a little red lipstick, called goodbye to her roommate and ran down to the streetcar stop.

She caught a westbound car on Queen, transferred to a northbound at Bathurst and got off at St. Clair. Dunegal Crescent was a residential street with brick houses and big maple trees. Her father's house was a duplex. Louise rang the bell for the main floor apartment and he opened immediately, as though he'd been waiting by the door for her arrival. He'd taken to keeping the curtains closed all day and wearing sunglasses indoors to hide his bleary eyes. He was always happy to see her, a little agitated and anxious to please – more like a bachelor unsure how to act around women than the father of two full-grown daughters. He ushered her to the sofa and poured two stiff drinks. He never minded her smoking in front of him, though it was improper for women to smoke in public. She lit her cigarette in the dark, stale-smelling living-room and they talked about her studies and the stockmarket and then they listened to opera. A passage sung by a soprano caused tears to roll down from under his sunglasses.

One spring afternoon her fiancé planned to join them for dinner. It was bright and warm – the gutters full of ice-water, slush and dirty snow. The trees' branches, though bare, were no longer a dead grey and had faint pink or green hues. On the sunny side of the street crocuses sprouted blooms of easter yellow and purple. She noticed a robin hopping from twig to twig. The smell of rotting leaves and dog feces frozen at the start of winter were released into the spring air.

She walked up the neatly swept path and knocked on the door, waited, and knocked again. She said to herself, he's in the bathroom, or in the kitchen or on the telephone and she knocked again and waited. The door was unlocked. She stepped quietly into the living-room. The needle of the record player bounced lightly at the end of a record. He lay on the floor, sunglasses askew, an almost empty glass on the end table and several empty liquor bottles on the kitchen counter – George, having that day finished a job he'd started twenty years earlier.

Two lonelinesses filled the dark living-room: the loneliness of his life, and hers now without him.

◊

Natasha loved looking at pictures of her grandmother Peggy: a little girl skates on Lake Ontario in a plaid suit with velvet cuffs; a teenager grins in a sailor suit; a young woman at a garden party with ribbons in her hair; her first married picture, the young bride looking like a water lily in her swimsuit with its modesty skirt floating on the surface of the lake; the middle-aged woman with her second husband and their drinking buddies – she looks like one of the boys in a plaid shirt and khaki trousers; and the widow in a shapeless mu-mu watching Natasha swing, back and forth, in the back yard.

In Peggy's day clothes matched. For every occasion a special outfit: dancing shoes, bowling shirts, lounging jackets, white gloves for summer, black gloves for winter and formal wear. Natasha reviewed her own clothes: torn t-shirts, faded jeans, everything second-hand and as old-looking as possible. She felt pleasure finding a beautiful lace shawl or antique silk slip at a rummage sale, an old checked lumberjacket, plaid pants or beaded sweater with three-quarter length sleeves.

Natasha treasured garments Peggy would have rejected as outmoded or beyond repair. She yearned now to be old-fashioned in a way Peggy, who had always been ahead of her time, never had.

◊

Dot was always a little bird of a woman, an annoying bird, clucking, strutting, pecking. She made her nieces think of the Wicked Witch of the East. She always bought Christmas presents at Boxing Day sales and when she wrapped them 364 days later they had a stale, yellowed quality. When the children complained, they were hushed. Their Auntie Dot had had tragedies in her life. "Poor Dot. Poor poor Auntie Dot."

After her father's death, Dot left school to support her sisters Peggy and Sylvia and her mother Naomi by giving piano lessons. Her heart shrivelled when her father died. She had been the apple of his eye – now there was only her mother, who loved the younger girls best. Then Dot got engaged to an Irishman called Freddy. Her heart sweetened and blossomed.

Freddy and Dot lived with Naomi and the women signed over the finances to Freddy as the new man in the house. Everyone was happy until Freddy ran off with the life insurance money. They couldn't even call the police. Naomi drifted into a world of dark religious figures from which she never quite returned. Peggy quit school and worked as a secretary to help pay bills. She and Sylvia, being young and extroverted, blamed Dot for their hardships.

Dot turned sour. She moved into a bachelor apartment and lived there as though it were a bomb shelter, cramming it full of everything. After ten years Dot could no longer bear her isolation and she enrolled in Arthur Murray's Dance School. She loved the lessons. She got a steady dancing partner, an insurance salesman named George Alcock, and they flirted for a long time. One day he took another partner. She'd mastered every step she could ever need in a ballroom by then, so she decided to quit. But the contract she'd signed had small print committing her to ten years of lessons so to get her money's worth she kept going long after any inclination to dance had left her spry feet.

When she died Dot left an unwelcome surprise for her younger sisters. The money from the sale of Naomi's house was gone. Dot had spent a lot of it on advance funeral preparations for herself.

It was magnificent. Several vestal virgins kept a vigil over her body. The coffin was mahogany lined with satin. Her nieces and great nieces and nephews and great nephews were fascinated as they filed by her open casket, gazing at her gaudily made-up face and doll-like hands folded one on top of the other. She wore a new gown and rhinestone necklace and on her bony finger was Naomi's wedding ring.

Libby and Louise got the job of cleaning out Dot's apartment. They felt self-conscious, as if they had wandered into a fairy-tale land where creatures completely different from themselves lived.

Her apartment was reminiscent of a giant nest. It contained every object that had ever come into her possession. As Libby and Louise separated out the things of value they were serenaded by Dot's budgie. The old bird tittered and squawked in a voice like Dot's. When they came to the pair of ruby red pumps their aunt had worn for her dancing lessons they hesitated.

◊

Sally took Natasha to see the killer whales. They went down to the underwater viewing chamber. A sudden wall of black and white glided past. Skin like human skin, hairless and smooth, but perfectly pigmented in separate fields of black and white – and the trick eyes: two white ovals above the real, warm-blooded eyes, black and seeing. The whales nuzzled each other, one burying its face in the other's soft belly and then sliding up to kiss. A third expelled a dark green cloud as it swam up for air. Their bodies were imprinted inside her, like the memory of her baby sister's round cheeks, the way her mother's face changed when she smiled, the taut smoothness of her grandmother's girdled stomach. She sensed their fluid curves the way she felt inside her own body.

The show began. Sally and Natasha ascended. The audience applauded and the whales held their heads out of the water, as if to listen. Sally wondered if they enjoyed the sound of clapping. Maybe it sounded like seals barking or rain tapping on the surface of the ocean.

◊

Peggy was married at 18 to George Bernard, a man in his early for-
ties. On their wedding night he did a strange thing that hurt; in the
six and a half years that followed she had four children – Neil,
Libby, Sebastian and Louise – and five abortions.

George Bernard was no happier a man married than he had
been alone. He fell in love with his children but Peggy was not
interested in being loved only as the mother of his children. She let
her resentment be known with smashed crockery and curses.
George was unprepared for the demands of young womanhood.

It wasn't until Peggy had an affair that she discovered sex was
enjoyable. She divorced George and married Sid Dandy. She and
Sid bought a cottage on Lake Wobegon and called it Nirvana. It
was the garden of their love and they shared it with her children,
grandchildren and great grandchildren, and with their friends, a
heavy-drinking rowdy bunch of poker players, sports hunters and
housewives with names like Hoppy, Babs, Claire, Frankie, Gordie,
Agnes. As 'the gang' entered their fifties together, some of the men
discovered they were no longer in good health. Sid's doctor told
him if he didn't quit smoking he'd die of lung cancer within the
year. He didn't quit, and in little over a year, Peggy became a
widow.

She'd become quite plump in her happiness and in her sadness
she became even plumper. Her favourite delicacies were the crack-
ling on pork roasts and the pope's nose. She became what the
younger women in the family feared becoming. Fat and old and
lonely.

As her sadness matured she settled into a new role – hostess of
bridge parties. While they played cards, the women ate Ritz
cracker treats, pastel mints, nuts & bolts; they drank lots of sherry,
rye and rum. Peggy lived in a one-bedroom apartment across from
the Golden Griddle Pancake House where she treated grandchildren to pancakes after "The Sound of Music" and "2001." She often
gave presents to her grandchildren and her two daughters. She
drove her tan-coloured Corvair out to her daughters' houses in the
suburbs to babysit. When she was 65 she fell in love again.

His name was Frank Waters. Peggy rekindled his desire and
they made love every day for ten months. Then one morning, after
they'd refrained for a week on doctor's advice, they made love

again. Frank lay down on the living-room couch complaining of a headache. He slipped into a coma and a few days later died.

Peggy's spirits descended to a dark place where they remained for a long time. Yet five years later she met Al Robertson and married him. They drove to Florida every winter and drank till the small hours with friends. One night Peggy had a stroke that paralyzed the right side of her body. She couldn't talk or walk any more.

◊

Louise had a dream after Peggy had the stroke. She saw a freshwater dolphin swimming among the roots and branches of a submerged forest. It was a pink dolphin floating alone, propelling its smooth pink skin under vines and over branches, brushing softly against a green leaf, neither stirring up the thick smooth mud and brown flakes of vegetation on the bottom nor breaching the surface, a mirror with the sky painted on. In the mirror, blue and white and warm, birds flew together, soaring and singing and eating and making nests, every once in a while turning their heads sideways to see the luminescent pink form gliding below.

Louise had watched a Jacques Cousteau special the night before on freshwater pink dolphins in the Amazon. As she witnessed the film on this creature, she was overcome. The earth could not really house such an animal. A pink dolphin. She felt like crying at the preposterous beauty of it – this misplaced mammal existing mythically in the middle of an enormous continent.

When she woke up she knew it had been a dream about life after death. She remembered Peggy trying to drown herself in the lake that cloudy afternoon in Northern Ontario. It occurred to her now that Peggy must have been in pain.

◊

When she sees her son-in-law, Libby's husband Robert, approach her bed through the women, Peggy groans and thrashes her head from side to side. With her good hand she makes a pushing away gesture and from the good side of her mouth comes the roughly formed word, "No." She doesn't want a man to see her like this. She'd rather no one saw her, but she accepts the women.

For the past twenty years Peggy has been saying, with a regularity her family found morbid and embarrassing, "When I die, throw me out in a garbage bag and leave me for the dump truck in the morning. I don't want a single cent spent on my funeral." This was a reference to Dot's extravagant exit, which Peggy never forgave. "Money is for the living to enjoy. I want my funeral to be a big party with lots of booze and music. I've had a good life. I've been very lucky and I want you to celebrate." And now here she lies, unable to do simple personal chores, helpless to end her life the way she wanted.

The hospital room is institutional, yet her presence fills it with something special. Since the stroke she no longer controls her feelings; every emotion is at full intensity. She weeps and moans in sudden sadness, she laughs and grins and her eyes sparkle with happiness. Her visitors are affected by this intensity and after they leave the cold green room, their emotions flow more freely.

Her body has lost its plumpness. She is a bird with light brittle bones, tiny feet and hands; her eyes are a deeper blue, prettier, her skin pinker. She is all blue and pink and soft soft grey.

◊

Dust and rock. Nothingness full of longing. The moon. A high piercing wail like wind from the dark side. The woman in the moon. Giving birth. Dying.

The moon is new when Louise and Sally and Natasha, wrapped in memory, leave Peggy staring at the wall in her hospital bed. It is the colour of a diamond or white hot sand, its shape – a nail clipping. As they pull out of the parking lot it is a white slit in a pale winter sunset and, as they turn onto the Parkway, it is a small tear in a deep blue veil and, as they exit onto the Lakeshore, it is the flap of a tent in the desert, blowing open in the gentle evening breeze and, as they park the car in their driveway, turn the engine off and get out, it is the luminous mouth of a dark envelope. They unlock the front door and enter the house and outside the moon becomes the female opening into infinity, a brilliant crown shining through a translucent dark sky.

THAT
SHAGGY LOOK

Suniti Namjoshi

THE WILD MARE had come to the moors so long ago that she had almost forgotten why it was she had originally walked out; but here was her niece standing before her and expecting to be given the right answers.

"It was because you were fed up with bourgeois respectability and creature comforts, wasn't it?" her niece demanded.

The wild mare hesitated; living as she did on the moors she had learned to appreciate warmth and shelter, not to mention food and water; besides, as best she could remember she had never had anything against creature comforts, and as for bourgeois respectability, she wasn't quite sure what it was.

Luckily her niece hadn't noticed that she hadn't answered. "And, of course, that shaggy look is a form of protest," her niece went on.

This was too much. The wild mare had never been vain, but she had never thought of herself as a sloven. "Do you mean my long hair?" she asked stiffly. She wanted to explain that it was difficult to get it trimmed and that moreover it kept her warm.

"Yes," her niece broke in. "Look, I've copied the style. Do you think it suits me? It's very much the fashion, since these days you are the fashion."

"What do you mean?"

"Your ideas and everything. Thank you for explaining them. I shall tell everyone when I get back."

"But I haven't explained anything," the wild mare cried out.

"Of course you have. All that you said about doing without and wearing your hair long – it's really caught on. Well, I must go now."

Her niece left, while the wild mare stood stock still and pondered the point that in the course of time she had gained acceptance, if not as an individual, then certainly as a tourist attraction.

HIDE AND SEEK

Carole Corbeil

W HAT IS or is not there depends on you. That's what the
magician counts on. He will make your eyes disappear, not
the rabbit; he will cut you in half, not the woman. That's the real
trick in his magic. His hands, your eyes. But what's the magic from
the rabbit's point of view, from the woman's point of view? It's
being scrunched up in a hat or a box while the guy in the cape gets
all the applause.

If I become the woman, legs straining against her support hose,
lips parched beneath red lipstick, if I become the rabbit, pink skin
moving beneath white fur, nose twitching like a blind man's cane,
you too can become woman or rabbit. That's another kind of
magic.

◊

The woman in the support hose, the skimpy satin outfit and the
stiff red smile is Jean. Jean is an orphan, and she's made a career of
loving men. She wants to find a way to love men without scrunching herself into a box or being sawed in half.

The magician's name is Terry. He's from Sault Saint Marie
where he's still known as a minor hockey star. In his dreams, he
passes the puck with grace in the glare of large arenas. He looks
beautiful in a black tuxedo and cape. He stuffs his long dark hair
into a top hat. He carries himself like a man who is used to being
watched. Even his clothes love him; his satin shirt trembles against
him when he waves his wand.

There's always a very soft look in his eyes just as he's about to
cut Jean in half. His eyes say, I want to put you together. His eyes

say, I know the gut I'm about to cut intimately. Jean loses herself in those eyes. But after the show, Terry pretends that nothing passed between them.

After the show, Terry goes back to his hotel room with a different girl practically every night. Everybody wants him; not just women, men too. Everybody wants to touch his beauty, to feed on it, everybody wants to disappear into him. No that's not true. Not everybody. Some men see him, and they start collecting spit in their mouths.

Jean, on the other hand, goes to her hotel room alone, opens a bottle of scotch and dreams Terry. Every night she says to herself I'm going to tell him what I feel. But she never does. Once she started to, and Terry looked away and folded his magic scarves with such wilful meticulousness that she felt choked. Her voice got so small it never even got out of her head. She was thrown back on herself.

◊

Jean turns off the lights of her hotel room, lights a cigarette, and watches big snowflakes falling against the glow of the streetlight outside. The town is white and mute. Occasionally a car goes by, wheels hissing like air and water escaping from a radiator. The snow makes Jean feel holy and fragile, as if she were about to witness a miracle.

She gets into bed and wraps the yellow chenille bedspread around her shoulders. She drinks scotch and free-falls. Her falls are not so free. Her mind is like a tongue looking for where a tooth used to be, feeling for the soft depression in the gum, the pocket of blood. She always ends up in the same place: the moment when Terry's eyes look into her own before he cuts her in half.

I want, she says. I want your arms around me, I want to press myself against your chest, I want to wrap my legs around you. You won't have to do anything, you don't have to do anything. I'm not like the others, Terry. I don't need anything. Really. I don't need anything. Just choose me. I want you to choose me. Me. Me. Just choose me. And then everything will be all right.

Oh Jean dreams his lips alive, and then tires of it all, and drifts off. Suddenly she remembers a summer when she was 12 and skinny and wearing a turquoise dress. A sleeveless turquoise dress. She was standing by the door of a green skating shack;

inside, the wooden floor was all scarred from blade marks. And this boy in jeans with a nice mouth and thumbs hooked in his belt loops was standing there too. And just as she was about to go in, feeling fresh in her sleeveless dress, he put his arm across the door. You gotta pay, he said in a soft, regretful voice. His blue eyes looked right through her. She could smell the soap and sunlight on his white t-shirt. And Jean caught something in his eyes and his arms opened for a second and she was in there like a flash, pushing herself against him and he liked it, and he kissed her on the neck and she buried her face in his t-shirt. But then he noticed some boys watching so he turned it into mock-torture, squeezing Jean so that she had to fight to get out of his grip. The other boys laughed. They kept laughing. But the boy, he turned towards her and smiled and winked. Look what I have to pretend to do, his eyes said, just to hold you. And Jean was in love with him for the rest of the summer. She didn't want to know anything else in life but the feeling between her legs when his arms opened and she slipped in. It was the summer of If You Go To San Francisco, and he put flowers in her hair.

Now Jean curls herself around a pillow and sleeps. Her neck is stiff, she feels like a coiled reptile drifting on a log down a fast-moving river. She dreams. She dreams she is drowning. She wouldn't mind drowning so much if she hadn't just this minute in the dream discovered what it was she'd wanted to say all her life. It is taking shape in her mind, a kind of crystal, clear and full of light. But just as her mouth is about to spit it out, she goes down glug, glug, glug, drowning in the blue, fading to black.

She wakes up crying.

◊

Touring magic in the winter is a cruel, impossible thing. The sky is blinding blue or grey, the roads slippery, the rooms overheated, the food canned. The rabbits get dry noses, and sometimes they even wheeze. Every day Terry and Jean climb into his red van after packing the tables and scarves and costumes and speakers and two caged rabbits. Jean sits in the passenger seat, smoking endless cigarettes and watching his profile. Terry does drum solos on the leatherette-covered steering wheel. They hit all the small towns and there, in bars, in cream-painted memorial halls, in run-down hunting lodges, they set up and wait for the groups to come. Nobody wants this magic any more, really, but sometimes groups of gas station owners, or Home Hardware salesmen, or Ladies' Auxiliaries don't know what else to book for their get-togethers. The men like to look at Jean in her satin and rhinestone bathing suits, and the women like to see anyone from out of town.

Jean was selling shoes at Florsheim's when Terry came through North Bay. He bought a pair of black velours slippers. She slipped one on his foot, but he insisted on putting on the other one by himself. He'd just lost his partner, June, in Sudbury. They'd done a show and afterwards June had gone to visit her sister and her kids who lived just outside of Sudbury. June said she wanted to stay with her sister. She told Terry she wanted to find a real man and get pregnant. "I want to get full," she said, looking very pale with the red costumes in her arms. "Here," she said. "You'll find somebody else easy. Just look for my size." Terry found Jean in the shoe shop. She was the right size.

"I want," Jean says now, in the smoky van, "to wear different clothes." Terry turns down the radio. "Why?" He looks worried. Jean wants to say because I can still smell June, but she says "it's too cold for those skimpy things." She's taken Racy the rabbit out of his cage and she's stroking him on her lap. Racy is a nervous rabbit. He doesn't like traveling so they always give him Gravol drops, and now he's nice and calm and warm on her lap.

"We could buy you a cape," Terry says.

"No, it's gotta be something else," Jean says. "I'm thinking gypsy." She thinks of the drapes full of big pink cabbage roses in the last foster home she stayed at. "And I kind of see an eyepatch."

"You're out of your gourd," Terry says. He cracks his gum, and looks at her. "We've only got two more gigs. I'm sure you can live through it."

"I've got a hunch," Jean says.

"You can't eat hunches," Terry says and drives straight through a red light.

◊

A couple of days after this conversation, Jean buys two yards of glazed cotton with pink peonies and a yard of eyelet lace at a dry goods store in Coldwater. In a Shoppers Drug Mart in the mall on the outskirts of town, she buys a black eyepatch. The woman at the counter says that they don't sell a lot of black eyepatches nowadays on account people prefer flesh-coloured ones.

Coldwater is their last stop. It is February now, and they are scheduled to take a break in Barrie for the next couple of months, and if Jean wanted, Terrry said they could set off again in late spring. "It's nicer then," he said. "We can plug the van in trailer parks." And Jean saw herself standing near big chestnuts by a river bank, her legs bare in the tall grass, her eyes small holes for the brilliant sky to shine through. She said nothing to Terry. She couldn't decide.

In her hotel room, Jean makes herself a gypsy skirt out of the material with the peonies, and a beautiful peasant blouse out of the lace. It takes her all afternoon to baste it together, and she figures basting's good enough for her purposes. She doesn't know what she wants to do, she just knows what she wants to wear. The light is fading by the time she finishes. A big streak of pink plunges like an arrow into the roof of the Zellers across the street. She sits in the dark watching it change slowly, the sky turning light green then violet. By the time the streetlights come on, she's drifted into a half-sleep.

What she has always wanted to say is there again, on the tip of her tongue. Something is pulling her down, weighing her down, as if she were spiralling into hole. And then suddenly, from nowhere, she is taken up by a great gust of wind, and she feels as if she is folding back on herself like a flag only to unfurl in whiplash fury, over and over again, folding in and snapping like a flag in the wind until stones start flying out of her mouth, hundreds of stones, as if she'd swallowed a gravel pit.

"There is nobody," she screams. "Nobody. There should've been somebody."

◊

Jean has a bath in the cold-tiled hotel bathroom. Naked, she rubs cream on her face, her breasts, her belly, her thighs, her arms, her elbows and knees. She brushes her long hair until it shines. She puts on her gypsy clothes, everything but the eyepatch, and then her black wool winter coat. She opens the door, walks back in to pick up the rabbit cages. She walks back towards the door, a rabbit cage in each hand, all ready to go now, ready to kick the door shut behind her. But something holds her back. On the threshold she closes her eyes, opens them and stares at the chain-lock dangling on the door casing. It rattles with the force of her slamming the door shut.

◊

Behind her or in front of her is the question. If she slams the door behind her, she finds herself gaudy and ripe sitting with her legs apart in the rented hall. She shocks the bejesus out of Terry. She turns herself into the one-eyed gypsy. She hexes Terry. She shouts the unspeakable. She's as bold and mean as a blackfly. She interrupts Terry's routines to show the audiences how the hinges on the tables work, how the special pocket in his top hat compresses the warm flesh of rabbits. See, see, she says, it's all a sham. She cackles and says what are you laughing at when others laugh. She pisses on Terry's parade.

In our story, Jean slams the door on herself. That's why she can see the chain of the lock rattling. She walks back into her room, takes off her black wool coat, and all of her basted-together gypsy clothes. She lies down naked on her bed, and bit by bit over months that turn into years, she dreams her body alive. Her hair turns white from the strain of growing into her original shape, but her face loses its sternness, the sternness of flattening her longing into a pillow.

When she feels ready, she hangs up her sign, and men and women come to her, eyes dead with fear, palms extended with need. And Jean takes their hands into her own, and burns the fear from their eyes by speaking their desires aloud. She writes their fortune.

MUSIC

FROM BELOW

Susan Glickman

"Hᴇ'ꜱ ꜱᴛᴀʀᴛɪɴɢ ᴀɢᴀɪɴ," she said, burying her head in her pillow.

"No he's not. You're getting so paranoid."

"Listen."

And then he too became aware of it, first as a subterranean rhythm which he felt rather than heard, but eventually as a melody, faint but unmistakable, filtering up through the floor of their dark bedroom.

They looked at each other, or tried to, seeing only silhouettes: heads and shoulders outlined in silver by the streetlamp outside their window. Outside, where all was quiet.

"Can you sleep anyway? Try," he said, stroking her hair.

"I will try," she answered, hoping she didn't sound petulant. "But why does he do this to us? I can't take it anymore – it seems like every night now."

"I don't know why, Sweetheart. The guy is ... strange. Maybe he can't sleep. He never goes anywhere; that piano is his only resource."

"But we've asked him and asked him and he always apologizes so *sincerely*! I don't understand why he keeps promising not to play late at night if he doesn't mean it."

"I know, I know. But what can we do about it now? You want me to go knock on his door again? It's freezing out there. I'm sure he'll

102

stop in a moment. Anyhow, he *is* the landlord. It's his home, whether we like it or not. We're only tenants."

"But it's our home too, and he's invading it with his insomnia and homesickness and bad dreams. And always that same song! I'm *sure* he's doing it on purpose – he knows we're listening, he's forcing us to listen. He wants to drive us crazy or drive us away."

"For God's sake calm down," he said, beginning to get irritated. "You let yourself get too worked up about this. He's just a lonely old guy. He keeps the house immaculate. He's responsible about repairs. Last summer he gave you flowers from the garden, remember? You thought he was so cute then, with all that 'old-world charm.' And *you* were the one who couldn't stop boasting about what an amazing apartment we'd found, so cheap, so beautiful."

"Well, maybe it was all an illusion. Maybe the price is too high after all." She rolled away from her lover, making herself very small inside the quilt, the way she did after being punished as a child.

They were both quiet for a moment. The music filled the silence where their angry voices had been, or that's how it felt to her; that they were being displaced, evicted from their home, by some unseen but relentless power. That song – he was playing it again, over and over. Occasionally he played others, but this was the one she found herself listening for with dread and expectation, convinced it was a message from the old man to her, to them both. It was a simple Eastern-European folksong which modulated from a major to a minor key half-way through.

"I tell you what," her boyfriend said, more softly. "I'll phone around tomorrow and see if I can get a good price on acoustic tiles. Maybe if we pay for them he'll put them up."

"Oh, don't be crazy! That will cost us a fortune. We've already spent more than we can afford on rugs for soundproofing – and *they* don't work. Why should we put money into *his* apartment too?"

"Look, I was just trying to think of something that would calm you down so we could get to sleep. There's nothing else I can think of right now! I'm exhausted! If you hadn't made me listen to that damn piano I never would have heard it anyway."

"Well, you might be able to filter out whatever you don't want to be aware of, but *I* can't."

"What the hell is that supposed to mean?" He sat up abruptly and stared at the huddled shape wrapped in patchwork. An hour ago it had been the welcoming body of his love, which delighted him with the smooth slip of skin over muscle, the contrast of softness and bone. Now it was an alien form, an obstacle. He wanted to pull the quilt off and shake her. He wanted to make her cry out in pain, to punish her for belittling him. He would show her who was stronger!

He caught his breath, felt his heart pounding. The music continued, reprising the merry beginning of the song. It sounded like the score to a documentary about happy peasants: he could see the scene clearly – the women's heads in bright flowered kerchiefs bobbing between rows of golden wheat. It was hot and sunny where they were. A few placid goats browsed along the edges of the field, twitching their short tails. A fly buzzed so close to his ear he flinched and shook his head.

"I think I'll sleep in the living-room," he said quietly. "I have a meeting at 9 a.m. sharp. I've just got to get to sleep, and we're both over-excited now. Let's just give each other a little space, OK?"

When she didn't reply, he picked up his pillow, pulled a blanket out of the closet and left the room without saying goodnight.

The song began its descent into the minor key. One chord: two: then a trickle of melody, a few notes played high up the keyboard with the right hand. She clenched her eyes shut against the scene which flickered against their lids. Night was falling on the field and it was very cold. The sheaves of wheat stood like abandoned cottages, a few birds pecking around their doorsteps for leftover chaff. And then she smelled smoke and they came, as they did every night, the soldiers; their greatcoats flapping behind them like black wings. Their torches, dipped in tar, burned brightly, and the wheat-sheaves flared bright orange against the black impervious sky.

In the distance a woman screamed. The soldiers stopped and waited until the sound came again. Then they set off towards it, stepping briskly across the scorched straw, holding their torches up like bouquets. They stepped forward gallantly as lovers through the burning field.

THE MEANING OF THE MARRIAGE

Cynthia Flood

MRS. PERREN MARRIES my grandfather on a Tuesday afternoon, late. Providing a wedding meal is therefore unnecessary. The guests drink tea and eat pound cake.

On the Tuesday morning, Mrs. Perren comes with her sister to inspect my grandfather's house. (I don't know where he is.) They find everything very clean. The oak floors shine, and the thin high windows. Mrs. Perren's sister is enthusiastic about a man who keeps house so. (My grandfather is a saddler.) The two women see the bedroom prepared for the motherless little girl, my mother, who is now to leave her grandparents' house. She can come to live with her father because he will have a wife, and thus she a stepmother.

The sisters end their tour in the kitchen. Glass-fronted cupboards go right up to the ceiling, so Mrs. Perren stands on a chair to inspect the topmost shelves. From her altitude she sees out to the back yard, where a nasty box-headed tomcat rolls about in the sun-dappled shade of the maple. She sends the sister out with a broom. Then the two leave my grandfather's house to go along to the village dressmaker.

During the many fittings of her wedding dress, Mrs. Perren had been narrowly inspected (she was not local), for this unknown bride was to replace my dead grandmother and to 'take on' my mother, then aged 5. Posthumously, she would also be "your stepgrandmother" in the stories my mother told to me and my brother.

Mrs. Perren's wedding garment was of mauve silk, for she had been a widow long enough to finish with black and dove-grey in their turn. The dress was the bride's 'best' for some time after the ceremony; it moved then through a sequence of demotions, years long, which led first to burial in the rag bag but thence to magnificent resurrection in the crazy quilt on the spare room bed. Mrs. Perren was a notable quilter. Of the rite I know only that it was Methodist, though I think Mrs. Perren herself adhered to a harder covenant.

Was my mother there, to carry flowers for her new step-mother? At the little reception, did she chatter and clown to get the attention she was accustomed to? Did my grandfather and his bride have a honeymoon trip? How did my grandfather feel as he stepped into the bridal chamber? He was after all a veteran. His first wife had died after childbirth, taking twin girls with her to the grave. His second, my grandmother, had proved no more durable. A beautiful 26, she fell victim to the same 'childbed fever' as her predecessor, although the offspring survived.

Looking at my grandmother's photograph, taken in her marriage year, made me feel strange when I turned 26. Years later I told my mother so. For her, the strangest time had been when she herself was 52. These jumping years unnerve me. Two days after my daughter's birth, my body's temperature rose. I lay cold and sweating, could not eat, wept feebly on the nurse when she arrived at last. *Chills, headache, malaise, and anorexia are common.* In no time flat I was out of the ward, into isolation, on antibiotics. *Treatment consists of debridement by curettage and administration of penicillin;* I don't remember being debrided. The baby ran a fever too. Nobody named the poison in us.

Could my grandmother's family bring themselves to attend the wedding? My great-grandmother did make the pound cake for the occasion. I know, because over the years Mrs. Perren was repeatedly plaintive to her new husband and his little girl about its impropriety. A fruit-cake would have been seemlier. Perhaps Mrs. Perren felt that the ceremony hadn't really 'taken'? I have wondered how my great-grandmother felt as she mixed the butter and sugar and flour, a pound of each for the wedding that featured the same bridegroom as their daughter's and the same church, where her funeral had also been conducted, with, as my mother always says, "the entire village in tears." This is a direct quotation from my great-grandparents, who told and retold to my mother the terrible story of their daughter's death. The narrative shaped the end of their lives. My great-grandparents also told my mother, repeatedly, that their dead daughter was a joyful woman. My mother still repeats this to me. Her voice lingers with the phrasing. "My mother made everyone laugh with her," she says.

That is all I have for the story's opening.

Next comes a story set in the same polished kitchen that Mrs. Perren and her sister see on the wedding day. (I never heard a thing else about that sister.)

My 9 year old mother wears a green checked dress. Her dark hair shines and her eyes are hazel like mine, like her dead mother's. Her cheeks are hot. In her hands is a small box, dark blue leather. (A favourite wedding present of mine came in such a box: eight coffeespoons with handles shaped like palm trees and alligators and scimitars. Later, these went to my ex-husband.) The silver clasp is stiff, my mother's fingers determined, and the opening lid reveals a set of miniature ivory-handled cutlery. Oh perfect, she sees, for raspberries on leaf plates with girlfriends in the back yard, for imaginary cat-banquets with the strays watching lickerishly from the lower branches of the maple .... The little things exactly fit her hands. (My mother looks with disbelief at her arthritic digits.)

Who has given her this present? Its extravagance suggests grandparents. My mother has never said. I don't think she cares. My step-grandmother snatches the box away. She throws it into the wood stove. With the toasting fork, she rams the gift well down into the flames. "Sinful waste," says Mrs. Perren, "and for a girl like you." Burning leather smells dreadful.

Why didn't my grandfather stop her? Maybe he wasn't there, in the story.

Then did my mother tell him, crying, when he came home from work? Why didn't he do something then? Or later?

Mrs. Perren did not approve of pets – I believe she was originally a farm woman – and so my mother played with the neighbours' cats and dogs, and with the strays that Mrs. Perren said were all dirty beasts. One such was the box-headed tomcat, which turned out to have been a female rolling about desirously in heat, and Tipsy's kittens caused the first full confrontation between step-mother and step-daughter. Yet my mother has always been vague about this episode; I don't know how my step-grandmother 'got rid of' the little cats. When – rarely – my mother talks about her step-mother, she usually tells about the poison.

This story begins in an act of straightforward evil: some person or persons unknown leave gobbets of raw meat daubed with strychnine up and down the village lanes. Dying cats and dogs writhe and yowl and froth. Now 13 years old, my mother is frantic to hold the dying animals, stroke, comfort. Not unreasonably (in her narrative, my mother is always careful so to characterize the action), my step-grandmother refuses permission.

What Mrs. Perren does instead is to walk my mother out to the back lane and hold her there, forcibly, to watch one of the cats complete its death. She does this to convey to my mother the meaning of the expression 'tortures of the damned,' for, as Mrs. Perren says to her, "You do not know yet that you are wicked, and it is my business to teach you."

I can never bear this part, and always break in. "But your father, why didn't he do something so she wouldn't be so mean to you?"

The answer never satisfies. "Well," my mother says mildly, "*she* was looking after me, you know. I was her job. And everybody said I was very spoiled. My grandparents – they were broken-hearted, you see. I looked exactly like my mother. My step-mother probably told my father I was difficult. I suppose I was. And he was a quiet man."

A twenty-year gap comes between this story and the next.

My mother, 33 years old and now the mother of a little son, my older brother, drives out from Toronto to the village. One pretty spring day, drives out to visit my step-grandmother. Why?

Mrs. Perren is a widow again. My grandfather died when my mother was 26.

Why does my mother, fully-orphaned now, make this journey to Mrs. Perren?

I still think of Mrs. Perren as Mrs. Perren. I try to use the accurate term, but she doesn't feel like a relation. I don't even know her first name. Only recently I realized that she must have come *from somewhere* when she and her sister walked up to that thin clean house on the Tuesday. What happened to Mr. Perren? Why were there no little Perrens? Why did she remarry, at 40? My grandfather presumably sought the stability of husband-hood and of having a mother-substitute for his child, and calculated that losing *this* wife to puerperal fever was unlikely. If age was one of her charms, what were those of a middle-aged man with two dead wives and a young wilful child?

So my mother drives out to see her step-mother.

All I know of my step-grandmother, this woman who has so influenced my own life and my brother's, lies in these stories and questions, which I tack together into the rough shape of Mrs. Perren's ignorance and hate. I believe they suffice. But the man is missing. My grandfather. Where is he? I do not know one single story about him. For me, the space where he should be is magnetic.

My mother tells me about my *great*-grandfather, a companion story to that of great-grandmother and the pound cake, about a time when he goes to England (why?). While there, he makes a purchase for my great-grandmother and her five sisters: beautiful silk. (Every decent woman must have her good black dress.) To get the goods past Canadian customs, my great-grandfather wraps the gleaming yardage around his waist and so passes, unscathed though bulky, under authority's eye. This story, pleasingly, takes the edge off the probity of my intimidating forbearers. I like to imagine my great-grandfather in his stateroom as the ship pulls in to Quebec City or Montreal, breathing heavily, winding the stuff round and round himself and pinning it solidly at his sides. Further back, I like to see him in the English shop – in London? a textile city of the Midlands? – looking at the black shining rivers of fabric. "Yes, Rachel will like this."

Those sisters – my great-great-aunts, are they? I know stories about them too, though not their names or what they look like. One has a daughter, Sarah, who dithers in her selection of a husband. Finally losing patience, my great-great-aunt declares, "Sarah! You will go round and round the bush, and choose a crooked stick at last!" I even know that Sarah's marriage in fact turns out well. And another great-great-aunt, designated to teach my mother tatting, finally takes away from her the small circle of grubby botched work and issues the verdict: "Some are not born to tat."

But I have not even a little story like these about my grandfather.

Mrs. Perren did not like the story about the smuggled silk. (In what context did she hear it?) My mother says simply, "My step-mother disapproved." Of the purchase itself? of the deceit? Yet she used strips of that silk to edge the splendid crazy quilt she created for the spare room in my grandfather's house. How did the scraps get to Mrs. Perren? Perhaps my great-grandmother and great-great-aunts sent them along as a compliment, intended to soften; competent needlewomen themselves, they recognized but did not possess the talent required to conceive such an extraordinary bed-covering as my mother describes. To follow a pattern – log-cabin or wedding ring or Texas star – is one thing, but to create *ex nihilo* quite another. Buying material would be waste. No. The quilt-maker must use whatever has come to her rag bag through the years, and thence generate a design that exploits those random colours and textures, displays them to their utmost brilliance. She is midwife to a metamorphosis. In her quilt, the scraps and bits and tatters fuse, and then explode into a shapely galaxy of shattered stained glass.

Perhaps my foremothers hoped to win influence over my step-mother. But perhaps my great-grandmother was not even aware how my mother felt – my mother, another scrap sent from house to house; I don't know, yet I can imagine. I can't see my grandfather's face, though.

So now my mother is 33, and her visit to Mrs. Perren may say, "You taught me I was evil. You did all you could to stop me from living my life. Yet I have vanquished. I am educated, a trained teacher. I have traveled. I am married, pretty, happy. I have borne a beautiful healthy son." The subtext is clear: "None of this is true of you, step-mother." Yet that is not the story of the visit.

She only told me the full story once, when I was young. Now my mother wants me to tell her how the story ends.

During the visit, my brother is noisily vigorous, running about the neat back yard and stomping in the kitchen and wanting to throw his ball in the living-room. Mrs. Perren says to my mother, "Take him away." My mother is angry, but she does not leave. Instead she leads my brother upstairs, to show him mummy's room when she was a little girl. Mrs. Perren does not go upstairs any more (arthritis), has not for some years; a bed has been placed for her in the dining-room. So she sits, alone again, in the chair by the window. How does she pass the time today, any day? She can no longer quilt. No novels – devil's work. Perhaps Mrs. Perren reads the Bible, perhaps she looks out the window and disapproves of passersby.

I can imagine thus about my step-grandmother, my great-grandfather, my great-great-aunts. I cannot imagine about my grandfather, because my imagination requires a toehold on the known world, and I know no stories about him.

Up the stairs go my mother and my brother, in the story, and as they climb they smell the musty acid odour of stale cat excrement, stronger and stronger, nearer and nearer. In the spare room, a branch of the maple tree beloved in my mother's youth has pierced the window. Later, after the wind shook out big shards of glass, the tree went on growing, and now a convenient cat-bridge leads to shelter and relative warmth. Right now, as my mother and brother enter the room, they find two animals dozing on the quilt. Silk and velveteen and grosgrain and muslin and polished cotton and gingham and corduroy and chintz, triangles and rhomboids and squares in all the colours – all are smeared, all stained, rumpled. Cat fur lies thick. A drift floats airborne as one cat rushes out the broken window into safe leafiness. The other purrs under my delighted brother's pats. My mother sees. The floor is littered, sticky, with feces. The down pillows drip urine. She goes quickly into the other rooms on this upper floor. The cats have been everywhere.

My mother no longer remembers what she did next. She can only get as far as what she thought of doing.

One choice is to tell Mrs. Perren, perhaps even to help her make arrangements for pruning, glazing, cleaning. (My mother wonders if undiluted Javex would work.)

The other choice is to say nothing, to leave her step-mother stewing in her stink. My mother worries about getting my brother's co-operation, so he will not cry excitedly to Mrs. Perren, "Kitties pee on floor!" Surely, she thinks, the coming summer heat will eventually let the old nose know. Or some other visitor will come. (She herself never went to that house again.)

My mother asks me now, "Which did I do?" But I don't remember. My brother was only 3. He doesn't remember. Neither of us can tell her what she wants to know.

I would like to, but for me as a child that story had little to do with the solitary woman waiting downstairs or the sharp resentful voice saying, "Take him away." No.

I loved the branch to the spare room, the branch where the cats ran back and forth in the moony night and through the green leaves of the day. Perhaps if that branch were sturdy, the window-hole big enough, a child might travel thus and hide in the heart of the tree, with the furry cats purring and snoozing and stretching their lithe long selves? I did not care, either, about the reeking sodden floorboards in the spare room, the precious quilt ruined, the golden double featherstitching all torn and frayed. This for me was just one of the wonderful cat-stories from Before Me, stories told and retold by my mother and my brother, like the one about Slippers the calico, who in her first pregnancy follows my mother from room to room, sleeps on her lap and on her bed. Her labour begins as my mother prepares for a dinner party; my brother strokes and soothes the cat as my mother finishes dressing, takes up her cloak. (This wonderful garment is purple velvet, cast-off church curtains. How has my agnostic mother come by this fabric? The purple is limp, the nap gone in parts, but my mother takes scrim and shapes a high dramatic collar to show off her high-piled hair.)

Seeing my mother leave her bedroom, Slippers struggles up and follows her, mewing, one scarcely-born kitten left behind in the basket and another's nose sticking out of her vagina. My brother retrieves the cat, but Slippers writhes and yowls and my brother, fearful, drops her. She runs after my mother and half-way down the stairs delivers her second kitten. My mother stops. She gathers cat and kitten into her cloak. She brings them back to the basket in her bedroom. My brother has to go downstairs and tell my father, waiting impatiently in the living-room with the fire going out, that she isn't coming. She settles down with Slippers, and the kittens are born in peace. When all are safely curled by their mother, she does go to the party, where she makes a fine story out of the event and my father almost forgives her.

And another story is of Johnny-come-lately, of a winter's dusk with thick snow falling and my brother standing by the living-room gazing out, half-dreaming with the white movement of the flakes. A red car comes along – an uncommon colour in 1930s Toronto – and stops by our house. My brother calls, "Mum, come look at the red car." The moment she appears at the window, the car opens, a black kitten is flung out, and the car flees scarlet down the street with rooster tails of snow and exhaust whirling behind it. Johnny was with our family for years. He was the first animal whose death I grieved.

My mother wants me to tell her the ending of the story about the visit so she will know whether she did – right or wrong, I suppose. Or: did she obey her duty or her desire? Which was which? Without the memory, she cannot judge herself.

I want other knowledge. I want to know why my mother forgot my grandfather.

Perhaps she even decided to forget him.

My mother has never in my presence used the words, "I remember when my father ...." The word *Dad* has never been used. No snapshot or painting is extant. No quotations survive, letters, account books, diaries. No stories. But that beautiful joyous woman married him. She must have had her reasons, and I wish I knew what they were.

Did my mother feel so abandoned that when she grew up she simply obliterated him from the stones of memory? Did she unilaterally declare herself parentless? Certainly one parent was always dead, dead from a few days past my mother's own day of birth. This parent existed only in stories, none told by the other. None of his words have survived. Nor has he.

I will try imagining. Let us suppose that after my mother's birth my grandfather sits by my grandmother's bedside, looking down at her lovely face, seeing with delight his living daughter. Likely he goes away then, to tell family and friends, perhaps to thank his God for the safe deliverance this time, to sleep at night and wake joyful in the morning. But by then the dirt, the poison, are thick in her blood. She feels unwell. The doctor comes. The milk stops. The baby cries. The smells begin. *The patient is toxic and febrile, the lochia is foul-smelling, and the uterus is tender ....* The young woman lies quietly. *Chills, headache, malaise, and anorexia are common. Pallor, tachycardia, and leukocytosis are the rule.* This rule holds. So as she dies my grandmother does not scream and writhe and froth like the cat, but slowly dazes and drifts, descending into a poisoned stupor (*Hemolytic anemia may develop .... With severe hemolysis and coexistent toxicity, acute renal failure is to be expected*) and so to her death. *The mortality rate is then about 50%.* But then there was neither debridement nor penicillin, so that rule did not apply.

The other parent sadly sends the child off to live with her grandparents. What else to do? My great-grandparents love the baby, painfully. They live nearby. He cannot be a saddler and care for an infant on his own. Paid help is not possible. So for five years the little girl lives with her doting grandparents. Then – inexplicably, to such a young child – comes the alleged reunion. In reality, my mother comes to a cold bitter woman who resents her step-daughter even before they meet, who teaches an innocent girl to believe herself to be evil, who burns her present and makes her witness the agony of the cat.

In his third marriage, how comes my grandfather to make such an error in judgment?

When I am 15, our plump tabbycat Mitzi with the extra toes dies on the operating table as she is being spayed. My mother collapses with grief, self-blame, rage at herself and my father for having determined that this cat should not kitten. "She mewed all the way in the car," my mother shouts, weeping, her sweating face contorted. "She didn't want to go. I made her. Because I was bigger and stronger. I took her to her death." My mother falls on the sofa and shoves her head into the cushions and hits the sofa arm repeatedly. My father and I look at each other. I start to leave the room. "You can't run away from this," he says, gripping my arm hard. "Come back to her."

I don't remember how we get through the afternoon. My mother does not make any dinner, and this is very difficult for me because my father likes no cooking but hers. Early in the evening she goes up to the spare room in the attic and closes the door. She stays there overnight. We hear her crying from time to time, and shoving at the stiff window; it gives to her strength with a harsh scraping rattle of glass against wood. In the spare room are stored non-working lamps, moth-nibbled blankets, stacks of magazines that my brother will sort through some day. The bed is not made up. Faded chenille covers its lunar surface. The heart of the house beats in the wrong place that night, and though the spare room is next to mine I gain no comfort from my mother's nearness. Thinking of her there disturbs me still.

I will sum up: My grandfather was a saddler. He was a quiet man. He had a small clean house in a village in Ontario, at the turn of the century. He married three times, lost two wives – one of whom was lovely and laughed – and gave his only surviving child into the care of a wicked step-mother. He died, for some reason, on the borderline between middle and old age. That's all I know.

MIRROR, MIRROR

Rachna Gilmore

S AROJ STARED at the storm raging outside. So much to do
before Mummy came, and here she was, stuck home. She'd
have to hustle and finish all her shopping tomorrow, no matter
what the roads were like.

"Footwear!" Shaking off the bubbles, Saroj wiped her hands
hastily on her apron and picked up her mother's letter again.

"Don't worry, Saroj. I'm sure I'll have enough warm clothes to
brave your winter. Jayinti has a coat that she bought in England to
lend me, also gloves and scarves. I'm dying to get my first glimpse
of snow."

"Just as I thought," murmured Saroj, "Mummy doesn't mention snow- boots."

Mummy couldn't possibly be prepared for a PEI winter – even
on the coolest winter day in Bombay you never needed anything
more than a light sweater.

She wrote down 'snow-boots' on her list and looked out the
window at the white blur. Mummy would see snow with a ven-
geance.

She'd be packing now, her mother, bustling around the big
house, locking up valuables and staples after portioning out *dahl*,
flour, rice and other necessities. You could never trust servants not
to gorge and get into things while you were gone. There were only
Mary and Willie now. Once there had been many servants.

There had been Unnu. She and Unnu. Unnu with the gentle,
luminous eyes.

"Mom," called Gita from the family room, "Can we watch 'The
Friendly Giant' now?"

115

Saroj looked at her watch and smiled. Dead on time. The children were enjoying the day off from school. They still loved to watch their old favourite shows.

"All right," she called back.

She heard the deep voice of the Friendly Giant say, "Look Up, Look Waaay Up!"

She let the water out of the sink and began to dry the dishes. It was a long, long time since she'd seen her mother. Thirteen years. That was when her father had died, just three years after she and Mohan had married and moved to Canada. Saroj had rushed back to India, the journey a blur of airport lounges and crowded planes.

Saroj wondered what Mummy looked like now. Photographs showed so little. Did she move swiftly and surely, or had age slowed her down? Somehow, Saroj still saw her not as the white-clad widow, face innocent of makeup and wan with grieving, but as she had been in Saroj's childhood. She had been tall, elegant despite her bulk; kohl encircling her eyes, always beautifully arrayed in colourful saris with lipstick and *bindi* to match, jewels sparkling on her ears, throat and arms. Back then, she walked quickly and gracefully, her movements alive and alert. Memsahib never missed a thing. Wherever she went, an orchestra of sounds announced her: the rustle of her sari, the clicking-flapping of her sandals against the marble floors, and the music of her gold bangles tinkling in concert with the jingle of the household keys tucked into the waist of her sari.

Saroj used to love watching her; she'd picture herself, all grown up, busy and important in silk and gold just like her mother. What grand plans she'd made, she and Unnu. No, not Unnu. Saroj was to be a princess at the very least, but Unnu, she was content to be just Unnu. Of course her name wasn't really Unnu, it was Anna. But with the Indian accent it became Unnu, just as Unnu's mother, Estelle, was called Istailla.

A gust of wind buffeted the house, clattering the trellis against the siding. Saroj shivered.

She put away the plates and sat down at the desk with the list, tapping the pencil against the paper. Everything must be perfect for Mummy; nothing but the best. Flowers for her room: something bright and sweet-smelling like freesias and roses, with sprigs of baby's breath and ferns.

"Groceries. I must get a nice eggplant and make up a *bhaji* for Mummy. Oh, the steak, I'd better hide that."

Saroj flew to the freezer. No, the last of the steak was gone. She'd have to remind Mohan and the children not to mention beef.

Saroj heard a rattling at the window. It was the bird-feeder blown upwards by the wind, banging against the eave.

"I'll have to fill it again," thought Saroj. Mummy would be enchanted with the blue jays. She still had the miniature glass birds she'd collected years ago when Saroj was little. They'd come from a glass blower in Bangalore; the most exquisite, vibrant pieces of hand-made perfection Saroj had ever seen. They occupied the place of honour on the top shelf of the china cabinet in the dining-room of the big house in Bombay. Saroj was never allowed to touch them, but she loved looking at them. But not Unnu. She was always morbidly nervous of anything fragile or forbidden.

◊

That sweltering afternoon in late May, Saroj and Unnu had swung on the heavy iron gate at the bottom of the garden. When the heat had become too ferocious, they'd retreated to the shade of the front verandah.

"Let's play Snow-White," said Saroj. "I'm Snow-White and you're the wicked step-mother."

Saroj always directed their games and played the glamourous parts. And Unnu never complained, glad to play with Memsahib's daughter. Glad to get away from the chores her mother thrust at her and to play in the big house away from the noisy, crowded heat of the servants' quarters. They played Snow-White, shrieking and laughing.

"You're not a very good witch, Unnu," said Saroj. "Look, you have to be scary."

Unnu smiled, "I don't know how." She wriggled her dusty toes. Her feet were large, the toes splayed innocently wide, as only feet unrestrained by footwear could be. Her heels had already begun to crack like Istailla, whose heels were slashed and split all around. And the stringy legs above just exaggerated the size of Unnu's feet.

"Look at your feet; they're huge. I know what, let's play Jack and the Beanstalk; I'll be Jack and you be the Giant."

Saroj rumpled Unnu's hair and said, "Now stamp your feet hard and this is what you say: 'Fee-fi-fo-fum, I smell the blood of an Englishman. Be he alive or be he dead, I'll grind his bones to make my bread.' "

Unnu hid her face and squealed with fright and laughter.

The afternoon wore on and, as the sunshine reverberated and pulsed, even the verandah became unbearable. They tiptoed indoors, clothes clinging to sticky bodies, faces radiating heat.

All was still in the big house. It was Memsahib's habit to take a nap every afternoon in her air-conditioned bedroom, and Saroj and Unnu knew better than to disturb her. Saroj got herself and Unnu a drink of ice-cold water from the refrigerator. Then, still hot and prickly, she came up with a new idea.

"Come on, let's go see the glass birds," she said, pulling at Unnu's hand.

Unnu hung back.

"Am I allowed in there?" she asked.

Saroj lifted her shoulder to wipe the sweat off her upper lip. Unnu was always so timid, like a little frightened calf.

"Of course you are; you're playing with me aren't you? Mummy allows me to go there whenever I want."

Unnu rubbed her bare dusty feet against the back of her legs.

"My mother will get angry," she whispered. "She said not to go anywhere but your room or outside. Memsahib said so."

Saroj clicked her tongue impatiently. "Don't be silly. She won't be angry. Not if I said you can come. Come on, stupid." She pinched Unnu and pulled her into the gloom of the dining-room.

Unnu wrapped her arms around her thin waist and stood motionless, lest the edges of her dress brush against something. The dress was one of Saroj's cast-offs. Unnu was three years older than Saroj, but she was smaller, so she came into many of Saroj's old dresses. Memsahib liked to look after her servants. Furthermore, she didn't believe in waste.

Saroj clicked on the overhead fan. The heavy, humid air reluctantly moved. Saroj flapped her arms and puffed out her dress to get the maximum circulation. Unnu, with wet patches under her arms and beads of sweat glistening on her forehead and upper lip, stared with round, pensive eyes at the teak-laden dining-room.

As the fan whirled, Saroj felt some of the heat and irritation evaporate from her body. She smiled at Unnu and smoothed the spot she'd pinched. She was sorry she'd pinched her but she didn't say so. Mummy never apologized to Istailla when she yelled at her. One didn't.

Saroj peered at the glass birds on the top shelf of the china cabinet. There they were: a yellow canary with a bright orange beak, a red parrot and a brilliant green parrot with beady black eyes, a few birds of startling plumage and dubious authenticity, but best of all, the iridescent turquoise and gold of the peacock. Saroj pressed her nose against the cabinet, her breath making a foggy smear on the glass.

"Saroj, don't do that."

Saroj grinned and breathed harder.

"Come on, Unnu, come and see the birds, see how pretty they are."

"Saroj don't."

"Don't be silly." Saroj flapped her hand at her impatiently. "It's my house, I'll do what I want."

"Please, Saroj."

"You're such a spoilsport." Saroj hated that cowed look.

Unnu chewed her lip and twisted her arms around each other.

"Memsahib might think my mother didn't clean that properly and then she will get into trouble and my father will get angry at her," she said in a low voice. "My mother cannot afford to lose this job."

"Gosh, Unnu, must you make such a big thing out of everything," groaned Saroj. "Mummy won't get angry; I'll tell her I did it."

But she wiped the foggy spot with her palm. Moving away from the china cabinet, Saroj flopped into a chair beside the sideboard.

Unnu simply didn't understand. Memsahib was fair and just. Didn't she give to the poor and go to the temple regularly.?

"You must always remember those people who are not as well off," Memsahib would say on holy days as she handed out small coins to the beggars outside the temple. "You must remember your duty and treat them well."

And in the temple Saroj and her mother would remove their sandals and join the ranks of wobbly women with yellowing-grey hair piously chanting, "*Ragupati Raghava Rajaram, Patitapavana Sitaram ....*"

And she even let Saroj play with Unnu, a servant's daughter. In fact, there were no other playmates nearby. That was one of the disadvantages of living in a bungalow outside Bombay instead of in a flat in the city. But there were compensations.

Saroj remembered a conversation she'd overheard between Memsahib and a friend as they had sat on the shady front verandah overlooking the flower beds. The garden had glowed with hibiscus, marigold and roses. The women had watched the gardener at work in the full glare of the sun as they sat on wicker chairs, sipping ice-cold drinks that Istailla had served.

"You have such a beautiful compound!"

Saroj's mother sipped her lemonade and scratched her stomach under the folds of her flowery chiffon sari.

"Yes, it's nice to have the space, but," she lowered her voice, "the *mali* is lazy and I have to keep at him and at him to do his job. That's the third time I'm making him dig that bed; he just won't do it right."

"Yes, yes. It's hard to get servants to work these days, but at least you can get them. Where I am, it's a real problem keeping them."

"We never have that problem; they don't want to go." Memsahib kicked off her sandals. "It's the servants' quarters here – it makes them toe the line. They'll think twice before leaving for the slums."

"You're so lucky! We don't have any servants' quarters and we just can't keep them, even though we pay well."

"Of course, it's not just the quarters, you know." Memsahib smoothed the fragrant jasmine garland wound around her bun. "They have it pretty cushy; I'm very good to them."

And Saroj knew she was. The day after one of Memsahib's lavish parties, Saroj would regale herself on leftover desserts. Memsahib, the dangling end of her bright silk sari tucked in at the waist, her bangles pushed firmly up her arms, would dole out the leftovers. Her strong hands flew as she picked the flesh off chicken bones, calculated how much rice was left, and portioned the umpteen curries, vegetables and *chapatis*, every now and again popping a morsel in her own mouth. Nothing was ever wasted. First she put aside the choice food suitable for the family, then she scraped and gathered every last crumb for the servants.

"Istailla, here's something for you to take home," she said, handing her a plate of fragments from the feast.

"Thank you, Memsahib." Istailla's glass bangles tinkled as she brought her hands together in thanks. Servants were always grateful. Istailla, along with the other servants, would finish cleaning up the party chaos. Then she would go home to the room she and her husband and five children shared at the rear of the compound.

◊

Saroj stared at the list. She'd been doodling. What had she drawn in the corner? Apples? Apples. Of course, she'd forgotten about fruit. Mummy liked apples. Red apples. Big, shiny apples.

"Mom, Ravi won't give me the remote control and it's my turn to pick the show." Gita bounced into the kitchen.

"No it's not, Mom, she picked the last one! She's lying."

"No I'm not, and it is so my turn," Gita yelled, a bubble of saliva forming at the corner of her mouth.

"For heaven's sake! Stop it!" Saroj snatched a kleenex and wiped and wiped the corner of Gita's mouth.

"Oww! Mom, you're hurting!"

"I'm sorry, ... Gita, but I'm very busy preparing for your Grandmother's visit. I don't want to hear your fighting. I won't. If you two can't work it out, there'll be no TV."

Gita and Ravi looked at each other, then went back whispering into the family room.

"Now where was I?" sighed Saroj. "Oh yes, fruit."

◊

In the dining-room, after every meal, Istailla carried the huge bowl of fruit from the sideboard to place on the table in front of Memsahib. It was a glass bowl kept covered by a fine mesh cloth weighted around the edge with an intricate pattern of beads.

Memsahib pulled off the mesh and folded it quickly.

With her elbows extended almost at right angles, she palpated the fruit – pears, papayas, apples, bananas, mangoes, figs, custard apples and others, depending on the season. With sharp-eyed, almost religious fervour, she picked the best and handed it out; first to Saroj's father, then Saroj and then herself. She liked best the red apples from Kashmir. She'd inhale the aroma with a "mmm!" and sink her large teeth into the firm, juicy flesh.

◊

"Apples" wrote Saroj. She didn't care for them.

She gazed blankly at the sheet of paper while her hand, as if of its own accord, stroked, dashed.

She was doodling again. She'd drawn a bowl under the apples. A wide, gently-curved bowl. Like the one on the dining-room sideboard.

◊

"Okay, so what do you want to do?" she'd asked Unnu crossly.

Unnu's eyes brightened. Now that Saroj had abandoned the china cabinet, she looked more cheerful.

"How about playing with your dolls, Saroj?"

"Nah! I don't want to." Saroj stroked the straggly ends of her hair away from her face.

"Then let's go outside again."

Saroj stared gloomily at the blinding sunshine. If only it would rain. The monsoon was expected any day now; it would settle the dust. Everything looked so dirty and faded in the savage heat. It was too hot to play outside. Besides, Mummy didn't like her going out in the worst of the heat; she'd get too dark. Unnu was fairer skinned, a legacy from her Portugese ancestors. But Unnu didn't have to worry about her complexion. Not Unnu. It didn't matter for a servant girl whose father would have to scrape to get up even a meager dowry.

"No, silly, it's too hot."

"Let's go into your room and find something to do."

Saroj dragged her gaze back indoors. Bright spots danced in front of her eyes. Unnu's face looked dark and blank after the glare outside.

"That's all we ever do," said Saroj. She was tired of playing with her toys. It didn't seem fair that Unnu didn't have any. If she had, then at least there'd be two lots of toys to get tired of. Anyway, Mummy would never have let her play in the servants' quarters.

"Saroj, please, Memsahib will wake up soon. Let us go to your room."

Unnu's very meekness sent a prickle of irritation up Saroj's back.

"For goodness sake, I've told you, haven't I, we're allowed in here."

Saroj moved her hips further back into the chair, her legs dangling. Her hand brushed the fruit bowl on the sideboard, and the beaded edge of the mesh covering the fruit flicked against the bowl, a rhythmic clicking sound, like a miniature pendulum, regular, inevitable. Saroj flicked it again, harder. The beads chattered frantically against the glass.

"Come on, Saroj," begged Unnu, "we'll get into trouble."

Saroj pulled the mesh off the bowl and groped the fruit as her mother did. She picked up a large red apple and sank her teeth into it.

"Here." She handed one to Unnu. "Have one."

Unnu shrank. "I don't think I should."

Saroj sat up and stopped chewing her apple. She swallowed hastily. "For God's sake Unnu, relax. You know Mummy says you can eat the same things as me while we play together."

Unnu bit her lip and traced small circles on the marble floor with her foot.

"Take it." Saroj pressed the apple into Unnu's hand.

Unnu stared at it. "It's beautiful."

"Eat it."

Unnu held it in her hand. "It looks too good to eat."

"Oh for God's sake Unnu, it's just an apple."

"We hardly ever get apples. They're special."

"Really?" Saroj stopped in mid bite and stared. An apple special! For Saroj, special meant the Indian sweets that Daddy brought home from the *mithai* shop. A surge of compassion and affection swept over her. Unnu was a good sort.

She smiled at Unnu. "Go on, it's all right. Mummy lets me have them any time. Eat it."

"Thank you." Unnu slowly bit into the apple.

"Take a bigger bite."

"It's so good," said Unnu as soon as she could speak.

Saroj laughed and rolled her eyes. Poor Unnu. Going on about apples.

Unnu ate her apple fast. Something about the way she nibbled at the core made Saroj say, "Like another one?"

"Oh no! No thank you. Come on, Saroj, let us go back to your room."

"Just wait. Now have another. Mummy won't mind, honest."

Eagerness and diffidence struggled in Unnu's eyes. Saroj saw it, and a strange sensation gripped her throat. There were four more apples nestled among the fruit in the bowl. Saroj snatched them up and thrust them at Unnu.

"Here," she said gruffly. "Take them home for later."

"No, no, I can't," whispered Unnu, aghast.

"Take them, Unnu," commanded Saroj. She glowed with the pleasure of giving. "Mummy's always telling me to share. We have plenty more in the fridge. Go on. Take them. You know Mummy won't mind. She really believes in sharing. And she's always giving your mother things. Go on."

Saroj saw Unnu's eyes widen as she balanced the apples in her arms.

◊

The pencil point snapped against the paper. Saroj slackened her grip on the pencil and stared at the jagged tip. She shook herself as if awakening from a trance and sharpened the pencil into a fine point.

She got up quickly and began to open the kitchen cupboards energetically.

"Let's see, what else do we need?"

◊

Images flickered. They must have been dreams.

Mummy yelling at Istailla. Shouting, "Thief!"

Saroj clinging to her mother, "Mummy, she didn't steal them. Mummy listen, please listen. Mummy, I gave them to her. No, Mummy, no. I promise it was my idea."

Memsahib's voice, icy, certain, "You don't understand these things, Saroj. That's enough."

Saroj crouching in bed listening to the screams as Unnu's father beat her.

Peering out the window, watching the tonga cart laden with a family's belongings slowly plodding away, the clip-clop of the horse's hooves kicking up a mist of dust. Istailla slumped on the baggage, weeping; her husband sitting up front with the tonga driver. Unnu's four brothers huddled around Istailla. *Where was Unnu?*

Saroj, wandering alone through the shimmering heat behind the servants' quarters. That strange silence; no radios blaring, no voices chattering in Konkani. Drifting aimlessly inside the outer fringes of the large compound, feet and sandals encased in dust, blinded by the sun, sweat trickling down her face. If only it would rain and cool everything off. The leaves on the shrubs were coated with dust, the flowers withered, scorched.

Through the wire fence she saw something. Just outside the compound. Something not quite behind a bush. Going outside the iron gate and scrambling through the shrubs pressing against the fence, parted branches snapping back.

She saw the feet first, grimy; wide-spread toes.

That must have been a nightmare. Not Unnu.

Unnu must have gone with her family. Not left lying bruised, battered, limbs askew, brown eyes half open, a glob of spit at the corner of her mouth. And clusters of blue-green flies, like jewels on Unnu, buzzing, buzzing, buzzing.

Running somehow, dry heaves tearing her throat, clothes ripping on branches as thunder rumbled behind.

Mummy tucking her into bed under the mosquito net, smoothing her tangled hair as the roar of rain filled her ears.

"You didn't see anything. You didn't see anything. You must have fallen asleep; it was the heat, and you're tired. Daddy looked and there's nothing there. Nothing."

Safe in bed, waves of fragrance wafting down from the wilting jasmine garland in Mummy's hair. It was so blissfully cool under the white, shrouding mosquito net with Mummy's hands gentle on her forehead and the rain lulling her to sleep.

◊

Saroj slammed shut the cupboard door and clicked her tongue. She'd opened and shut all those cupboards and she hadn't noticed a thing. What a dreadful imagination she had. Wasting time. Childhood memories were so refracted, like images in a hall of mirrors. Crazy, rippled glass twisting reflections into ogres and monsters. Mummy was right, she was too sensitive, too morbid.

Saroj sighed. Now she'd have to go through all the cupboards again. Was there enough whole wheat flour? Anyway, those kinds of people always landed on their feet, Mummy said so.

She finished writing the grocery list, then checked it over. Yes, she'd remembered everything. She looked out the window at the storm, still shrieking unabated. No hope of getting out today; the groceries, the flowers, everything would have to wait until tomorrow. Everything. And she mustn't forget to remind Mohan and the children not to mention they ate beef. Mummy would be so disappointed.

SOONER OR LATER ALL BODIES TEND TO MOVE TOWARD THE CENTRE OF THE EARTH

Libby Oughton

S HE CUPPED her hands around the earth spinning under her palms. Sometimes there was no centring this small bit of earth or herself. By closing her eyes she could search the faintest tremor in her world. Seismograph. Imagine, Lucy thought, a fancy machine hooked up to this wheel, the needle etching out in code: you're off centre, on centre today. She pulled her attention back to the spinning wheel. Only hands, hands on. Listening with fingers and palms.

The clay forced her to connect to a centre within, wrapped up tight and hidden away, discarded. Until now. Connecting her inside and down, deep down, down beyond. Like the apple! That one that had bopped Newton on the head. Grave, he thought, indignant. Then sat and reasoned under the tree and the notion of gravity had burst upon him ... the attractive force by which all bodies tend to move toward the centre of the earth her father had said. But *that* didn't satisfy her. As a child she threw lots of balls up, dreamed of them stopped up there, hovering, free, caught in forever. And why didn't angels crash to earth? Her Sunday School teacher had laughed that adult what-a-stupid-question laugh and answered that it was god's will. She'd clung tightly to her own truth that one day something would not come down. Did Newton consider the angels ...? Now, almost half a century later, she smiled at this memory. Memories. Pocketfuls returning to her. No. A much larger container, a transport truck speeding across the prairies on the Transcanada, racing its huge shadow cast by the falling sun. A blur of letters on the side:

LUCY'S MEMORIES

But what opens the doors? Who decides when this or that memory pops into the present? So here she was with the gravity of Newton on her mind again and the earth a little off centre slithering under her palms.

There I go again, she thought. Wandering. Must shut off the tick-tock of my head, let it wind down.

With the slightest pressure she slowly slid her interlocked fingers up, raising an almost perfect cone, cupping her thumbs over the tip to rest, to listen. No tremble, no wobble. How curious it felt, moving yet still. With caution, she lifted her hands to observe this first success. Strike me down, she mused, a perfect phallus! Wouldn't Freud have loved it. "Lucy, a patient of mine for twenty-four years, finally, after much resistance, confirmed my theory and discovered that having her own penis did indeed bring her joy and contentment ... although her solution was highly unorthodox." In mock tribute to Freud, her eyes closed and her fingers sought the soft clay. She cupped the bottom of the cone, stroked and squeezed toward the tip. Gentle. Caressing. Then with care her thumbnail created that little ridge. Perfect, straight (no question of arches of course), a beauty created by her own hands. As easily made and fine-tuned as it was destroyed by two thumbs and careful pressure down. Phallus to pancake with utter ease. Back to phallus again at a touch. Simple, so simple.

And unexpected. This satisfaction. The library book beside her with the step-by-step instructions was pretty matter-of-fact on this point. "The student will find it useful in the art of centring to raise the clay into a cone and bring it back down by pressure on the top at least three times to get any imperfections such as air pockets out of the clay." Nothing at all about the erotic freedom in her own hands. She was thoroughly pleased with herself.

What instinct had lead her to pottery? A grasp, a straw, a needle lost on a mountain. Her body tensed and shook. Fear unseated her hands. Those days, those nights, her private black holes ... after her one and only lover had stalked out the door shouting that she was nothing but a stupid drunk, hopeless, useless. And right after that she was fired, or "let go" as the boss said, "for her own good." What good, she'd wondered. The only two things that kept her connected with the world, with living, gone. No good was really what she was. To anyone, except liquor store sales and her dog.

That night she found herself weaving up the steps to the library. Drunk again and infinitely lonely. Convinced she could carry it off. Fool the librarian. She practised the words she would say, trying to remember how normal people would talk. Should be simple. Nothing was simple. "Do you have any books on pottery. My friend wants to learn about it and can't get to the library." Lying. Again. Try truth. "I want to get a book on pottery. Where are they?" That should do it. Unless the librarian smirked at her with that poor-soul-what-would-she-ever-do-with-a-book look that would make her dissolve and flee. Reaching the top of the stairs she spied the bench there, with the usual collection of drunks keeping it warm, passing the paper bag, shouting at her to join in. *I'm not one of them.* Although the bench looked appealing. Time to get her speech exactly right. The sidewalk leading to the heavy glass doors had a nice straight crack right down the centre. Her test would be walking it steadily, step by careful step. Simon says .... If she passed she would be ready, normal. Oh god how complicated everything was. What if the librarian asked her questions. The doors were getting close. Yes, she would have to. So scared, so much to plan, just to go to the library. For a book. That's what libraries were for. She had rights too. Right? Wrong. The wrong was that she was drunk and doing it, she told herself. Libraries weren't for drunks. Drunks only use them to get warm if they can sneak in.

She passed her own test, and gave her request in the quietest of voices. The librarian showed her two books. She took the one with the largest type and walked out the door, her head just a little higher as she passed the bench.

How heavy that book had been. And the idea she could learn anything new. She remembered exactly where she'd put the book that night. Spread out an old lace curtain on a stump she hauled in from the woodpile. Set it exactly in the centre of the kitchen. An altar for the book. She added a small jar of Queen Anne's lace to keep it company. The flowers bent their heads, sprinkled pollen on the book. Each night she and her trusty bottles of sherry would watch the book, fascinated by what might be between the covers. For someone. Not her. In her last conscious moment she would touch it once. Thumbprint. Ownership. A dust jacket of thumbprints. The library sent pink cards to her mailbox. She sent them unread to her wood stove.

How many days weeks months had it been? Soon after the disasters, someone she barely knew had cornered her in the lineup at the co-op store. Said to her point blank that she drank too much and that if she wanted help it was available. She remembered saying no thanks to the floor. But she stopped going out much after that. It was getting too complicated to lie any more. Living with the living. But those words stuck. Choking her night after lonely night until the sweet sherry soothed them away. But never as far as she wanted.

Then the letter from a school friend she hadn't seen for twenty years arrived. Catching up, the letter said, because we'd lost touch. (She knew this person had been sick. In and out of hospital since graduation. Suicide attempts she'd heard.) Her friend spoke of discovering weaving, of sitting at her loom for seven years after she'd been kicked out of the hospital with a supply of pills to keep her quiet. Kept her hands busy and anchored her body. To get the time and the space for memory. To search what had really happened in her life. Yards and yards of silk collected at the end of the loom until she'd woven her truth. Her father had done it first, abused her. Then her brothers. She didn't even hate them. They weren't worth that. But she needed to get away, far away for awhile. Could she come and visit.

Visit? The letter was never answered. It sat beside the book and the weeping flowers on the altar. How long had she been bent over the wheel, the clay spinning and her hands idle? (How thoughtful and kind of the earth to wait for her. Patient the earth.) Funny. How life goes. Now that she'd retraced the library steps through the body of her mind, they seemed easy to negotiate compared to the next steps.

Opening the book. No. Get it straight, she prodded herself. No, then it had been that little pamphlet. Pink too. Crumpled inside the mailbox. "Are you an alcoholic? Try this simple quiz and find out." No way, she thought, but couldn't throw it away.

Like the book and the letter it found its way to the stump. One night she put a Magic Marker beside it. Decided that after each bottle of sherry she would answer one question. Sooner than she meant, the empty boxes were filled in. She read the rules ... if you answer yes to more than .... The pink paper knew (and she'd even cheated, well ... stretched the truth on a few). It said at the end to call a certain number if you wanted help. She sent the quiz to the wood stove. She took a matchstick and printed the word HELLp in the dust on the book.

One full moon night, drunk and desperate because the dog had knocked over her last bottle on the rug where she couldn't scrape it up, she found herself dialing the number. Secure that no one would answer at that hour. They did. Talked to her for hours on the phone, said they understood, said they knew. How it felt to be so lonely, even how it felt to be so angry about the empty bottle. And they sounded kind – no one had been so kind to her for so long. They wanted to come and see her in the morning. She couldn't believe she said yes. But she did, as if the person who dialed the number was beginning to inhabit her.

She waited that endless and horrible night, clutching her dog to keep at bay the great hairy monsters that stalked around the room, grinning.

And they came in the morning

She only remembered that they wrapped her in a blanket and took her away. To the city. Days without memory. Days without.

Unhinged.

Detox. Hospital.

They visited her every day. Took care of her dog and brought it to the window for her to see. They said in their kind and measured way that she could change, begin again. If she wanted. Did she choose? Actually choose? Or did the light choose her?

When she returned home she put the Queen Anne's lace in the stove, bought the wheel and dusted the book.

The last rays of winter-red sun were slipping under the frozen ocean. She raised her face to the fire in the window. Her eyes closed as she placed her hands on the clay, feeling the centre of her, umbilical threaded deep into the fiery core of the earth. Connected. Is this what Newton intended? She digs in her thumbs and opens the universe.

MIKALYN

Frances Rooney

T HEY MET in the spring; coupled as leaves the colour of her love's hair fell to the ground. By the next spring they were homing together, and Mikalyn's life had begun.

And so passed four sets of seasons. But with the fifth snow, her love said she needed to be alone, needed to feel her own strength in solitude. Once more Mikalyn homed with other women, or alone, but she no longer homed with one woman, no longer homed with her love.

She raved at her love, at the love that would not die, at the soundlessness of her alonehome, at the woman who did not need her, at the sky that did not hear her, at the moon that did not smile on her. And her love needed her less, needed to be away from her.

Mikalyn worked and played, and found her own need for the healing and strength and joy of solitude. She took other lovers, and one season followed another. She thought less about her love, but came to know that the love she felt had become one of the strongest threads in the cloak that let her meet the world. Sometimes, when the moon was approaching the fullness of her love's breasts and the colour that her love's hair was turning, she would go out and look across the snow to the sea and become aware of the joy and the longing that she carried with her always now. They were as comfortable to her as her arms, and most of the time she neither noticed them nor revelled in the joy nor minded the sadness; they were part of her.

Mikalyn changed. She grew in herself. Her needs changed, and she grew restless. She stopped going to the sea when the moon was

132

growing. She sometimes forgot about her love. When they met she did not feel the anger she had felt at first, nor the humiliation of the later repeated turnings away, nor the tug on her heart that the sight of her love always had brought. Though she decided that she did not quite understand it, she saw and accepted the thread in her cloak, knew that its warmth was necessary to the continued beating of her heart.

Mikalyn left her home. She crossed the mountains and kept going, far far to the east. She left the sea and the moon; she left the colour of her love's hair and the remembered pull of her body.

Her new life engulfed her. She mated. She lived happily with her mate, and prospered.

The seasons followed one another, many times. And as her own hair took on the colour of the moon, she found herself thinking of the dance of the moon and the sea, and gaining peace from the thought.

One day a friend from beyond the mountains, a friend from the land beside the sea, came to her door. Mikalyn saw that she was deeply troubled.

"I come with bad news," the woman told her. "Your love has died."

Mikalyn knew this to be a lie. She also saw that her friend did not know that she lied. She asked why her friend thought that her love was dead.

"She went, as she always did, to the mountains in the fall. She took food and clothing and shelter, and went. She never returned. We searched and searched for her and found nothing – not her shelter, not the cloth from her back, not the bones of the fish she took. At the first snow we went again, hoping that there might be some tracks, but it was already many weeks, and she must have died by then. We found only animal tracks, heard only our own calls and those of the birds which echoed our search and our grief. All through the winter we kept fires burning on the slopes of the mountains she usually visited. In spring we closed her home and gave away her belongings. The old women decided that I was to come to tell you. We know that she was necessary to you, as you were to her." And then the friend wept, for she had made a long journey with such bad news, and she was tired and saddened.

Mikalyn laughed. Her obvious delight frightened her friend. "No, dear one, I am not mad; neither are you," said Mikalyn. "There is no need to mourn or be sad. My love lives; you just did not know how to find her. I will find her."

The friend dared not hope that Mikalyn was right; she decided grief must have clouded Mikalyn's mind. "I will come back with you," Mikalyn told her. "I will find her. Be glad." The friend was too tired to do anything but sleep by the fire, so she curled in on herself, sick with sadness and this new worry, and hardly knew when Mikalyn covered her with a very old, very soft blanket.

When she woke the sun was slanting through the trees and Mikalyn was ready to leave. She had been up all night, talking with her mate, telling her that she had to return to the sea. Her mate was sad and quiet; Mikalyn was her love as surely as the woman who had gone to the mountains was Mikalyn's love. But Mikalyn's mate had always known that this time would come; though she had lived under its shadow, she had been happy. The time of living with her love had made her strong; she could now take a mate or be alone and still have the peace she had found in her centre.

◊

It was summer when they reached the sea. When the moon grew full Mikalyn looked out across the water at its reflection and waited. She grew stronger and quieter with each sunrise. Her hair grew long and thick and took on more and more the gleam of the moon. The others recognized that what was happening was right and good and they said nothing.

Mikalyn missed her mate, she missed the warmth and comfort of their life together. She missed the enclosure of the trees. Her heart pulled in two directions. She waited for the turmoil to end, or to become bearable, part of her. As her arms.

Fall came, and with it leaves the colour her love's hair had once been. And then the snow. It was time.

Her friends, her love's friends, and the other women, who had said nothing until now, could remain quiet no longer. They asked her, begged her, told her not to leave in the snow. They threatened to shut her in, to keep her among them until the spring. She said only that now she must go, it was time for her to go to her love.

Then the others decided, as her friend had feared, that her mind had become unclear in grief. They wanted to shut her in her house until she was better, to feed and stay with her while she learned to accept.

The oldest of the women knew better. They saw that what Mikalyn was doing made sense in the rhythms of the world. Since their knowledge of things real went beyond that of all the others, since they knew more of sight and sound and time and space and the seasons than the rest, the other women accepted that Mikalyn must do this thing.

They dug a pit on the beach and lined it with blankets. In the centre, where ordinarily they would have built a fire, they borrowed water from the sea in which the moon could dance. They prepared to wait for the sign that the oldest knew would come, and that the others hoped would: that Mikalyn had done what she needed to. And they tried not to be fearful when the old ones told them, "Say farewell to Mikalyn, as you did not to her love."

The morning she left, Mikalyn asked the women to spend the night dancing for her and her love and their reunion. The women promised with all their minds and half their hearts. But when the time came, they surprised themselves: their cries reached the sky, their joy built upon itself until the moon herself felt it and smiled. Alone on her way inland, Mikalyn saw the smile, shook her thick silver mane, and laughed to the sky.

The journey was hard, but anticipation made Mikalyn's feet quick and her load light. She had taken little, knowing that though she would travel through snow and over rock, she would not travel for many days.

In the day the snow gleamed. At night the moon danced on it in front of Mikalyn's shelter. Each night she watched the path the moon made, and the next day she followed it. Tracks of deer lay frozen in the ground. Small birds accompanied her, their summer song silenced. The bush, parted by the moon's charted path, whispered shut behind her. The sun was pale. The moon set late in the morning.

She found her love on the fifth day, and then the tears that had never been shed burst from her, the joy that had lived silently ripening in her soul shot out to shatter the cold air. And her love smiled her welcome.

That night she slept in the snowless brambles of her love's legs. She needed no blanket. The next day she searched until she found the smooth depths between her love's breasts; she spent the night enfolded, safe. And on the third night, finally, she found the mouth whose breath was the source of her own life, whose kiss was the blessing of her existence. With their kiss, Mikalyn's tears began again, then she and her love laughed together. Her length stretched to match her love's, and she lay down beside her. Their legs and arms gripped each other, and they wrestled in the urgency of their need.

The mountains rocked with their tumult; their passion sent the thunder as far as the sea. On the beach, the women looked at one another and knew that their vigil was ended. They would see Mikalyn no more; she had found her love.

When the sun rose, Mikalyn and her love slept, at peace. It snowed on their stillness that night, making them all over the colour of their hair, the colour of the moon, the colour of their blinding joy. When spring came, small, rich and wildly tangled bushes, of a kind never seen before, grew everywhere, their bark pale, their leaves silver, their tiny flowers gleaming white. And Mikalyn and her love slept and laughed and cried, and their fervour rocked the mountains often.

◊

The women named them the Twin Monadenocks, though they were not really twins at all. The northern one was larger and rougher, and shaded the smaller from the north wind. The vegetation of the smaller grew more lush, that of the larger more sturdy. The crescent lake that joined their eastern slopes bubbled warm sparkling water in winter no less than in summer. Knowing that they were always welcome, the women went frequently to bathe or play or rest, to vent their high spirits or to feed their tired ones. This place they named Laughing Springs, and they passed the knowledge of its location to the young ones, as they passed the story of Mikalyn and her love in the lullabies they sang on the nights when the moon shone in the winter sky.

AGAINST THE TOOTH OF TIME

Ruth Millar

T HERE ARE TIMES when the ticking of minutes becomes the
enemy and hesitation the final act. For the woman who was
running and plunging through snowdrifts, inhaling brutal air that
sandpapered her lungs, this was the source of the nightmares that
nightly catapulted her from sleep into a state of semi-conscious
terror.

It was a race that was all too familiar.

the dream quicksand
I'm going to miss it
I always miss it

        it's only a ruddy bus

and an appointment
important

        he'll wait if he values
        your friendship

have to catch it run
I promised

She climbed aboard the waiting bus, aware of the interested
stares of the people who had watched her stumbling through the
snow. Hers was an attractiveness that was beginning to be eroded
by the contours of approaching middle age. She settled into her

seat half-way down the aisle, and retreated into her own inner dialogue.

I always sit in the middle
what's the matter with me
what does it signify?   *fear*
of solitude?

> *more like an obsession*
> *with conformity*

I am not a conformist   *it's*
just my place   *in the middle*
age   class   stature

> *we're not discussing your age*
> *we're discussing your inertia*
> *your obsessive moderation*

but I always see both sides
if we were all raving fanatics
the human race would have long since
obliterated itself
somebody has to be a
reasonable negotiator

> *ambivalence is double-think*
> *it has no integrity*

but hard-liners just alienate
their own allies

> *if you don't take a position*
> *you're just wishy-washy*
> *you have to choose*

stop   I won't listen

Justine was still musing about her middle-ness when the bus arrived at her stop outside the restaurant where she had promised to meet him.

"Ernest!" The tall man leapt up to embrace her.

he sparkles   Africa has
changed his life

"You look wonderful! It must be going well, your project in Africa. What are you doing here, and how long will you be home?"

"Africa is marvellous, breathtaking. I'm only home for a briefing, a little over a week, then back to Somalia for another year."

"Do you ever get homesick over there?"

"Not a bit. Too busy. On the contrary, I'm homesick for Africa right now."

"You've only been home for a few days!"

"Ah, but it gets into your bones, wanting to do something with your life. Not only that, it's blissful to escape the raging bureaucracy here, the stunting stultifying narrow-mindedness of complacent bourgeois idiots obsessed with their sickeningly trivial concerns ... their bloody lawns and their insurance policies and their forms in triplicate every time you go to take a pee."

Justine giggled. "Ernest, you're such a cure for the blahs. I envy you this adventure."

He examined her face for a moment. "Don't waste your energy on envy," he said at last. "Why don't you come to Somalia?"

She sighed. "I can't afford a holiday like that."

"I don't mean a holiday. I mean work. I'm offering you a job. We could use you over there at the university."

"Me? What would they do with a bleeding heart with no practical skills in the middle of a country dying of famine?"

"We don't need your bleeding heart. We need your skills. We need books and teachers, and professionals to organize the flow of information."

"I.e., librarians."

"Exactly. Could you come for a year? Eight months? Six months? I think I could help you get a posting if you're interested."

adventure!

no, terror   inadequacy

"Oh ... maybe ... I don't know. How could I? There are my children and my house to be taken care of. And my job. How could I leave?"

"Take the kids with you. It'll broaden their horizons, turn them into international citizens with compassion for the human condition, not horrid squalid little suburban brats. As for your job, get a leave of absence, rent out your house. I did. Do you think it was easy?"

"I'm not as intrepid as you are. I'm used to ... conveniences ... hot showers and stereos and microwave ovens, all that."

"You got along without that sort of thing when you were growing up. You got along without it at graduate school, too. I seem to recall you took only a trunk, a radio and a camera."

"But Toronto was civilization! I'm spoiled by city living. I need theatre and cinemas and libraries."

"So do I. They'll be here when you get back. In the meantime you'd be living what theatres, cinemas and books only reflect."

"Don't you think you're an impossible romantic, Ernest?"

"Perhaps. But so are you."

"Let me think about it for a while. My decision-making process is achingly slow."

> *romantic!   for*
> *him it was right*

"You have until next week to decide, Justine. I'd need a few days to arrange things here. My flight leaves on Friday."

For Justine it was an uneasy trip home, and a restless night, followed by more restless nights. At the library she pored over glossy illustrated books and tantalizing articles about Africa. The inner voices harangued and prodded.

> *Somalia   Somalia*
> *I'd love*
> *to live amongst those stately*
> *people*

> *emaciated people, you mean*
> *drought   starvation*

> *no   that's Ethiopia*

> *next door   close enough*

> *Ernest wasn't emaciated*

> *no   of course not   he's a*
> *professor   esteemed, privileged*
> *not like me   more importantly*
> *he's a man   I'd just be a*
> *woman alone   vulnerable*

> you're not weak   you've
> taken care of yourself
> and the children for
> years

I'm a woman!   women in Islamic
society   shrouded in veils
repressed

> no   you'd be a Canadian
> ex-patriate   you'd be
> safe

no!   danger!   exposing my
children   unnatural mother
must protect my young

The days passed by, and still a decision eluded Justine. Now she was seated, again, half-way down the aisle of a bus, still engaged in her silent debate, when one of those stunning flashes of synchronicity startled her from her reverie.

A tall African had boarded the bus with two handsome children.

It's Rashid   I thought he had left
for Vancouver months ago

There are times when the coincidence of events is so startling as to defy credibility. Perhaps it is only heightened awareness, but at such times the realization intrudes: what if I had missed that connection?

Rashid caught her eye and eased into the seat beside her, propping the little girl on his lap so that the older boy could nestle beside him.

"Good morning, my friend," he said.

"Rashid! I'm surprised to see you here. I thought you had moved to Vancouver to be with the children."

"It was not necessary. I obtained the custody."

"How did you manage that?"

"Their mother ... is not educated, you know. She could not give them much ... much future."

he pulled rank on her
dazzled the judge
played on his prejudices
I can imagine the scenario

don't be such a bleeding heart
he'll go on to a distinguished
career back home among the
privileged classes of his people
for her it would be a struggle

"But it is a hard life," Rashid was continuing, "trying to do post-graduate study and attend to the care of the children."

"I know, I know. Tell me about it. The life of a single parent is tough."

especially for a woman   and I'm
lucky   good job satisfying career
why do I want to sacrifice all this
for some nebulous fulfillment

"It will not do. I cannot do my research, and run back and forth to the daycare centre all the time. I have decided I must take them home to Africa."

it's not their home! they've never
been there   and what about the
mother-child bond   it will
damage them

"How will it be better there?" she asked.

"My family are there to help. And I will have a wife to take care of them."

"A wife?"

"My family will arrange a marriage. A girl I knew when I was younger. She will be a good mother."

"How do you feel about an arranged marriage?"

"It will be all right. It is the custom."

"You don't mind marrying someone you don't love?"

"Romantic love is a western illusion. We will grow to love one another. In time." The passengers swayed as the bus rounded the corner, then skidded in the icy ruts. They were approaching the university.

"Rashid, last week I was ... you won't believe this ... but I was offered a job in Somalia."

"Wonderful! You should go."

"But the thing is, my children. They would miss their year in school."

"There is an American school near the university. You are going to Mogadishu?" She nodded. "But the experience itself would be worth five years of regular school. I hope you go. Perhaps we shall meet again over there."

He rose. "Come, children. Goodbye, Justine." The children smiled shyly as they left.

The bus lurched on, accelerating to enter the intersection before the lights changed. The engine's rumble was beginning to nauseate Justine, and she was relieved when the bus reached her destination. She stepped gingerly down on to the slippery, hard-packed snow and headed toward the low building ahead. She leaned against the door until it yielded to her pressure, and walked down the hallway.

the stench! old age? illness?
incontinence? every time I come
here it nauseates me how can
they bear it?

　　　　　　　　　　they must get used to it
　　　　　　　　　　they have no choice

She passed clusters of silent, white-haired figures huddled in wheelchairs in the lounge, gazing at the television set with unknowing eyes.

At the door of the last room down the hallway she paused, and then entered. The old man propped in the wheelchair looked up from the spot on his gaunt lap where his gaze had rested. He stared at her for a moment.

oh dear　　he doesn't know me today
that defeated haunting expression
where have I seen it before

She searched her memory, in vain, and then suddenly, recognition.

> *Peru   the blind beggar*
> *the old woman selling trinkets*
> *the legless man wheeling himself*
> *on a dolly, pleading   all of*
> *them helpless   and hopeless*
> *all dignity gone*

Then a momentary awareness animated her grandfather's face. His capacity for speech had disappeared, ever since the stroke, but he uttered an inarticulate cry of greeting, his eyes gleaming. Justine avoided the sight of the catheter that emerged from his pyjamas. She leaned toward him to place a kiss on the pale, translucent skin.

> *gaunt cheekbones   sunken eyes*
> *hopeless   that's it*
> *those faces   Ethiopia   starving*
> *that's what's happening to him*
> *he hasn't much time left*
> *time   where did it go   what*
> *did he accomplish   did he*
> *achieve his dreams*
>
> > *probably not*
> > *he was afraid of*
> > *taking chances*
> > *afraid of risk*
> > *he always wanted to be safe*
> > *then life struck him down*
> > *divine retribution for his*
> > *cowardice? karma? blind fate?*
>
> *his time just ran out!*

Suddenly her mind switched tracks. The dream, the nightmare. Always the same, a promise made and not fulfilled. An appointment missed. A cosmic commitment neglected.

> *I was going to do it   I meant*
> *to do it   I forgot   there wasn't*
> *time   I was so busy*

Its form was palpable, an unnamed presence. *God? Nemesis?* An accusation devastating in its finality. No hope of appeal. Something so unspeakable it always jolted her awake, leaving her trembling with horror.

>   *nuclear holocaust*
>   *Armageddon*
>   *the end of time*
>
> *or just a warning that*
> *personal extinction comes too soon*

With a stab of insight, she knew what her decision must be. There was still time.

THE EARTHQUAKE

Lake Sagaris

THE EARTH TREMORS have become a part of life, like the newsstand on the corner or the soldiers who come out at night, standing with blackened faces, guns ready, guarding the darkest corners of the city.

I don't try to control my fear any more. It's not in my best interest, as the Chicago Boys would say. The family is a free-market enterprise and you have to grab what you can and squeeze the most out of it. I know they don't love me, but they owe me, and that's more important. This raggle taggle bunch of children, grandchildren. Not one of them has come out right. Except maybe Mariluz, and she's gone now.

Of course, some of them are better than others. He's the worst. Stubborn crusty old bastard – not the sort of word you could say out loud but that's what I always call him in here, where I'm with myself. This is just between you and me and you are me. That makes everything all right. Normal. Correct.

Sometimes I think I'll kill him. Or he'll kill me, or himself, or maybe I'll kill myself. We're so entangled in each other, years, decades of hate have passed between us. I could have left him. After he screwed around – that's how Licha would say it, if I let her, but I won't let her – with that bitch – another Lichism. That woman! How could my Luis marry anyone so vulgar! Even here inside my own head she has to put her obscene tongue. I heartily dislike her, as my mother would have said, but still her gestures, her words, circle inside my mind as if it were a drain.

But it doesn't matter. Nothing matters. The old man and I, we're just a couple of old bonebags, good for nothing but eating.

So why doesn't he admit it? Why does he insist on carrying on, with his foolish clandestine meetings, his 'comrades,' his forbidden news broadcasts, the rumours, the hope? We buried the future ten years ago. There's nothing for us now. We had our chance. We were really building something then. Even I could feel it, at home, with the kids just beginning to grow up and get out on their own.

Goddamn. There's another one. All the pictures shaking and the china clinking. The kids hardly notice. Except that little birdbrain of Carlos'. Scared of me, he is. And he ought to be. He may be Carlos' but he's not mine. I never even met his mother. And Carlos never married her. Well, prison, the camp, they changed him. What could you expect?

But they were so committed then! Even little Luis away at university. Who knows what he was up to. The old man and Carlos, even Mariluz always out at meetings until late at night. Members of the same party and all and they still fought about what time she'd get in at night. But I covered for her. They act as if we women didn't do a whole lot, but we did in our own way.

And after, when the old man and Carlos were in jail. Who took over then? The only time the old man's wine industry made a profit was when I ran it. I really had it together then. With Marta Contreras, Jaime Aravena's mother, Mrs. Jimenez. Every one of our prisoners got Christmas dinner that year, even the ones with no family. We made shirts for every one. We sold *empanadas* and *dulces* and pastries to raise the money. Mariluz was with me then. Carrying messages to and from jails.

Even then, even then! they couldn't stop monkeying around with this party business. In jail, being tortured, on their way to concentration camps, the island, death some of them, those b...'s just kept at it. Rebuilding the party, they said. What for? I asked myself. Everything's over. You haven't seen what things are like now, outside.

The *sapos* on every corner, listening even to us women when we ran into each other, till we stopped saying hello, settled for a nod, or looked the other way.

There goes another one. If something breaks .... It took so long to put the house back together. And you never knew when they'd come searching again. Breaking things. My mother's picture, in that lovely little frame, hand-carved by my brother before he died. Smashed to pieces like everything else. God it was awful.

Beginning from nothing, again and again and again. Just like an earthquake. Rubble and dust. Looking for guns, they said, slamming the door behind them.

The books, burned or buried. The posters, I had to take them all down and hide them, even the one the president signed, right after the election, when he was here, in our house. I wanted to tell them it was all over but they wouldn't let it end. They kept it alive, packed into boxes, forced to eat their own excrement. My own sons never said a word. But someone always knew, and had to talk.

That's when I joined the Red Cross. Because they went into the stadium and got people's names and told others what these thieves were doing. Hoods. Trained to kill. Turning their guns on their own people. And when they finally got Mariluz! After so much time had passed, I thought, somehow they'll leave me this one. They've taken my husband, my oldest son. Luis's gone. Just a baby. I really didn't know where he was. I could only imagine. But up till then I had Mariluz to hold on to, to explain what she could, to keep me going. But they took women too. When we finally got her out, the lawyers, the Red Cross, the psychiatrist .... Just one quick visit before they put her on the plane. I couldn't stop crying. I stared at the dirt on those ugly old blinds in the waiting room and felt her stunned and motionless in my arms. All the lumps and horrors I couldn't squeeze out of her any more. She wouldn't tell me what had happened. I read it in the reports. The men. The dogs. The rats. The doctor told me physically she could maybe still have children. By caesarian. But she never will. That's clear from the reports. In all these years abroad, she's never married, never had a boyfriend, never will. My only daughter.

◊

The old lady's in a terrible mood today. Scared shitless by the tremors, I suppose, although there hasn't been an earthquake in ages. Snapping at the kids. Getting into a fight with Luis when we're hardly in the door. Because we were so late I suppose. Because I didn't have time to change the kids' clothes. Because ... because ... because .... She moves that cast around as if it weighed a ton. Groans a little once in a while. Complains. I don't know why. Usually she loves to have us all here at once. It hardly ever happens. And here we all are, three generations worth, sitting around her lovely eucalyptus table, eating off her precious English china, listening to the damned TV in the background. They never seem to turn it off. Barrier of sound, probably keeps them from each other's throats. They should have separated twenty years ago. But they didn't. So she's angry and resentful and he's got to have some lovely old lady hidden away somewhere, maybe that one who's always typing up documents for him, or maybe someone else .... He's thriving. The dictatorship's given meaning to his life.

And taken it from hers. That picture of Mariluz. Why does she always sit me under it? To compare I suppose. Or maybe just so she can look at it instead of me. What's that knocking on the wall? Another tremor. She almost jumped up that time. She wants us to feel sorry for her. But when she gets like this she just pisses me right off.

Luis's watching. He knows she's angry and he knows that always makes me impatient. His fingers warm in mine. Then moving to take something away from the baby. Then tickling the back of my neck. I know I'm starting to smile. She hates that. I hardly had time to tell him about the demo' today. I could tell he was proud. Of me! I thought my knees would never straighten. But it felt so good. To speak out loud. We've all been thinking and no one dares to say anything any more. And to hear people clapping afterward, and shouting.

Mariluz used to do stuff too. Luis's told me. So why does the old witch get so angry? So the clothes don't always get washed. So I'm not always there when she comes to visit. So what?

And the old lady could do something too. There are a lot of women like her around. She could try and get permission for Mariluz to come home. Luis even arranged that interview for her once. But she didn't go. Said her arthritis made it too hard. And now with the broken arm and all ....

Why put up a fight to cook, to clean, to care for? The arthritis is liberating her, she says. I say it's beating her. You have to fight it inch by inch or one day you can't move anymore. Like the dictatorship.

But it must be hard for her, stuck with the old man. They don't really have a lot in common. She could still separate. I've told her that too. But she says she won't. Things are different for her generation. Only because you let them be, I tell her. They've only changed because some have dared. Maybe that's why she hates me so much.

And he is a pain sometimes. The way he goes on with his rumours and this and that. To listen to him the DCs and the CPs united years ago and they've all got their weapons stashed away ready to go at a signal from ... well, god or marx, it would have to be, depending on the party. Someone has to apply a little pressure on the old man.

◊

"But how can you say that the military are up in arms, that they're ready to dump him? It's clear there are some disagreements, but that's minor stuff." Licha presses the old man.

"Listen," he says, with the heavy courtesy that always makes Licha wriggle with impatience. "I have a friend whose wife is the secretary of a department manager in the ministry. She says she actually saw the petition demanding his resignation. Well, not actually saw it, because her boss, who's a captain, covered it up when she entered the room, but ...."

"Rumours! Rumours! Don't you ever get tired of all these damned rumours!" the old lady shoves at him. "You've been predicting the end of this for the last ten years."

"At least I've tried to change things!" He bites, as usual.

"I've done plenty!" she flings back at him. "What about when you were in jail!"

"That was a long time ago," he drowns her out. Their children watch uncomfortably. Their children's children watch television.

Luis' hand leaps over Licha's, holding her back. The old lady turns on her.

"And you! Who do you think you are anyway? Always late. Look at your husband's shirt. When he lived with me he looked respectable!"

"That's not worth a damn. Women can't stay home anymore! We have to get out and fight too!"

"Nonsense! Someone has to be around after the arrests!" the old lady slaps back. "That's our role. That's what we do best."

Licha jerks to her feet.

"When the protests started we hid in the house. I was so scared, I'd throw up all night. But the police came anyway. They searched our houses, smashed the radios. They took the kid from next door and dumped him naked, after curfew, god knows where ...."

The table seems to stagger, then steady. No one notices.

"Today, I spoke on the street. People listened. Applauded. I felt free, proud of myself for the first time."

"You're absolutely worthless," her mother-in-law says coldly. "You don't care about your husband, your children. You'd rather be out looking for trouble!"

Licha raises her hand. It comes down hard, water smashing stone.

Silence rings between them.

Luis grabs his wife. "Let's go get some bread."

"We don't need any more bread," his mother shouts after them, but the door has closed.

◊

On the way back, Luis hears a noise like a heavy truck bearing down on them, gears squealing, clutch smoking.

His mother screams when she feels it.

Licha's about to tell him the lights have gone out.

The old lady leans hard on the shoulder of Carlos' son, screaming over and over. This is the end! We're all going to die! Grieving or exultant, who can tell.

Luis grabs Licha's hand.

Shut up, the old man says.

The windows to their left explode, one by one. They stumble, panicked, away from blasted glass.

The plates shudder against the table. Walls groan and arch. Shelves begin to vomit books, painted plates, china dogs, salt shakers.

The earth tormented, wild beast, shaking away human fleas. An adobe wall collapses beside them, crushing a dappled horse. Stone and bone mixed with blood. Not life. Not —

Death! she thinks. As usual, he hasn't understood. Maybe this will be my test. She straightens to face it, joyfilled and bitter.

Houses crumble. They jerk to the left. A car screams to a halt. A glimpse of civilization being swept from the tabletop of earth in one sharp gesture.

Pictures drop like bombs and smash on tiled floors. The wall gapes open, bricks and mortar spat out like smashed teeth.

The wires! Licha screams and they veer right, crashing into a wall, falling to the ground. The childrenohmygod where are the children?

Screams echoing in the stairwells. The old couple, Carlos, his boy, herding the younger children before them, down the stairs, which suddenly part like a broken jaw. Carlos! the old woman screams and he pushes the baby into her arms and jumps after. Outside. The buildings sway like belly dancers. The baby a live weight unmoved and giggling in her arms.

We've got to get home. Luis pants. But they can't move. Drunken clowns, sprawled on upheaval. The sidewalk a twisted slab of asphalt, thumped by a giant, raging fist.

Darkness falls between them, vibrant with screams, echoes of screams. Silence. Alone. Until Carlos lights a candle. His face flickers, projected like a ghost on the night air.

We couldn't be safer, Luis tells her, releasing her. She stares at an old man banging his head against the blood-spattered cart. All that running— we didn't get anywhere! His tears streak the grey wood. My mother must be terrified. Luis starts to run. The children .... Sees her livid face.

◊

"Are you okay?" She nods as the cars begin to push their way through the rubble and they stumble, climb, crawl back up to the apartment.

The door grinds open. The English china is scattered across the floor, mixed with earth from the spider plants and the wandering jews, white petals of shattered flowers and heads and paws of smashed dogs. Pieces of a puzzle that will never fit again.

"They've gone," Luis says.

Licha turns to leave.

"Wait." He rummages in the back of the closet. Pulls out a small burner, relic from family picnics. Licha, understanding, finally, plucks the kettle from a pile of metal on the floor and fills it with water.

They slide down the stairs, clambering awkwardly over the gaps.

Licha looks for her mother-in-law, finds her, the baby propped against the cast, rocked gently, painfully, back and forth by the other hand.

Licha opens her mouth, shuts it.

Now the old lady hands the baby to Luis, taking the burner, standing clumsily on the uneven ground. Licha comes closer. Hands her the kettle and fumbles through her pockets. As the old lady opens the burner Licha offers her the match and the gas hisses into flame.

The two women stare into each other's eyes. Licha's smooth,

short fingers brush the wrinkled, patchy hand that holds the burner.

Then she kneels on the ground, improvising a bed for the baby.

The children are picking up fragments of glass, trading the larger pieces. Gently, Carlos spreads out the blankets torn from beds bucking like wild animals. Luis pulls the cups out of the old picnic basket. Jars. A can of milk.

The kettle begins to murmur. The old woman straightens. "At least we're all together," she says, breathing deeply, filling her lungs with tea-fragant steam.

"The radio's smashed," the old man's voice has a sob in it. "No more shortwave news reports ...." He watches her stirring the leaves, pulling their flavour into the hot water. He remembers the shelves, frozen in a quick glimpse before the lights flashed out. They looked twisted and drunken, their cargo of china emptied on the floor.

"Everything's gone," he says. "Again. We'll never have enough money to replace all this, not with my pension ...."

The old lady doesn't look up.

He mutters, "Again and again and again. How much longer? We're getting old ... too old to rebuild. This has all lasted so much longer than we thought. History doesn't wait for us to catch up with it."

◊

We've been through worse, I'm thinking. We've been through worse. And here I am, with a cup of shattered tea and all the tears in the world hissing in the kettle. We women were made for this; for picking up pieces, over and over again. That's what Mariluz was doing, is doing still, far away. And Licha, even Licha is doing it, in a different way. Maybe she wants to change things. Break the circle. Stop the earthquakes. Once and for all. The old man thinks we can't go on. But we've done it before and we'll do it again.

Bring the sugar over, the milk. Let the tea scald its way into your cold bellies. Every beginning is an ending, my mother used to say, and every ending ...

CANADA DAY

Maya Khankhoje

CLEMENTINA SANCHEZ stepped into the world. The sun shone, her red and white cotton dress was cool and it was Canada Day. Canada Day! Canadian. Clementina Sanchez, Canadian Citizen. She rolled the words from one side of her tongue to the other.

It was a perfect day. She was now one of the land and this land was hers. No one could tell her to go back home, because this *was* her home. If only Abuelita could be here to light her way.

◊

Tina was 11 when she came of age. That night, the grown-ups had been in the kitchen drinking tequila and arguing. Uncle Chema with his plump wife Maria; Pepe and Tito, her two brothers; Laura and Marta, the two fiancées.

Normally, Tina would have slept through the whole commotion in her cot in the pantry behind the kitchen. Nothing would have woken her up. Not the sound of the TV set, nor the music wafting through the courts and alleys, nor Maruca's muffled cries, which meant her husband was at home.

But these had not been normal circumstances. Tina had awoken that morning with cramps in her lower abdomen and a red blotch on her panties. She had run scared and crying into Abuelita's arms.

"Nothing to be afraid of, *muchachita*. Just make sure you watch out for those boys out there. Their pretty words and smiles will be poor comfort if you have a baby to feed and your milk runs dry.

154

Yes, I know, it's tough to be a woman, but the good Lord chose us to carry his children because we have broad hips and our feet are firmly planted on the ground. He also gave us brains, though, and it is up to us to use them properly!"

So that night Tina had been lying in bed trying to solve the riddle of life.

◊

The sky had suddenly turned grey. A drop or two hit Clementina Sanchez on the face and jerked her back into the present. She didn't want her hair wet. For many years she had worn it long, loosely braided down her back or tightly coiled into a bun. The young men who had hovered around her had loved it.

"You remind me of an Aztec virgin climbing the steps of the sun pyramid," one had blurted as he followed her up the wooden steps of Mount Royal.

"Your eyes are like roasted coffee beans; your skin like ripe corn," another had whispered as they drank steaming coffee in a sidewalk café on St. Denis.

But she'd tired of the ethnic look, shorn her hair and practised with hair rollers until she got it just right: a hint of a casual curl and no more.

Clementina unfurled her umbrella and tightened her step as she crossed Westmount Park. Mrs. Bierce did not like to be kept waiting.

◊

The voices in the kitchen rose as the level of tequila in the bottle dropped.

"My wife has diabetes! You can't expect my Maria to look after Tina. After her own mother walked out on her!"

"Chema!"

"It's true, mother. She says she's too busy working ... working the streets of La Zona Rosa ...."

"I forbid you to talk like that about your own sister! Where were you when she needed help?"

"Abuelita, please, please calm down. Of course Tito and I will look after our little sister."

"What do you mean, Tito and you? What you really mean is Laura and me when we marry you two machos. If we do. I'm not quitting my job to look after somebody's else's little brat!" Marta gulped down her tequila as if to make her point.

"Enough!"

Everyone turned to Abuelita. They had never seen her so angry.

"My grandchild goes with me. Together we can make it. We don't need the charity of our own blood."

The Sanchez family said nothing. A haze of shame floated about like tequila fumes.

"Abuelita," ventured Tito, who had not spoken as yet, "how can we let you go off to some foreign land to wash some stranger's laundry?"

"I have washed my family's clothes all these years and I shall now wash them for some stranger. I am now going to bed. Tomorrow will be a long day."

◊

Mrs. Bierce sat in her living-room sipping sherry with Mrs. Kilby, her childhood friend. Sherry was one of her few pleasures nowadays. Except for the orange juice laced with champagne that she sometimes had at Spatches, over a Sunday brunch. Mary Bierce and Amanda Kilby hadn't seen each other since their lives had changed. That is, since John Bierce had suffered a stroke and Ian Kilby had run off with the company accountant.

Amanda Kilby had been left with three children and a fat bank account. Mary Bierce had no children – only a fixed income from a trust fund, a lovely house and a husband who was a shadow of his former self.

Life could have been better for these two graduates of The Study. But then again, it could have been worse.

"You'll just love her, Amanda. And she is so good with children and so neat and proper. It's true that she's also very pretty, but now that you don't have to worry about Ian, I guess it doesn't matter."

Mrs. Kilby choked on her sherry.

"Oh, my dear, I didn't mean to ... I'll get the door. That must be her."

As Mrs. Bierce opened the door, Mrs. Kilby discretely poured herself some more sherry.

"My dear Clementina, you needn't have bothered," exclaimed Mrs. Bierce, as she took the sherry bottle that Clementina had been hugging to her chest.

"Didn't I tell you, Amanda, that Clementina was a very thoughtful young woman? Come on in, come meet Mrs. Kilby."

Clementina shook her soggy umbrella and left it in the porch. She then wiped her shoes carefully on the welcome mat and stepped gingerly into the house.

◊

It had certainly been a long time till tomorrow. Preparations for the trip to Canada had in fact taken several weeks. Birth certificates, passports, letters of recommendation, trips to the pawn shop, farewell parties. Even a special mass in the neighbourhood church, paid for by friends and relatives. A new 'winter' wardrobe which was to prove totally inadequate. And then *adiós*.

All had been forgiven. All had been forgotten. Blood was thicker than water, after all. But the facts remained. The old woman and the young woman were going to the cold north for an indefinite period. Until things got better.

As they packed their suitcases into a borrowed pickup, Tina turned back to look at the house. The house where she was born. The house where her own mother was born. It had started out as two adobe rooms and a large yard. As the family acquired new members, the house sprouted new accretions: a room here, a verandah there, indoor plumbing. As the house expanded and the patio shrank, they had decided to build on top of the flat roof. The municipality had vetoed the project. Not until you start using concrete and solid baked bricks, they had said.

Ultimately this was done.

Tina stood in the patio, trying to etch the image in her brain: the wrought iron gate; the nopal cactus in the corner of the patio; the tortillas drying out in the sun on an old newspaper; the red geraniums in brown earthen pots on the windowsills. And Chucho, the family mutt, who had obstinately buried his muzzle in his paws and refused to look up.

"Tiiina ... hurry up ... we'll be late for the bus station ...."

◊

Clementina was now a qualified secretary, thanks to Mrs. Bierce's support and her own hard work. It is true that Mrs. Bierce had helped her a lot, with her papers, with a loan here and there, with words of encouragement. But it is also true that she, Clementina, had been Mrs. Bierce's lifeline. Looking after the old man, wiping his drool, trying to decipher his slurred words and convert them into coherent thoughts.

He was old and partially crippled, but his left hand could still stray and fasten itself onto parts of her body. Was her silent complicity an act of charity? A gesture of compassion? Mere self-preservation? She didn't know. She didn't want to know.

Now that she was a qualified secretary and a Canadian citizen, she would no longer be just the housekeeper's granddaughter, the girl who had stepped into her grandmother's job. She had been invited to dine with Mrs. Bierce and with Mrs. Kilby, to enjoy the evening like three old friends, in spite of the differences in their upbringing and their ages.

Things had moved so fast. They would all be spending the summer in Mexico, in a rented villa, up on the mountains that overlooked the valley.

"You might as well get used to calling us Amanda and Mary, my dear. After all, we shall be one big happy family! Of course your relatives can come and visit."

As Clementina wiped the dishes she had offered to do, and while the coffee perked, she thought of home, of how proud Abuelita would have been.

◊

The Sanchez household had prospered. Uncle Chema had been promoted to foreman at his factory and had been able to buy a secondhand car. The two brothers had married their sweethearts. The nopal cactus had given way to a neat bed of roses and tortillas were no longer left out to dry in the sun.

"It doesn't look good," Laura had sniffed. It was Laura who, as the mother of two boys, had inched Maria out of her role as lady of the house. Laura had installed a brand-new electric range in the kitchen. The tortillas would be dried in the modern way. Marta's salary as a nurse had helped pay for some of these improvements.

It had been on an August evening in Montreal that Abuelita had suddenly announced that she wanted to go back home.

"I want to meet the boys," she had said. "I want to die in Mexico. I want them to bury me there."

She was granted her dream.

Abuelita had gone back to Mexico to embrace her great-grandchildren.

God had embraced her to His bosom.

She was buried in Mexico City, right under her house, when the newly constructed second storey had proved to be too much. Too much for that roaring, mad, hungry earthquake. The earth had let out a deep and plaintive rumble and gobbled up many of her children.

It was Chucho who had sniffed her out. Her and poor Maria, both buried under tons of rubble. Laura had just taken the children to school; the rest had already gone off to work.

Nothing. Finished.

◊

The aroma of coffee brought Clementina back to the present. With a corner of the dishcloth, she dried her eyes and then busied herself setting the coffee tray.

"Don't ever look back," Abuelita had said. "Never."

As she headed for the living-room she caught a few stray words.

"Won't she *mind* looking after the children? And let's face it, Mary, that girl won't want to have to take care of John for the rest of his life. He is your husband, after all, not hers."

"Amanda! Stop moralizing! You were always lecturing me in school and you still seem to be doing it now. I know it's been tough for you, what with Ian running out on you like that and three little children to look after. But you can start all over again. I can't. My life's finished! Finished, do you hear!"

Clementina stood at the kitchen door. The dinner invitation, the-big-happy-family-in-Mexico, "call us Amanda and Mary, my dear ...."

How could this Westmount woman say her life was finished!

What did she know about the harshness of life! What about Abuel-ita! What about the Mexicans whose lives had suddenly stopped on that September morning!

Clementina turned slowly around, placed the coffee tray carefully on the kitchen counter and opened the back door silently.

Mrs. Bierce caught a glimpse of Clementina's red-and-white figure through the living-room window. She jumped up, opened the front door, grabbed Clementina's umbrella and, waving it, yelled:

"Where are you going, girl! At least take your umbrella with you ...."

Clementina held her head high and looked straight ahead. The summer drizzle had turned into a downpour. Her curls were now heavy strands that clung to her forehead and the nape of her neck, sending rivulets of rainwater down her nose and mouth and back. Clementina Sanchez, Canadian Citizen. The words left a bitter aftertaste in her mouth.

SUMMER WAGES

Caroline Woodward

FIRST OFF, LET'S put it into perspective, as Josie used to say. I, Geraldine, have worked nine waitressing jobs and I have taken the vow never to do it again. Sure, I make these tired old jokes about support hose and roller skates supplied by management but I've got other things I can do for less work and more money. No more shiftwork either.

I do the books for five businesses right out of my own home. Claim office expenses for one-third of this double-wide trailer under the self-employed category on income tax and I sign off with a nice flourish, let me tell you. It's better that the money comes back to me, hard-working mother of three, than to the lousy government just lusting to squander it on their corrupt friends or some US kiss-ass submarine thing.

But here's the kicker. My oldest, Carrie-Lynn, wants to get a job. Fine. Grade ten, smart as a whip, takes after Ab for brains and Josie for looks, like she used to look before she got into the booze. But the job she wants is waitressing up the highway this coming summer "just like you and Aunt Josie did" she says to make herself a big point (wrong move) in this long drawn-out battle we're having.

I'm building up to spilling the beans on her, to sit her down in the next hour when she gets home and telling it like it is. Was, anyway. She's too innocent and the world is meaner and trickier than it was in 1969. I'm going to let loose with the scuzzy side of me and Josie's adventures in Service With A Smileville so she'll clue in and get a decent job. Like being a lifeguard. That's classy and the

161

money is two and a half times minimum wage. She's still got time to get the swim ticket she needs. I'd pay for it, no ifs or buts.

She wouldn't get tips unless she served booze and she's still underage so that's that. The kid's only 15 now, 16 in June, runs like a deer, swims like a guppy, brings home ribbons every sports day and swim meet. Lifeguard badge be a cinch for an athletic kid like her.

Getting the damn pool job is another story though. I got to be realistic on that score. Carrie-Lynn doesn't have a high-up Daddy, or Mommy, to pull strings up at City Hall. Ab is the *janitor* at City Hall for crying out loud. Plus he invents things like the automated scarecrow last summer. But until he makes some indecent amount of money, people will just laugh at him. "How's it goin, Ab?" "Built a better mousetrap yet, Ab?" And Ab will just miss how entirely mean they really are and smile and say he's not that interested in mousetraps, his current project is this or that, keeps me busy, keeps me busy, he says, nodding and smiling at the snickering sons of bees. They don't know who they're talking to. Ab's halfways a genius and he's got the kindest heart in the West, not a mean bone in his body. Me, I'm mean, let me tell you.

Me, I should join the Business and Professional Women's Club, get on the power lunch and business card swapmeet circuit but I'm afraid they'd turn me down. I couldn't take that. It kills me because I'm so proud to finally get to be a bookkeeper but that might not be enough for them. A chartered accountant and on up is what to be for them. Carrie-Lynn, Carrie-Lynn, that's where you come in.

◊

I started by default, waitressing, because they hired me to chambermaid. It was new then, it's closed now, a gas station and about ten cabins plus a café with a good reputation. Exactly halfways between Fort St. John and Fort Nelson with Pink Mountain looming up out of the muskeg some miles away. The Beatton River began a hundred yards from the café, just a little brown stream coiling around the willows and stunted spruce trees.

Josie was actually thrilled to be a waitress even when she found out there was no uniform, just a long green apron to tie on over her blouse and jeans. Still, she fixed up her hair and did her nails and worked a full shift an hour after we got there. Petticoat Junction is what the truckers called our place on account of the five young women between 16 and 18 working there.

By the first of August, Josie and I were the only employees left. The Mister had picked a fight with Henry, the gas jockey whose girlfriend was the head waitress and whose sister was the second cook. The second cook's best friend was the main cook, a farm kid from Tom's Lake who had cooked for her family since she was 11 and that Esther could cook, let me tell you.

All four of them left in a huff because of Henry being fired. They headed back to Dawson Creek and big summer dances with The Crystal Ship and maybe even Anthony and The Romans. Lucky bums. They were fun; we didn't realize how much fun July had been until we watched them leave in Henry's souped-up car and the café was suddenly dull. No more Social Centre. Josie and I were on our own with the Mister and the wife.

The Mister drank at least once every two weeks and was out of commission for three or four days at a time. The Wife was a bible-thumper and an excellent cook but she holed up in one of the motel units whenever he hit the bottle so he wouldn't hit her. Josie and I had orders to leave him be and to bring her meals three times a day. No problem. We avoided him like the plague, sober or drunk.

We never told our parents. We needed the dollar ten an hour and all this booze and sex (those Dawson Creek kids not us) and violence just like the TV only made us feel more grown-up and on our own. We didn't want to worry the folks. Hear what I'm saying? You got that little smile on.

So. After the big You're Fired! Like Hell I Am, I Quit! We All Quit! episode, Josie and I pretty well ran the place. We'd get up at 5:30 a.m., dash from our unheated shack to the café, get the grill and the coffee on, eat a stack of toast, and go our separate ways. If a tour bus to Fairbanks pulled in, Josie would holler from the back door of the kitchen. I'd set down my toilet scrubber or whatever and run over to ladle out soup and make a bunch more pots of coffee. Josie kept a clean green apron by the door for me so I'd look more or less like a waitress. We'd go flat out getting upward of fifty people fed and watered, answering their dumb questions about where we went to school and how come we didn't have pecan pie and was the soup in the crockpot homemade like the sign hanging over it said?

In July when all five of us worked, a couple of us could have a break, walk up to the Sikanni Chief airstrip, climb up the old forestry lookout until we lost our nerve around thirty feet up. Henry made it to the top once and so did Josie. It took them forever to get down and I had to run back to cover her shift which pissed me off. It was a whole day off for me and something didn't sit right with me, down on the ground, looking up this ancient creaking tower, and them up there laughing. I don't know why I remember that now, haven't thought about that for years and years.

Josie and I would hitch the one hundred miles down to Fort St. John every Friday afternoon at four o'clock and on Sunday afternoons, we'd get a ride up to Mile 54 and hitch back up to work in less than two hours usually. We got rides fast. Two blondes with our thumbs out with no *idea* we were two blondes standing with our thumbs out on the highway! I can't believe it but no kid of mine would stand out there, male or female, not in these times. Only so many angels on duty per innocent kid.

By mid-August we figured out that we were putting in close to eighteen-hour days and then it dawned on us that we'd just worked seven days a week for two weeks straight. We were missing the really huge parties at the Old Fort and we had romances to tend to. Or we liked to think we did. Pink Mountainview Motel or Pink Elephant Lookout as we called it behind the Mister's back was seriously interfering with our futures. We each had two hundred dollars clear, a small fortune.

Now listen up. Our Dad phoned us right at a busy lunch spell and told us to quit if we'd had enough, give them a week's notice, come home and have a week off before school started. The Wife came in and gave me a dirty look for being on the phone, my only phone call all bloody summer for maybe three minutes. So I look at her, said "Uh, huh," when Dad said goodbye and then I said, "Dead?! Where?" Beat. "Mile 109? Mile 136? Omigod!" Beat. "Hitch-hikers? Have they got the murderer yet?" Beat. "Okay. Yes. Okay. Yes, we will. Bye Dad."

The Wife pretended she wasn't eavesdropping and scuttled out the door again. Something fell in the garage (closed again) and the sliding door came up and banged down. No Mister though. We waited a couple minutes, cleaning up the last of the lunch specials for a bunch of campers from Idaho and then it was just the two of us.

We got spinny, plunking quarters in the box and dancing to Little Green Bag three times in a row. Dancing like a pair of banshees until another camper pulled in. I settled down and marched out to where the Wife was holed up in Cabin Three and told her through the door that Josie and I had to quit.

I heard the toilet flush. Quit! Flush! Like an exclamation mark. Spent half her life on the can I swear. She opened the door and glared at me.

"There's two weeks left in the season," she says in her snappy boss voice. Her breath reeked of American cigarettes. Took me hours to air out a cabin after she'd holed up in it.

"Our Dad says you owe us 4 percent holiday pay," I say in my most polite and careful voice.

"But you girls didn't give us two weeks' notice," she says, folding her big huge arms over her big huge bazooms.

"Our Dad says it's the law and you didn't give us notice to work fifteen days straight either." Her mouth makes an O.

I take the plunge and make a decision for Josie and me. "If you give us our pay with the 4 percent tonight, we won't charge overtime. Our Dad," I say, watching her squinty little eyes, using my most extremely polite voice now that I'm lying like a sidewalk, "Our Dad will come up tomorrow morning for us and I guess he'll talk to you about it if Mister isn't, ahh, around." I raise my eyebrow at her with this last bit.

That did it. She gave me a long, hard look and slammed the door in my face. I started running up to the kitchen, leaping from plank to wooden plank so I wouldn't sink into the mud lake between the cabins and the café.

There were some customers, the geologist guys from the Pink Mountain site, so I held it in until Josie took out their orders and came back into the kitchen. I retell the whole exchange with the Wife and we both get so excited our whispers shot up to squeaks and we tried to jump up and down without making noise, her in her wooden clogs and me in my gumboots.

Josie had big dark circles under her eyes and she'd lost fifteen pounds in a month and a half. She was more burnt out than me because short-order cooking and waitressing and night clean-up was all inside work, breathing a steady diet of grill grease and Pine-Sol. At least I could cart towels and linen in the fresh air between cabins. For the first few weeks there was a truck, the Alaska Highway Laundry Express, but then it folded and yours truly used an industrial washer and an outside clothes line about fifty yards long because their dryer had broken down. I liked doing laundry better than making beds and scrubbing toilets.

Outside the air smelled like spruce tea with the late summer mists hanging low and the roots dangling into the little river, steeping it a coppery brown colour. I could hear trucks downshifting miles and miles away, that throaty motor sound with a silent breath between gears. I'd stand up on the laundry line perch, singing my head off, pulling wet sheets, towels, pillow slips and kitchen cloths out of my basket and onto the line, or vice versa.

But back inside, to that time, I tried to keep my mood light and summery, battling relief and giddiness and drawing a blank when it came to what to do next. I put the apron on to help Josie with night clean-up, strolling over to the juke-box to punch in some Creedance and Three Dog Night and Greenbaum's Little Green Bag, our theme song. The geologists chit-chatted abut rocks and bone hunters, one of them insisting that this place was smack in the middle of an ice-free corridor during the last glacier age. I poured their refills and kept my ears open because these guys had the most interesting arguments always. Then I heard the Wife giving Josie hell in the kitchen and so did the customers. I set the coffee pot down none too gently and marched into it.

Josie was looking white and shaky, holding a piece of order pad with some figuring on it.

"You got your hopes up, girlie," says the Wife, standing with her feet splayed apart and her arms hoisted over her bazooms, launched into a major bullying session with a tired little Grade Ten waitress. Honestly! Some people's kids!

"And what's the problem here?" I snap out in a loud voice that shocks even me. Josie looks at me like we've got one last chance to live and hands over the slip of paper.

"I figured out what I've got coming to me and they won't give it," she says, close to crying.

Josie is very smart with math and so I (no genius) quickly check the end result. I pause just a few seconds. Not for nothing was Drama my best subject last year.

"Looks right to me," I say in my new loud way and stare the skinflint down. By this point I am amazing myself!

"I'm paying her for nine hours a day and that includes breaks and meals," she says, looking past me at the heads of the geologists who are lining up at the till. She starts to move but I jump in front of her, wanting witnesses in case Mister crawls out of his cubbyhole in the garage and things get really weird. The Wife is scary enough but I got to her earlier with the yak about our Dad and the law and I know it.

"This poor kid works more hours than the fourteen a day she's claiming," I say. "She's opened up and closed down this joint for half the summer and she better be paid for it." Then I step aside so she can face the geologists over the cash register. Let the old bag simper and coo about how they like her homemade soup now, the frigging hypocrite!

To make a long story shorter, we did get our cheques that night without one word of thanks. We had our thumbs stuck out by 7 a.m. the next morning, facing a chilly north wind blowing gravel grit in our faces. In no time flat we were climbing into a big fuel tanker truck and listening to Buck Owens and Merle Haggart on eight-track stereo.

It was a deluxe truck with a cabover for sleeping, tons of seat space, tinted windshield, little orange balls across the top that some truckers called Calgary willnots, don't ask me why, and swinging dice cubes in oversized green and white foam stuff. And then there were the naked ladies.

Once I saw them I couldn't stop staring at them out the corners of my eyes because they were cut up into parts and glued onto the dash and the middle of the horn and the ashtray. Mostly breasts, no heads or arms. I was glad the trucker, Al, he said he was, didn't want to talk much because I was sitting next to him. Josie always pulled the shy act when a ride slowed down for us and started whining for the outside seat. The music blared out of four speakers and Al tapped one finger on the wheel but he didn't keep time with the music, just kept the same beat. I had to make myself stop staring at that finger too.

I made myself look out at the scenery rolling by, the miles of stunted muskeg spruce and swamp tamarack giving way to taller spruce and pines and poplars. We passed a jacknifed rig and a squashed station wagon, burnt to a grey crisp. Ugh. There was a bunch of wild-looking horses in the ditch, at least twenty of them escaped from who knows where, up to their bellies in good grass, sly and happy-looking the way horses are when they're on the lam.

The sun was pouring into the cab even with the tinted windshield. Al put on sunglasses which made him look even more sinister with his pock-marked jowls and hooked nose, an overweight parrot in an Hawaiian shirt and dirty jeans. He asked Josie to reach into the glove compartment for his pills.

"Gotta speed up my eyeballs," he said. "Hyuh, hyuh. Don't know your ass-pirin from your elbow, do ya, girlie?" Josie's giving him a confused, rabbity look because she can't get the lid of the flat black pillbox open. He asks her to fish two pills out for him. She still can't get the bloody little box open. I could scream.

The inside of the glove compartment is completely papered over with cut up women's crotch shots from magazines. You've got to understand that I'd never seen anything like this filth in my entire 17 years. This was beyond the regular girlie magazines in the drugstore in 1969 is what I'm saying. I know, it's everywhere today, the TV, everywhere. Makes me puke.

Josie broke a precious fingernail and finally opened the pillbox. Al gulped down two and sucked on an orange he kept up on the dash within reach.

He was really booting it, pedal to the metal, wanting to get to Edmonton by midnight. We roared through the village of Wonowon at eighty miles an hour. That's way over a hundred and twenty kliks to you. Too damn fast. Little Indian kids on trikes and dogs and gas stations and trailer courts blurred by us until a siren drowned out the Buckaroos.

Josie dug into my ribs. When Al cursed and started pumping the airbrakes and downshifting, she mouthed, "Out, out, out." Her face had gone white and every zit she'd ever had sprouted in purplish scar galaxies across her forehead and chin. I'm saying she looked worse than awful.

When the rig ground to a halt, we jumped out with the big brown suitcase we shared and yelled our thanks. The young constable waved us on and motioned Al down from the truck for their little talk. Josie yanked at the suitcase and my arm at the same time and broke into a run for the side of the highway well ahead of the truck.

"Do you hafta pee or what's the panic?" I yelled, tripping over the Soft Shoulders highway sign we'd sawed off the night when all of us young workers got drunk for Mister's birthday. A red stock truck slowed down before I could even catch up to Josie and in it were two young guys with cowboy hats on. When I got closer I could see it was the Wayling brothers, rancher types from near the Blueberry Reserve. I didn't know them except to look at them and that was fine by me. Dark curly hair, cut short except for sideburns, grey eyes, gorgeous noses. They were, I told Josie later, like Zane Grey heroes minus their buckskin stallions.

We hopped in the truck and tried our damndest to get them to talk in full sentences for the fifty miles into town. Josie loosened them up with jokes about jogging on the highway to keep the pounds off and I, usually the yappier of us two, sat back and laughed and laughed. Josie was never funnier except they didn't get the one about hippies being living proof that cowboys screwed goats, which was just as well considering their occupation. I don't think they liked girls to swear or talk dirty and Josie picked right up on that and said all the right things after that. Like disasters in the kitchen when the only thing left to cook was freezer-burned hamburger and stale white bread. I bragged about her and Esther turning out fifteen pies at a time, cherry, apple, blueberry and lemon meringue. Josie flirted with them way worse than I ever did with the geologists. I had the outside seat too, did I mention that? Anyway, it was amazing what a summer of waitressing did for her confidence!

But once we got to Fort St. John, the brothers asked us to go cabareting and that's when they found out we weren't old enough to get in the bar and that was the end of that but it was fun while it lasted. They dropped us off at the end of our block like we asked because we didn't want our folks to see the truck and get ideas and besides, we had to talk.

She told me there was a convex mirror on her side of the window and she'd looked into it and seen a pair of eyes between the curtains of the cabover, staring at her. That was just as we started to barrel through Wonowon. She stared back at the eyes, paralyzed with fright, and then the police siren saved the day. When I asked if it was men's eyes or women's eyes, she said she couldn't tell because of the warping of the mirror. Holy doodle. And here I was freaked out by the dirty magazine scissor work!

We tried not to dwell on it and we didn't tell our folks because the chances of us going further north to, say, Muncho Lake the next summer and earning really decent money would be shot down for sure. See? Not a brain in our heads – or more guts than brains is a better way of putting it.

◊

Look, I'll spare you my grown-up jobs, 19 years and up, the classy night spots like the Silver King Cabaret where I pranced around in red polyester hotpants. Sure, laugh. Where I got bonked on the head by a flying beer glass for stepping between my friend Ella and a very hefty, very drunk woman who already yanked off Ella's frosted blonde short'n'curly wig. Poor Ella standing there in her red hotpants suit with bobby pins holding down her greasy brown hair. Don't laugh. A little giggle is all you're allowed. Now that's enough.

You could be a lifeguard. Or go down to the Tourist Information booth. You're smart, you're pretty, you've got a nice personality. Don't leave this godforsaken town until you're 18. Promise me that. You got the rest of your life.

Please?

ME AND MINE

Sara McDonald

I

KRAFT DINNER, they say. We want Kraft dinner. This isn't just any old soup, I tell them. This is Campbell's soup and all the Campbell's Soup Kids have fat rosy faces. They look at me. They don't know what I'm talking about. Mom's been drinking again, says Buddy. He's been watching too many soap operas.

Can we go to McDonald's for supper? they ask me with angel faces. Sure, I say, Daddy can take you and I'll stay home. No, says Suzy, you have to come too. I can't, I say. I'm having a rendezvous with the telephone repair man. Wait until Daddy gets home, Suzy says. She believes everything I tell her. I tell her things like God is a huge woman who wears silver bracelets from her wrists to her elbows. We saw her on the bus one day.

Suzy and I are watching Coronation Street and drinking tea. I have milk in my tea and Suzy has tea in her milk. Buddy always hides when we are watching Coronation Street because he can't stand to be ignored, and prefers to think he is ignoring us. The phone rings just when Stanley's telling Vera about the girl in the white MG. Suzy answers it. Mommy's taking a piss right now, she says. Can she call you back? Sometimes I really do love that kid.

II

Suzy has decided to change her name. I can't really blame her – it's not such a great name, and parents shouldn't have the power to slap a label on you that you have to carry around for the rest of your life. My parents named me Mary Ellen and I still can't understand how they could've taken even one look at me and said: She's a Mary Ellen all right. The problem with Suzy is that she wants us to call her George. St. George, actually, but she'll settle for George.

When Bob and I first started talking about the possibility of having children (which was around the time I was three months gone with Suzy), we fought endlessly over names. He favoured family names, but as far as I'm concerned everybody in his family has stupid names. I probably could have found a better way to tell him that, but being pregnant makes me a lot of things, and tactful isn't one of them.

I'd always dreamed of having kids named Phoebe and Holden after the characters in *The Catcher in the Rye*, but Bob's mother had once burned a copy of that book because of the F-word. So we compromised and came up with Suzy. Buddy is really Robert Junior, but I think if you're going to call a kid Junior you might as well call him Lesser Than and be done with it. As for the nickname Buddy, I don't think Bob's mother ever made it that far with Salinger.

So now I have a daughter named George and I feel like I'm living in a Johnny Cash song. I know that it's only a phase but it's bound to have repercussions. When I send her off to camp this summer she'll probably come home with no panties because even now she is printing *George* with a Magic Marker in all her little pink unmentionables.

III

Buddy has been crying all day, ever since Suzy told him about the Easter Bunny. He didn't take it this hard when she told him about God. The worst of it is that he's locked himself in the bathroom and won't come out, and I've had to send Suzy over to Old Lady Finnegan's twice already. Mrs. Finnegan thinks I'm an unfit mother and whenever she gets near my kids she tries to stuff them full of apples and muffins.

It's hard to ignore Buddy when he's yelling this loud, but it's doubly hard to try and talk to him. Every time I get near the bathroom door he screams through the keyhole: You lied to me, you old cow. I guess I'm not supposed to find being called a cow amusing.

Buddy has a mouth on him like a truck driver, which Bob says is all my fault and I guess it is. Still that doesn't help Bob out any when his mother comes to visit and Buddy asks where his fucking Tonka toys are.

It seems to me that Bob's mother lacks a sense of humour and managed to raise Bob the same way. The only thing I don't understand is why I didn't notice it sooner.

I'm feeling pretty guilty about this Easter Bunny thing and the only way I can rationalize it out is that it wasn't my idea in the first place. But try telling that to a screaming 5 year old. Meanwhile, I'm just waiting for the moment where he figures out this means Santa is a hoax too. My kids aren't dumb and I know he'll get it sooner or later. Poor Suzy may never pee in her own home again.

IV

Suzy came home today and announced that she was through with school. I tried to tell her about careers and options and all that guidance counsellor crap which you shouldn't have to lay on your 7 year old. I don't want a career, she said. I'm going to be a mommy. Try to argue with that. Try to explain how my degree in Art History prepared me for Sesame Street being the high point of my day, and for putting clown faces on cupcakes when one of the kids had a birthday. I thought my cupcakes were pretty innovative, but Suzy gave me hell when one little girl started to cry because her cupcake clown only had one ear. Six year olds don't give a damn for Van Gogh.

So I let her spend the afternoon at home and watch Coronation Street with me, just like it was summer holidays. I was pretty depressed by this point anyway, and thought I could use the company. I figured I'd let Bob sort this all out when he got home.

When both of them were safely tucked in for the night, Bob said to me: Well, she's your kid all right. She doesn't believe that one and one always makes two, and never anything else, said Bob. She refuses to go any further with math until someone can prove it to her.

Yeah, I thought, she's mine all right. And I wanted to laugh, but didn't because I knew I'd never make Bob understand how proud I was. As far as I was concerned she didn't ever have to go to school again. She could stay home with me and we'd watch Sesame Street and Coronation Street, and eat Fruit Loops right out of the box. We'd sit around and she could tell me all about life and one and one could be whatever the hell she wanted.

V

Buddy has decided he doesn't want to be a boy anymore if it means that he has to pee standing up. When Bob caught Buddy using his little stepping stool to drink water out of the toilet he hid it in our closet. I'm sure that somehow all this makes me a bad mother. So now Buddy has to stand on tiptoe to reach it over the edge, and today the inevitable happened: the lid fell down.

Masculine pride on his part and a knowledge of Greek tragedy on mine prevented me from kissing it better. He howled for about an hour and I would have done anything to make him stop crying, which was how we came to be having animal crackers and jello for supper.

Bob got pretty pissed off after about his third giraffe and went out to pick up hamburgers. I thought that being a man he would be more sympathetic to Buddy's whimpering, but I was wrong. Although maybe not entirely because when I went to use the bathroom the stepping stool was back where it belonged.

VI

My old coffee gang came over for coffee this morning. It was kind of strange at first because our main topic of conversation used to be boys. That and the cities we were going to visit, and what we would name our kids if we had any, and how we were never going to be like our mothers.

I heard this song on the radio the other day and the chorus went: "At the age of 37, she realized she'd never drive through Paris in a sportscar, with the warm wind in her hair." I cried for about three hours and really freaked out my poor kids who hadn't seen me cry like this since my Mom died. By the end of it I was buried in all their little sympathy gifts: Suzy's stuffed animals, and Buddy's Hallowe'en candy that he'd been hoarding somewhere for months.

That was when I decided to call the old coffee gang, and somewhere in the back of my mind I think I must have been doing it to punish myself for some long-forgotten sin. Maybe the time I slept with Carol's boyfriend.

Carol was the first one I called. Have you been to Paris yet? I asked her, and when she said no, I invited her over for coffee. Sharon hadn't been to Paris either, and Jill had been to London, but I invited her anyway.

The funny thing was, after talking about our respective kids, careers, and minor nervous breakdowns, we talked about boys. We laughed more and cried less than we used to, and once in a while we even managed to tell the truth.

I guess I thought talking with the old gang might bring me to the inescapable conclusion that I'd made all the right choices in life, but it didn't of course. Mostly it just gave me a clearer idea of what I'd been missing out on. But if it came down to a choice between Paris and my rotten kids I couldn't give them up. As Suzy would say, I'd rather drink spit.

SPRING FORWARD, FALL BACK

Sarah Sheard

for Margaret Dragu

S HE CUT THE MOTOR, rode her wake in to the dock and jumped out. Jay stirred uneasily in his pack, aware that he was no longer in the rocking boat, and she absently stroked his head with her free hand. She didn't want him to wake up and demand a feeding until she'd gotten things organized.

She piled their stuff on the end of the dock. Dew began to darken the bottom of her canvas pack. Damn. Her clothes, her books. She picked it up. Put it down again. As long as Jay's stuff was dry on top. Six fifteen. If the bus wasn't on time she'd have to breastfeed him against a piling. She looked at her hands hugging Jay in his pack, visualizing them in ten years. Maybe it was the light. Even her clothes looked elderly.

She heard the generator whoosh up and the sign over the marina door snapped on, blue-white against the light outside. They work a long day, she thought, shifting the harness on her shoulders.

It was finding that goddamn golden hair. One, long, golden hair. Where it shouldn't have been. It left her no choice.

She had a habit of resisting persuasion. Her intuition told her something was going on but she tried to ignore it. When Dutchie insisted that he was toeing the line, her gut told her he wasn't, plaguing her with doubt in her own judgment. She'd been wondering, ever since Jay was born, if she was as intelligent as before. When her friends remarked at how quickly she'd regained her old self she looked away, wondering why they were misleading her. She couldn't shake the conviction that no one was coming clean with her. Was she such a difficult person to be truthful to? And the more they protested the less she believed them. A 100 percent pure paranoiac predicament.

Until she found the hair.

She squatted against the wall of the marina, pulled up her shirt and began nursing Jay. She looked down at his head, white as a ptarmigan's breast, and his nursing mouth and she felt herself surrender to him totally, her whole being flowing out to him like a genie swarming above its bottle. If she unclenched for only an instant, her maternal pouch would spread like some tropical lizard's and engulf both their lives, smother outsiders, push history backwards.

Each time she caught a reflection of her new self, mother of Jay, she remembered how she had once looked upon mothers – the fleeting judgments – plain child, this one, or – my god, the fatigue on that woman's face, ribbons on those twins was a big mistake etc. Now, each time she turned a corner, it was her own judgmental self she confronted to explain that she too had surrendered, that she'd acquired a taste for the happiness that unconditional love brought. Jay and his stroller were a delicious weight to push against. She had entered the thoroughfare of human history, was no longer watching from the curb. All embarrassment was gone. She didn't know how better to put it than that.

A faint line in the open bay showed where she'd crossed. A wrinkle in carbon paper. Little ruffles in the water. The breeze that dawn brought pushed the tethered sailboats around on their strings. Pretty toys.

Dutchie would be so pissed off when he saw she'd left him on the island with only the canoe. Aren't you glad we won't be around to hear that, she whispered into Jay's ear, rocking him against her shoulder. But she had to go when she did. Before they talked this thing between them to death, waiting out the six days between buses. Dutchie would have done the same. He was a means-justify-the-end kind of guy. Anyway, they were both too beat to get mad over a detail like this.

Ah, the golden hair. She had pulled the sheets off their bed, thrown his pillow into the hall, rolled herself up in a blanket and slept the rest of the night on the couch. The next morning, she had flown at him, pushed the piece of paper at his face. With the names of all the women she knew for absolute fact he had slept with. Coming to, her fists pummeling his chest, she saw she was throwing what he called a Mediterranean Tantrum but she couldn't help it. She was loco with disappointment. Who are you, she remembered shrieking, over and over.

She covered one foot with sand using the other. Sweet Jay. And what would he make of all this one day. She smiled, remembering those first few weeks when she and Dutchie used to tiptoe into Jay's room at night holding hands, just to watch him sleep. His face was better than a movie. The way expressions flitted across it like weather.

That part of their relationship – the one that went into creating Jay – was bone-true.

So why can't you just trust that and forget about the rest, he asked her. She tried to explain why not by reversing the details so he'd see it her way but he only shrugged and went blank. Wouldn't bother me, he said. I'm not jealous. So she squandered energy instead trying to analyze Dutchie from his point of view. It withered her ego.

When Jay arrived he lay between them, a little negotiator, his indexes jabbing them each in the nose urging them to thrash it out, solve this thing, once and for all.

The re-*demp*-tive power of love, the preacher intoned. Approach your set now, *touch* the screen and feel the re-*demp*-tive power of love. The power that moves mountains, crumbles walls, makes the dead talk, the crippled walk. Be-*lieve* on it ....

She had groaned and bopped the TV off but not before her hand grazed the screen furtively, curious to feel something. They both sat in the dark, in silence after that. She really wanted to believe this thing had finally broken like an abscess and that from now on, things would be different. Not perfect, she didn't insist on that. Just different. Something to indicate progress. So they could believe that people changed if the price was right.

But after the hair incident, there was nothing more to say and the failure, a gigantic spider's sac of all their time together, hung in the dark room, between his couch and hers, reproaching them, as Jay himself ultimately would. There was nothing either of them could say. He couldn't promise to change, he said, without understanding himself better and he began to cry. She told him she couldn't wait any longer. He couldn't ask her to. Aching to hear something different, they were overcome with tenderness towards one another, knowing their time was up.

Jay, the little fossil of their intimacy.

Jay, by the light of the full moon. Jay, who took ten moons to make. The scent of Jay's head – salt milk and crushed ferns – through the mosquito netting. Jay's garbled cry of hunger in his sleep, a sound she called Fox in the Henhouse that sent a reflex of burning needles into each nipple. The ghost sobs that echoed in both their ears long after the real Jay had fallen back to sleep. The back of Jay's head a swelling shape as though undergoing mitosis, pulling away from the forehead. Dutchie proposing to draw cat whiskers on him. Peering down to inspect the inside of his perfect throat the first time he yawned. Jay's fists relaxing in sleep to reveal wrenched-out tufts of Dutchie's chest hair. Jay, whom Dutchie took in to weigh each Friday on the marina fish scales. (A fresh sheet of newspaper in honour of the occasion.) Jay, the baby who spoke an actual word, *igloo*, at five weeks – she overheard Dutchie crow to the guy at the scales who actually believed him. Jay, of the bad smell that seeped under the door of his bedroom into theirs, taking them two days to trace to its source, each accusing the other of lapsed personal hygiene, a very bad, lost sock etc. Jay, whose hydrochloric spit bleached an exclamation mark onto the bedspread. Jay, who farted whenever his arms were stretched, like a squeezy toy. Jay, who preferred to lie widthwise across her chest clutching her throat while he slept. Jay's face, born old, growing younger, day by day. Jay, whose body returned to hers each time he went limp in her arms. Her flesh again, repossessed.

She propped the haversack against a tree and stretched herself with eyes closed listening for the bus. The sensation of dying, she wondered, and then of coming to, would it feel anything like this? Like in those magazine stories. Would it feel like this morning in the boat coming over?

She opened her eyes. Dutchie was reading her note.

He would have made breakfast as usual, smoked his first cigarette, now he would be scanning the water, in some sense looking
for her boat, but also planning his future. Although he would deny
that.

Later, they would meet down in the city. By then she and Jay
would be settled at her folks. Her letter made it clear how much she
wanted Jay's wellbeing to dictate the terms for them all. They'd
both agreed that Jay should grow up in the city. This was just a little
earlier than they'd planned. She knew money would not be an
issue between them.

Jay's head shifted and he pursed his lips in a perfect O, his O-
mouth. An indication of alert attention, the baby book said – except
he was sound asleep.

Ultimately you went on instinct and whatever smarts heredity
endowed you with. Forget the books.

She stood up and waited for the door of the bus to swing open in
front of them and indicated her luggage to the driver who nodded
and stepped down to load it in. She chose a window seat. A taste of
iron seeped into her mouth which she swallowed and then shifted
Jay's head so they could both look out the window, cheek to cheek.
She could almost see across the water to the island, up the rocks to
the cabin. To Dutchie, sitting at the table, stubbing out a cigarette,
his eyes meeting hers, her note in his hand. A smile. A wave. Of
hello and, of course, goodbye. Ambiguous as always.

She wondered at – was it her fickleness. No, not quite that. Just
the gradual displacement of romantic love with realism. Virtually
invisible from the outside, what had happened to her. Her shape
was quite the same, colouring, inflections, handwriting, even her
sense of humour, but she had undergone a kind of petrification.
One cell after another had been penetrated with a flux of new wisdom that gradually hardened to stone.

PRETTY GOLDFISH

Libby Scheier

D URING BRAN FLAKES Sam notices that Pretty Goldfish is belly up. "What's the fish doing, Ellie?" he asks.

"I'd rather be called Mom," I say. "Why do you keep calling me Ellie?"

"Because that's your *name*," Sam says. "Don't be dumb."

"Maybe you could try Mom once in a while."

"Everybody's called Mom. Nobody's called Ellie. It's special."

"But Mom makes me feel like I'm special to you," I say.

Sam sighs. "Okay, I'll try and do it sometimes. What about the *fish*, Ellie. What's the matter with the fish?"

I look at the goldfish bowl. "Oh no. It's dead."

"What do you mean he's dead. How come? How come he's dead? Is he really dead? How come?"

After a minute, I say, "I think it was just time for it to die, you know. Fish don't live a really long time. I think it just died because it had lived as long as it was supposed to."

Sam's eyes get red and wet. He's going to cry. Okay, I say to myself, say the right thing. I think hard about the effective parenting workshop. Validate feelings. I'm supposed to validate how he's feeling, that's right. Don't say it's nothing, that it is the fish's time to go, say he is right to feel whatever he feels. Right.

"I know you feel sad," I say. "You liked Pretty Goldfish a lot. You can cry if you want, it's okay, you know."

Sam immediately dries his eyes with a napkin and gets himself under control. "You don't care that he's dead. It's not fair," he says,

181

angry. "It's too short. It's not like people. People have a long time. It's not fair for Pretty Goldfish."

I panic and regress to pre-workshop thinking. "It seems longer to a fish than it does to you," I say. "For the fish it feels as long as a person's life feels to a person." It seems like a good thing to say in the circumstances.

◊

Pretty lived for six months in fact, which is longer than I expected. We bought it one day in Woolworth's, after me and Sam and Norman had all jammed into a twenty-five-cent photo machine booth and made fools of ourselves in front of crowds of Saturday shoppers. When we came out of the booth we found ourselves face to face with a huge tank filled with hundreds of goldfish.

"Let's get a fish!" Sam screamed.

"Yeah, all right!" Norman and I shouted back at him. "Your first pet!" Sam had just turned 5.

It took Sam twenty minutes to study all the fish. To me, each one was a perfect gold twin of the last, but Sam could grasp their individual essence.

Finally, he pointed to one toward the bottom of the tank, swimming away from the pack. "That one," he said. "That's a pretty one."

It was with relief that I watched Sam take a mothering attitude toward the fish. I figured that meant I was nice to Sam, even if I hadn't studied effective parenting until he was 5, and that the reason Sam was turning out so good had something to do with my mothering. Maybe, on the other hand, I told myself, Sam had a wonderful nature that no amount of fucked-up parenting could destroy.

Pretty lived on the big wooden kitchen table where we took all our meals. We'd bought one of those ordinary small goldfish bowls and the fish twitched and darted around and was always hungry. You're supposed to feed fish once a day or they get overfed and die, Norman said, but it became obvious that Pretty, like the rest of us, took three regular meals. If it hadn't been fed, it would slam itself against the sides of the fishbowl as it swam and jerked back and forth. When you picked up the red fishfood can and approached the bowl, it stopped dead for a moment from its sideways darting back and forth, then swam straight up to the surface, nose first, as though suddenly pulled there by a heavenly fishing pole.

Looking back on it, I think I was a little insensitive to Pretty. I didn't buy any greens or plants or other things that fish like. The fish looked lonely in the barren bowl one morning, so I took a green marble frog from the mantelpiece and plunked it in. I guess I expected Pretty to swim over and give it a pucker, but instead the fish seized up, darted to the other side of the bowl, and stayed there, dead still, for an hour. Finally, it slowly approached the frog and nosed around it, then began swimming around as usual. I felt better about nearly scaring the fish to death when, later, Pretty began to use the frog to hide behind when it felt anti-social.

Pretty quadrupled in size in about a month and, at its death, it was at least ten times bigger than when we had bought it. If we had put it in the bathtub, it probably would have become as big as a cat. So we fed it well, but it was still nervous, even when it wasn't hungry. I took this as a reflection on me, of course. But then, I asked myself, how come I don't have a nervous kid? It was nature-nurture again. The old question.

Maybe it was Norman's effect on the fish. Norman and I had lived together for six months, and he was playing stepdad to Sam. Norman was nice but had high anxiety about his health and his conversations with other grown-ups. He was great with Sam and had almost gotten used to me, though talking with me still made him nervous sometimes. He also had a touch of the passive-aggressive in him, never being one to raise his voice, but preferring to lie down in bed with the covers over his head in the middle of an argument. He was a tall, thin man who ate tons of food but, unlike Pretty Goldfish, never gained weight. But if Norman had made the fish nervous, how come he hadn't made Sam nervous? To tell the truth, I have not been a calm individual myself, but rather the high-strung, explosive, heart attack type, averaging one burst of temper a week. These often took place in the kitchen where there were more breakable things to choose from. Since the fish bowl was in the kitchen, you could have pinned Pretty's nervousness on me. Then again, I had not managed in five years to stress my son, or least he didn't show it. So it was either that nothing could make

Sam nervous because he was such a remarkable, centred child (*my remarkable, centred child*) or that nothing could make the fish calm because it had such a fragile, nervous nature to begin with.

Sam became attached to the fish, of course. More than that, he granted it a natural and rightful place in the house in a way that never occurred to me or Norman. We were playing a number game at dinner and Sam gave us a question: Who's the youngest member of the family? We guessed him, then each other, each time Sam saying "no" with a big smile. We gave up and Sam shouted, "It's the *fish*! Ha, ha, you lose!"

◊

"How do you know Pretty Goldfish felt that way"? Sam says, his wet eyes staring at the upside-down fish. "How do you know he felt his life was long. Maybe he felt short."

"I read it in a book," I say, feeling guilty.

"I want another pet," Sam says. "I want a pet that doesn't die fast. How about a cat? Does a cat die fast?"

"No, a cat lives about fifteen years," I say.

"Okay, let's get a cat."

This seems a disrespectful conversation over the not yet cold body of Pretty Goldfish, but Sam had a deeper emotional relationship with the fish than me, to say the least, and I'm not about to criticize him. "Let's talk it over with Norman," I say. "Cats are more work than fish, and cost more money, and are more trouble. We'll have to think it over."

"Okay, we'll talk with Norman tonight," Sam says.

Norman has a meeting at work and doesn't get home till Sam is asleep. I can't give him the bad news straight. "Guess what?" I say, after he's taken his coat and shoes off and collapsed on the sofa.

"Animal, vegetable or mineral?" he asks.

"Animal," I say.

He sits up. "You're pregnant," he says, his face grey.

"Nope, try again."

"Okay, you said it's animal, right?"

"Right."

"Animal-human or animal-animal?"

"Animal-animal."

"The fish died."

"Right."

Norman looks genuinely sad. I tell him how it went with Sam. "Maybe we should talk to him some more about it," I say. "Death has been a big topic of conversation this year. And now we have our first practical example. Show and tell. The only thing is, I don't really know what to say."

"Just don't give him that 'everything dies' stuff. I don't think he's conscious of his own death yet. He's only 5."

"Oh yes, he is, he's conscious of it, there were some conversations that went on around here before you came on board," I say ungenerously. "What's wrong with saying 'everything dies.' It does. Dying is part of living, you know," I say, wincing at my cozy motto.

"I don't think putting it like that does much good," Norman says. "I think we should just tell him it's okay to be sad, that we're sad, too, and that we all miss Pretty Goldfish." Norman has also attended the effective parenting workshop.

"He wants a cat."

"Well, maybe we'll get a cat."

"What should we do about the fish?"

"I guess the three of us could bury it in the back yard tomorrow."

"Can we leave it overnight in the bowl, or is it going to rot and stink up the kitchen?" I ask.

"Oh, I don't think fish rot so fast when they're in water. Besides, it's so small. How much of a stink could it make? We can wait till tomorrow," Norman says.

We go into the kitchen to get ourselves a drink, and it has already begun to smell from Pretty Goldfish. "Looks like we have to do something tonight. I'll empty the bowl and put some ice in it and put the fish back in," I say. Norman scoops the fish out of the bowl with a soup spoon and puts it on a dish.

The bright gold colour has already faded to a pale yellow. The belly is white and a greyish translucent jelly coats the perfectly round eyes, white with solid black centres. Where the belly has begun to rot, in the centre, it is pinkish brown. The tiny-scaled skin looks slimy and sticky. The fish lies completely still on the dish, like a sardine, like any dead fish, its nervous spirit gone and departed.

Norman grimaces. "You wouldn't think such a small fish would smell so much," he says.

He washes out the bowl and I fill it with two trays of ice cubes, scoop Pretty up again and put it on the ice. Its nose slides down between two cubes. "This is really stupid," I say. "Why don't I just wrap it up and put it in the freezer. This ice is going to melt, by morning the water will be warm and smelly. Putting it in the freezer is easier, anyway."

"Just wrap it in tin foil and put it in the fridge, that's the best thing to do. Then we can bury it inside the tin foil," says Norman.

"Can't we just bury it as is? Do we really need a coffin?" I say.

Norman's face shows suffering. "Ellie, how are you going to carry it out to the garden – by its smelly tail?"

"Yeah, okay, you're right." I get the tin foil and try to get the fish out of the ice cubes. This is hard, because as they slowly melt, it keeps slipping between them. I'm afraid if I spill the whole thing out, the cubes will fall on the fish and break it to pieces. But I can't get it out and finally I tip everything into a large dish. The fish emerges in one piece. I touch its side with my fore-finger and it feels surprisingly solid. I suddenly feel a catch in my throat.

"This is ridiculous," I say to Norman. "I'm getting upset."

"I know," he says, "I'm upset too."

"God knows I've seen a lot of dead fish."

"You know," Norman confesses, "I saw the fish up near the top of the water last night and it looked like it was gasping a bit for air and I told myself maybe I should change the water and then I was tired and decided to do it the next day."

"Oh, for Christ's sake, don't start guilting yourself about the fish," I say, "We didn't expect it to last a month. I thought you said six months was a long life for a fish."

"I don't know," Norman says. "I don't know how long fish are supposed to live. My brother kept fish and they died every month. He kept buying more. He loved fish."

I get some tin foil, nudge the fish onto it with my finger, wrap it up and put it in the freezer.

In the morning when we get up, we find Sam pretend-reading to his stuffed bears. I'm in the bathroom when I hear Sam say, "Norman, I've got some bad news for you."

"What's that?" Norman asks.

"The fish died."

Norman has forgotten all about it. So have I.

"I know," Norman says. I can feel him gathering up his internal resources as he next says, "Let's sit down and talk about it."

"Wait for me!" I shout from the bathroom. "I'm coming too." I rush down the hallway and Norman is sitting on the bed with Sam on his lap, asking him how he feels about the fish dying.

"Sad," Sam says. "I want a cat."

"It's okay to be sad," Norman and I say simultaneously. Sam stares at both of us.

"I'm sad too," I say.

"Me too," says Norman.

"The fish's spirit is still alive," I say.

Sam looks at me and says, "*Ellie.*"

"Do you want to talk some more about it?" Norman asks.

"I want to get up," Sam says. He gets off Norman's lap and goes to play with his bears.

"We'll talk with him some more later," Norman says to me, and gets his coat to go to work.

He comes into Sam's room to say goodbye. "I'll see you later," he says. "I'll see you tonight."

"I'll see you tonight," Sam says, cheerfully. "And tomorrow too. And the next day. I'll see you forever."

Norman goes down the stairs.

"I'll see you till you're dead," Sam calls after him.

PICTURES

Gertrude Story

A S SOON AS she'd left Arthur Alfred, Emma got interested in
sex. In the thirty-seven years she was married to him it was
something done in the dark between hot sheets (or cold ones in the
unheated bedroom of the A-frame farmhouse that hadn't seen
even the insulation of a coat of paint since Arthur Alfred's father's
time); Arthur Alfred's 'conjugular rights' were exercised rarely
and, mercifully, quickly and they had become just another chore
from the first time he availed himself three months after the wedding. Yet as soon as ever she left him, took the eight hundred dollars she had saved, mite by veriest mite, over twenty-seven years
in a jam jar hidden in the pickle section of the cool cellar and simply
walked out to the grid and hitched a ride to Winnipeg with the Co-
op fuel delivery truck, she got interested in sex.

She didn't even have the need to flip the switch in the mind that
turns the words off – turns *the* word off; turns the pictures off too.
So all the way to Winnipeg she let the pictures roll about the Co-op
fuel delivery man, whom she didn't know from Adam, who was at
least twenty years younger and who spoke a lot about his wife and
three kids and bet she had grandchildren to visit in Winnipeg, well
he would sure just deliver Granny right to their door and wouldn't
they get a nice surprise? She let him talk and let the pictures roll
and she smiled to herself about all the things the Co-op fuel man
would never know.

She got him to let her off at Eaton's, the only place she really
remembered. Then she didn't know what to do next and so she

found a telephone and looked up Doris' number and told her what she'd done.

Doris would have taken her in. "Sister or not," she'd said, as soon as the car door was closed with Emma in the passenger seat, "I kept out of it all these years. Though Mother must have turned over in her grave a hundred times the way that little pip-squeak made you work, milking cows by hand, if you please, in this day and age."

"It's all right, Doris," Emma had said. "I like cows. I didn't mind." And then she closed her mind to Doris' talk, talk, talk and looked at the pictures. And an hour later Doris was still talking and there was a teacup with tea in it in Emma's hand and she couldn't quite remember how it had got there. She placed the teacup onto its saucer quietly. She had never liked noise of any kind. And Arthur – Arthur Alfred; he was named after two kings, was Arthur, and he often told you so – ever since his hearing wasn't what it used to be Arthur did everything loudly.

He played the radio loudly to catch the morning news and the weather; he ate his breakfast loudly; he grunted into his boots loudly; he gave her her orders for the day loudly; he banged the door the same way and started up the old truck with clatters and clangs and curses that penetrated the kitchen, quiet as soon as he'd left it, setting her teeth on edge, her heart a-flutter twenty times before he finally roared up the lane and was gone.

"I said you can come and live here," Doris was saying. "Can't you listen once? Fred won't mind; you know Fred."

Emma knew Fred. Of course. Quiet, patient Fred. Who had milked cows for their father once. How quiet and peaceful it had been in the barn those times, just the two of them (and fifteen milk cows, of course!), she and Fred, one as tongue-tied as the other so there was no chitter-chatter to invade the warm contented steaminess of quiet cows and clean straw and fresh new milk. Until Doris would come barreling in, yodelling à la Wilf Carter at the top of her lungs, stealing Fred's cap to collect the eggs in, tying Emma's braids to the tail of the cow she was milking.

"Look, Freddie," she'd say, "Emma and old Jess are twins, you can't tell where one leaves off and the other begins."

"You shouldn't," Fred would say. But he would smile just a

little, and Emma would feel awful, just awful. And he would get
up off his milk stool and come over and undo the knot to free
Emma's braids. And his hand would brush her hair sometimes,
lightly.

And too soon he and Doris were married and had moved into
Winnipeg, all that way, and Papa bought them a little place.

"It was nice," she said now, placing a hand palm down over the
teacup to prevent Doris from filling it again. "Your first little house.
It was nice."

"Nice?" Doris said. "It was a mousetrap. But I will say, Fred
made good on the railway always, and as soon as ever I went to
work at the hotel – not where I am now, I mean the Fort Garry –
well it sure didn't take us long to pay Papa back and get something
decent, I cleaned a lot of crappy toilets let me tell you, to do it. And
Fred fixed and painted on the new place, and made his own
lunches even going on the midnight if he had to, and never once
complained. You know Fred."

Emma knew Fred. And that's why she couldn't stay there.
When Doris went gallivanting off to bingo and she and Fred
played cards or watched TV together and it was all so quiet even if
it was a shoot-'em-up they were watching, it was all, well, so *nice*,
and the pictures would start.

And the feelings. She would be holding a nice hand, planning it
out, when the cards would become a house right there in her hand.
More like a cabana by the sea, maybe – whatever a cabana was.
This one had a thatched roof.and was open to the sea and the sun
and the salt breeze. And it had a hammock swaying gently from
the beams. And she and Fred were in the hammock. Wearing not
very much. Wearing, in fact, as she looked, nothing.

She hadn't seen Arthur Alfred in nothing in all the years they
were together. Except in the bathtub when he yelled at her to come
wash his back. And then he always had the washcloth spread out
like a floating garden over his personals.

As if she would so much as be tempted to pluck his thorny rose!

But with Fred it was different, so she had to move out. Even
though Doris said, "Don't, where will you go? they won't even hire
you to sew pockets in men's pants when you're 58, well OK 57, 57;
stay here I tell you; if old A.A. comes looking leave it to me to read

him the riot act." And the first thing Doris did when she came home off shift was to call "Emma!" and she didn't even take her coat off until she had found where she was.

One of the good things about the city was a paper that came every single day. There were ads in it. Doris would read some of them out loud and laugh. "Adventuresome male seeks like-minded," she'd say, "I bet it's not the mind he's after!"

In Emma's mind danced pictures of a young couple, as sunbrown as in the TV ads, dancing together on a golden beach, then sinking entwined below white-capped waves, their bodies hot, hot despite the coolness of the water. She wasn't sure if she was the young woman or the young man, but it didn't matter – she was there.

"A little adventure never hurt anybody," she said.

Doris rolled her eyes. "Listen to her," she said to Fred, "57 years old and an innocent. In this day and age! Emma, it means he wants another *man*!"

The pictures on the TV screen inside Emma's head became a jig-saw puzzle and then made a new picture. The sun and the waves still felt good. "So?" she said. Doris rolled her eyes.

She tsked her tongue loudly. "*You* better not read the want ads," she said, and put the paper aside. She hoisted her body out of the deep soft sofa and went to make tea. She brought it in on a wide tray along with real cream and with real sugar and with a high stack of the raisin bread Emma had made that day, well-buttered and with sugar cinammon sprinkled thickly over it.

In spite of herself Emma ate two slices. When the late news came on she sneaked the paper off with her to her room. Every night Emma soaked in the deep tub in the white, white bathroom connected to her room. It's yours, use it, Doris had said; soak the cow smell out of your pores – I know, I *know*, you *like* cows, you've said so a thousand times since you came.

And she'd rolled those famous eyes in the way that had always made their mother laugh and had driven the boys in the schoolyard to tease her so she would tsk her tongue, hands on hips, toss her head and give them that exasperated eye roll. Fill the tub, Doris had said, enjoy it; baby yourself a little. Call me if you want your back scrubbed. Or Fred. He's good at it!

The pictures, the feeling, the good smells of Fred doing that bothered her too much and she had to make her mind think of cows instead. It worked, until she felt again the firm-soft teats drawing the good warm white milk into the shining pail.

HOUSEKEEPER WANTED, FARM BACKGROUND PRE-FERRED. Emma knew she would phone the number in the morning as soon as ever Fred and Doris had gone to work. She saw the Wanter already, though: medium-tall, thickly muscled; clean shaven, balding; neat as a pin; quiet-spoken. (In fact, Fred.)

Mr. Arnold was tall and skinny actually, and he spoke loudly, with a lot of old country Eh wot? lass's and constant tinkering with his hearing aid. He had white bushy hair and white bushy eyebrows and a moustache that had once been a waxed military one, judging by the old photos of him that hung everywhere on the walls of the sitting-room. The moustache was now quite droopy and spilled over into Mr. Arnold's teacup if he did not "exercise eternal vigilance over the demn thing."

Mr. Arnold used a cane and was obviously relieved when Emma suggested she make the tea he offered. He went before her to the kitchen, whacking a swath through loose newspapers and empty grocery bags; in the kitchen he swung cupboard doors open with it, pointed out the 'company tea' with the tip of it, talking, talking, talking – eh wot? lass – the whole time. She thought he was kind of cute.

Emma would have liked a little hot buttered toast with the tea, she'd been too nervous to have anything that morning before she left, but she didn't want to be forward and suggest it. No milk, no sugar in the tea for Mr. Arnold, so she said she didn't take it either. Once back in the sitting-room, though, with its old-fashioned solid good wood and the deep plush big old sofas and chairs, every one antimacassered to the hilt, Mr. Arnold smacked a round blue and silver tin box out from under a chair with his cane. It said Olde Englishe Biscuits on it and was, thankfully, half full. Mr. Arnold, also thankfully, was quick to say, Come, come, another one won't hurt you.

Mr. Arnold liked farm girls because he had worked on a farm when he came to this country and he had indeed married one of the farm daughters, bless her soul. He knew farm girls were clean and they were hard workers, eh wot? lass. Emma's mind didn't make a single picture of hammocks hanging from the roof beams of a cabana or of hot golden bodies entwined in the depths of cool-blue ocean waves, but she took the job anyway.

In fact she stayed, then and there, and cleaned the bags and papers and old pizza cartons out of the kitchen in no time flat. It was actually a neat and tidy and pretty room once that was done, clean except for the cookie and toast crumbs that matched the counter tops and so Mr. Arnold kept missing them. You can't clean what you can't see, eh wot? lass, he kept saying. He bungled about the kitchen the whole time whacking papers out of the way with his cane just as she bent to pick them up, bellowing, Let me do that for you, lass, until she took the bull by the horns and said, "Now, Mr. Arnold, you're paying *me* to housekeep, remember? So how would it be if you sat right there in that nice captain's chair and put your feet up and tell me again what the sergeant major said when they found out you'd lied to get into the army? And when I'm done here we'll go for a walk together, what do you say?"

So they did that. They walked through a little park – Mr. Arnold was quite a walker, it was a good thing he was deaf and couldn't hear you puffing – and then they cut over to a little grocery store for "war supplies" ("against Hunger, the stalwart enemy"). By then Emma was having a good time and the rest of the day flew by; she almost forgot to phone Fred and Doris; did, in fact, forget until Mr. Arnold offered her cab fare to go and get her things.

After she phoned they brought them over so fast it was plain they hadn't even stopped for supper. "Well now, aren't you the cool one though?" Doris said when Emma answered the door. "Mama always said you were a deep one." But she didn't roll her eyes at Mr. Arnold or his big gorgeous old house with the handsome shiny wood in it, she sat primly erect on a hard wooden chair, ankles crossed (to keep the skirt where it belonged, according to the rules laid down by Miss Caroline Warkentin in grade six in Clover Leaf School in northern Manitoba a good few years ago); she mouthed precisely the carefully chosen words she directed, well-modulated, Mr. Arnold's way so efficiently that he rarely had to twiddle with his hearing aid the entire evening.

Fred sat quietly, of course. And smiled and winked at Emma (she had hammock pictures the minute he did that), and hooked a thumb in sly look-at-them-will-you? style in the direction of Doris and Mr. Arnold now loudly enjoying the old military photographs on the wall, each old buddy reminisced about being smacked soundly on the head by Mr. Arnold's cane. He ignored Fred and Emma completely, except to whack the biscuit tin into view from beneath his chair and suggest Emma make tea.

So she fore-fingered Fred into the kitchen with her and made ham sandwiches to go with the cookies, starting Fred off with a big thick one, light on the mustard, before she even plugged in the kettle for tea.

By the time Mr. Arnold was booming, Come again! Come again! and hanging on to Doris' hand so that she almost never got to *go*, let alone come again, it was late news time eh wot? lass, but all Emma wanted was to close the door on herself in the cozy big room on the third floor that had once belonged to Mr. Arnold's studious third daughter. Who was also good and practical, for she had had the big hall closet-that-was made into a young lady's modern-day bathroom with her first salary cheque from the library. Because she said she was going to live with her parents forever.

"Never so much as took a bath in the bathtub," Mr. Arnold said, "maybe never so much as washed her hands in the sink or looked at herself in the fancy mirror." She had been struck down by a speeding motorist running a yellow light – "They all drive here like Parisians, demn them all," Mr. Arnold said – and she never opened her eyes again though Mr. and Mrs. Arnold took turns and stayed with her every minute of the twenty-seven days it took her to die.

"*She* never called it *dying*," Mr. Arnold said. "The missus never called it *dying*, she said you *translated* into other worlds. And when our baby was gone her mum simply decided she wasn't staying behind and so she up and translated too, just like that, not even a headache when she went to bed, just slipped away as smooth as butter and with a smile on her face."

The droopy moustache had drooped even more limply while Mr. Arnold told that story while they waited for the kettle to boil once they'd got home with the war supplies. There was so much of everything – pictures, sounds, smells, feeling – spinning through Emma that whole first day that now, with Doris and Fred safely gone, all she wanted – and what she desperately needed – was to simply slip out of her clothes and at once into the cool-blue waves of the blue cotton bed-ocean and let it all roll her into a sleep that would have no room for cows or the farm life she had left behind so recently. Or for Arthur Alfred whose loudness was of a different order from Mr. Arnold's. Mr. Arnold's did not set the teeth on edge.

At least not yet.

Six months later she had heard the same war stories so many times she could put herself on automatic, like the fancy oven Doris had taught her to use, and cook supper to the tune of Mr. Arnold's loud voice and be ready to set it on the table with his last but-we-showed-the-blighters,-eh-wot?-lass. By now she knew every nook and cranny of at least a half-section of Winnipeg around Mr. Arnold's place because they walked a good part of it daily, his cane whacking stray Colonel Sanders' boxes and sections of discarded newspapers and even unalert cats and dogs out of the way. Once he let fly at a child's abandoned go-cart and she had visions immediately of a child being in it, but of course there wasn't.

And she began wondering what Mr. Arnold had looked like, felt like, in his hammock days. She began looking at the ads again but she didn't really want to leave Mr. Arnold's handsome old house with the third storey room full of studious books – not that Emma read any of them, but she liked the feel they gave the room, as if they were pleasant and kindly people – or maybe it was more that they were a sugar trap for pleasant and kindly people. Like Mr. Arnold's librarian daughter who came maybe to be with her books again, or even to watch the late news on the tiny colour television set and then say, somehow, to Emma: It's too bad, I know, all that trouble and killing, but it doesn't matter, when all is said and done, here.

Sometimes, if Mr. Arnold's cronies had been there all evening playing poker and smoking up a storm, Emma's head felt as though it at least wanted to 'translate' somewhere else, she didn't care where, as long as it was away from tobacco smoke. At first she had been pleased to be asked to play, to be coached from all sides of the table and allowed to get away with murder as far as the rules were concerned. It was even kind of exciting to have these old men telling you how quickly you caught on and offering to put up the nickels for you.

Eventually though, the smoke got to her, and lately, back in her safe upper storey, the door closed tightly, the window open to spring and opening apple blossoms, the night visitors became, somehow, more real and their words began to ring in her head. First they were simply the voices of the card players saying again over and over, Oh don't go yet, Emma, it's early! But as she sat silently there came the voices of ... well ... of 'others,' maybe even of Mr. Arnold's daughter, saying Leave here; go, go, go!

She didn't really want to but she started reading the newspaper ads again. There was no feeling of any kind, only a dullness in the heart, when she was reading the Help Wanted kind, but one night, her head filled with poker smoke, her eyes happened to fall on COMPANIONS WANTED and in less than a snap of the fingers her heart welled wide in the chest almost to bursting. For she could hear, could see him, a man of medium height, with greying hair, lots of it; dressed in a blue-grey suit, a three-piecer; saying in quiet, kindly tones: Are you a mature lady who puts friendship at the head of the list but isn't afraid of a little adventure? Let's make a new life together; age, colour and status no problem, I'm an Equal Opportunity Employer! Phone number please.

Then and there she sat down at Mr. Arnold's daughter's beautiful pale oak desk and wrote to the man. She never for one minute thought he might not answer.

For three weeks the time flew again and she even began listening once more to Mr. Arnold's war stories, saying Well, you don't say! or, Who would have believed it? in all the correct places. Then one morning very early, Mr. Arnold's daughter's phone rang, the phone Mr. Arnold now called Emma's phone. But it was Doris.

"Arthur Alfred is after you," she said. "Finally, after all this time, he phones. I bet he has another woman on the hook because he's threatening divorce unless you come back, he's just looking for a way around things, nowadays they have to give you half, get yourself a lawyer and don't let him wiggle out."

"Does he know where I am?" Emma felt she had to say *some*thing.

"Are you crazy? What do you take me for? I said we hadn't seen you, I said he'd better try the girls."

Emma's heart turned over. Topsy-turvy completely. She even saw it, a valentine heart, flopping itself end to end so that its rounded shoulders were bottom and its sharp bottom point was now the top and sticking like a knife-point into her breastbone. She hadn't thought of Arthur Alfred's daughters in a long time.

"He said he *wrote* them long ago," Doris said. "Leave it to good old A.A., he wouldn't get loosened up enough to phone long distance unless there was money waiting at the other end and guaranteed to pour out gold at his end. He was in Winnipeg he said to pick up a new honey wagon he said; maybe he thinks you'll hear the news and be impressed; if you go back to that miserable excuse for a polecat Emma, I swear to God I'll never forgive you."

"It's all right," Emma said. "Mr. Arnold has been asking when you're coming to see him."

"For God's sake, Emma, this is *important*! What are you gonna do? What are *we* gonna do?"

"No, really Doris, I told Mr. Arnold I'd ask the next time you phoned." Emma saw pictures of Doris' mind. It was scattered lightning. Red. Maybe the word was more like scarlet.

Then the lightning went blue and Doris said, "Oh I don't know, I get so bored with the old fart, make me some excuse, OK? I don't want to hurt his feelings, but ... oh for God sake, why are we talking about Mr. Arnold? Are you gonna be OK?"

"Yes," said Emma. She looked around the large bright room. The window curtains were a pale gold in the early morning sun; the books on the many shelves wished her kind words; outside, reaching towards her window, new apples were forming on sound new limbs. Mr. Arnold's daughter's room was becoming hers and she did not want to leave it, even to go below and cook Mr. Arnold's old-fashioned oatmeal breakfast or even to walk alone in the large greening garden in the early morning sun.

But she did those things anyway. She put Arthur Alfred out of her mind. And that night the man phoned. She almost didn't answer. She thought at first that maybe Arthur had tracked her down, how could he? the phone was still listed as for Mr. Arnold's daughter, but maybe Doris gave in? or Fred? the thoughts scatter about your head so, like lightning dancing on a white wire fence in a late summer storm while the phone rings once, twice, three times.

You reach over as in a dream, as if it is another you doing it, and he says – his voice like a movie star's or a preacher's – "Emma? I'm so looking forward to meeting you."

They met at McDonald's. He was so goodlooking, so neat and clean and so smiling with good white even teeth, and so quiet, that Emma knew he was the Companion she had wanted all her life. The hammock pictures did not even put themselves to the trouble of presenting themselves.

He asked if they could go to her place so they could talk better. Emma said, well, she kept house for an older man, but the kitchen there was very nice, how about that? He said, no, no, no, that really wouldn't do, they might be interrupted. Emma said, "Well, yes, it's true Mr. Arnold is quite a talker and if he comes and gets started, well! So what about where you live?" And the man said no, no, no, he had this teenage son and he could come home any time. And Emma said, "I'm looking forward to meeting him." And the man said, no, no, no, he's all upset about the divorce and that would make him angry. And Emma said, "Well, let's walk in the park then, there's one close by." And the man said, no, no, no, there were often bad people in the park, drunks and everything. "But," he said, "I really, really want to talk to you so don't you know some place we can go?"

She took him to Doris and Fred's. It was a week both worked days. And the man got very fond and for a while it felt very hammocky and everything although there weren't any pictures. But all at once Emma didn't feel good about it and she said, "It's too early, it's too quick, I wanted a friend first."

But it happened anyway. And it was really no different than with Arthur. And Emma offered to make tea so they could really talk and get to know each other but the man had an appointment and had to go.

"Maybe we can talk on the phone sometime then?" Emma said. "I have lots of time at night."

"Sure," the man said. "I'll give you a call."

"Or you could leave me *your* number," Emma said.

"Oh," said the man, "I live with these teenagers, you know, and you know these kids, always hanging on the phone, no, no, no, I wouldn't put you to the trouble, it's best if I do the calling." And he was gone.

She knew his first name. That was all. Well, and his face. And how he fit in a hammock, you might say. The words about that surprised Emma so, she had to smile in spite of herself.

She had a shower. Scoured herself with lots of lather. She washed the bedsheets and re-made the bed. Somehow she still smelled the good clean man smell of him. She locked the house behind her carefully, stowed the key carefully in a zippered side pocket of her purse – she'd promised Doris to take good care of it always – and found a bus to take her back to Mr. Arnold's place.

Three weeks later the man still hadn't called. The only pictures she was having lately were of gardens, green and diamond-sparkled with dew, and with flowers she didn't know splashed gold and crimson and purple slap-dash throughout the greenness.

Then, at breakfast, she was surprised to hear herself asking Mr. Arnold if she could have two weeks off for a holiday. "Not that living here isn't a holiday!" she was saying/somebody was saying (maybe, somehow, a Doris?).

She had already looked up the paper Doris had given her with the lawyer's name on it. Her bank book she left behind and anything new she had bought since she'd come to Winnipeg. She took a cab to the bus station and gave the driver two dollars for himself too. She didn't phone Doris. She would do that, long distance, from the farm.

The first thing she would say to Arthur Alfred would be, "Arthur, you talk too loud!"

She bet herself ten dollars there was an electric milking machine by now in the barn.

THE TALLEST MAN IN THE WORLD

Susan Swan

I WASN'T FRIGHTENED the day I met the tallest man in the world. My mother always told me men are the weaker sex. Of course, you have to be careful. If their aggression doesn't get you, their vulnerability could cripple you. Naturally, the tallest man in the world was a little bigger than I had counted on. I gulped when I saw him duck so his head didn't hit the marquee of the Wax Museum as he lumbered out to meet me. Look here, I told myself. He isn't a pop-eyed ogre from a children's fairy tale. He has on running shoes and jeans like you. Besides somebody your size has no reason to be scared of a man. You are six foot one in your stocking feet, and if a man sidles up and starts to pester you, you look down and give him the Toller Fish Eye which is famous in your town for making fools stop dead in their tracks.

"You must be Milt the Stilt," I called up, standing my ground. The giant shuffled closer in a clumsy, lurching gait. Then he jerked to a stop in front of me and I couldn't help noticing my eyes were level with his fly. I stared straight into his foot-long zipper and for a second or two, I admit, I felt impressed. The next thing I knew I heard a rumbling noise like water gurgling down a drain pipe and two rubbery lips flapped open above my head, exposing a palisade of teeth.

"You must be from the Bulletin," the giant said, staring at something across the street instead of looking down at me. "My real name is Milton Shakespeare O'Brien."

"And I'm Judy Churchill Mackenzie King Toller," I said. "My father was partial to politicians."

"Don't hold my fancy moniker against me. My ma fancied poets, she did." The giant extended a huge hand and I shook two of his long, rubbery fingers. Then I craned my neck to see if he was friendly but the giant's eyes were hidden behind a pair of kid's sunglasses. The tiny white plastic frames divided his huge moon face into two halves of sweaty, porous skin. "It must be fun to show yourself off for a living," I said.

"I'm an accountant, Judy. I only do a gig like this when I'm short of cash." The giant sighed and stared over my head again so I sneaked another look at his fly and then I saw what lay hidden behind the teeth of his zipper. *It* was the length of a telephone pole: a club of flesh that could split a woman in two with a single stroke.

As I stared, the giant hitched up his pants, smoothing out the wrinkles across his hips and I thought, watch out, the brute knows you're looking there. Then he raised his hand as if he wanted to grab me by my hair so I moved back another step or two, not enough for him to notice. Look Milt the Stilt, I wanted to say, if you so much as lay a finger on me, I'll punch you in the balls.

I waited for Milt to make his move but nothing happened. Instead I felt a breeze by my ear and I realized Milt's hand had soared far into the air. Just by his chin, it paused, and a silver gold line of sunlight lit up the edges of his swollen fingers. The next thing I knew the hand alighted on the skin of his perspiring forehead and five big fingers walked down the bridge of his shiny nose and adjusted the tiny green sunglasses. I dropped my head way back so I could see what the hand was going to do next and suddenly it fell out of the sky, right at me. I dodged to the side and the hand stopped at his belt and old Milt hitched up his pants again.

"How much are you getting for the Shriners picnic?" I asked hastily.

"Not enough," he groaned.

I am an experienced reporter with a slew of interviews under my belt and I know there is no way to force somebody to talk before they're ready. I usually stay friendly and maintain eye contact. Of course, the latter was a little hard to do with the tallest man in the world. Whistling, I stuck my notepad into my purse, careful not to look at his mammoth zipper. Think of something ridiculous, I told myself – like the British giant Milton Shakespeare O'Brien in

Stanfield long underwear. But do you think I could conjure up a picture of Milt in long johns? Not me. Instead, I saw him from the waist down in nothing but skin-coloured briefs, and the sight of ordinary nylon stretched out of shape like that made my skin start to creep. To settle my nerves, I turned my back and began to fiddle with my camera.

"You're a photographer too?" Milt sounded impressed.

"I'm a two-way reporter," I said. "The union lets me take pictures. There isn't another woman like me in the newsroom."

"I bet," he chuckled. "It's not every day I get to meet a tall girl like you."

I made a scoffing noise, then I pulled myself up to my full height and we began to walk slowly up the hill. Only a pair of Shriners dressed in tasseled fezzes and ruby jackets stopped to stare. It was very humid for June and perspiration was making my blouse stick to a spot between my shoulder blades. Ahead of me, Milt's immense shadow swayed on the pavement. I began walking very quickly, so my shadow didn't disappear inside his.

Halfway up the hill, Milt began shuffling his feet and making funny, puffing groans as if he was in pain. "I say!" he shouted. "Would you slacken your pace?"

I turned and a lanky, blonde girl in a store window turned too. One of her hands steadied a camera around her neck while the other hand held a long brass hunting horn. She wore a wide-brimmed hat with a drooping red feather and a green tunic with pointy calfskin boots. On her belt, embroidered in letters of gold, I read the words:

> *Judy the Giant Killer*
> *Here's the Right Valiant Niagara Girl*
> *Who Vowed to Slay the Monster Milt.*

The girl's fierce young face stared at something beyond the edge of the glass window. I stared there too and saw a goggle-headed monster, a cyclops in sunglasses, standing ankle-deep in Shriners. The Shriners wore their funny red coats and tasseled hats and they were climbing hand over hand up the hairs that grew as thick as rods of iron from the giant's calf. As soon as the little men reached the giant's bald kneecaps, the ogre laughed with a funhouse menace and brushed them to the ground where he squashed them under the heels of his seven-league running shoes.

I looked higher and the next thing I saw were ten shrieking Shriner women strung to the ogre's belt. As I watched, the giant plucked up one of

*the screaming women and, holding his victim by the hair, drew her toward
his gaping, snaggle-toothed mouth.*

I turned away from the store window and the giant caught up,
breathing hard. "The old joints aren't what they should be, Judy."
He pointed apologetically to his knees. "You'd think a man my size
would be able to go twice as fast, wouldn't you?" His large head
wobbled slowly back and forth. "Well, looks can be deceiving."

We stopped in front of a steakhouse and he rested his hand on
the top of the doorframe.

I stood back to take a picture. But even from this distance, it was
impossible to get all of Milt's long-legged body in the camera
frame, and the tiny, white-rimmed sunglasses made his face look
odd.

"Take off your sunglasses, Milt" I called.

*The blonde girl put the horn to her lips and blew. Tantivy, tantivy. The
ogre seemed not to hear. Instead, his mouth yawned so far apart his green
bespectacled face appeared astonished, and then, with a flick of his two-
foot tongue, the giant licked up the tiny screaming woman and sucked her
in through the arch of his flabby, grinning lips.*

*Once again, the blonde girl blew her horn. Tantivy, tantivy! The ogre
stopped chewing and sniffed the air, an arm drooling from the corner of
his mouth like a noodle of spaghetti.*

I hastily put my camera away and walked into the restaurant.
The mouth of the maître d' made a small O of surprise and I knew
Milt was standing behind me. Then the maître d' led us to a dark
corner in the shadowy room. We sat down and I ordered mineral
water for me and wine for Milt and made it clear I was paying. Men
think you owe them a favour if you let them buy you things and I
didn't want Milt to accuse me of leading him on.

"So let's get down to business," I said with the old Toller
confidence and pulled out my notepad again.

"Rightie-ho, Judy!" Milt smiled and took off his weird sunglasses and I noticed for the first time that his eyes were brown.

"I say, this is pleasant!" he said. "A tall gent like me coming to a
toney joint with a girl like you."

"You claim to be the world's tallest man," I said, ignoring his
attempt to butter me up. "Isn't the American giant bigger?"

"The American giant hasn't been measured in years," Milt
leaned toward me, and for a second I could have sworn he pressed

one of his huge knees against mine. Then the pressure went away and he hissed, "The poor blighter can't stand up to be measured for the title because he has spinal curvature."

"Why, that's terrible!" I said and Milt nodded at my solemn face.

"At least, he doesn't have to strut about like me." Milt held his glass to the light and swirled his cheap Niagara wine as if it was imported, and I realized he was nice-looking in a white-skinned, dark-haired, English way. "You don't know how bored I get, Judy, saying the same things over and over." He began to speak in a sing-songy rumble. "I'm Milt the Stilt, the world's tallest man." He paused and mimicked a glazed smile. "I'm seven foot six and the main reason I'm so tall is that my pituitary gland went a bit berserk and didn't know when to call it a day."

The giant laughed and picked up the bottle to pour himself another glass. "I'd wager you know what it's like. You're tall for a girl."

"Boys used to try to measure me at school dances," I said.

"Not very chivalrous of my sex, was it?" He leaned over and filled up my glass with yellow wine before I could stop him.

"Or maybe you don't drink on the job?" Milt grinned. "It leads to shenanigans with the blokes I bet."

"Nothing I can't handle," I said and then I took a sip just to show him wine has no effect on us Tollers because alcohol takes twice as long to make it through our bodies.

"Bravo, I knew you were a sport the moment I saw you." Milt patted me on the shoulder and I felt the damp heat from his fingers through the material of my blouse. The warmth felt nice in the air-conditioned restaurant but I frowned and he took his hand away. I looked down at my own hands with their slim, tapered fingers. Just because I'm a little taller than ordinary, people think I like men big. But a woman like me has no interest in tall men. Their stilt-like legs and flapping elbows digging at you through the air are waste-ful and sloppy! Tall men are too demanding. Even their height is an order: take me seriously. I like small men, the shorter the better. Their size is more economical and they fit in so nicely anywhere.

I glared at Milt but he just kept smiling and filling my glass with more wine. "I may be oversized, but the last thing a bloke like me wants is for my height to come between me and my friends," he winked. "Did you know, Judy, everything in my house is normal size? You could visit my home and sit on a regular sofa."

He pointed to his sunglasses on the table. "Just like my shades," he said proudly. Milt paused and poured another glass of wine for himself. "I tell you it was a bloody thrill to walk into a store and buy something off the rack like everybody else."

"So that's why I thought you were wearing kid's sunglasses!" I said. "On you, average size looks small!" Then I scowled in case I had hurt Milt's feelings.

Before Milt could answer, a man in an orange clown suit and horn-rimmed spectacles put out a hand and grabbed our wine bottle. Milt said, "Oh-oh" and the man lifted up the bottle like a trophy to show two men standing behind us in Shriners' fezzes.

"It's a dead soldier all right," one of the men said, the tassel on his ruby hat jiggling.

The man in the orange clown suit banged the bottle down on the table.

"My name is Ed Ernshaw," he grinned. "We're here for the big fella."

"You're Milt's manager?" I said.

"In a manner of speaking," Ed Ernshaw snickered. "Our temple's rented him for the evening."

"Your temple can wait," the giant said suddenly. "Judy and I are going to have dinner."

"You can have dinner with her after the show. Can't he, Judy?" Ed Ernshaw smiled at me and I was too taken aback to say yes or no and then Ed said, "Come on, boys, do your damndest."

"Ups-a-daisy," one of the Shriners said and began to tug at Milt's elbow. The other man laughed and pulled at the neck of his t-shirt the way a parent will tug a child.

"Just between us, Milton Shakespeare O'Brien is a little uncomfortable with show business," Ed said in a loud voice.

"Pipe down, will you!" Milt groaned. Standing up, he was twice as tall as the Shriners whose fezzes came to his hips. Then I stood up slowly, grabbing the back of my chair to steady myself.

"Will you look at the size of her!" Ed Ernshaw said and the other two Shriners laughed. "Milt the Stilt has found someone almost as tall as himself." And suddenly I felt as if I was in a small body, not my six-foot-one Toller body which gives me confidence.

Ed drove the long way to avoid the crowds so nobody could see Milt before the show. We circled around past the falls which frothed thick as milk in the distance. And then Ed parked the Volkswagen in a back alley and Milt said "I'll see you after the show, Judy," in an excited hopeful voice that made my breath catch in my throat and I followed Ed into the museum. My legs shook a little as we walked down a long, dim hall. Not that I was frightened. Who me? With a case of nerves? I was all right even if I'd polished off a glass of wine or two I'd have been better off without. On either side of me I saw things in badly-lit display cases but I couldn't make out what they were. Then we entered a circular room called the Human Being Gallery. Its walls contained more of the display cases I'd seen in the hall, except now I could make out their contents.

The first glass case contained life-size wax replicas of the world's fattest twins. The next case contained a miniature woman in an old-fashioned gown holding hands with a miniature man. Next to the midgets I spied something too big for a display case. It wore glasses to hide its empty eye sockets and a tie and a shiny green business suit, and on its chest a sign said: Mount the steps and see the world through the eyes of an eight-foot-eleven man.

Then I saw Milt sitting beside the effigy in a huge chintz armchair and the way he was sitting, lost and alone, made my confidence start to slip. I wanted to shout – Milt, for God's sake, do something. Anything! Just don't slump there in your chair with a miserable look on your huge moon face! As soon as Milt saw me, he winked one of his brown eyes but I gave him the famous Toller scowl and looked off in the other direction. Then the fezzed heads of the Shriners tilted back and the crowd made a collective "Oh" and I knew Milt had stood up.

"I'm the world's tallest man and my name is Milton Shakespeare O'Brien. My ma fancied poets, she did," I heard him begin and I wondered if he was wearing the same glazed smile he had mimicked for me at dinner, but I didn't turn want to turn and find out. I took a breath to steady myself and stared up at the slowly revolving blades of the old wood fan on the ceiling. The heat from the crowd of bodies was making me faint. Then I heard a Shriner ask, "Why aren't you married?" And I heard Milt say, "I'm working on it, aren't I Judy?" And the Shriners laughed way too loudly and he lifted his free hand and beckoned for me to join him and I felt the last of the old Toller confidence run down my legs and out my toes.

Judy the Giant Killer was in peril. Dozens of miniature hands were carrying her toward a thick beanstalk that stretched high into the clouds. The poor girl couldn't move. The wretched trolls had fed the valiant giant killer a drug that had sapped Judy of her strength. It was very dark because the towering stalk blotted out the sun. As Judy's eyes grew accustomed to the darkness, she could make out the spidery ridges that swarmed up the base of the thing. It seemed to give off a pulsing heat that grew more unbearable the closer they came. At the top of the strange stalk sprouted a giant mushroom-cap.

"Ups-a-daisy!" the trolls cried and they pushed Judy onto the rubbery vine. She threw her arms around it and the thing wobbled, once, twice, and then was still.

"Climb! Climb!" the little men shouted. But the valiant girl clung to the stalk and did not move.

I shook my head to show Milt he couldn't play on my sympathies. Then I turned and jostled my way through the Shriners. Once I was outside the door of the Human Being Gallery I stuffed my notepad into my purse and ran down the dim hall as fast as I could, my long legs trembling. At the door of the museum office I stopped and caught my breath. To my surprise, Ed Ernshaw appeared behind me.

"You're not leaving?" he said. "The big fella's counting on dinner with you after the show." Then he took my arm and pulled me into an office. He picked up a phone and yelled into the receiver: "Get the big fella down here! The reporter has to go!"

He jumped in front of the door to keep me from leaving and in the next second, I heard heavy footsteps crashing along the hall. Then Milt rushed in and the other two Shriners rushed in after him and then everybody rushed out of the room so Milt the Stilt could be alone with me.

Milt stopped panting and said, "Will you come up for a pint? I have a deluxe hotel room, Judy, with a kitchen suite."

"I have a boyfriend," I said quickly. "I don't see anybody but him."

"I say old girl, you're not scared to come up for one little drink, are you?" Milt said smiling. "How can one little drink hurt?"

"Us Tollers are not afraid of anything," I said. And I followed him back down the long hall and then up the fire escape until we were standing in a room with long red brocade curtains and a fridge with a sticker on its door that said "Good things come in big packages." The bed lay beside the fridge, normal-size. Milt sighed and took off his t-shirt and lay down across the middle of the bed resting his feet on a chair placed next to the bed for that purpose. He pointed to the fridge and said, "Be a luv and fetch us some pints, will you? I'm a little nackered after the show."

I did what he said as if I didn't have a care in the world, but out of the corner of my eye I couldn't help noticing his big red nipples which stuck straight up in the air like suction cups you see sometimes on the tips of darts. Then I lay down beside him as if I had sex with a giant every day and when he reached over and began to unbutton my blouse, I didn't object. I closed my eyes so I didn't have to see what his long fingers were up to and I felt very noble and very kind and very desirable – all three things at once because I was giving in gracefully, so to speak, to a man the size of an elephant.

The pulsing heat from the rubber stalk was beginning to make Judy sleepy. The poor girl could hardly manage to cling to it while the trolls pinched her bottom and yelled "You lazy girl! shinny higher!" Suddenly, she heard the noise of thunder. She stared up as far as the eye could see and a droplet of rain wobbled down the hood of the mushroom cap. For a second, it hung suspended on the rim of the cap – a pear-shaped drop as big as a cathedral – and then it fell, drowning three trolls at once. There was another clap, and then another, and then another, and a voice called out "What big hands I have!" Now Judy realized the sound of thunder was the noise of the giant crying. "What big teeth I have. And what a big ...." The giant sobbed again and Judy wanted to put her hands to her ears ....

"Need you have," the trolls answered. "All the better to impale her with, O Great Blunderbore."

And finally – oh and finally – I got my nerve up and opened my eyes. Then I looked down and there it was pointing east to the refrigerator, small and soft above a springy growth of dark hair, like a sleeping dormouse. Milt looked down too and his perspiring moon face crumpled as if he was going to cry. So I touched its pink nose and made a cooing sound as if I was talking to a baby or a kitten and then I kissed it and did some other things besides until I could feel the sweat running down my forehead onto my nose. Then I noticed the shaking bed and I realized Milt was crying. And I said, "It's normal," and he sobbed, "Not to me. I haven't had sex for three years." And I started to tell him there were other things we could do if he wanted to fool around but he wouldn't listen and he began to moan, "Judy! I have hurt you! I have let you down!" I said I didn't mind a bit but he kept on sobbing until the sheet was drenched and the pillow too. I swore on a stack of bibles that I wasn't disappointed, not me, but he only howled louder so finally I gave up trying to comfort Milt. And I put my blouse back on and my pants too and all the time Milt lurched around the hotel room, sobbing, and plucking at me with his long rubbery fingers. "Judy! Judy! Say you forgive me! I had too much to drink!" he wailed and I said, "Milt, you don't understand me. I'm not the type to hold a grudge." Then I walked out into the hall and Milt followed me, wailing to beat the band, so I started to run, taking the steps down the fire escape two at a time, and Milt began to hurry too. At the front of the museum, a bunch of Shriners stood watching a sword-swallower do his act. A roar went up through the crowd as soon as they saw Milt lumbering toward me with his long arms outstretched and a terrible pleading look on his face and Ed and his two assistants swarmed around the giant and pushed him back inside so the Shriners didn't get to see him for free. I walked away as slow as you please and when I got to the end of the lineup, where I could see the Bulletin office over the tops of the Shriners' fezzes, I stopped and called with my old Toller confidence, "So long, Milt."

TO A FAIRER PLACE

Helen J. Rosta

T HE NIGHT BEFORE we visited my brother's grave, we sat
with the Langfords in their garden. David and Eva Langford,
hosts of our bed-and-breakfast. Thomas and I were the only foreign guests and the Langfords had made something of a fuss over
us. They talked of a holiday in Canada and we invited them to visit
us, said we'd drive them through the Rockies.

My brother never saw the Rockies; he went from the prairies to
training camp and then to England and the Second World War.
He's buried in the Thames Valley, at Oxford Cemetery. Flying
Officer Allen Richard Bancroft of the Royal Canadian Air Force.
He was 22 years old.

That evening in the curiously-muted light, the Langford's garden seemed an alien place, the plants strange to me, part of an unfa-
miliar terrain. But, suddenly, unexpectedly, in the pervasive fragrance, I caught a note that reminded me of a prairie flower – the
tiny yellow star of the silver willow.

I asked Eva Langford if I could take some flowers from her garden to place on my brother's grave.

She shook her head in a slow, side-to-side motion.

"No."

I felt as if I had swallowed a stone.

◊

It is the fall of 1936 and my brother is leaving home. He's starting
high school and is going to board in Clintin. Clintin is only thirty
miles away but when blizzards close the roads, it might as well be a
hundred.

210

"I've seen enough drought and depression for the two of us," my father says. He winks at Allen. "With an education under your belt, you'll be driving around the country collecting mortgages."

Mother looks up from packing Allen's suitcase. "And the neighbours will hate us."

"Never mind that. He'll be so flush, he can help put Susan through."

"Aw, Susie doesn't want to go to high school," Allen teases. "She's going to marry Delbert Black."

Delbert Black is mean and snotty but aside from that, I'm not going to marry anyone. I pummel Allen's stomach.

Allen sweeps me over his shoulder and holds me there, arms and legs flailing.

Susie's mad and I'm glad and I know what to please her.
A bottle of wine to make her shine.
A bottle of ink to make her stink.
And ...

Allen gives me a bear hug as he sets me down, "Delbert Black to squeeze her."

"Susan isn't going to marry Delbert Black," my father says. "She'll go to high school just like you."

I smirk at Allen but inside I'm cowed by my future, town boys and girls, the big red, brick school in Clintin.

◊

Thomas broke the silence. "This house," he said, "wears the patina of time. It's absolutely charming."

I looked up at the Langford's home – ivy-covered, dark and mossy, as if its brick walls had grown out of the earth – and thought of the only brick building in Clintin, Allen's school, my school. I recalled it, at that moment, not as the grand and forbidding structure of my childhood, but as a thing reduced, a raw, exposed brick box dropped on the edge of town.

◊

Allen is gone and my mother is getting me ready for school – the little one-room schoolhouse a mile from home. She runs a comb through my ringlets, reties my belt, pats me reassuringly. "There." Hands me my lunch pail. "You're on your own now. Better hurry. I don't want you late the first day."

I start across the field, following the path that for two years I had walked with Allen. The path is narrow. We walked Indian file, Allen leading the way, brushing aside barbed rose bushes, breaking trail in winter.

I want to turn back and run home when Greenfield School looms before me. I climb through the fence.

The boys are playing ball, Delbert Black pitching, Bill Whitney at bat, Edna Gilbert's brother, John, with his big catcher's glove raised, squatting behind the plate. The Bouchers – one, two, three, four, five, like steps on a ladder – are on the bases and in the outfield.

Edna and Amy wave to me from the school steps. We are the only girls in Greenfield School.

I walk across the yard, feeling vulnerable even after I reach the steps and we three link arms.

"Our new teacher's name's Miss Bennett," Amy tells me. "And there are new kids. The Corys."

"Girls?" I ask hopefully.

Amy holds up one finger. "But she's only in grade one."

"They moved into that old MacDonald house," Edna says. "Lock, stock, and barrel over the weekend."

The MacDonald house sits north of the school, just beyond the fence. It may have been painted once, but now it's weathered black and some of the windows are broken; the house has been empty a long time.

"They're renting," Amy says.

Edna lifts her eyebrows, tilts her chin the way her mother does. "We're footing the bill. The Corys are on Relief and the rent's coming out of our taxes."

"That's because Mr. Cory is turning to stone," Amy announces.

"Stone!" There's a picture of a stone man in Allen's history book – Admiral Nelson standing on his column. But that's in England, a million miles away. "Stone!" I repeat in awe.

"My dad says Mr. Cory can't even get out of bed, that he's just lying there in a back room, turning to stone."

"Where'd he start turning?" I ask.

"Who knows? Maybe he's just petrifying like an old tree."

Edna grimaces. "Ugh! Makes me sick. And that old MacDonald house ... I bet it has mice and bats and bugs. Bedbugs!"

Miss Bennet, a short, plump woman in a white blouse and navy skirt, comes out and rings the bell. The boys yell and throw the ball back and forth as they run toward the school. We girls walk sedately through the cloakroom, the little antechamber to the building. It's called the cloakroom but is never used as one; it's full of flies in spring and fall and too cold in winter.

The new kids are hanging there in the dim light of the dirty window. They draw back as we pass.

"Phew!" Edna exclaims.

Jason, Edgar and Nadine Cory. Edgar is the one who smells. He wets his pants. Wets them the minute Miss Bennett asks him to read; she doesn't notice.

Edgar and Nadine are plain and sallow with drab brown hair and flat, pale eyes. But Jason is beautiful; he has dark, wavy hair, deep blue eyes and the longest eyelashes I've ever seen. I think he should have been a girl.

I notice right away the boys don't like him. When Miss Bennett's back is turned, Delbert Black slides a note onto Jason's desk.

Jason turns red, crumples the paper into a small wad and drops it.

"Sissy," Delbert hisses.

Miss Bennet stops writing on the blackboard and glances around. By then, Delbert is hunched over his scribbler, looking innocent.

At recess, the boys get the ball and bat. Jason trails after them but John Gilbert pokes him with the bat.

"We don't want no Relief bums."

"No bums and no sissies," Delbert mutters.

"No bums no sissies, no bums no sissies," the Bouchers echo.

Jason shrinks back at the door and Edgar and Nadine sidle up to him and huddle in a clinging way.

Miss Bennett, who is reading at her desk, looks up. "All of you go outside and get some fresh air. And close the door quietly behind you."

Edna tugs at Amy and me. "Come on."

The Corys follow us but hang back in the cloakroom.

"London Bridge," Edna proclaims.

We skip down the steps. Edna and Amy join hands and raise their arms.

> London Bridge is falling down,
> Falling down, falling down.

London Bridge is falling down
My fair lady.
I pass under their arms and am caught.
The Cory kids come out onto the steps.
I take Edna's hands and Amy passes under.
There aren't enough of us girls to play any game properly.
"Hey, Nadine," I call. "Want to play?"
Jason pulls Nadine from behind him and gives her a light shove.
"Don't come near me," Edna shrieks. "I don't want lice."
Amy drops her outstretched hand.
"Hair lice," Edna chants, "fleas and bedbugs." She grabs Amy and me and spins us around. "Good night. Sleep tight. Don't let the bedbugs bite."
We whirl, dizzily, in our small circle.

◊

We bade the Langfords good night and climbed the stairs to our room.

"Well that was strange," Thomas said. "A garden full of flowers and she couldn't spare even a little bouquet for your brother's grave."

I lay awake in the heavy darkness, remembering the slow motion of Eva Langford's head, the precise "No" falling from her lips. Its meaning was hidden, as concealed from me as the mysteries of my childhood – the look that passed between my parents that Sunday evening when the radio voice announced Britain's declaration of war; Allen's Air Force portrait disappearing from the cluster of pictures on the sideboard. Something I shouldn't ask about.

Years later, my mother told me, "After the telegram came, your father couldn't bear to look at it."

◊

Thanksgiving weekend, we pick up Allen in Clintin. When I see my brother coming down the steps of his boarding house, dressed in good clothes and carrying books under his arm, I think that higher education and town-life have changed him.

Allen tosses the books onto the seat and slides into the car.

"I hope," Mother says, " you don't plan to bury your head in those books."

"Worrywart," Allen laughs. "I have a few assignments. They won't take long."

Assignments? "Homework," he would have said before. But then he grabs a ringlet and gives a gentle tug, "How's Delbert Black?" and I relax.

We drive slowly down Main Street.

"There's Mrs. Gilbert," my mother says and waves.

Edna and her mother are coming out of the Star Cafe. Behind them – and this is what catches my eye – are two town girls. I know they're town girls by the way they're walking, sort of like high-stepping horses, prancing along and tossing their heads.

"Those girls in your class?" I ask.

"They're sophomores."

I ignore "sophomores" which I don't know the meaning of and poke him with my elbow.

"You're blushing."

"Am not."

"Are too," I say and add, "Mrs. Cory has hair like that."

"Who's Mrs. Cory?"

"New people," my mother tells him. "They've moved into the old MacDonald house. Poor woman, she's got a hard row to hoe. Three children and a sick husband."

"And yellow hair," Allen says.

"Yes," my mother laughs. "And yellow hair."

Tuesday morning, the Cory kids are late again and Miss Bennett scolds them.

They're late because they linger across the fence until the bell rings. At recess they'll get as far as the cloakroom. The cloakroom is dim and dusty in the October light and its windowsill is covered with dead flies.

Miss Bennett doesn't make us clean it up. She spends recesses and noon hours correcting our scribblers or writing exercises on the blackboard. She goes out only to ring the bell or – rarely – to the toilet.

The first recess, we girls are at the back, getting snacks from our lunch pails. We'll eat them outside in the sun and talk about the weekend – where we went, who came to visit, what we ate.

We open the classroom door and step into the cloakroom.

The boys have Jason down, pinned to the floor in a snarl of bodies. John's hand is clamped over his mouth.

Jason is struggling. His eyes bulge and clammy sweat stands on his forehead.

White-faced, Nadine and Edgar cringe against the wall.

"What's going on?" I ask loudly.

"Shut your mouth," Delbert snaps. "And shut that door."

John Gilbert crouches over Jason. "Bet you didn't get no Thanksgiving dinner."

"Yah," Delbert adds, "bet your Mamma spent all that Relief cheque ...."

"Our money."

"Yah, our money. Bet she spent it on pretty petticoats and underpants. Lacy ones from Eaton's catalogue. And you didn't get no turkey."

"We won't see you go hungry." John Gilbert jumps up and scoops a handful of flies from the windowsill. "Open wide."

The Bouchers pry at Jason's jaws.

I hear strangled retching.

My stomach churns; bile rises in my throat.

Finally, John says, "Guess he's had enough."

Moaning and spewing vomit, Jason rushes outside.

I clench my hands into fists. I want to light into them, blackening eyes, breaking noses, pounding those smirks into their faces ....

Instead, I stammer, "If my brother was here, you couldn't do that. You wouldn't dare."

"John, that's awful," Edna says, disgusted. "I'm going to tell on you."

John grabs Edna and shoves her against the wall. "You keep your mouth shut or it'll end up full of flies. And that goes for the rest of you."

My mother is kneading bread at the kitchen table when I walk in.

As always, she asks, "What happened at school today?"

I hang my coat on the peg by the door and empty my lunch pail before I answer.

"I saw an airplane."

That too. We heard the drone, at first faint and then louder and louder. Everyone strained toward the windows and Miss Bennett stopped talking in mid-sentence.

"It went right over the school. Teacher let us all go out and look at it. It flew west and got smaller and smaller until it was small as a bird and then it disappeared."

My mother takes her hands from the dough and dusts them on her apron.

"I wish I'd seen it," she says in a disappointed voice. "I always wonder what keeps them up there."

◊

We took the train at Paddington station. I held a bouquet of roses Thomas had bought at a florist's, twelve perfect roses, long-stemmed with blunt thorns and dark-red blossoms.

Allen cut roses for me from the tangle of bushes along our path.

Prairie roses. Five pink unfurled petals, a golden heart. Thorns like needles. He'd wrap the stems in a handkerchief, his scarf, anything that was handy. "Careful, Susie."

He wrote a poem about thorns and roses in my autograph book:

> This life that we are living in
> Is mighty hard to beat
> You get a thorn with every rose
> But aren't the roses sweet?

The train passed into a gentle countryside.

A foreign, but a familiar landscape. After we sang "God Save the King" and saluted the Union Jack, my eyes dropped to the old print hanging under the flag. A misty sky, a fairy tale castle framed by great brooding trees – unlike any trees I had ever seen.

An English landscape imprinted on my mind. And English poetry committed to memory.

> I saw the spires of Oxford
> As I was passing by,
> The grey spires of Oxford
> Against a pale-grey sky.
> My heart was with the Oxford men
> Who went abroad to die.

◊

January 3, 1937. The holidays are over. Allen is gone and my mother and I are taking down the Christmas tree.

I made a New Year's resolution to stick up for the Corys, but backed down on that and decided instead to give Nadine a doll for her birthday.

Mother places the glass balls carefully in their box and puts the popcorn strings into a bag to be taken out to the birds.

I stand on a chair and reach for the silver star at the top of the tree.

"Starlight. Star bright. May I get this wish I make tonight. Wish I didn't have to go to school tomorrow."

"You're lucky you can go to school," my mother scolds. "There are plenty who can't. I hope Allen remembers that. While you're wishing, wish he didn't have such a crush on that girl. I worry it'll affect his studies."

"What girl?"

"That blond. And she's older than he is."

"The yellow-haired girl! So that was her picture in his wallet. I thought it was a movie star."

"Susan! You're not to snoop in Allen's things."

"I didn't," I say, offended. "He showed it to me. He said she was a movie star."

I jump down from the chair and dance around the room. "Allen's mad and I'm glad and I know what to please him. A bottle of wine to make him shine. A bottle of ink ...."

"Susan," my mother snaps. "Stop that nonsense. This minute. Right now. You hear!"

◊

Allen's history book became mine. He'd written on the fly leaf: Allen Richard Bancroft, Grade Seven, 1933, Greenfield School, Alberta, Canada, North America, World, the Universe.

The day I stood in Trafalgar Square and looked up at Admiral Nelson, the stone man, gazing down from his column, I could feel that book in my hands, touch the crackle on the face of the photograph, smell the must of the yellowing pages.

"With pardonable vanity the gallant Nelson had arrayed himself in full uniform, and had worn his stars and orders. He was thus a mark for enemy sharpshooters and fell with his backbone shot through. 'Now I am satisfied. Thank God I have done my duty.'"

◊

On Saturdays, when my parents buy groceries at the Greenfield Store, we stop at the Corys on our way home. I'm glad it's not a school day so that no one sees our car there.

My mother always inquires about Mr. Cory's health and when she does, I glance toward the dark hallway that leads to the bedrooms. I long to see him.

But Mrs. Cory never takes us in. She smooths back her pale yellow hair and says, "He's about as well as can be expected."

My father sits at the kitchen table, sipping watery tea and looking uncomfortable until Mother gets around to the real reason we dropped in.

She starts with a nervous laugh. "I visited at the store while John did the shopping and, my goodness, he bought so many oranges ... they had a good price on dried fruit today ...."

Then my father exclaims that he'd better bring in the groceries "or before you know it they'll be frozen." Soon, there's a little pile of our groceries on the Corys' table.

As we drive away, I picture the back room, Mr. Cory lying on the bed, turning to stone. One day, I tell myself, he'll make a fine statue. Everyone – even the Gilberts and the Blacks – will come from miles around to see him. And his children will be proud.

◊

Thomas took the bouquet from me and held it to his face. "Odourless," he said sadly. "They've bred the smell right out of them."

◊

We are eating supper when the knock sounds. My father answers the door and comes back with a telegram, the envelope unopened, in his hand. His face is white.

My mother doesn't speak. She gets up and starts clearing the table with quick, jerky motions. Then my father takes her arm and leads her to the living-room.

I follow.

Their heads bend in the circle of lamplight. When they look up, their eyes don't see me.

"Allen's gone," my mother says.

Gone?

She means "dead."

Still, I search for Allen. Every time we go to Clintin, I peer around the corners. I make excuses to walk past the school, expecting to see him coming down the steps.

At night, when I can't sleep, I sneak out to look for him. Sometimes the sky is so full of stars, it makes me dizzy.

◊

Outside the train window, a tidy landscape glided by. Scars healed – or hidden in a mantle of green. A peaceful landscape.

> They left the peaceful river,
> The cricket field, the quad,
> The shaven lawns of Oxford,
> To seek a bloody sod –
> They gave their merry youth away
> For country and for God.

The train picked up the rhythm and ran the words over and over in my head.

◊

"Wednesday, June 30, 1937," I write in my scribbler. Last day of school.

The Corys almost sparkle.

At recess Miss Bennett writes out report cards. She looks up sharply when Amy approaches her desk.

"All of you get outside. You Corys too."

The Corys leave their desks reluctantly. For a long time now, they've dawdled in class and Miss Bennett has been keeping them in recesses.

"It's a beautiful day," Miss Bennett says. "Why would you want to stay inside on a day like this?"

The boys are playing Aunty High Over, throwing the ball over the school. They never let us girls play that; they say we can't throw high enough and we'll break a window.

John Gilbert sees the Corys first. "Hey guys," he shouts, " the bums have come out. Let's get 'em."

As one, the Corys shrink back toward the classroom but John cuts them off.

The boys burst past us. They grab Edgar and Nadine and throw them to the cloakroom floor.

"You guys didn't get no din-din last time," John Gilbert says. "We've got a real treat for you. Fresh flies."

"Yah," Delbert laughs, "fresh born in horse shit."

◊

We changed trains at Redding. I had bought a paperback at the station but it lay beside me, unopened. I took the book I'd brought from home out of my tote bag. "At the Oxford Cemetery, there are more Canadian airmen buried. In the military portion of the cemetery 98 members of Canadian bomber crews rest among 743 graves of their comrades-in-arms."

> God rest you, merry gentlemen,
> Who laid your good lives down,
> Who took the khaki and the gun
> Instead of cap and gown.
> God bring you to a fairer place
> Than even Oxford town.

◊

My father and I are in Clintin's general store. I've picked a doll for Nadine, a red-cheeked doll with blue eyes, blond molded waves for hair and a pink ribbon tied through a hoop at the top of her head.

My father is trying to talk me out of the doll. "For that money, we could get them a box of groceries. Something for the whole family."

"I want the doll."

"Think of the others," my father says. "I know that poor woman goes hungry so her children can eat. Wouldn't you rather put food on their table than buy a doll?"

I shake my head. "Nadine's never had a doll. She told me." I feel my eyeballs sting. In a few minutes, I will start to sniffle.

"Oh, all right." My father lifts the doll from the shelf. "I'll buy the doll. But it's against my better judgment."

◊

Allen and I are driving to Clintin.

He's looking pleased with himself, proud that Father's let him take the car.

"Now don't let Susan out of your sight," Mother told him and Allen had laughed in a grown-up way.

"Heck, Clintin's not big enough to get lost in."

We pass the Cory house and I catch a glimpse of Mrs. Cory on the steps, shielding her eyes and looking toward the road.

Allen sees her too. "Dad says they're poorer than church mice. The Relief cheque doesn't stretch to the end of the month. They must be scraping the bottom of the barrel by now."

"I gave Nadine Cory a doll for her birthday," I brag. I don't dare say anything about the Corys eating flies; he'll tell our parents and they'll go to the others. I feel sick at the thought of flies in my mouth. I put the Corys out of my mind.

The sky is bluer than a robin's egg. A hot wind blowing through the open windows ruffles our hair. We are driving south, straight into the blazing sun.

Allen takes a hand from the steering wheel and pats his pocket. "I'm feeling flush today. After we've picked up that piece for the mower, I'll treat you to an ice cream in the Star Cafe."

"I want a banana split!"

"Wow! You'll break the first guy who dates you."

"Takes a long time to eat a banana split. Maybe the yellow-haired girl will come in. 'Allen's mad and I'm glad and I know what to please him ....' I bet you've kissed her, haven't you?"

"Me to know and you to find out."

"I bet you have. Your face is red as fire."

When we leave the café, we pass the girl on the sidewalk. She's with a boy. He has his arm around her waist and she's laughing up at him. As they swing by, she pretends she doesn't see us.

I don't look at Allen until we're in the car.

He grinds the starter and the engine roars. We head out of town, his hands white-knuckled on the steering wheel.

I scrunch down beside him.

We drive in silence.

Suddenly, Allen blurts out, "The principal says I'm university material."

"What's university material?" I ask anxiously.

"Someone who can go in for higher education."

I'm puzzled. "Clintin's higher education."

"University is higher than Clintin. I'll have to go away to the city."

I don't want Allen to go away. I hear the echo of my mother's voice. "Where's the money coming from?"

"The principal said I can get scholarships. Scholarships are money, Susie."

The banana split suddenly flounders in my stomach. "I'm going to throw up."

The car stops in a spray of gravel. Allen leans over and flings open the door. "Out Susie. Jump. Quick."

Afterwards, I'm tired and cross. I lay my head on the seat and brood over what Allen said. There's a hurt in my chest. He's going to leave us.

"Will you ever come back home?"

I feel his hand on my hair. "Of course, Susie, I'll come back home."

◊

We took a taxi to the cemetery.

The military section lay in a corner – a private place enclosed by a hedge of yew. Yew – for sorrow.

If Allen had lived, where would he be now. Whom would he love? I thought, then, of the yellow-haired girl ....

On his last leave, perhaps Allen didn't even think of her as he swung down from the train.

I looked out over row after row of tombstones.

"Will I ever find him?"

I felt a tap on my shoulder and turned. An elderly man had come up behind us. "Sorry to startle you, my dear, but I think I can be of help. Name's Watson. Donald Watson. I come here every day."

"Canadians," the old man commented, as he led us among the graves. "Then I expect you recognize those trees. Fine specimens. Those maples were given to us by Canada after the Great War."

We progressed slowly, the old man halting now and then to call out names, make comments. "Gordon Landry. Bomber pilot. Flew a Lancaster. That lad there, James Robinson, was a rear gunner. And Russell Kerwin .... My James was an airman too. He went missing in action June 6th, 1942 – over Africa. It's hard not being able to visit him. I make up for it by coming here, getting to know these lads."

He stopped and drew our attention to a stand of silver birch. "This is a beautiful cemetery, isn't it? Look, over there. The City of Oxford erected that monument after the Great War. It's called the Cross of Sacrifice."

◊

The car stops. I awake, groggy, the taste of vomit in my mouth.

Allen is rolling down the window. "Can I give you a lift?"

I raise myself on my elbow.

It's Mrs. Cory standing on the road and she looks like a clown, red spots painted on her cheeks, bright red lips.

She flings an arm across her face and shakes her head. "I, I didn't recognize your car .... I was just taking ... a walk."

I watch her as we drive away. "She's going back to the house now. Why'd she have all that red stuff on her face?"

"I don't know why, Susie," Allen says. "Let's not talk about it."

◊

Row after row of tombstones embossed with the maple leaf. Our dead.

My brother's name.

Mr. Watson stepped back and bowed his head.

I knelt and placed the roses on Allen's grave.

After a while, the old man spoke in a formal manner. "Flying Officer Bancroft was a brave man. I know something of his story. It was a night sortie, a low-level bombing raid over rail yards. He dropped his bombs on target and was climbing when he was intercepted by enemy fighters. His Wellington was badly crippled but Officer Bancroft brought it under control and headed back to base. Over British soil, he ordered his men to parachute. He stayed with the aircraft. Officer Bancroft died a hero's death trying to save his machine."

I clasped my hands over my ears. "You made that up," I cried. "You're lying. I don't believe you."

◊

Now I am satisfied. Thank God, I have done my duty.

No!

I push the old man's lie out of my mind. Whatever Allen saved in this war, it wasn't a machine.

Storm troopers standing over them ... dim dusty cloakroom, Jason pinned to the floor, the handful of flies ....

My child-voice. "If my brother was here, you couldn't do that. You wouldn't dare."

Retching sounds. Smell of vomit.

Taste of vomit. My head resting on the car seat. Allen's hand on my hair. "Of course Susie I'll come back home. Of course ...."

Miss Bennett's, "Close the door quietly behind you. It's a beautiful day. Why would you want to stay inside on day like this?"

"Hey, guys, the bums have come out. Let's get 'em."

Let's get 'em.

They were rounded up in the streets, forced to their hands and knees, forced to clean gutters, toilets – to scrub Schuschnigg signs from the streets of Vienna. As the name disappeared under the brushes Schusch Schus Sch, they wiped clammy sweat from their foreheads and looking up, saw pairs of boots facing them.

I gripped my husband's hand and looked down at my brother's grave.

GUATEMALA

Susan Perly

A ND SO IT WAS TOLD:
There was a place called The Place of Forgetting. And to that place came the suffering souls: it was where they ran, it was where they flew, it was where they found their shelter, it was where they found their voice.

Their story belongs to our time, children, and to every time before – it is the story of a people who had to abandon their land, and who lived out their time in one place longing for the place they used to be, and how they used to call it home.

And so they tell:

The next one to arrive was the old woman from San Francisco the High One, she whose place had been burned to the end of death.

She came, and she spoke from her perch on the tree, and the listeners sat in a circle beneath her, under the flickering shade. The green leaves were seen in the water, in the river which gentled at the shore. She was the blue flash which appeared on the green and spread wide, a gentian stain flapping on the river's tree as up above she stammered out the events which had brought her here.

"Kill us ... army army, kill us away ... from the land kill us, army, from the sun ... give blows to our ... army, to our ... slice our ... little, stop they never ... the children, bodies ... army kill us ... stop, army ... killing us ...," was the story she sucked up in sobs and pushed out in squeaks through her one lung left her, in skirls of her language Chu, to say what happened in the highland place, the town they burned to the ground, the town where she saw her daughter's man

226

with his head on a stick, the army passed it around, they started burning them, the little grandmothers ran with the children, they hid inside the mountain, the helicopters came after them, they looked close to find them, the sound of helicopters would not leave them alone.

She saw spinning again the fan in the cantina where they used to come for a drink, right at the edge of the plaza, and the fan there. The broad blades of it, silent and still in the cool days, and they twirled lazy with the first rains and spun twirling up to speed with the season of the hot days in full, and the amber bottle of beer she held in her hand – it was so cold, and the feeling of the breeze of the fan blowing her hair away from her face, the jokes and the stories, and the bartender leaned over to tell one of his, then they burned him.

Twirling, turning, spinning like the inside of the wind were the helicopters, they came in the air with their sound, they burned it all, they followed the Indian people up and down the mountains. Trying to find a place where they didn't kill them was what they were trying to do, those who left running before they could turn into those who remain; for they kill those who remain.

They run, they leap, they fly: she told the story.

And the other half-human half-bird creatures listening to her, we breathed along with her tale, which was our tale too: how she had run as we had, and how she had flown – when finally after many days of running the gods gave her wings to fly – and how she had flapped and flapped with so many others made birds, to reach a gliding blue span high through the sun.

"Kill us," she speaks, "... we had no wish to, kill we who they ... we who, who remain they, those who they make enter the living places, they burn us; we go to the church, we go to the house of goodness to be together, the army gives us beatings, the army cuts us up, all the young men they kill. Twenty number the dwellings on our hill; where we go to gather in one, they kill this daily place of fire and bread, they burn it with gasoline. Children witness this, their lives are fear now. They hear about it in the next forest, they tell each other: the army are taking away the spirits of those they kill. In pickups they transport away the dead Indian people.

"On the nearby hill, they take away five small children. They kill them. It is six moons since they left, six moons and the death of six suns. They died of shame, *army, army*, says the river, was why the suns died of shame in that time. The army, they took the five little ones from the nearby hill, they took them in the month of taking. Now, all my place is finished. It is over. The place is over.

"Five children they take away, first they take one out to kill him, and they say he is the one and next the human beings in uniform kill all five; it is above us, that place of mine, and along the way. When I run ahead of the family, I don't know if they are killing them, first a day and a night they die. Various beings that belong to us, running, small little children, little girl children and the boy. The youngest of ten, they took him out to show his dying, we saw. Tiny cows, the poor females, and the parrots dead, all the birds, they kill them, they never stop killing them.

"We go apart from our place, we are empty of it. The sound of seven, and seven again helicopters, the army arrives to be gazing at the people, they arrive to kill us, they keep on killing us, the Indians of San Francisco the High One, where sits the church of the very same name.

"The children stay inside the mountain, our hearts are where they huddle, the mountain keeps us days and nights in the month of hiding, the little ones don't know what, they are bleached, their sleeping is crying. Burning is what has become of our home, we tell them, now our home is over. The helicopters chase us, sent by the government of them. They follow us past the border, and past over-there and anywhere. They keep on following. They want to follow to kill all the people who lived in our place, because they don't want any returners.

"We aren't thinking of returning. There is no place. There is a place in the stories, there is the telling-about place, but there is no place.

"Three are too full of missing it. They wander back to go see it, to be there. They see nothing. A place a place no more. They run, afraid, they say: We saw the death, we saw it. The uniforms come out of the trees and shoot them. One is lucky to fly back. It is he who tells the story; we heard it from him.

"This is our place: a home of death."

She of the many shriveled skins, and then she rested. She rested a moment from gasping remembering, from uttering her life in her born tongue: and we listeners with her, with her pause found our racing lungs slow down, and our quick breath broken into half-even rhythms steady, and we saw in the smooth glass river some peace we might have: a canoe gliding by with no sound; then our breath with hers grew from easy to shallow and out of quiet she began to suck up air to continue her witness of what it was that had happened to her, and hers.

"Him ... the head, her husband, my little girl's man, his children, they were on my shoulders, we ran down the volcano for hiding, the little ones saw him alive, then they saw his head they saw cut across the neck, *army, army,* cries the shame, the army passed it around in the plaza, we ran to the mountain of the ancestors and into the cave, they saw their father, the children, like this, the eyes of him falling from his head in blood, and she could not enter the church, their mama, the army put it on fire.

"They said: Watch, and they did not kill her. She looked. They were too cruel to kill her. They were too cruel to kill my daughter.

"A living beauty of a thing. My little girl. The name of her I cannot speak. My one. The children, he was their father.

"At the worship place the people gather to enter within. They have come to be together. They pray outside the church with no protection. The army shows them the head on the stick. Then the army takes the head of her man to show to the ones who are not at prayer and not in the house of goodness, and they show them the head.

"In the plaza they show it. They enter into the cantina, they show it to the women. Who have fear, they leave that death running. Every child is a creature of fear, they complete the killing of all young men.

"Their father, they pull the brains from his head like grey snakes. Human beings in uniform do this, they make the children watch. She was my little one, their mama.

"They put his brains down their throats, this happened, in front of the ones who are standing at the door of the church and her, my baby, she is made to see, she is a thing full of fear. And the people do not go in to pray. They are made to see the place of prayer burning, and him, a dead one, they keep on killing him. The women see this, the children, they kill all the men.

"Us ... they take us away from the land, away from the corn they take us, they keep organizing us together on earth, they kill us, they never stop killing us, the church dies to sticks, the priest is dead in the lake, they kill us and they kill us to be killing us, then they put up a flag.

"Helicopters, helicopters in the black sky they ... we heard from the ancestors there is a place where you can cross through the sky to a river past a rock and past next to that place you can arrive to where the sound of helicopters calling *army, army* to the stars will finally at long last finish and be over and leave the Indian people once and for all alone.

"We heard the news that there in that place it is safe for Indian people. We heard the news that in a place they call The Place of Forgetting, they won't be following us to be killing us. We heard that this is that place."

◊

An old woman once, now a half-bird of many many years, it was she who squawked out her sounds so hurt and so hurt, her red two eyes in a human skull two blood beads looking down on us so kind, and so kind. She told the story.

To the dead priest in the lake, she said, *Forgive me,* as she flew away. The land which had nurtured her, and held her and showed her the colours of first things – her mother, a corpse she was abandoning.

She was empty. Emptiness filled her, it ached her. She flew.

The clear sky reminded her of everything there was going to be to miss. She was already back, even as she flew fast to get away she saw herself back there, and longed to be there with that her. Sitting in the cantina and having a beer, and telling the latest to the bartender, and listening to him in her ear, at home in her life at home, not knowing how unbearable it was to not be there with all of it until she was on her way and she grasped she could never come back to be with any of it again, ever. The place which had caused her so much pain: it was lost to her.

We were also birds half-human, we knew the ache. We knew it, and knew no one could know it; and she, she had known it. By the river, under the tall treed canopy, she named it in words born of the human race, and the sounds of her words were a music entering us inside, touching lost things. Being of there. Belonging. Dying into its soil.

We had sanctuary, but here was not our home.

We wanted home back, we wanted back what we had given up, what we had flown fleeing from to be safe, and, yes, we were safe, but inside us was a hurt which wanted no place but back home to go to to hurt.

Each sound she made, and the sounds she forced together to make words, made our brains rush through our bodies, giving birth to buried thought-pictures: children once upon a time – us, running down the hills to town from the fields of corn overlooking it, down to the plaza, down to the market, down to our friends: our children, running too fast down the hills from the corn, to the plaza, to the market, to their friends, to the church, to the burning, we carried them away, we ran. We leapt, we held them, the seeds of us in our arms, in our new wings, each a child who will never grow up to say: *Once upon a time, when I was young.*

We knew the words she was speaking. They were the words we had never spoken out from inside. Her lime-green throat began to vibrate again, and out came her grief.

"I took her, took her my little one, my own, saw her then, the church was on, boy took her little, boy too, fire the children, *!pum! !pum!*, caught her we ran, caught her helicopter, helicopter, this going ... her ... his head shot my ... on fire all things, army ... my girl, army, gun they, my daughter, my own, my small one, *!pum!*, she, my baby, they ... too cruel to kill her, army makes her see the dying ... makes her watch her own ones – she sees, she dies in her heart: *!Pum!* Now they come kind, she dies in her body. Her body is over.

"I cannot say you the name of her. She is one of the dead ones. Her – my little life.

"The children, I took them with, we came, I am their little grand-mother. Here they are. I crossed over with them, I came with their bones in my arms, we flew. Here they are here with yours of yours, and all the ones of all your little daughters. Here they are in this place, gone to earth."

The river ran along in ribbons of sky and sea. We sat beneath the tree of the wide and many branches, the tree grown by the shore. Some of us, falling a long way alone, rocked only in our very own arms; others of us, feeling too orphaned, moved closer to each other for the comfort it might bring.

The sun dropped red into the river's shimmering sky, and over the spreading red a canoe skimmed with no sound, paddled by two human-birds, and they paddled it silently back towards shore, as the hour had come for the end of the day.

◊

And so it is told:

Once there was a place called The Place of Forgetting. It was there the long reign of silence ended. It was there the first one spoke of the death by army of Indian places. She was the old woman from San Francisco the High One, where used to sit a church of the very same name.

She was chosen by the gods to be first. The gods gave her wings, and the others had wings to fly. But the gods did rip her heart open, and her life was a thing spoken, and the rest had hearts torn by her words, and they followed to speak.

So it was that the listeners became tellers. So it was that the hurt was caught, and named, and this scared off the silence.

Green throats shook, green reflections waved on the green leaves gentling in the water, and gentian stains, wings, spread across the branches where all had flown to speak, and all spoke, from the tree they call the Tree of Forgetting.

And we said:

"My place is gone and all my people are gone and every thing of mine is gone. It is gone back to dust. My place, it was my home, I used to be there. It is a nothing I weep for, my lament is for something which used to be. It is nothing but a nothing now. I call it, where is it? My ear is waiting. I hear no answer.

"Dust, you were trees. River, my veins leaked red to your bottom. Body, once I was you, now I am here. I am a thing with wings; I flap through the air. Who am I, but the pain of humans? What am I, but this sorrow?"

THE ORPHAN BOY

Marina Endicott

WHEN PEOPLE were unhappy, they often came to our house with food. Sometimes they came secretly and left something on the back porch, a pie, a lemon loaf or (one wonderful time) a bucket of fried chicken. At Christmas, big laundry hampers full of cans and bottles of exotic food and drink. But Ariadne Keller came in the middle of the night and pounded on the door and they let her in – how could they help it? She was a tornado standing on the front porch, laughing through the little pane of glass, snapping the knocker back and forth and beating time with her heels, too.

My room, the room that Cecy and I shared then, was right over the front porch. But we had not been asleep, of course, we had been lying in bed arranging our hair on our pillows for the delectation of the Arabian Knight who was going to leap through the window on his charger and carry us off – one knight each: we had got into an argument that evening over whose knight would arrive first, and I was feeling dreadfully certain that mine would be late, and I would have to watch Cecy lifted up into arms of steel and plumped delicately down, sidesaddle. Then there would be that spring, the hind legs of the horse swelling downwards to rebound upwards into the air forever, no need of a magic carpet, and me left alone in our maiden bedroom waiting for who knows how long, covered in humiliation. So when the noise began, the pounding and the rapping and the heels on the wooden porch floor, I was glad enough to disarrange myself and beat Cecy to the window.

"It's Ariadne Keller," I whispered back to her. We always called

233

her by her full name when we talked about her, because my mother did, as if her name was a spell and couldn't be left unfinished. It does sound melodramatic, but so was she melodramatic. Cecy shivered in bed and pulled the blankets back up; they had lain in romantic dishevelment awaiting the shining one.

"What's she doing?"

"I don't know yet, she's dancing, I think."

Cecy scrambled up, stamping on the giveaway board, but that wouldn't matter with all the noise.

"Let me see a little."

Ariadne Keller was calling through the door, "Little pigs, little pigs, let me come in!"

That was a little scary and I began to hope that she would go away, but my father was switching on the lights and letting her in. It was his job, of course, to give succour and sanctuary.

My mother stood at the top of the stairs fully dressed by the time Cecy and I worked up the courage to edge our door open a crack. Without turning around to look at us she said, "Back to bed, girls, I mean it."

But Ariadne, coming into the bright hallway with parcels and packages in her arms, looked up the long angle of the stairs and lit up her brilliant eyes at us, and cried, "Oh, no, let them come down too – look at all this I've brought! You can't be so cruel ...."

What was my mother to do? My father standing behind Ariadne with his arms out for her things, us waiting for the word, the baby beginning to make little cranky noises, even my brother, who slept like a frozen man waiting for medical developments, had come sliding out of his door.

"Robert, it's nearly midnight ...."

Cecy and I looked at each other with wild surmise – that was practically a capitulation.

"I should be taken out and beaten, I know," said Ariadne Keller, bowing her long body in shame. "But look what I've brought you! Spaghetti!"

She dropped a bag on the carpet in the hall and began pulling things out of it: long, long spaghetti, longer than we ever got, in a blue and white paper bag; jars and tins, and bunches of garlic, a beautiful string bag full of onions and peppers, a long stick of white bread and a pound of butter, cheese in wrapping, a bottle of wine.

My mother turned around and looked at us. She looked a little pinched and tired, but she smiled. "Are you hungry still?" she asked us. She put out an arm to my brother Sam, and he walked into her. "Hungry, Sam? Spaghetti?"

"They'll be sick for the rest of the night, Ariadne," she said as she started down the stairs.

Real spaghetti, not just out of a can, was still almost an ethnic food. We were thrilled.

My father shut the door and helped gather up the parcels again and we skipped down behind my mother to help. Ariadne was holding on to my mother's arm, coaxing her into the kitchen, thanking her, waltzing her a little, her hand smoothing up and down on my mother's sleeve or clasping her to her for a minute and then pushing her away again. She's hectic, I thought, like Ruby dying of consumption in that Anne book.

"A party, a party!" she sang as she flung cupboard doors open and shut, hauled out big pots and little pots, snapped the stove on, found the corkscrew. My parents looked at each other, calculating how long she would stay, glad that the dishes had been done that evening, apologizing to each other. Cecy and Sam sat on the bench behind the table, very subdued, but I sat on the stool by the fridge, practically in the middle of all of it.

She stayed until dawn, telling stories and making us all laugh. She taught Sam how to do a time-step, she sucked her spaghetti in through the space in her front teeth, she dazzled my father and hocussed my mother, and she gave me secret smiles as if we were the only ones in the world who really understood sophistication. Even Cecy sat on her lap for a while – she hadn't sat on anyone for years. I despised her for doing it, but knew exactly why she let her standards slip. Ariadne carried her upstairs when she fell asleep, her little legs drooping to one side and her head drooping to the other like a broken lily – exactly the effect I worked for when arranging myself for the Arabian to come and take me away.

I followed after them and contented myself with the swing of Ariadne Keller's skirt and the beautiful tendon in her heel which stretched sharply away from the bone at every step. The backs of her legs were beautifully brown and smooth and strong, from dancing, I thought. Her arms, too, were strong and thin and fell into exquisite shapes carrying Cecy, easing her gently around the newel post at the bottom of the stairs, pulling her in closer during the climb, lightly raising her over the end of the bed.

"I long for someone to carry me," Ariadne Keller said to me, pulling the sheet up over Cecy. "Not since I was 9, like Cecy. Or someone to swirl me around in the air, you know, like an airplane?"

I nodded, shy to be in the room alone with her except for Cecy sleeping.

"If only someone really big would come along and carry me away I could stand it. As long as there's someone who can pick you up you're still okay, I think .... It's only when you get too tall that you're in trouble. On your own."

"I'm 11," I said. I could have killed myself for saying that. What a dumb thing to say, it didn't even go with what she had said. Now she would leave.

"It's a strange year," she said, looking at me with her sidelong eyes. "Magic. I remember being 11." She said nothing for a minute. I tried to think of something to say to keep her there, but nothing came.

"Did you know I have a twin?" she finally said, looking in the little mirror.

"No."

"Well, I do. My dear twin, my second soul, my spirit-mate, Ardith the Beautiful ...."

My father looked in the door, carrying Sam. "Sleep now, Laura."

Ariadne Keller leaped off my bed where she had settled for an instant and bowed me into it. Then she stretched her fingers up, up, and grazed her fingers on the ceiling. "Too big to be carried, no one will come and take me away, my own sister deserts me – how will I live?"

She had forgotten me already, but that was part of her glamour – to be forgotten by her was a privilege.

She went downstairs with my father and they both walked straight into his study without even talking about it. She stayed in there with him for a long time. My mother came upstairs slowly after she cleaned up, and she stood in my doorway for a minute to listen to our breathing. My rhythm didn't change, but she came over anyway and kissed me. Her hand stuck clumsily as she smoothed down my hair and it made me feel desperate, too big for the room. Downstairs we could hear Ariadne Keller crying in the study.

After a little while my mother went to her own room, but the crying noise continued into my sleep.

◊

Sam told me she wanted to adopt a boy, that's why she came over in the middle of the night.

"That's silly, why would she want another boy? She's got six children already." It was hard to believe that she was really their mother, but there were six children at her house and they did look a bit like her. More like her husband, the Commander, who was never there. She didn't act like a mother either – what mother would come to our house and make spaghetti in the middle of the night? What were her children doing then?

Sam said solidly, "I know, but that's why she came. His name is Michael Rowe, and he is 3."

"That's not a real name. How do you know all this stuff?"

"Daddy told me."

We were sitting on the bank at the side of the house, the side with no windows, eating cookies which I had said we were allowed to have.

Cecy said, "Why did he tell you without you asking?"

"Because he's the only boy, that's why," I told her.

Sam just laughed and looked ordinary, which was annoying. He was aware of things like that, but not much affected by them.

"Well, why don't *we* get the little boy?" said Cecy. Our parents had tried to adopt a boy to have a brother for Sam, but they didn't have enough money, apparently. But my father was still a good reference for someone who wanted to adopt; being the minister, he looked good on the forms.

I didn't understand yet. "Why does she want one particular boy? I thought you just got what came out of the bin."

"I don't *know*, I said, I wasn't even listening," Sam said, getting up to leave. "Maybe she knew his parents. I'm going to ride the scooter." He left.

"So why would she cry?" I asked Cecy.

"When did she cry?"

"For ages after you were asleep. I was awake."

"Liar."

"It's true."

Even later, Sam wouldn't pump Daddy any more, and although Cecy and I talked about it for a while, we didn't really like talking about Ariadne Keller. She was out of bounds, maybe because she was too powerful. She lived on a street called Whitlock Edge, and my mother called her the Witch of Whitlock Edge when she was being unguarded. My father used to change the poem: "On Whitlock Edge the wood's in trouble," he would say solemnly, and you could tell he was feeling a bit of a devil for laughing at one of his parishioners.

◊

About three months after the spaghetti night, we had our portraits taken. A very good photographer came out from Halifax and set up in our living-room. The dining-room was turned into a dressing-room, and we had to wear curlers all morning. It had been arranged through friends of friends, but we had a songbook filled with the photographer's photographs, and she was obviously the real thing. Cecy and I were very impressed. We watched her from the corner where we were sitting quietly while my mother got the baby ready. Miss Howard strutted around fixing up white umbrellas and reflecting sheets and fancy lamps on tripods, and finally got out her cameras. She paid no never mind to us at all, just got on with her work. When we were ready to sit, she sat us, took some pictures, re-sat us and took more. We changed our clothes and did it again. She took three sets of pictures, all in different clothing, and then she took individual pictures and pictures of pairs of us. She had just settled on me and Cecy as the last set of all when the doorbell rang, and my father sent Sam to open it.

The woman photographer was fiddling with the film. She had posed Cecy sitting on a chair and me sitting on the arm of the chair with my arm round Cecy's shoulder and my head over her head.

Cecy didn't even have to move her lips to talk to me. "Maybe I'll be a photographer. I bet she makes lots of money."

"How much is she getting for this?"

"A whole bundle, Daddy's mad about it, but Mommy said it had to be done anyway for the Christmas letters."

There was quite a noise out in the hall.

"It's the witch," Cecy said, squirming suddenly. The photographer's working eye caught her moving.

"Just sit still for six more shots," she said reasonably. "Then you can run off."

She must have decided to make the last ones good pictures by talking to us. Maybe she thought she would put them in a book.

"What's it like, you two, being sisters?" she said, just as Ariadne Keller put her head around the archway from the hall. "You must have special secrets, you two. Do you share a room? I always wanted to have a sister, to have a special friend."

While Miss Howard was talking, Ariadne Keller left her body in place, but bent her head away behind the arch and then bent it back, only when she bent it back she had two heads, both nodding and smiling.

Cecy shrieked and jumped up. Her head banged me in the jaw and made me bite my tongue so I smacked her and she howled.

My eyes were watering from the pain, but there were certainly two Ariadnes standing in the archway, both laughing. The photographer didn't know what to do – we were older than her normal range of children, I guess, and wouldn't have paid much attention to a sucker or the birdie. My mother arrived and told us both to be quiet.

"I am ashamed of you," she whispered fiercely, pulling the cushion of the chair back into place where Cecy had kicked it out in our fight. "Not only is Miss Howard here, we also have guests. I don't want to hear another word until she has finished and you have changed out of those dresses, is that clear?"

We nodded, keeping our eyes on her to assure her of our goodness – also to avoid looking at the door where Ariadne Keller stood with her twin sister like those photography studios where for an extra dollar you get two prints of each photo.

It was soon over – the photographer didn't ask any more questions about being a sister and was probably glad not to be one herself. She packed up her gear while we put on our normal clothes, and my mother and Sam and my father, who had all changed while Cecy and I were getting done, put out tea in the garden.

When Cecy and I got downstairs again, the living-room was empty of equipment and the house of people. We looked out the balcony window by the boxy fireplace and there they all were, having tea down below on the small lawn. Behind our house was a tiny garden and then a row of big rocks, and past the rocks the swamp began – several acres of marsh and bog, rocks and reeds and muck. It was quite pretty, but the mosquitoes were very bad at certain times of the year, and of course there was a smell. But if the wind was the right way, people could sit in wicker chairs in the little garden not even knowing there was a swamp out there.

Ariadne Keller had brought her sister and also the new little boy who we (Cecy and I, and Sam) hadn't seen yet. My parents had been to dinner at her house and he had been 'on display' my mother said; she also said he was a very ordinary little boy.

The first thing he did was walk around the rocks and straight into the swamp. Cecy and I, looking over the tops of them all from the balcony, saw him heading for the middle along the tussocks of grass and scrub. He was wearing white knee socks, and they were streaked and soaked already. We should have raced down and caught him, but in fact we knew he would be all right; it was not a dangerous marsh. Instead we stayed leaning on the rail and watched him.

"How old?" Cecy asked me.

"Three, I think."

"He looks older than that, don't you think?"

I was leaning too hard on my chest, I had to get up, so I swung my leg over the rail and sat balanced on the top. "I think he looks like a changeling, a goblin child."

"And Michael Rowe, that can't really be his name."

"Not possibly – where is his boat ashore?"

That made Cecy laugh, and the adults looked up at us, and my mother gestured for us to come down. Sam held up a plate of goodies. Ariadne Keller and her sister stared up at us from their doubled faces, somehow reproducing even the angle of the glance. And a third of the way into the swamp, the child Michael turned around and looked at us too.

It all made me want to show off, but I couldn't think of anything really good to do, so I just stood up on the railing. Cecy made that little squeak noise she makes when she's scared that always pushes me further, so I did a little soft shoe, prancing along the narrow board. Normally I know this would have been no big deal, but the balcony itself wasn't very safe and the railing was particularly rickety, and we had been expressly told never to sit on it, even. Having stood up, walked, done the little dance, there wasn't much available for a finale – but then a little flash caught my eye out in the swamp. It was the Michael boy's white socks flicking through the air as he fell off a rock into one of the water spaces.

I turned to Cecy to say, "Don't be worried, I've done this before," and then I launched out. It seemed to take a long time to get to the ground, as it always does. I hadn't actually jumped from standing up on the railing before, only from standing outside the railing hanging on with my toes to the little bit of extra platform. The four-foot difference nearly ruined me.

But I landed (on all fours instead of gracefully like the goddess from the machine), without breaking either my bones or the tea set, and set off for the swamp.

I had certainly made an impression. My parents leaped out of their chairs, and my father nearly brained Miss Howard with the camera he was examining. Only Sam caught up with me, though, as I was delicately, quickly, bunnyhopping from hillock to hillock, mound to root to stump to rock, to where the orphan boy had gone in.

We stopped short about five feet from him as if he was an animal and might bolt at a sudden movement. In boring truth he was in no danger of drowning. There was only a foot or so of water. But he was only little, and didn't know how to get himself out of the mire. His pretty suit of shorts and shirt was ruined.

"What's that secret word you use for horses and fairies," I said over my shoulder to Sam. He snorted, because really the little boy did look like a brownie, all filthy and pointed. His nose had stayed clean somehow, and it stuck straight out, and his dark hair grew in swoops all over his scalp. You could see the patterns of its growth, unlike most people's thatches. His skin stretched over his face bones more tightly than usual in little kids, and it gave him a knowing, old look. That look dissolved suddenly as we watched him, though, because he started to cry, and he held out his arms to be picked up. I didn't have much patience with babies and never ever played with dolls or anything sentimental, but he made me feel very sad for him, so I did go over and pick him up. I was big enough to hold him almost comfortably. He got muck all over my t-shirt and pants, but he tucked his head into my neck and wrapped his legs around me, and it made me feel strange – huge, like a terrible, kind giant. Cecy had leaped across the swamp from the other direction, and came up to us just before my father reached us.

"That was just stupid," she hissed at me. "You did that just to show off. Let me hold him."

"Don't be crazy, I've got him!"

She started yanking on his legs and made him stir and murmur, and that made me furious, so I whacked her with my free hand and she fell into the swamp herself. Before she could grab my ankle to pull me in, which she was trying to do, my father got there, and he took the boy from me and told Sam to help Cecy up.

While he was lifting the little boy off me, he looked at me seriously and said, "Really well done, Laura, you could have saved his life. I'm proud of you, sweetheart." He smiled and rumpled my hair up and walked back along the safe path.

Cecy was left wallowing in the mud and scratchy branches. She really hated the swamp, too – for her to come flying over a new path as she had done was a desperate feat. Sam gave her his hand half-heartedly; she ignored him and pulled herself out of the sucking slime by roots and rocks. I don't know why I stuck around – I wanted to follow after the boy and be petted and paraded.

She looked at me as she was clawing out. "You want to watch out, Laura," she said. "You could become a horrible person if you don't be careful. Then you'll be old and no one will like you and Sam and I won't live with you." By that time she was standing up, dripping, looking even more like a swamp-thing than Michael Rowe had. Her pale hair was slapped to her face with dingy water, and her eyes were frog-jewels.

"What did I do?" I asked Sam. I knew that would annoy her more.

"I'm going to the barn, do you want to come?" she asked him. He looked back and forth between us for a second, but he would have been a fool to refuse her. She was really mad, and if he sided with me she would be mad for days longer. So he went off with her through the swamp over the path she had cut coming in.

They were both pigs, anyway.

I went back by the safe path. My feet hurt from jumping all that height. It must have been twelve feet with the railing added in. At the head of the path between the two guard stones, my mother was waiting for me.

"We're going to have to have a talk, Laura," she said in her quiet, dangerous voice. Nothing got by her. She put her arm around me, leading me into the garden as if we were the best of friends, and smiled for the guests.

It had only been a second, I guess, since my father arrived back with the kid. He was holding him under the garden hose, rinsing the worst of the black muck off him, and Ariadne and her sister were standing anxiously by, not looking at each other, only at the child. Ariadne rushed forward, dragging her sister, when my mother sashayed me into the garden.

They were both wearing flowered things, long and full in the skirt, made of vague, ghostly cloth which sharpened their own vividness. Some of the colour was paled, though, in both of them. I was surprised to see that they'd gotten so fond of a little orphan boy in just a few weeks – or maybe they just felt guilty about him, like I did about the baby if I dropped her when I was supposed to be babysitting.

"Laura, thank you a million times," she said, but she wasn't really talking to me at all, she kept looking back at the boy. "This is my sister, Ardith. I want her to meet you, she's staying with me for a little while. Ardith, I think you'll love Laura ...."

Ardith put out her hand for me to shake, and as soon as our hands touched, Ariadne leaped back to the little boy – it was like the fizzy light leaping between two metal sticks in an electricity experiment. Ardith snapped her head around to watch her sister, but she turned back to me soon enough for politeness – well, more than politeness, because I was only a child anyway, she didn't have to talk to me.

Seeing her out in the garden made it clearer why Ariadne had talked about her so strangely. They were the same, only Ardith was more of it. She turned her eyes on me, and they were so beautiful – slanted and deeply set, with shadows around them. Her hand, still holding mine, was long and veined and well kept, and she had a ring on that glinted. Just one ring, no wedding band.

"I expected to see wings on your shoulders," she said to me. "Wings for an angel, wings for a bird! You must have been practising flying."

"No, but I dream I'm flying," I answered her, and that was a lie – only Cecy ever dreamed she was flying, I never got into the air no matter how hard I tried.

"Oh! So do I, always!" she crowed, and her eyes glinted at me like her ring. For a minute I was glad I had lied about flying in dreams, but then I suddenly thought that she was lying too, that she didn't dream she flew either. "Over cities and towns, like the dark man in Chagall, or like the Queen of the Night." She went on about flying, talking in poetry almost, but she wasn't talking to me at all any more, although her eyes were still on me, keeping me in place. All her concentration was going behind her to Ariadne and the boy.

My mother touched me lightly as she went by, and said quietly, "Change your clothes again, please, and find Cecy." She helped Ariadne clean the last bits of mud from Michael's face.

Ardith said, to call me back, "Before I leave we'll have to take her out for a treat, won't we? Something really wonderful."

I couldn't understand what she meant until I realized she was talking to Ariadne, about me. I only got that because Ariadne came closer, still holding the little boy, with her arms wrapped right around him. She looked at me over Ardith's shoulder, and smiled, and I thought for a minute that she was much more beautiful than Ardith. "Yes," she said, "Oh, yes, we will! What a good idea!"

I took a gulp of whiskey once, when I thought it was apple juice. Those women made me feel like that most of the time.

◊

Sitting on the roof of the garage one evening later on, when Cecy wasn't mad at me any more, we were trying to decide how high the balcony railing was exactly without getting out the measuring tape. Sam was talking about a theory of his to do with shadows and string, and Cecy thought if we got Daddy to walk underneath it by some ruse and then estimated it—her formula wasn't quite worked out. I campaigned fairly hard for the sixteen-foot theory because it was after all me who had jumped off it without breaking anything.

"I bet that Michael kid is her sister's baby, and she's pretending to adopt him," I said.

"No, because Daddy signed the papers."

Sam said, "He did, I was a witness."

He needed to be squashed, he was getting out of hand. "You are only a child," Cecy told him.

"You couldn't be a witness, you silly baby, you're only 8."

"And he's not her sister's baby," he said, getting a little mad. "He's her own, that's whose baby he is, and she got him back, and Daddy thinks it's best that she have him back, and me too."

"What?"

"Really?"

"I just *told* you, do you think I lie or something?" Sam was stalking down the roof to the branch to get off. "You guys are so *old*, well, you don't even remember when she went away to Montreal for a long time and they thought she wasn't coming back but then she did, and I remember that."

"Be careful on the branch," Cecy told him. "Don't jump from too high."

"I know how to do it," he said, but he wasn't really mad any more. "I'll get some graham crackers."

"Bring oranges too if you can," I said, but Daddy caught him going in the kitchen door; we could see them both outlined in light, Daddy bending down and Sam bending up – then Daddy picked him up and tossed him in the air and came out to the porch to call us.

"When they take me for a treat, you can come too," I told Cecy while we climbed down through the dusky air inside the shell of leaves.

◊

They came to pick me up on the second Sunday after Trinity, in June, after lunch. I didn't know they were coming. We were all sitting at the table still. Sam was making us laugh, with his eyes two circumflexes but his mouth straight, not laughing with us. We had our arms on the table to lie on while we laughed, and my mother was gasping with laughter, helpless with it, cutting loose – my father having to wait for a breath before he could add to the joke. The baby was banging with a spoon on her tray and singing – no wonder we didn't hear the car grating on the gravel, we were in our house, laughing.

The first we heard was heels on the step outside the kitchen door and rapping, rattling on the pane, and different laughter coming from outside. Two faces, the same face, and two panes of glass. My mother hiccupped and nearly laughed again, but she pulled herself up out of what she liked best and whipped the cloth off the table before she opened the door. My father stood up too and put his glasses on. Cecy and I untangled our legs from each other and left the table – she going towards the hall door, me into the middle of the kitchen. Sam stayed at the table; he still had his pudding bowl in his lap to finish.

They came in laughing, but we had all stopped for guests, so they were laughing alone now, and Ardith was singing something.

"We've come to take Laura for her treat," Ariadne said, "If you'll let her come? Ardith wants to see the sea, we're going to drive down the south shore, maybe as far as Chester. But I promise you we'll have her back in time for dinner – let her come with us, please ...."

She sounded more like the spaghetti night again, all urgent and flattering, humming like a telephone wire. I think there were sparks of light coming off her, but I may just remember it that way. Ardith, too, still singing, "I want to be, beside the sea ..." and both their skirts dancing around their legs, high staccato shoes dancing on our tiles. I wanted to go so badly, I couldn't see anything but the two beautiful women, and my mother standing like a tree in the kitchen, not laughing, but smiling for company. I was afraid to look at her face in case she wouldn't let me go, but she just said, "Run up and put on your warm sweater, Laura, and brush your hair, darling."

I ran before she changed her mind – why should she have changed her mind? To get to the stairs I had to pass Cecy standing in the archway to the hall, and she didn't move when I went by, not even to look at me, but it was worth it. I was the oldest, it was fair, I could get her back later.

When I came down again Cecy was gone and so was Sam, and my mother was in the kitchen with the baby, but no one else.

She called me back before I was out the door. "I love you," she said. "Be home on time." She held the baby lightly on her lap.

Back into the dark hallway, past the study door (no sound at all, that I could hear). I pushed at my hair in the hall mirror for a minute, but I still couldn't hear anything. No sign of Cecy, they must be in the barn already, but then through the balcony windows I saw her and Sam sitting on the head rock in the middle of the swamp. He was staring towards the house and she was talking to him with her chin stuck out forward, kneeling on the bumpy rock in her bare knees. Too many windows in this house, I thought.

Ardith was sitting in the driver's seat, playing the radio softly and smoking a cigarette with her arm out the open window. I was a little shy to come up to the car, but she saw me and made me get in the front seat with her.

"Never wear stockings in June, Laura," she said. "Just too hot. Did you know that nylon is an excellent insulation? That's why I always wear stockings in the winter. Your legs stay warm! But as soon as it's summer, I just put them away."

I looked down at my own legs, pale brown and scratched, and I thought of my mother, wearing a girdle and nylons every day of her life, squirming into the tube of gripping in the morning, laughing with us at how silly she looked, folding the edge up to attach her stockings.

Ardith's shins were brown and as smooth as Ariadne's, maybe a little thinner. She stretched them towards me and twisted the ankle to examine it, in her stiletto heel. No one else would have worn those shoes to go and be beside the sea. "New York, Paris, London – walking through great cities has lathed my legs, Laura," she said (and she said it for poetry). "What am I doing here, is the question I ask myself. She had a brilliant future, you know, she could have done anything – and instead, she lives in a back-water with all those children .... It is sordid, isn't it. Have you read *Brave New World*? You'd love it. Luckily Lisle is old enough now to take care of them sometimes. Thank God I didn't do the same – I look at her life sometimes and just sigh, I just have to sigh – you know what I mean, don't you Laura?"

I nodded. "And now another child," I said, trying to continue the conversation.

"Yes, well, you know all about that, of course, being your Daddy's daughter ...." She looked at me as if I was a woman, so I nodded again. "It's an awkward situation, I feel terrible about the whole thing. It doesn't seem to be working out too well, if you want my untutored opinion ... so much to feel guilty about! Sometimes I think I will have to take him back. He's a difficult child, I see that, and the Commander doesn't make things any easier." She laughed – I would have to say ruefully, shaking her head slightly.

By this time I was completely lost. It seemed best to just let her think I knew everything, so I rolled down the window on my side and stuck my arm out too. No cigarette, unfortunately. She flipped her envelope bag open beside her on the seat and went through it like a filing cabinet, looking for something. Her bag matched her shoes, and they were green, the same green as her dress. Her nails were polished coral and flicked over the things in her bag: leather covered books with a purpose, compacts covered in other leather, a bottle of perfume, a gold lipstick. She looked up and smiled at me watching her and a dimple came in her cheek, a tight, perfect dent.

The front door banged, and Ariadne came headlong down the steps. My father was still standing in the door, watching her run. And then she was at the car, opening the front door beside me, and I made to get out and get in the back, but she stopped me.

"No, no, this is a sight-seeing tour! We can all sit in the front. Let's go, Ardith."

Ardith held my knees over towards her to make room. "We'll go and get Michael first," Ariadne said as she slammed the door.

My stomach did a snake thing. I looked at the dashboard. If she was going to bring Michael on this treat I should stop the car and ask to bring Cecy. My legs pinched because I'd pulled my knees together when Ariadne got in, but the underskin had stuck in its old place. Ardith had already backed out of the driveway, and the yellow forsythia bush by the door blocked out my father. Then around the corner of the house I could see Cecy on the rock, by herself now. Sam was probably on the scooter.

"But what about Laura's treat?" Ardith asked the air outside her window. She flicked her fingers on the steering wheel. I sat still.

Ariadne leaned forward and banged the glove compartment open. "I don't want to leave him with Lisle."

"She's 14 – she's all right with him."

"Where are the maps?"

"We don't need a map."

They looked at each other for a minute. We had come to the turn-off to St. Margaret's Bay Road, and I sat very still. Then Ardith turned the car to the right instead of the left, and we went to get Michael. If I'd known how, I would have gotten out of the car and walked back to our house.

At Ariadne Keller's house the road curved into the trees, and the land sloped down from the road to a small lake behind the house – they had a dock. Ardith stayed in the car while we walked down the path to the lake. Ariadne Keller ran ahead to where Lisle and Michael Rowe were sitting on a blanket. Lisle stood up when she saw us, holding Michael – they both stared at us with the same expression, something closed and serious.

Ariadne lifted Michael high in the air so his legs spun out and said to Lisle, "I'm taking him with us after all – Laura doesn't mind, do you Laura?" She was all sparkling again, and she smiled, but she looked so unhappy underneath it that I didn't really mind. "Just wait while I get his runners ...." She flew up the path to the house.

Lisle folded up the blanket and stood by the tree with her dark hair falling over her face. I was a little scared of her. She never spoke, she just swam. Out in the water, her brother Derek floated on a tire tube, his back to the shore and sunglasses on. There were pine needles sticking to the blanket, and Lisle picked them off with brown fingers while Ariadne ran down to the dock to call to Derek. He was 13, he stuck his hockey stick through my skate blade while we were skating the winter before and made me fall down. It was dark and cool under the pine trees, there wasn't any noise, and I wanted to go home.

Ariadne Keller came back up the path with Michael Rowe on her hip and made him wave goodbye to Lisle. She had all the pine needles cleaned off the blanket, and she walked behind us back to the house. My mother said she was shy and very intelligent, and my mother wanted me to be friends with her – it wasn't my fault that she didn't talk. She was a very good swimmer.

In the car, Ardith was listening to the radio again. Michael was put in the back seat, and he lay down and went to sleep right away, before we had even driven away from the house. He curled in on himself like a fiddlehead fern. He was cleaner than the last time, but he still had a cast of brown over him, a cloudy bloom.

We drove for nearly an hour. One or the other of them would occasionally point out pleasant vistas, but I was glad when Ardith pulled the car off on a side road and stopped at the edge of a short cliff. Over the rise of the cliff we could see the sea.

Michael was still asleep, and they decided to leave him in the car with all the doors locked and only one little window open slightly for air. Then we climbed down to the shore and the two sisters took their shoes off and walked barefoot in the crumbly sand. When we got down to the water-line where the sand was wet and firm I took my shoes off too and walked behind them in the double line of their footprints. They made long, delicate feet in the sand, wavering towards the surf and away again. Long toes and a thin edge, and then a narrow heel. I was watching their prints rather than them, going slowly, and when I looked up they were far ahead of me, walking close together, their bodies bending towards and away from each other. They seemed to have matching magnets within their breasts which pulled them together or shot them off from each other, never at peace.

The noise of the water swelling up and subsiding and the screeching of gulls blurred their voices. Sometimes part of a word would be caught by the moving air and carried back to me. They were standing still now, close, as if they had their poles correctly balanced for a moment. If I thought about them I was frightened by them, so I just looked instead of thinking.

"Catch up, Laura," Ardith called, twisting back to me. Ariadne bent to pick up a shell and they walked on, separated, the path of their feet a great Y yawning larger.

When she thought we had gone far enough, Ardith looped back and waved at Ariadne walking in the curling lip of the sea, foam to her ankles.

"Race you to the car," Ardith cried.

It was not a fair race, Ariadne was farther out, but she lifted her head and they both ran like horses. I was up on the dunes and I took a shortcut overland to get there before them to watch the finish. Ardith ran easily, in rhythm, not putting herself to too much trouble, stride falling into stride. She was way ahead by the time they were in sight around the curve of the bay, and Ariadne was already bending forward too much, trying too hard.

I heard a little noise behind me – Michael Rowe was standing up in the back seat, leaning against the car window. He couldn't get it open, and the doors were locked, so I couldn't let him out. He pressed his cheek on the window, it must have been cool. You could see how hot he was inside that car, his hair was stuck to his head, damp and curling. I stuck my nose against the glass to make him laugh, but he only moved away from the window and shut his eyes.

Down on the sand Ardith was coming into the home stretch and Ariadne was closer, running as if a fire followed her. Abruptly, Ardith stopped and looked back, and called sweetly, "You will never, ever, ever, catch me, and you know it."

Ariadne fell down on her knees, but was up again in a jerk and running again.

Ardith hit the car with her ring hand, it made a little mocking ting! loud enough for Ariadne to hear as she stumbled up the dune.

"I got him first," Ardith said.

"But it's my car." Her voice was harsh and thick.

"But I have the keys."

I really hated her then. I wasn't crazy about either of them. Michael was locked in the car still. I walked around the car away from them and waited by the back door, and after a minute Ariadne snatched the keys out of Ardith's hand and unlocked the front door.

"I have all of my body," she said in a fury – and as soon as she'd said it she laughed once, ha! as if someone had punched her in the stomach, and then looked sick. Ardith took the door handle from her gently, smiled at her, and opened it. She reached in and unlocked the back door, and she held out her arms for Michael. He walked over the seat to the opposite window, where I was, but not looking at me, and leaned against the seat in the corner.

Ariadne laughed again, and Ardith suddenly lunged into the car and grabbed Michael out by the back of his shirt, and shook him – it was so quick and neat that for a second it didn't look mean, but it was, because he didn't want to go to her.

He stiffened, and Ariadne put out her arms to him, but he wouldn't look at her either. I wished so badly that I wasn't there that my head hurt, and my chest, but I crouched down lower so I could look through the car to see what they were doing. Ardith held him out stiffly away from her, half-way between them, and if they spoke, it was so quietly that I couldn't hear. But after a little time she bent down and put Michael back in the back seat, and leaned farther forward and unlocked it for me. Then she walked around to the passenger side, and Ariadne (who was still standing by the door, watching her) waited until Ardith was inside the car before getting in herself.

She drove.

After about ten miles Ariadne suddenly spoke; no one had talked till then. "Ardith couldn't have children, Laura, that's why she gets angry." Ardith had her pointed face turned to watch her sister, but Ariadne only looked at the road, and glanced up fiercely to catch Michael in the rear-view mirror.

"I can't believe you're saying the things you're saying," Ardith said.

"She needs to have her cake and eat it and have it and eat it and have it, and a picture of it, and a recipe for it, and the *candles* always burning but never burning down ...."

"Everything, I need to have everything, that's the thing, Laura, and I think she's right. I'd like to have Michael now. Michael, climb over the top, sweetheart – come and sit on my knee, baby."

He did try, I was shocked. He scrambled up and leaned on the front seat and tried to pull himself over, and Ardith pulled under his arms, but at the same time Ariadne was stopping the car, making the brakes hiss but not squeal, and I was yanking on the waist of his pants to keep him in the back.

Ariadne got out of the car like a snake, like a fuse, and opened Ardith's door as fast as light. She held it and waited, and Ardith got out, and they walked behind the car and talked to each other in low voices for a while. Michael and I sat still. He wouldn't talk – I hadn't ever heard him talk.

After a while they came back into the car and Ariadne drove off again, and nobody spoke at all. Ardith sat beside her in the front and did her lipstick and flipped through her bag and rustled generally all the way home.

Michael and I sat in the back with the windows open a crack. He looked awful, but he didn't want his hand held or anything. They dropped me at my own house without coming in.

"Laura, this has been a bad treat," Ariadne said when she stopped the car. "Wait a second. Thank you very much for jumping off the roof to your peril – take this and be better sisters than we are." She gave me a five-dollar bill.

◊

I stood on the grass until they had driven away and I was just going to go in when Cecy came around the corner of the house crying.

"Somebody stole the scooter," she said, forgetting to be mad at me.

"I'm not going to fight with you any more," I told her.

"Okay," she said. "Or Sam?"

"I never fight with him anyway, he won't fight."

"Do you mean it?"

"If I start, you tell me."

We went inside and down into the hidey-hole under the porch stairs where we kept the flashlight, but we used a candle instead to save the batteries. It was a fancy candle, beeswax with a willow pattern in blue wax wrapped around it by some amazing process, which we had broken by mistake and then hidden in the hide before a dinner party. The smell was particularly good in the narrow angles of the hide, and the yellowy light was comforting to me.

"We'd better get Sam to tell you if you start," Cecy said.

"Okay. And I'm not going to lie any more."

Sam came in with three peaches which he said Mommy had said he should bring and eat with us, really ripe ones just washed so some of the fuzz was smoothed off.

"Daddy had to go to a confession," Sam said.

"I remember when he went to one when we were in Manitoba and I thought it was a confession from a crook, remember? And you told me it was an axe murderer?" Cecy knocked me on my arm for a pat, not hitting me.

"I thought it was an axe murderer. Something he said, he said something about it that made me think it was so terrible ...."

"It was a man who had hurt his wife," Sam said. "He'd hurt her really badly, stabbed her with a knife when they were fighting, you were right."

"I don't know how he knows all this stuff," I said to Cecy.

"He gets told. And then we tell him things too, and he puts them together."

"This time, I am telling you to take my peach pit upstairs and Cecy's too and bring us something to read and steal another candle."

"Okay," he said, and he went.

"Something terrible is going to happen," I said to Cecy.

We never found the scooter, it was a bad day.

◊

Cecy and I were on the no-window side in the afternoon eating Vachon cakes with caramel in them from my five dollars, and it was the last cakes of the five dollars, so it must have been at least two weeks since the drive. Sam was running round and round the house ten times so we would each give him a bite, and we were laughing at his knees going by each time pump pump which we could see from between the yellow flicks of the forsythia. In between passes we leaned our heads back on each other's shoulders and let the caramel run out of the tops of the cakes onto our tongues and chins, and we had our shoes off so that the sandy dirt would force up between our toes.

Before Sam had gone round seven times my mother came out of the house with the baby in the basket and called for us – we could see the basket dangling from her arm, so we only waited till she rounded the corner to the back, and scrambled out to follow her. I gave Cecy my cake to hold; she didn't want to because the chocolate had melted partly from holding it, but I shoved it at her and ran.

"Laura!" my mother was calling. She had put the basket on the low table and she was peeling back the blanket just enough to give the baby air. "Get your shoes, Laura, I need you to come with me quickly – where is Cecy? – Cecy, we'll be back as soon as we can .... I've left a message for Daddy and he'll come home as soon as he gets it, so don't worry."

Cecy was trying to hide the Vachon cakes behind her back and listen both at the same time, but she didn't need to bother, because my mother wasn't looking at her anyway, she was searching for her glasses in her summer purse.

"Laura, quickly, I said! Run and get your shoes, I'll be in the car."

"Where are you going?" Cecy whispered.

I tried to look mysterious, but she knew I didn't know, so I ran to get my shoes from the forsythia and she stayed by the baby's basket looking lonely, with the Vachon cakes oozing out of her hands.

In the car my mother said, "I need you to come with me because I don't know what is happening exactly, and I may need you to help with the children. If I can, I'll leave you in the car, but if I call you you'll have to come immediately, and keep calm and be helpful and quiet."

"Where are we going?"

"To the Kellers' house."

"What's the matter?"

"I don't know yet, Lisle phoned to say please come."

"But what do you think?"

"Laura, don't talk now. What I think is that something terrible has happened, and you will stay in the car till I find out."

It didn't seem like a very long ride to Ariadne Keller's house this time. But it was quiet, and heavy, and the air was different out under the sky than it had been under the forsythia. When my mother parked the car and walked down the steps I tried the old trick of smiling to make the sun come out, which if you do slowly enough can sometimes happen, but it didn't work. The whole street, all Whitlock Edge, was still. No doors banged and no one rode by on their bikes – you could hear the water lapping at the dock. I saw Lisle open the front door, but it was so far away and so hidden by leaves that I couldn't see what was wrong. My mother took her shoulder and went inside with her.

I was getting scared out in the car. The windows were all down and the seats smelled because it was so hot, and I didn't want to sit there anymore. I didn't want to go into the house either, because I suddenly started to think about the axe murderer who Daddy had heard the confession from, and how all the noise in their house must have stopped after he was finished. But that wasn't real, I remembered that we had made that up.

My legs were stuck to the seat, and when I moved them they stuck again. Then I heard a door banging finally, but it was the Kellers' back door, the screen, and I couldn't stand it any longer, so I thought I would run down to the lake to see if some of the children were there and they might know what was the matter.

I pushed the car door shut carefully and quietly so my mother wouldn't hear me leaving, and I skimmed around the side of the house running low so she wouldn't see me through the windows – I was going so fast I didn't stop till I got to the pine path though the trees, but then I did stop.

I couldn't understand what it was for a minute, they were all standing around a lump. Lisle and her brother Derek and two of the littler children and my mother, only my mother was bending down. I didn't dare go any nearer, but my eyes refocused like a telescope and the awful shape resolved itself into something I knew. It was Ariadne Keller with her hair unbound lying on the pebble shore with the boy Michael in her arms, and I thought they were both dead, they were so drowned wet. Not wet and shining like you would be after swimming on a hot heavy day, but just drenched like from rain, their bodies left on the shore in all their clothes, slimy and dark from the wet. Her hair was black and fell all around her face and neck, and some of it fell on Michael too. My mother rose up with Michael in her arms, or tried to, but Ariadne's arms came up too, and all the other children moved away a little in slow fright. My mother said something low, and then she looked up and saw me standing there, and she said, "Come down, Laura, I need you."

There were still no other people there, and Lisle and Derek couldn't do it, but all by herself it would have been awkward to remove Ariadne's arms from the boy, it would have made it worse for the others. So I went down to the mound on the shore and Lisle and Derek parted away. My feet moved by themselves in a prim trot, sure and light on the needles, and I didn't need to be told what to do. I took one hand of Ariadne Keller at a time and pried the fingers open – it was not too hard. I kept my back in between the fingers and Lisle and Derek, and my mother was looking at the smaller girls to calm them.

Her fingers were cool and a little flabby without her excited grasping appetite inside them – but she wasn't dead, she was just unconscious. I never thought she was dead, dead people are supposed to look happy. I laid her fingers down on her stomach, and one of her hands fell away upwards and grazed her breast, and someone winced. It sounds so slow, but really it was all done quickly, as if my mother had changed the way time went so that nothing would be jerky or frightening for the children.

She was already turning away with Michael, moving swiftly away up to the verandah, and she looked over her shoulder to me.

"Chafe her hands and cheeks, Laura, try to keep her warm. Derek will bring down a blanket in a minute. She will be all right, Lisle. You can watch Michael with me until help comes now ...."

Lisle was still standing where she had been, staring down at her mother, and she looked so desperate that I started to cry for a second but I stopped it in time before it got up into my face.

"She went into the water because he was drowning," she said, and she walked up after my mother. She glanced at Derek as she went by and made him go with her. The two little girls stayed down with me – I could never remember their names.

It was pretty calm under the trees with everybody gone to the house except me and the little girls and Ariadne Keller who looked now like she was sleeping, less dead. I kept rubbing her hands between mine, and we all kept our eyes on them. There was sand in patterns on her arms, like the baby game where you draw your name in spit on your skin and then shake sand on it. Way way in the distance we could all hear a siren, and it surprised me, I thought maybe this was all going to be quiet, that my mother had fixed it so no one would know something awful had happened.

"Will they lock her up and throw away the key?" one of the little girls asked, the one who didn't have her three fingers stuck in her mouth.

"Why?" I asked her.

"That's what she said, that's what she says all the time. Because she walked into the water with him."

The other one took her fingers out of her mouth. "I think Lisle should have left her in the water."

It was quiet for a minute. She still had her shoes on, sandals with thin straps. I tried to decide what colour they had been before they got dark with wet.

"She walked right in there with him," a voice came out of a bush behind the girls – the younger boy who had been hiding there came out walking like a frog to have a look now that my mother was gone. "Right into the lake, right in ...." They all nodded, not looking at each other, just looking at her.

They were really scary, they made me want to throw up, but instead I kept looking at Ariadne Keller's hands, all long and pale brown now, and the children didn't say anything more. She had never looked like she had any children at all, and they didn't look like they had any mother at all.

The siren got louder and louder and then cut out at the turn-off from St. Margaret's Bay Road – even though it was so far the sound was clear in the silence. We heard them drive up, and the crunch of the red clay bits in the far driveway, and then we heard doors shutting and opening and people moving, and the front door, and my mother's voice, and all this time, hearing all these important moving things going on and about to happen, we just sat on the shore with Ariadne not stirring, still. I got worried suddenly that they would forget about us, about me, and I would have to stay there with those scary kids until dark and then they would probably eat me or get out their axes.

My mother came to the top of the path and called the little girls by name, I don't know how she remembered them. They ran away up the path and past her, and out through the trees to some hide of their own. She wavered as if she might follow them, but she came down instead, with the ambulance men following her. She was still holding Michael in her arms, and he lolled over the edges like Cecy had drooped over Ariadne Keller's arms on the spaghetti night. Nothing on him was broken, but now that he'd been out of the water for a while you could see where the blood was coming from that had washed over him before. One split on his forehead was leaking blood down over his eye, still pinkish and weak over his pinchy face, and there were dark bruises on his skin now purpling round the edges.

Lisle had followed the men down, and she saw one of them staring at Michael in my mother's arms.

"She went into the water because he was drowning," she told them. "She went into the lake to save him, he was rolling on the log and getting hurt so she went out to get him," she said, and then she turned right straight around and threw up in the bushes.

I was all right until the ambulance men told me to let go a little rudely, and one of them pulled my arm, and I hit him really hard as I got up, and then I had to say, "I'm very sorry," because I hadn't meant to hit him at all, and I was amazed that I had done it and also very ashamed. But my mother was there and she had given Michael away to one of the men, and she held on to me and said I could wait in the car, and that Lisle was there already and she would be glad if I would help her and Derek, so then I had to move away from Ariadne Keller, lying on the shore.

◊

I was fine when we went home, and I was fine later on, and I was fine when my father took me into his study to tell me what had really happened and to say that Ariadne Keller was very unhappy and had wanted for a little while to die, and that she would be going to a sanatorium, which I knew was the loony-bin. And the whole time he was talking to me and trying to explain how it could have happened without frightening me, I wasn't frightened. There was no need to be frightened. I was just miserable.

I had a nightmare in the middle of the night, I think because of hitting the ambulance man by mistake. I dreamed that I was beating up somebody. I'd gotten in a really bad temper and I just started beating up people. It was a backwards dream – I could have dreamed that I was beating up someone and woken up to find I was punching my pillow, but in this dream I began at the pillow, which made me terrified to wake up, because I thought if I've been dreaming that I'm beating up a pillow, when I wake up I will really be beating a person, who will I be beating? Then the pillow I was holding became a child, and I thought, I can't beat this child, I can't be doing this – so I know what I'll do, it's not happening, I'll take us under the water. I'll go under the water and it will not happen. You can't beat somebody up under the water, and the water will comfort him.

But under the water it was so awful, it was so thick. I couldn't move quickly, I couldn't get my long brown thin legs to move, or my long arms to untwine from around Michael Rowe. If I'd thought to go into the ocean it would have worked. But the ocean was far away, and the lake was right there.

Cecy woke me up, I was curled right down at the bottom of the bed, and weeping. She sat on my bed with me for ages and I told her about the dream, and she played with my hair until I stopped crying.

"Do you know what?" I said to her. "I love you to pieces."

"Yes, and I love you back together again," she said.

◊

The ambulance men had pulled a stretcher down the path and they were going to put her on it. She looked so sad even with her eyes closed that I thought she might be pretending. She might just be wanting someone to carry her, like she had said to me a long time before.

CONTRIBUTORS

JAN BAUER is a freelance writer whose fiction has been published in *Whetstone* and *Waves* and has been broadcast on CBC Radio. Articles have appeared in the *Globe and Mail* (co-written with Susan Crean) and English PEN. Through her association with International PEN, Article 19 and the Network on International Human Rights she has become deeply involved in the international effort to promote and defend the rights to freedom of expression and intellectual freedom. She is presently working on a project with Article 19 and The Canadian Centre of International PEN to establish an international database on constitutional and case law as a resource for the defense of rights articulated in the UN Universal Declaration of Human Rights and the Covenant on Political and Civil Rights. In the last three years she has worked on cases of rights violations in countries as diverse as Chile, Sri Lanka, China, South Africa, Taiwan, Ethiopia, the United Arab Emirates and Colombia.

BETH BRANT is a Bay of Quinte Mohawk from Tyendinaga reserve in Desoronto, Ontario. She is 48 years old and began writing when she turned 40. She is the editor of *A Gathering of Spirit*, a collection by North American Indian women. She is also author of *Mohawk Trail*. She is a mother of three daughters and a grandmother of two grandsons.

CLARE BRAUX has had her short stories published in *Waves*, *Cross-Canada Writers' Magazine*, *Quarry*, *Zymergy*, and *Kalliope*. She is currently working hard at her second novel.

CLAUDIA CASPER writes in Vancouver, British Columbia, where she runs a one-woman typesetting and word-processing business called CCWriter. At present she is exploring what the concept of 'heritage' means in a country like Canada, where the ancestry of most is hybrid and discontinuous, severed from place of origin and broken with history.

MARLENE COOKSHAW's fiction and poetry have appeared in a number of Canadian periodicals. *Personal Luggage* was published in 1984, and her second collection of poems, *The Whole Elephant*, will be published in Fall 1989. She is assistant editor of *The Malahat Review* in Victoria.

CAROLE CORBEIL has written for *The Globe and Mail* as well as for magazines such as *Saturday Night, This Magazine, Canadian Art* and *Impulse*. She is presently writing a novel.

DEBBY DOBSON was born in 1953 in New Brunswick and attended university in Halifax, Toronto and England. In England she received an MA in Modern African Literature. She taught English for two years in Nigeria and five years in Yellowknife. Presently she works as an English Language consultant for the Department of Education, Government of the Northwest Territories. She was one of the founding members of the Yellowknife Writers' Group, a small group, mostly women, which kept her going as a writer. Dobson has lived in the Northwest Territories for nine years and has two daughters under two and a half years of age.

MARINA ENDICOTT lives in Saskatchewan and works in the theatre as a director and dramaturge.

CYNTHIA FLOOD lives in Vancouver where she teaches English at a community college. Since 1970 she has been active in the women's movement and in left-wing politics. Her short stories have been published in *Atlantis, Fireweed, Journal of Canadian Fiction, Matrix, Prism, Queen's Quarterly, Room of One's Own*, and *Wascana Review*. She has also had stories published in four anthologies: *Common Ground*, NEW: *West Coast Fiction, Baker's Dozen* and *Vancouver Short Stories*. *The Animals in Their Elements*, her collection of short stories, was published in 1987 and was very well received.

RACHNA GILMORE was born in India, spent her teenage years in London, England and now lives in Charlottetown, PEI with her husband and two children. She is the author of *My Mother is Weird* (1988) and *Wheniwasalittlegirl* (1989).

SUSAN GLICKMAN was born in 1953. She teaches English at the University of Toronto, and is the author of three books of poetry: *Complicity* (1983), *The Power to Move* (1986) and *Henry Moore's Sheep* (forthcoming in 1990).

CLAIRE HARRIS was born in Trinidad, and came to Canada in 1966. Her books include *Fables from the Women's Quarters* (1984), for which she won a Commonwealth Prize; *Travelling to Find A Remedy* (1986), for which she won both the Alberta Culture Poetry Prize and the Writer's Guild of Alberta Poetry Prize. Her latest work is *The Conception of Winter* (1989).

MAYA KHANKHOJE was born in Mexico City; she and her two daughters have made Montreal their home since 1978. She is a member and co-founder of a feminist group for South Asian women in Montreal. Khankhoje started writing book reviews and articles in New Delhi in the early Sixties. Her first short story was written in French in 1977; her latest article, on the Aztec woman who became Cortes' mistress and interpreter, was published in Spanish in the new Montreal publication *Raíces.* Her main interests are languages, literature, philosophy and anything related to new frontiers in knowledge.

JOAN MACLEOD'S first play, *Jewel,* a one act one woman show which she also performed, was written four years ago. It has had eight productions to date and has been translated into French, Swedish and Danish. It has been published as a book along with her second play, *Toronto, Mississippi. Toronto, Mississippi* premiered at Toronto's Tarragon Theatre in 1987 and has also received productions in Vancouver, Victoria, Kamloops, and London, Ontario. In addition to her dramatic works, MacLeod's prose and poetry have been published in numerous literary periodicals. She has been playwright-in-residence at the Tarragon for the past three seasons.

LEE MARACLE, while raising her own four teenagers, has also mothered numerous nephews, nieces, children of friends and the odd 'stray.' Throughout these years her writing developed and matured as a result of our continuing dilemma: how to creatively impart knowledge to these little beings that they may achieve their humanity in what can be a largely inhumane society. She is currently working toward a degree that will enable her to pursue her great love of teaching the young. Her first book, *Bobbi Lee: Indian Rebel*, was published in 1975. She has had numerous poems, essays and short stories appear in a variety of publications over the past twenty years. Two poetry books and a collection of short stories are scheduled for release in the next year. Her most recent work, *I Am Woman*, was the top selling book at the Third International Feminist Bookfair in Montreal in June of 1988.

SARA MCDONALD is a writer from Saskatoon currently living in Montreal. Her work has been included in various anthologies including *Sky High* and *Open Windows*. Some of her stories have recently appeared in *Grain*, *Prism* and *The New Quarterly*.

RUTH MILLAR is a former journalist, single parent and sometime freelance writer who currently earns her living as a librarian. She grew up in Saskatoon, where she now lives, after brief periods spent living in Winnipeg, Toronto and London, Ontario. A lifelong concern about Third World issues prompted her to write "Against the Tooth of Time," her first attempt at fiction.

SUNITI NAMJOSHI was born in India in 1941. She has worked as an Officer in the Indian Administrative Service and in academic posts in India and Canada. Since 1972 she has taught in the Department of English of the University of Toronto and she now lives and writes in Devon, England. She has published numerous poems, fables, articles and reviews in anthologies, collections and literary and women's studies journals in India, Canada, the US and Britain. She has in the past published five books of poetry in India and two in Canada, *The Authentic Lie* (1982) and *From the Bedside Book of Nightmares* (1984). Her first book of fiction, *Feminist Fables*, was published in 1981; her second, *The Conversations of Cow*, in 1985; and her third, *Aditi and the one-eyed monkey*, written for children, in 1986.

In the autumn of 1989 a volume of her selected poems which covers a period of twenty years will be published in England.

LIBBY OUGHTON was born in Women's College Hospital, Toronto, grew up in Guelph, lived many places and many lives, and in 1980 settled on the red soil of Prince Edw(ina) Island, where she became owner of gynergy books and Ragweed Press. Taking her own writing seriously only began to happen in her fiftieth year. Her first book of poetry, *getting the housework done for the dance,* was published last year. Poems have appeared or are forthcoming in a number of journals. "Sooner or Later All Bodies Tend to Move toward the Centre of the Earth," her first try at short fiction, won first prize in the PEI Literary Awards.

SUSAN PERLY was born in Toronto and spent twelve years in the Maritimes as a journalist, photographer, a founder of the Halifax Women's Bureau and author of *Women and the Law in Nova Scotia.* In 1980 she went to school in Guatemala at Quetzaltenango (Xale), a Mayan Indian community in the north-western highlands. She has made numerous trips to Central and South America, including a year in which she did documentaries for CBC Radio's Sunday Morning from Ecuador, El Salvador, Costa Rica, Guatemala, refugee camps in southern Mexico, and for CBC Radio's Morningside the series *Letters from Latin America.* During the early Eighties she also worked in Argentina and Uruguay for the Centre for Investigative Journalism documenting the repression of journalists under both military dictatorships. Since 1985 she has been writing fiction and freelancing. She helped translate a book of poetry by Guatemalans in exile, *Exodus* (1988). Her short story "Jesus and the Toucan" won second prize in the 1987 CBC Literary Competition.

FRANCES ROONEY is a writer and editor who lives across the street from the only farm in downtown Toronto. The cows, pigs, ducks and sheep, as well as Meg and Mika, help to keep her in touch with the important things in life.

HELEN J. ROSTA was born and raised in Alberta and lives in Edmonton. Her stories have appeared in various magazines and short story collections. A collection of her short stories, *In The Blood,* was published by NeWest Press in 1982.

childhood in Ontario before moving to Vancouver and university (at 16) and, four years later, to Alberta for work. In 1981 she graduated from the University of British Columbia with a Bachelor of Fine Arts, major Creative Writing. She has lived in Santiago, Chile, since 1981, where she works as writer, translator and foreign correspondent for the London Times, and assorted magazine and radio programs in Canada, the United States and England. Her book of bilingual (Spanish / English) poems, *Exile Home/Exilio en la patria*, was published in Canada in 1986. *Un pájaro es un poema*, an anthology of Canadian poetry edited and translated by Sagaris, was published in Santiago in 1986. Her poems and short stories have appeared in many magazines and anthologies. 'Circus Love,' her second book of poems, is currently in search of a publisher.

LIBBY SCHEIER is the author of two books of poetry – *The Larger Life* (1983) and *Second Nature* (1986) – and is completing a third (working title: *Sky*). Her poems, short fiction and criticism have been published in numerous periodicals; her fiction has been anthologized in *Love and Hunger – An Anthology of New Fiction* (1988); her criticism in *In the Feminine – Women & Words Conference Proceedings* (1985); and her poetry in *Poetry by Canadian Women* (1989), among other anthologies. She teaches creative writing at York University.

SARAH SHEARD'S short fiction has appeared in various Canadian literary magazines. She is the author of a novel, *Almost Japanese* and is completing work on her second.

GERTRUDE STORY was born in 1929 near the town of Sutherland, Saskatchewan, which is now a suburb of Saskatoon. After completing high school, she worked as a bank clerk, then married and moved back to a rural community. In 1976 she began her university career by taking a half-course at the University of Saskatchewan. Subsequently in 1980 she convocated as the most distinguished graduate, and was awarded the Arts Prize and President's Medal. Since her first book of poems, *The Book of Thirteen*, published in 1981, Story has become one of Saskatchewan's best known storytellers and most acclaimed writers. Her immensely popular

Alvena Schroeder trilogy of short stories draws on her German-Canadian background and has earned critical praise. This highly original writer has produced four impressive collections of short stories and a recent memoir, *The Last House on Main Street*.

SUSAN SWAN, novelist, poet, critic, playwright and journalist, was born in Midland, Ontario in 1945. Her first novel *The Biggest Modern Woman of the World*, about the Victorian giantess Anna Swan who left Nova Scotia to exhibit with P.T. Barnum, was published in Canada, Britain and the United States and was a finalist in the 1983 Governor General's Awards. *Unfit for Paradise,* a collection of short stories on northerners in the tropics, was published in 1982. Her play, *Queen of the Silver Blades*, examined the public adulation of Barbara Ann Scott. Swan's next novel, *The Last of the Golden Girls*, will be released in September, 1989.

RHEA TREGEBOV was born in 1953 in Saskatoon and was raised in Winnipeg. Her first book of poetry, *Remembering History*, won the 1983 Pat Lowther Award for the best book of poetry by a woman. "I'm Talking from My Time," a performance piece she produced on the emigration story of a 95-year-old Russian Jewish woman, was presented in Toronto, Winnipeg and Ottawa. Her second collection of poetry, *No One We Know*, was published in 1986. A third collection tentatively titled *Faith in the Weather* is forthcoming in Fall 1990. She was a member of the *Fireweed* collective in its early years and she has been part of the feminist community since she arrived in Toronto in 1978.

CAROLINE WOODWARD's first collection of short fiction, *Disturbing the Peace*, is due in Spring, 1990. Work from this collection has been published in *The Malahat Review, This Magazine* and *Prism*. She was raised on a homestead in the Peace River region of northern BC and presently lives with Jeff George and Seamus Woodward George in Nelson, BC, where she attended the David Thompson University Centre for one glorious year of writing, theatre and hell-raising before the provincial government shut it down.